NINE LIVES OF AN URBAN PANTHER

DIARIES OF AN URBAN PANTHER NOVEL

AMANDA ARISTA

Second ebook edition 2021, ISBN: 978-1-7375481-2-6
Second print book edition 2021, ISBN: 978-1-7326143-9-0

First Avon Impulse ebook edition 2012, ISBN: 9780062207869 (out of print)
First Avon Impulse print book edition 2012, ISBN: 9780062207876 (out of print)

Cover design by Najla Qamber, Qamber Designs

PROLOGUE

D *ear Diary,*
        *Eight months ago, I was attacked in the back alley of
my townhome and rescued by an uber-hot guy named Chaz. He told
me there was a prophecy about me and that I might turn into a
werepanther. He was right on both counts. Then Spencer, the guy who
bit me, tried to convince me to join the dark side. It didn't work.*

*So he poisoned me and left me for dead. My best friend, Jessa, an
undercover fairy princess, saved the day but bonded us together as the
dynamic duo for opening and closing the Veil.*

*Six months ago, in an epic battle against my maker to save the
world, Spencer jumped through the Veil into the Neveranth, and I
ended up killing his father. As Haverty lay dying, he gave me the
Haverty Legacy and the hellfire that comes with it.*

*I thought life was going to get better. After four assassination
attempts, I finally changed my mind. When the Haverty pack needed a
new leader and I was the one holding the Legacy, I quickly found
having loyal followers really helped when the elemental Carlisle
started killing his way through all other competition for leader of the
Dallas Pride. When push came to claw, Carlisle got thrown into
mirror jail and I got crowned as the Prima.*

Yep, I think that's about it. All I have to do is keep sane from the prophetic dreams I keep having, run a pack, keep my "real" job, and have some sort of personal life with my fiancé.

CHAPTER 1

*B*EING A QUEEN was exhausting. This was the first of four meetings for the day, the first of three appointments with new pack members, and my second latté with an extra espresso shot.

As I waited at my favorite coffee shop for my caffeine and my ten-o'clock appointment, I stretched my neck and slipped off my pointed heels. Cute but deadly. Now that I was a Prima, looking like a leader was starting to get tiring as well. The life of jeans and T-shirts was behind me. I had to look more responsible now and my feet were paying the price.

The cool wooden floor soothed the pain burning up my legs and let me relax for just one moment. This place was my second home and I'd single-handedly brought it back from extinction with a string of new customers by maybe making it the unofficial hotspot for the new Dallas Pride.

Secret club has to have a clubhouse, right?

I looked down at my watch, my dreaded new accessory, and played with the charm at my neck. My ten o'clock was late. It had been hell to pin him down for a meeting. He was the last of the new members of my little family that I had to meet with before our first full moon together. I actually had to call his office to get an appointment. Neither of us was very happy about that.

My frustrated thoughts were quickly redirected by the feel of coarse fur brushing up my spine. I turned around to see a tall man enter the coffee shop and pause. His dark suit and briefcase were a stark contrast to the bohemian feel of the cafe.

He looked around the shabby chic décor, and when his cool blue eyes landed on me, I knew him, even though I'd never seen his human form before. This was my ten o'clock: Peter Delmont, lawyer/wolf.

He wore his power like he wore his sharply tailored suit and slick blond hair, on the outside for everyone to know he didn't mess around. As he crossed the small space in long, purposeful strides, I was frozen in his gaze. The look. The suit. It was damn effective, and for a split second, I almost thought I didn't have the claws for this one.

He stopped just short of stepping on me and I had to look up at him. Something my five-foot-eleven frame rarely needed to do. He didn't bother with putting up borders to contain his power, and his scent overwhelmed me. Under the cologne I was sure he wore because it made the women in his office swoon, his power, his wolf smelled distinctively of leather and sandalwood.

"Miss Jordan?" His voice was low and deep as his eyebrows rose with his question.

My spine reacted to his power, going stiff and straight. "Mr. Delmont."

"May we sit?" His eyes flicked to the open table in the back.

"I was just thinking the same thing."

He strode over to the table and I looked back to the counter for my drink. The young girl behind the counter had my coffee in her hands, her mouth wide as she stared at Delmont. Good. So it wasn't just me.

I waved my hand in front of her face so she would relinquish my coffee. The girl jumped and spilled a bit of the coffee as she sloshed the white porcelain across the counter.

With a sigh, I took the mug and headed back to the table.

Usually, I would have said something about the waste of good caffeine, but I was going to need my strength for the conversation ahead. I had a feeling my usual spiel to all the other new members about safety in numbers and checking in and full moon responsibilities wasn't going to work with this one. I sealed my borders, keeping my power close to my vest, and knew the macchiato would get me through this.

This man had his suit, and I had my twelve ounces of hot coffee.

Delmont had turned my usual table into his personal office, his briefcase on the small table already popped open. "I'm sorry this meeting is so delayed."

An apology? Now that was unexpected. I sat slowly on the chair across from him and waited for him to stop shuffling papers. "No problem. I've had a few things to organize."

He closed the briefcase, opening up the space between us. In the day light, he was handsome, slender and broad shouldered. But I knew underneath this forced perfection was an animal, a silver-mantled wolf easily the size of my panther. His energy had been primal when we bonded six weeks ago, when he had pledged his power to me, and that pledge connected our magical souls. Even now, as we sat civilly across the table from each other, Peter Delmont was different. The connections to the others in my pack were silvery threads that I gently nudged this way and that. His was a rough-hewn twine that bound me to him as his Prima.

Now, more than with any of the other fourteen, I was wondering why me. He was powerful, in this incarnation and his animal form. He had been a high-ranking member of the Haverty Pride before I came in and destroyed it all. Yet, when push came to claws in the battle between my few and the darker Wanderers, he had chosen me as his master.

That was the story I wanted to hear. The story I was slowly coaxing out of all the Wanderers who had given me a piece of themselves, chosen me as their leader.

Delmont looked down at the papers in his hand. "I was the lawyer and executor of Haverty's will." His voice was quick and succinct, with so very little affect I would have believed his act, if it weren't for the twisting of the twine between us, something undulating under the coifed façade that pulled at me.

"Must have been an honor, being so young."

All he gave me was a curt nod as he slid the stack of papers across the table toward me. "Reade Haverty had it set that the next leader of the pack should get all of his properties and assets."

A sudden void of white formed in the space between my ears. "What?"

Delmont licked his lips. "Of course, he meant it to be his son, Spencer, but, well, we know that didn't quite work out, you throwing him into the Neveranth and all. So, it seems that as the new leader, chosen by a majority of the pack by one, you are now the beneficiary."

"I didn't throw Spencer into the Neveranth. He jumped," I corrected. I looked down at the stack of papers. "I always got the impression Haverty was loaded."

"A full list of assets is included." He folded his long fingers into his lap. "Including houses, foreign accounts and domestic holdings, it comes out to around one point three billion if you were to sell everything. Which I don't recommend in this market."

I gulped and set my coffee down on the table. No need to waste the coffee by spilling it all over my new dress, though I think this meant that I could buy a million more cups of coffee if I needed, and a million new dresses for that matter.

"Why?"

His steel blue eyes finally rose to meet mine. "With the crown comes the kingdom."

His words settled around me like an ice cold blanket, and my skin prickled. It had taken me over three months to assume the title of Prima. I wasn't ready for a kingdom.

"I never asked for this."

The smooth monotone of his voice didn't help. "No, you didn't."

I licked my lips and cursed Haverty. Yet another burden to leave me with. Like the Legacy, his collected family power he forced upon me as he lay dying, this fortune was just another trap to tempt me in the direction everyone else in my line had gone- straight into the darkness.

"I know this is a lot to take in, Miss Jordan, but I will need a decision on the next step fairly soon. The property has been in limbo far too long."

"Of course." It had been in limbo for five months, since last December, when I'd killed Reade Haverty and his cowardly son had jumped into a parallel dimension. Don't imagine they have paperwork for that sort of thing.

A million story lines ran through my head about wealth, including a few scenes of Scrooge McDuck swimming through his money piles and all the horror movies I'd written with insane benefactors and large mansions and late-night feasts. But wasn't that one of the special little bonuses to being Violet Jordan: knowing the darkness so I can avoid it?

I wrapped my hands back around the hot coffee. "I'll need a little more time to think about it, Mr. Delmont."

"Very well. Call my office for an appointment."

He moved to leave the table, as if this meeting was over.

I chuckled and wrapped my fist around the charm on my necklace, the little charm that masked my real power. It usually kept me hidden from other Wanderers, specifically any baddies out for blood. But covered like this, it let me push my power out and flow over Delmont.

He froze six inches from the seat as if I'd pushed the pause button on his movements. His eyes darted to me as he felt my power again and smelled the burned magnolia fragrance of his Prima.

"Not so fast, Stretch. I booked you for an hour."

He gulped and his tanned face went pale. It was the first crack I'd seen in his façade since he came in. He returned to his seat and smoothed out his jacket.

I released the pendant and leaned back in my chair. Like this, the world was a little duller, but I'd gotten used to it. It was better than jumping at every shadow in the window convinced the undefined *they* had found me again.

"I do appreciate the business portion of our meeting." I tried to ignore the packet of potential just sitting between us and get down to the real meat and bones of this confrontation. "But I coordinated this to learn about you."

Delmont licked his lips and was seemingly speechless. He finally mustered, "What do you want to know?"

I figured we'd start simple. "Did Haverty place you in your law firm or did he get to you afterwards?"

He adjusted in his seat again. "You really don't play around, do you?"

"No," I answered quickly. "But I'm also not testing your alliance. We both know what you did. I just want a little more as to why."

Delmont's eyes dropped to the stack of papers. "Haverty treated me very well. And yes, he did help me get a place at the firm. In return, he only asked that I wave my retainer fees."

I frowned. "That seems tame for him."

"I was a little fish in his very big pond."

I nodded. "And what do you think about the pond now?"

He looked down at his briefcase and measured his words,

seeming to roll them around in his mouth before he spoke. "I've been told you appreciate honesty."

"Almost above all else."

Delmont cleared his throat. "Dallas isn't better, just different. There are still holes that need to be filled, and if they aren't, I predict there will be chaos."

I was glad for the charm around my neck that helped keep my power reigned in, because it also helped me hide when my emotions made my power jump, as his comment had just made my whole being tense in fear. What could he know that I didn't know?

I took a sip of my drink to bide some time with my answer. The coffee soothed my frazzled nerves. The sheer power of him was making me fray by the second. "Chaos is a strong word, Mr. Delmont."

His blue eyes were brave enough to look straight into mine. "It is an accurate word, Miss Jordan. You may have secured the affections of the Shifters in Dallas, but what of the witches and the vampires and the elementals, some of which are still nursing their wounds from six weeks ago?"

"They can't all be treading on the dark side. I watched them fight against Carlisle's men. They helped us defeat him."

"That just means they didn't want *him* to control things. Only the Shifters chose you, we just happen to be the majority in the pack."

I ran my fingers through my hair in frustration. It was a habit I'd picked up from no less than three men in my life. "None of them have made a move to try to challenge me."

He began to pinch the flesh of his pinkie finger as his hands lay in his lap. "They might not see a need to. The Shifters have their own way of doing things, other breeds have theirs. I wouldn't be surprised if the elementals were naming their Akasha as we speak."

I would have let the sentiment go as a concern, but the

fidgeting of his hands got me. Little things, like the fall of a shoulder and the pinch of a pinkie, had greater meaning to a person who had spent most of her adult life watching from the outside than a string of words put into a sentence. "You're not telling me everything."

His eyes darted down to his hands and he spread them wide on his thighs. He knew I'd caught his tell.

I was right. He was keeping things from me. Dangerous things about the others in the city. I could force him to tell me, literally pull the information from him, but then where would I be? Connected to an embittered pack member? Not the best way to start out this whole leader thing.

"The other breeds have not made a move. Dallas has been quiet. I'd rather focus my efforts on my pack, making them feel safe, protected. I don't know what you knew of Haverty's methods, but after the stories I've heard in the past month, these people need healing, and I won't use them as pawns in another war."

"For now," he said.

I straightened, looking into his eyes steadily. I knew them to be almost silver when he shifted. "Excuse me?"

"To protect them, you will need to use them, their strengths and their weaknesses."

"And how are you so sure about that?"

Delmont took in an unnervingly calm breath. His long fingers went traced the edge of his briefcase. "This is not my first pack. Been in one or another my whole life, Miss Jordan. It will happen."

I licked my suddenly very dry lips. "If you knew this, then why choose me? Why bind yourself at all?"

Delmont opened his mouth. A sliver of cold wavered around him and pushed against my own radiating power. He shut his mouth just as a cold, stony look covered his face and he hid behind his borders for the first time in our conversation, creating a void before me. He was nowhere near the confident man who had strode through the place, power out all willy-nilly.

I knew in an instant there was a story there, a painful memory he shut away with his steel-trap border. Those bound to me were like books, and stories like that are best served up willingly. Just like the information that I would need to get from him about the others in the city. Mother always said you catch more flies with honey.

I took in a breath and exhaled, again formulating the right words to use. "Unfortunately, I will need to use your legal skills. And if you happen to see a little of that chaos, I might want a heads-up."

Delmont nodded. "Yes, ma'am."

I grimaced at the ma'am but went on with the same speech that I had given all of my new wards. "I want you to feel safe. I want you to live your life. But I do expect you to be at the next full moon."

"I'll have my secretary put it on my calendar."

I smiled. I doubted he could resist the full moon. It was just a line to make him feel more important and used probably out of habit more than necessity. "I'll get her the information."

He moved again to stand, and I nodded. He rose, buttoned his suit coat, and picked up his briefcase. He turned to me and paused.

I expected for him to simply say goodbye, but as of late, I wasn't about to assume anything about anyone. Nearly cost me my life last time.

He spoke slowly and with a little hope, if I was reading his tone correctly. "This was an interesting conversation, Miss Jordan. I'd like to do this again."

I was in a little state of shock for a moment. "Well, I do have some papers to sign for you."

"Thank you." He nodded and walked across the coffee shop, leaving the faint scent of sandalwood in his wake.

As his exit from the shop sent the bells on the door into fits, my entire body relaxed. I was exhausted. The others had been easy. Mothers, students, hermits. No one had set me on edge like Delmont, testing me like he did. And no one else had as much information I desperately needed to maintain this peace.

TRYING TO DECIDE on what movie to watch with my boys was like trying to braid hair with seven hands: it's not pretty and nothing gets done. Ultimately, I won and decided to rent an action movie and order pizza. Pizzas. We had to call for another two supreme pizzas when the original four weren't enough for Nash, Tucker, Shadow, Chaz, and me.

"It's been a while since I've seen you guys eat like that," I joked as I flipped through a few of the boxes on the coffee table to grab another slice. I'd been through a whole pie by myself and still was hungry.

"It's been a while since you've sat still long enough to notice."

Tucker handed me another box with two slices sliding around in it and then reached down to see if Shadow was done with his. The dog growled and seemed to raise an eyebrow.

"Okay, okay," Tucker said as he put up in hands in surrender and sat back next to Nash on the couch.

Shadow chewed on a slice of pizza between his paws. He ate all the way up the crust and then nudged it to the edge of the plate before getting another slice from the box next to him. He was careful to not get the sauce on his black fur and was even more careful about pacing himself. I tried to ignore the irony that the man who had been turned into a dog did not like pizza bones.

My day had been long. My feet still ached from the heels, but being surrounded by my boys soothed every neuron. It almost felt right, all my boys around me, well fed, no demons chasing us down, at least none that we were aware of.

But even in the warm and furry living room, we all felt the missing piece. Tower of empty pizza boxes in hand, I went into the kitchen to throw out the trash but took a moment to lean against the counter.

Tyler was close. Our connection was raw, like an exposed nerve after a broken tooth, but I still knew him. He wanted to be here with us, but he still couldn't look at us. Especially me. Not after I'd practically pushed him back into Cristina's arms. Not after Cristina's death. Not after her sacrifice to save me from myself.

I still saw her sometimes when I closed my eyes. Her dark hair that curled around her sharp chin. Her nearly black eyes that turned white when she saw the future in her tarot cards and the part of her always red lips as she gasped when the blade was buried between her ribs by Carlisle. The blade that was meant for me.

I sent Tyler a warm thought through our connection, strumming the thick golden strand softly so he'd know that I was still there, we were still here waiting for him to come home. But I knew that it was selfish. I needed to know that he was okay. That I hadn't lost another. I couldn't lose another.

Nothing came back at me. No *I'm alive*. But the sentiment wasn't rejected. That was a first in the past month.

I took in a deep breath and wiped the brief moisture that had formed in my eyes. I got some cold sodas from the fridge, put on my brave face, and walked back out into the living room.

"You need to write for bigger movies," Tucker said. "The dialogue in this thing is horrible."

I laughed. "Didn't know we were watching this for the dialogue. I thought it was for the espionage and the slinky cat suits."

"You know I like me a good cat suit." Chaz smiled as he reached out for a soda but instead captured my waist and pulled me onto his lap.

I tossed the sodas to the boys and snuggled in to enjoy some action-adventure where I was neither actioning nor adventuring.

MY BUTT VIBRATED with the incoming call. I slid the phone out of my back pocket and frowned at the caller ID.

"Hello?" I answered as I rose from Chaz's lap and walked into the kitchen.

"Prima Violet?"

"Kandice?"

"Um, remember when you said that you could help us?" Her East Texas accent was thicker for the panic in her voice.

"What happened?"

"It's my boyfriend, see he sort of . . . and then I maybe . . ."

I closed my eyes and reached for my power. Sorting out through the dogs and wolves and snakes, I found her bird, a hawk, and strengthened my tie to her. She was panicked but not scared. It was new. "Are you at home?"

"Yeah."

"Text me your address and I can be there in ten minutes."

"Thank you, Prima."

I ended the call, and the glowing phone went dark as I continued to stare at it. This might be my first mission as a Prima. Dallas had been quiet since the battle against Carlisle. The other calls I'd gotten were more like "I'm going to be late" and "Can you pick up dinner, because Tucker ate the last bit of food in the house?"

This was a real pack member in need.

Almost giddy with the thought, I turned around to see the four men standing in my kitchen doorway, like a dark, furrowed curtain. They'd abandoned the action movie to listen to my conversation.

"What's wrong?" Tucker asked first.

"Kandice needs a little backup on something."

"On what?" Nash asked.

"Don't know."

"Then let's go," Chaz said.

They all moved toward the front door in sync. They had been spending way too much time together.

"Stop," I ordered.

The group actually stopped.

"I don't need an entourage," I said as I walked past them and slipped on my Chuck Taylors in the living room.

"You're not going alone," Chaz said.

I knew I wasn't going to get past the Brow Brigade. I also knew I was tempting fate if I went alone. I had actually learned a few things from getting my butt handed to me on a number of occasions. "Fine. Thumb wrestle over who's going with me. Taking more than one might blow this whole thing out of proportion. But if the proportion is already blown, then I promise to call."

As I hopped upstairs to grab a sweater, I was still excited about someone calling me to help out. It felt natural. There was trouble; I was here to help. With a sidekick.

So when did I get that super cape?

CHAPTER 2

"SO HOW EXACTLY did you get the short straw?" I asked Nash as he directed me to the address Kandice had sent.

He looked relaxed but cramped in the front of my Miata, his knees hitting the glove compartment. "Chaz got ruled out because it was pack stuff. And Shadow, well, there's only so much a border collie can do. So it was really just me and Tucker, and I told him I wanted more field experience."

"Contrary to what I might say and how I might say it, we aren't the X-men. There is no field experience needed."

Nash looked down at my phone and pointed to the next street. "Turn here. And I disagree. I think we need to get more experience in using our powers for good."

I followed his directions. "And what's your super power that needs to be honed for good?"

"Hounds have a nose sensitivity three times that of a Labrador."

"Huh. Didn't know that."

Nash sat up in the seat. "It's this one."

I parked at the curb outside of a simple white tract house with three cars in the driveway, two on cement blocks.

Slowly, we got out of the car and approached the house. Chaz had pressed my pepper spray into my hand as we left. And now, I held it tightly. I knew how these dark houses worked. I also knew I could probably kick the ass of anything that went bump in the night.

Didn't mean I wouldn't take the easy way out.

I slipped off my dampening charm and stuffed it in my pocket. Like releasing a muscle, I let the borders around my power drop to see if there was anything lurking. As I sent it out before me, the power echoed answers back. The house was cold and dark except for the scared little bird inside.

"Anything?" Nash asked.

"Just Kandice."

I carefully knocked on the door and listened, with a capital L. Panthers have pretty darn good hearing, and the walls of these houses are pretty darn thin, so I what I heard confirmed what my power had told me. The patter of flip-flops echoed across the house and Kandice's energy fluttered on the other side of the front door.

"Violet?" she asked.

"At your service."

The door flew open, and Kandice launched herself at me. "I'm so sorry."

For a moment, I was on the defensive as I caught the ninety-pound waif easily in my arms.

She tucked her head into my shoulder, sobbing. "I didn't know what to do."

"It's okay, Kandice," I cooed. "We're here now. Just tell me what happened."

She pulled away and wiped the tears from her already tear-streaked face. Her dirty blonde hair hung limp around her face and her pink tank top had seen better years. But it was her wide, pale blue eyes that told most of the story, especially the one with the purple bruise around it. "Better come inside."

As soon as I walked over the threshold, I smelled blood and beer. It wasn't a good combination. I stopped in the middle of the living room and looked around. I'm not one to judge the state of another's living arrangement, but this place was a wreck. The coffee table had been turned over and there was a broken NASCAR picture hanging sideways on the wall.

And in front of the muted TV was who I presumed to be her unconscious boyfriend. Or at least I hoped he was just unconscious.

I walked between his frame and the TV and focused on his throat. Still had a pulse, despite what the rest of him looked like.

He'd been beaten up pretty bad and there were some vicious scratch marks down his cheek and his chest. He wasn't out of shape; his T-shirt spread across his chest pretty well. A tradesman maybe. But the paunch of his belly told me this wasn't his first party.

"Now would be a good time for a story, Kandice."

"He got into another fight with some of the guys down at the bar"

Kandice stood in the middle of the living room with her hands so balled up into fists I thought she might break her frag-ile-looking fingers. "And then came home and started yelling at me and I don't know what happened. I just freaked out and I hit him back."

Even with the dim living room lights and the erratic jumping of the TV screen, I saw her already healing bruises on her upper arms and neck. I was getting the feeling this wasn't a shifter thing at all.

"And then?" I asked.

"And I got so mad I shifted. He doesn't know about any of that."

My stomach tied into knots. "He didn't know?"

"No, and I know there are laws against others knowing so I shifted back, hit him on the head with an iron skillet and called you."

I didn't know whether to laugh out loud or cry for this poor girl. "Nash, do we have laws against people from the outside knowing?"

"Haverty had a strict policy, and his punishment was severe. There were no exceptions."

I looked from Nash to Kandice. I'd already broken that rule. My friend Devin had already played doctor for a few of our wilder nights and was pretty understanding when I told him to wear two sets of latex gloves when he sewed up Nash's wounds. Wonder how many other rules I'd broken without knowing.

"I'm not punishing you for this, Kandice. But I need a very specific answer and I need you to be as honest as possible."

I walked toward her, stepping over a pizza box and no less than a dozen empty beer bottles. I focused in on her and her energy and felt her trembling from two feet away. She was so frail. So delicate. Like she would blow away.

"Why did you fight back this time?"

My loaded question hung in the air as she looked down at her hands, at her small purple wrists.

"I didn't want this anymore." Her voice was careful, slow. "I want a life I can be proud of and this ain't it. I want a choice like you gave us a choice." She pointed at her boyfriend's unconscious figure. "He just wanted to keep me at home and . . ." Her voice faded.

I put my hand on her shoulder. The truth hummed across our connection. "It's okay, but are you willing to leave, for good?"

"What?"

"If I said that we could make you disappear, would you stay away from here, from him? We're talking new job, cutting all ties—"

"Yes."

It was her lack of hesitation that convinced me. I stepped away and looked around the house. My creative brain kicked into high gear, looking at props and resources for the scene I was about to create.

"Violet? What are you thinking?" Nash asked.

"I'm thinking he just saw his girlfriend turn into a bird."

"And?"

When the plan hit me, I smiled. It was flawless and Boyfriend would never come after Kandice again. "I'm going to tell him the truth."

"Violet, you can't," Nash gasped.

"In this state, he won't even believe it, let alone anyone he would try to tell."

Nash stepped between me and Boyfriend. "We've had people come after us before and there really is only one way to stop them from continuing to come after us."

It surprised me that Nash was advocating violence. My little bookworm. For a moment, I was torn. It was nice to see he was growing a backbone, standing up for his pack, but what had he experienced that killing someone was his Plan A for rule breakers?

I appealed to his logic because I knew he would concede to that.

"I need proof. If he tries to come after her, I'll be more forceful next time. I really do like the iron skillet idea. But I'm not going to behead a guy unless he really needs it."

"Won't do much good. He didn't use it much anyway," Kandice put in.

I snorted but Nash maintained his stern look before he backed away. "Fine," he said.

"Thank you. Now. I need you two to get going. Keep your cell phones on and find a pay phone. If there are such things anymore."

"What are you planning?"

I put my hands on my hips and looked at him squarely. "I write horror movies for a living, Nash. I'll think of something."

I CLEANED. I would never admit that I was nervous, but after Kandice packed up a few things and Nash took my car keys, I picked up pizza boxes, beer bottles, and junk mail to clean up the living room.

Frankly, I needed the room to pace.

I'd checked Boyfriend's wound. He was going to be all right. I'd taken worse hits at the dojo with my wind elemental sensei. This was just a bump on the head.

Along with a few other adjustments to the scene, I secured his wrists with duct tape and waited. I channel surfed. Read through a magazine. Texted Chaz to let him know I was fine and would be home before the movie marathon was over.

Boyfriend moaned and I ran my sweaty hands down my jeans and took my hair out from its ponytail. My dark hair fell across my shoulders and into my face. Though I trusted my plan, I still didn't want to give this guy enough clues to chase. There were a million tall brunettes in Dallas.

I stood between him and the dancing glow of the TV.

His head lolled from one side to the other. His dull brown eyes opened slowly. When he realized he was gagged and taped to a chair, he began to jump around, struggling against his restraints.

"Hey. Stop. You're going to . . ."

He knocked himself over. At panther speed, I rushed to his side to catch him and my super strength almost wasn't enough to get him upright again. Boyfriend had a few extra pounds on him.

"Stop wiggling. I've just got a few things to say and then Kandy and I are gone forever."

He mumbled something that I interpreted as "Where's Kandy?"

"Well, due to your persistent mistreatment of my girl, I'm going to take her away from this and give her the kind of life she deserves."

He mumbled something close to "She's a freak."

"Yes, Kandy is very special. And there are a lot of very special people in this city. Could be your neighbor, the policeman who writes you a ticket. Could be your boss." I stood before him again. "And us very special people take care of our own and we don't like it when inebriates come home and beat on those smaller than them."

I leaned into him and smelled the fear and the liquor as it ran in rivulets down his forehead, down the cleavage underneath his white tank top.

I rested a hand on either of his arms. "I'm taking Kandy and you won't be coming after her."

Boyfriend yelled something that I was going to interpret as "But Kandy is a lovely girl and she's my pride and joy," and not what he actually said beneath that duct tape.

"Remember what I said. We protect our own."

I opened up my power and shifted down into my panther form. It was like relaxing all my muscles at once and falling into my other four-legged form.

The man fought his duct tape ties, screaming through the muzzle as he looked down at my bright green eyes.

I paced around him and looked throughout the house. There was an echo here that I hadn't picked up while on two feet. Not a good one. It was the slime that I recognized from the Haverty estate.

Bad things were done here. It had tainted the energy of the place. Where my lair filled with my boys was always warm and welcoming, this place was cold and the ache of it tugged at my bones.

I slinked back around, rubbing against the man's arm as I came to stand before him. I took in a breath and forced myself upward into my two-legged form. Fully dressed. Not a stitch out of place and my cell phone still in my pocket. I was good.

"Did you know that a panther's bite is four times as strong as that of a lion?"

The man shook his head.

It was a boldfaced lie, but with the way this man was shaking, I could have told him that pigs actually could fly but chose not to and he would have believed me.

I moved slowly toward him. "So I'm going to take Kandy. You will not come looking for her and if you do . . ."

I ripped the duct tape from his mouth, not feeling bad about the layer of lip that came with it. "Do you know what will happen to you if you come after Kandy, if you tell anyone about this?"

His mouth opened and closed a few times with some false starts. "You'll eat me?"

I smiled. I might have been having a little too much fun with this. "Precisely. So I'm going to go now and you will just tell everyone the truth. Kandy left you because you're a drunk ass. Say it after me."

"I'm a drunk ass."

I patted him on the head. "Good boy."

I let a slender claw slip through my nail, and I reached down and with a quick slash, undid the tape at his wrists.

Leaving him frozen in the living room, I wiped my prints from the door handle and then slipped out into the night. As I walked down the dark street toward home, I called Nash.

"Violet? Are you okay? Did it go as planned?"

"Went great." I walked down a few houses and leaned against a light post. "Think I've got a knack for intimidation."

It wasn't four seconds later that Boyfriend went screaming out into the night in his tighty whities and hot pink socks.

I smiled. The devil was in the details.

"Do you need someone to come pick you up?"

"Nah, I'll just take a run. Can you call the cops from the pay phone to come pick him up?"

I hung up and shifted and headed down the street after lover boy for just a little more fun.

CHAPTER 3

*S*HE KNEW WHAT *sort of men they were when they came into her Gifts and Things shop; the kind that were looking for the things part. She carefully locked the cabinet beneath the cash register and greeted them in the middle of the showroom floor.*

"How can I help you?"

"We're looking for Mrs. Goodwick," the older of the two young men said.

"I'm Miss Goodwick," she said, folding her hands at her waist like her mother used to do.

A curious look passed over both men's faces and the older one smiled and shook his head with a strange laugh.

"We must be looking for your mother," he said.

"Then try the church on Main. She's buried in the family plot."

The men looked at each other with a mirrored raised eyebrow. "I'm sorry, Miss Goodwick. Our father spoke of a Mrs. Goodwick, who helped him out of a few tight spots. We were hoping that she could do the same for us."

With a deep breath, she looked up at the two men and couldn't figure out why she hadn't seen the resemblance the moment they came into her store in the first place. Maybe she was losing her touch. She should have known those golden eyes anywhere.

"What can I help you two with?"

"We need some special ingredients for an old recipe?" the older brother said as he handed her a small slip of white paper.

Serena's eyebrows jumped when she saw the names of two very rare and dangerous roots. She swallowed hard and looked back up at the men.

"I'm not sure I've got the second one," she said, biting her tongue. She was a terrible liar. But she just had to know why they needed these two ingredients together. "I've got the first one in the back."

She led the men to the darker corner of the shop. Not too many people ventured back here. There was a reputation about the corner of Goodwick's Gifts and Things—that strange and dangerous things lay behind the glass countertop and on the shelves with locked doors.

She stepped behind the counter and took the key from around her neck and unlocked one cabinet.

"So you're a witch then?" the younger one said.

Serena just laughed softly as she reached for the darkly colored, unlabeled bottle. With an extra smile, she pulled two more unlabeled bottles out of the cabinet and locked it up.

She set the bottles on the counter and looked very hard at the younger of the two brothers. He had his father's eyes but not his features. He must take after his mother, she thought.

"I'm not a witch, young Mr. Garrett. I just know a lot of things other people have forgotten."

She opened up one of the extra bottles she had pulled out. "Like if you boil this herb in water from a fresh stream collected at dawn, it will stop the headaches that come after visions."

The young man gulped and his face paled.

She turned her gaze to the older of the brothers; he was his father's son down to the dark look in his eyes. She opened up the other bottle and pulled out a dirty brown root. "And a teaspoon of this one ground up in Neosporin will heal almost anything, not that you need it."

She set the root down on the counter and lifted the dark glass bottle. "And this, mixed with that other ingredient, will raise the dead."

She set the bottle back on the counter and clenched her jaw. "But no, I don't practice witchcraft."

"We'll take the lot," the older brother said. "And can you get us the other thing?"

"Maybe," was all she said as she began to package up envelopes with enough of the plants in them for their purpose.

"Money is no object."

"It's not the material cost I'm thinking about," she said as she left the counter and walked up to the cash register. The boys followed.

"Spells like these cost more than just money, gentlemen."

Serena looked down at the ingredients and looked squarely at the young men.

It was the elder's words that convinced her to find that other ingredient for them. "She's our sister. We'd do anything for her. No matter the cost."

I WOKE UP and stretched along the couch. Dreaming normal dreams again. Well, normal for me. That was nice. And dreaming in full-blown writing fodder to get back into the groove again. That was even better. I needed to get writing again. I needed something juicy to wave underneath my boss's nose to make sure he always loved me. The movie that I'd written for Drew and Cloak & Dagger Productions was awesome, but I needed to make sure that the awesome kept flowing so those mortgage payments kept getting paid.

I took in a deep breath and stretched. I sat up on the couch and scratched my head. No one had started breakfast yet. Maybe I could see if I'd picked anything up from my domestic god.

. . .

I SMELLED CHAZ before he ran his hands around my waist. "When did you get in?"

I leaned back into his strong chest. "Don't know. Went for a run and then crashed on the couch."

"You should have come to bed so I could greet you properly from your quest." Chaz chuckled and I felt his laughter in the muscles of his stomach and in the soft ebb of power that he'd opened up around us.

He reached beyond me and flipped the pancakes I was making a mess of. "Have you seen your planner for today?"

"Skyping with the boss at ten, meeting with two from the pack around lunch, and dinner with Waylon." I gulped at the mention of the last appointment. I wasn't quite ready to deal with the emotional hiccup that was the impending visit of my long lost cousin.

"And it's nine thirty. Let me finish these or you will starve. You need food, otherwise you're a monster."

"I'm a monster either way."

I pulled away and grabbed my coffee. I went to sit on the counter next to him as he worked on a stack of pancakes that could have fed an army, but really would only need to feed me, Shadow, and Chaz.

"I'd like to put something on the table," he said as he flipped the pancake.

"Butter? I can get it for you." I was being purposely obtuse.

"I think we should move in together."

My brain went a little foggy and my skin chilled. I rested the hot coffee on my bare leg and stared blankly at him. This was one of those steps that I was still amazed I was actually taking, and actually taking with a male model by day and gun-toting Guardian by night.

"I don't like having to schedule time with you. And if we lived together, it would automatically be more time together. I could rent out my house and get some extra income. And I think I can build my gun cabinet in that little storage under the stairs and . . ." He looked up at my blank face. "Violet?"

A million things were running through my head and, of course, I latched onto the wrong one. "I don't think you should get rid of your house."

"You don't want me to move in?"

"No."

"Oh." His eyebrows jumped and he moved away from the stove. "That didn't go as planned."

I hung my head. "I really shouldn't be allowed to talk before coffee."

"Maybe you're just more truthful before coffee." Chaz walked out of the kitchen.

I set my mug on the counter and turned off the stove. The taste of foot in my mouth clashed with the scent of cinnamon in the air.

"Chaz," I called out through the house.

He hadn't made it far. The place was pretty small. He was standing in the middle of the living room, his hand on his hip and the other running through his light brown hair.

"How are we supposed to be married under two roofs? I mean, unless you're having second thoughts about the whole marriage thing."

My skin tightened at even the mention of breaking of our engagement. "No, Chaz. Never. I want to be married to you. I just don't think you should let go of your house."

"Why not?"

Here we go. I was just about to launch into another diatribe where I got to mention that I hadn't told him everything, breaking rule number one in our relationship.

"First of all. It's your family house. Secondly, we might need a safe house."

"A safe house?

"And not just for when we have fights." I sighed and went to sit on the arm of the chair. "It's recently been brought to my attention that having places to retreat to around the city is not a bad idea."

"And who brought this to your attention?"

"Peter Delmont. The executor of Haverty's will. When I officially took on the responsibilities of Prima, apparently I inherited more than just the Legacy."

"What are you talking about, Vi?"

"I inherited everything. Seven safe houses, including the Forest Farms property and about a billion dollars more in different bank accounts and other investments."

I'd never seen that particular shade of pallor on Chaz's before. The blood rushed out of his face and he wobbled on his feet. I jumped up from the arm of the chair and guided him to the couch.

"When'd you find this out?" he asked.

"Yesterday morning?" I squeaked.

Chaz defaulted to frustration mode. "We were together last night, Vi. How do you forget something like that? Or were you just going to wait a few more days to tell me you're a millionaire."

"Billionaire?" I shifted on the couch to look at him. "See, that's where I'm having a problem. It's not my money. It's the pack's money, blood money really."

Chaz looked at me and I could almost feel the rush of questions across his brain.

"I also haven't signed the papers to officially have everything handed over to me."

"Why not?"

"Because I don't know what I'm getting into."

Chaz sighed and looked away from me and across the living room. "It's ten o'clock."

"I need to know what you're thinking. Screw Drew."

Chaz chuckled. "You've never said that before."

"I just wrote that man a summer blockbuster that spawned a TV show. I'm golden for the next fifteen minutes before he spazzes out and calls. Right now, I need you to tell me what you think."

Chaz scratched his head and sighed. "A billion dollars?"

"According to Delmont."

"Blood money?"

"Might as well be from the Mob. Think bloody horse heads."

He licked his lips. "What are you going to do?"

"What are *we* going to do," I corrected.

Chaz shook his head. "This doesn't feel like a *we* thing."

"Well, when we are married, according to Texas state law, half of it would be yours."

Chaz raised his eyebrows. "That doesn't suck."

"But I'd like to use it to help the pack. Maybe buy the property next to Iris's and build another house out there."

"Might be nice to build her a new barn as well."

"No one touches that barn."

Chaz frowned. "It's falling apart. The next big storm and it's going to be a wreck."

I smiled at him. "No one touches the barn, okay?"

"Sure? It's going to look a little odd with the yacht inside it though."

"Who says there's going to be a yacht in it?"

"I'm expecting an awesome birthday present this year."

I laughed and snuggled in next to him on the couch. He put his arm around my shoulder and I closed my eyes as I rested my head on his shoulder.

"So what are you going to do?" he asked softly into my hair.

"I thought about taking a shower. I think I'm starting to smell."

He kissed my forehead. "About the inheritance."

"I want to take a look at the properties. See if any of them are useful. But Forest Farms is going."

Chaz was silent. He knew why I could never use that place again. Why none of us could ever step foot in that place again. He tightened his arm around my shoulders.

"Should be an easy million from that one and as I stumble through this Prima thing, I'll figure out where the money needs to go and maybe where the money all came from. I can see legal fees, bail bonds in my future."

"I could look into that for you. I do have a few contacts."

"Don't you have a sacred destiny to fulfill?"

"The Avion is being more cautious about my jobs. She's still pissed Yasmina used her like that."

"Don't think anyone foresaw a time loop rigged by the leader of the Cause."

"Andrea just wants an invite to the wedding."

I groaned and sat up. "Can't we just skip that part?"

"There's always Vegas," he suggested.

I stood. "Jessa would kill me if I eloped. And then where would the pack be after that? No, I guess I'll have to go through with it for the sake of the pack."

Chaz ran his fingers through my hair. "So you're going to take the money, right?"

"You going to do this with me?"

Chaz sighed. "Guess I'm stuck with you."

"Don't you forget it." I snuggled in even closer to him and closed my eye eyes to listen to the beat of his golden heart. Everything was going to be okay. With Chaz beside me, I could do anything, even be rich. "I can make an appointment tomorrow with Delmont to sign the papers. How's your day look?"

"It's a Saturday. Do lawyers work on Saturdays?"

"I'm his Prima. He'll work on a Saturday."

~

I STOMPED AS I tossed the three shirts I had been holding on to my bed. "I have nothing to wear," I yelled at my poor defenseless closet.

"You're starting to sound like Jessa," Chaz said, appearing in the doorway of my bedroom.

"Well, we are the Key Holder and Keeper. I'm sure there is some personality osmosis."

Chaz walked across the room and my entire body smiled at him.

My day had been crap. I'd had to hand-feed Drew the script for the TV pilot *MoonBlood.* I'd had to walk two pack members through getting a driver's license. Another one called to see if he could take a job at a fast-food place, and I'd had to catch Tucker up on what had happened with Kandice's boyfriend to make sure that the guy was going to stay gone.

And now I was about to see a cousin I hadn't talked to in three years.

Chaz slid his hands around my waist and pulled me against his strong frame. Without my charm on, he was warm and goldenly and my radiating power beat like a heartbeat around us. He kissed my nose and smiled. "You'll look beautiful in anything."

I snorted. "I have to look great. I haven't seen Waylon since Aunt Glory's."

Chaz pulled away, catching my hand and pulled me toward the bed with a playful glint in his hazel eyes. "If you need a little relaxation . . ."

I resisted his advances regretfully. "We've still got company."

"We've always got company." He sighed and let my hand go. He flopped on the corner of the bed and watched as I went back to searching through my closet, which was better than it was six months ago, but still didn't have quite what I wanted to wear.

"Is this you being nervous?"

I stopped flipping through my tops and looked over at him. "It's just dinner with Waylon. Not a wildebeest from the other side of the Veil." At least that was the line I'd been repeating to myself every time the thought of dinner tonight crossed my mind.

"Didn't answer my question."

I sighed and finally pulled out a billowing black top to go with dark jeans. Waylon's call three weeks ago was not frantic, nor did it require silver daggers or claws. He just wanted to know if I wanted to see him and meet his twelve-year-old daughter. Nothing odd about that.

Except Waylon and I hadn't really talked to each other in a very long while and hadn't been close since he went off to college.

And now he was back. Out of the blue.

As I pulled on the needed tank top, I thought about it. Was I nervous? "I'm not any more nervous than meeting with the new pack members."

"Then why aren't they staying here?"

I pulled on my shirt and ran my fingers through my hair.

"Because they are staying at the Ritz-Carlton. What's my little place compared to the Ritz-Carlton?"

Chaz sighed, that little furrow between his golden green eyes forming. "Did you even offer?"

I sighed and put my hands on my hips. "What are you getting at, Chaz?"

"You have Shadow here all the time. Nash crashes at our place more than at Tucker's, and three times now, I've almost walked in on Kandice in the guest bathroom, and she's only been here a day."

"And?" I asked as I went into my bathroom to figure out what I was going to do with my hair.

"Could there be a possibility you see your pack as your family and Waylon as just someone you're related to?"

I stopped brushing my hair. Crap. The pretty boy might be right.

He did have a tendency to call me out when I was acting stupid or not thinking things through. I didn't know Waylon, not anymore, and he sure didn't need me like the others in my life needed me.

Chaz appeared in the doorway to the bathroom. "Vi? Family is more than just the people who rely on you."

I turned around to face him. "You know I hate it when you get all philosophical."

"That's right," he smiled. "You just keep me around to help you find your keys."

"And don't you forget it." I turned back around to look at myself in the mirror.

Chaz came up behind me and wrapped his arms around me. As he rested his head on my shoulder to look at me in the mirror, every muscle in my nervous frame relaxed against him as I rested my head against his. I was petrified about meeting Waylon and Lexie.

"I don't know if shame is even the right word for how we've just let each other float on our own for so long."

"What's the backstory here, Vi? Do I need to hate this guy? I've got that rocket launcher I'd never used before."

"No." I sighed. I let the warmth of Chaz soothe my narration. "I guess the blurb of it goes like this: My parents died. I got shipped off to my aunt's. Waylon came in all white knight with his comic books and canvas high tops, being the brother I never had, but two years later, I was back on the porch, cheeks wet with tears as he headed off to college and I was left, again, by someone that I love. I promised myself after that I'd just take care of myself and not rely on anyone."

Chaz nodded through the story, making little therapist sounds in my ear. "Because they always left?"

"Because they always left."

Chaz tightened his arms around me. "But you've grown up."

"I think I've had some help."

He rested his head on my shoulder. "You two are the only ones left in your family. He's a single parent and he's turning to you. He's not asking for power. He's not asking for protection. He just needs you here."

I nodded. "But I can do protection. I'm good at the slash and *grrr*. It's the emotional stuff I'm not too sure about. What do I know about kids? I was so emotionally blocked at Aunt Glory's funeral I missed that Waylon even had a daughter."

Chaz kissed my temple. "All you need to be is the adorable, loving, funny cousin Violet."

"What about Aunt Violet? I always wanted to be Aunt Violet."

He smiled. "Be the adorable Aunt Violet and I'm sure he'll tell you what he needs. You Jordans are a little blunt sometimes."

I slapped his arm but pulled his arms tighter around me. The warmth of him was almost as good as a double latté to soothe my jittering nerves. The sparkle off my engagement ring caught the bathroom light and twinkled merrily against the black shirt.

"Crap," I sighed as I pushed away from Chaz and went back to my closet.

"What?" he asked.

"I wore black last time I saw Waylon."

LEXIE WANTED TO have dinner at the Cheesecake Factory. Being a Friday night, there were a million other people who seemed to have a hankering for cheesecake as well. The foyer alone was deafening, especially to a person without super hearing. For me, it was like the front row at an AC/DC concert.

I had to ask the hostess three times to see if our party had arrived. The young girl shook her head, and I took my table buzzer.

Chaz and I wriggled back out of the crowd and stood on the

sidewalk outside. I gulped in the quiet air not saturated with date-night perfumes.

Chaz dodged another couple walking into the restaurant. "Do you think he'll consider someplace else?"

I shrugged. "This is what she wanted."

"Don't they have one where they live? Which is where again?"

I had to think. "It wasn't Illinois. He split from that place before I did. I think he mentioned Chicago or Boston or Pittsburgh. One of those."

Chaz jammed his hands in his back pockets. "So that wandering thing is a Jordan trait?"

I crossed my arms and huffed. I knew what he was asking. He was trying to see if Waylon had a talent like my mother had a talent, like I had a talent. "I don't know, Chaz."

"Does he know about you?"

"Bitten by a werepanther in my back alley isn't exactly first conversation stuff."

I knew the moment the pair arrived. There was a shimmer of something like cold pebbles rolling down my spine as I watched the two walk toward us. I didn't know if it was magic or nerves. I tugged at my red top and adjusted the charm at my throat.

Waylon looked like he had three years ago at the funeral. Sandy hair and sun-kissed skin, everything that wasn't me. He was saying something to his daughter, and as the two of them laughed, they shared the same smile.

The girl was already up to his shoulder, taking after her cousin Violet already. Her long brown hair was swept up in a ponytail and she pushed her glasses up on her nose as she said something about a four-inch cheesecake that this boy in class said he ate in four bites, but she was sure he was lying.

Got to love that super hearing.

When Waylon saw me, he knew me too, despite the loss of poundage and glasses. He smiled as he approached. "Violet."

His smile was wide and clear as he stuck out his hand. His hand was like his smile, warm and honest as I slipped my hand into his and squeezed. I knew a normal person would have hugged their long-lost cousin, but I wasn't ready for that yet.

"Waylon, this is Chaz Garrett, my fiancé."

"All right, Violet. Congratulations."

The two men shook hands and Chaz opened up his borders to greet him. I knew what he was doing, trying to see if Waylon got any of my family's psychic blood. Right now, Waylon was as normal as the next guy.

"And let me introduce my daughter, Lexie." Waylon's hand rested on his daughter's shoulder and he beamed. No magic involved.

"Please to meet you, Lexie." I stuck out my hand.

The girl pushed up her glasses as she reached out her thin hand. I shook it gently and smiled. The girl relinquished a small smile. There was a bit of Violet in there somewhere, but there was more Waylon.

"How's the line?" Waylon asked as he looked toward the door.

"About thirty minutes," Chaz said.

"But it's crazy loud in there," I said.

Waylon frowned, and again, cold stones rolled down my spine. "Right, well. Why don't we find another place for dinner?"

"But I wanted a four-inch cheesecake," Lexie said.

"We can get some later, honey. It's too loud for your Aunt Violet."

The moment he said *Aunt Violet* I loved the sound of it. It was one of the few titles that I didn't mind, and I found myself smiling for no reason as I imagined no less than three ways to spoil her.

Maybe there was something magical to this family thing.

Waylon squeezed his daughter's shoulder. "Do you guys know of another place close?"

"There's Maggiano's, at the mall," Chaz suggested.

"There's a mall?" Lexie's eyes brightened immediately, the thought of gigantic cheesecake but a distant memory.

"Why did you have to say the 'm' word?" Waylon sighed as he rolled his eyes.

CHAPTER 4

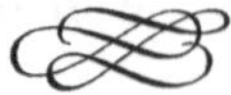

$\mathcal{C}$HAZ KEPT UP with Lexie as she darted through the stores in the mall like a hummingbird on crack. Only his super speed explained how he was able to keep up with a twelve-year-old girl.

And we let him. Waylon and I hadn't really gotten a chance to talk during dinner. I was too busy catching up on everything teenager. Lexie did not inherit my shyness as she rattled on for forty minutes about this and that. The memories of why I preferred my college tenure over my high school years came rushing back quickly. Boys and cliques and homework, oh my.

Waylon and I leaned against the railing outside of the store Lexie was currently rummaging through. He took another bite of the ice-cream cone that Lexie had wanted, taken two licks from, and handed to her father before her mad dash. Now, we were both using the ice cream as a way to avoid talking about what really needed to be talked about: Why now? Why, after thirteen years?

I savored the tiramisu gelato a little too long and tried to get the conversation started with some small talk. "So Ritz-Carlton? That must be nice."

"The company is paying for relocation."

"Do they need a staff writer?"

Waylon let out a small chuckle. The familiarity of him danced down my skin and I couldn't help but smile myself. For an instant, I saw the Waylon I remembered, sparkling eyes and charming smile.

"Since we are in between schools, if you know of any educational things to do here in Dallas . . ."

I nodded. "I know loads. Wrote a bunch of articles for *Parent Dallas*, this local magazine. I could email them to you if I had your email."

Waylon's shoulders dropped. "Let's not beat around the bush, Vi. I'm sorry. I knew what you were going through and I left anyway because I was selfish eighteen-year-old. You shouldn't have been alone."

The fear and hate and anger swirled around me for a moment as he brought up memories I thought I'd long suppressed into oblivion. With the memory of the crying chubby girl on the porch, the Legacy crept out and swirled around me protectively, and the heat of it started to melt my dessert.

I managed a few words. "I did have Aunt Glory."

"Let's be honest. You needed me and I left."

I licked my lips and looked down at the quickly melting cup. I took in a deep breath and calmed my borders. The power was soothing like a protective blanket of power that knew I was stressed.

"Please say something," Waylon pleaded.

I didn't know what to say. No quippy remarks, no snappy comebacks.

"I practiced that speech in front of my mirror for two days, Violet."

I chuckled. I could see him do it, because I did it.

"I kept seeing you at fourteen, looking back at me, those green eyes, just like your mom's."

"What did I say in these practice sessions?"

"I was a detestable mole-rat that should be flung out into the desert and left to live off its own urine."

I laughed.

"You always did have a way with words. I wanted my practice session to be accurate."

I took in a deep breath and looked up at him. I didn't see the boy who left, but a completely different man before me. Maybe with a hint of the boy who used to do Mad Libs with me when I couldn't sleep and made sure I was never in need of spiral notebooks for my stories.

And Chaz was right. I wasn't that chubby little girl anymore and I had managed to put together a family here in Dallas.

And most importantly, he deserved a second chance. Everyone else in the pack got one, why not us?

Waylon looked down at his cone. "I just need someone in my corner right now, Violet. I'm not asking for help. A familiar face, someone Lexie can rely on. It's been just the two of us since Mom died and I'm exhausted."

"Would it be too forward of me to ask about Lexie's mother?"

"Dancing away in Vegas, I suppose."

I plucked a napkin from Waylon's fingers to catch a drip of gelato from the now completely melted cup in my hands, but when my fingers brushed his, the story flashed across my brain so fast that I didn't have a chance to secure my dessert. They met when he was young. He was on a roll at the tables. They got married, had a baby, but the nuclear life wasn't for her and she left them to go back to the bright lights of the big city, leaving him only twenty years old with a baby to take care of.

After the sharp sting of the vision, brain party, whatever you wanted to call it, I had to pry my eyes open. Waylon was kneeling before me as he picked up my cup from the floor.

"You okay?" He frowned up at me.

Uh-oh. I've re-known him for a whole two hours and he already had the furrow. "Fine. Brain freeze," I lied. I didn't like doing it.

Waylon tossed the half-eaten gelato in the garbage and returned to me. "I know it's going to take small steps. You've got a life here, a big fiancé, and I don't want to ruin whatever peace you've finally found."

The comment elicited a laugh. Peace. Right.

Lexie and Chaz exited the store we were outside of as if on some fated cue and Chaz's golden eyes sparkled up at me. That's right, there was my peace. There was my reason to fight.

In that moment, Lexie darted off in another direction and Chaz jumped after her.

We laughed as we slowly followed them. "It really is good to see you all grown up, Violet."

"Who said anything about being grown up?"

WHEN WE GOT HOME from dinner, I paused at the sliding glass door of the patio. Something was off.

"Vi?"

I unlocked the door and opened it.

Chaz, being the Marine I'm pretty sure he was in another life, pushed past me and drew his gun from the hidden holster at his hip. He walked stealthily through the first floor of the house, peeking around corners as he cleared the bottom floor.

"Really?" I asked as I tossed my keys on the table and closed the door behind me.

"What?" he asked as he put his gun away and looked at me.

"You looked like something was wrong."

"Nothing's wrong," I smiled. "Take a listen."

Chaz cocked his head, but I knew he didn't feel what I did throughout the house. "We have the house to ourselves?"

He raised an eyebrow.

I jumped him. It wasn't pretty. Between the lack of guests and the newly acquired confidence from my recent foray into being a decent Prima and Aunt, I was more than a little eager for some Chaz time.

He caught me easily as I wrapped my legs around his middle. His lips were just as greedy as mine were as he walked us across the living room and dropped down to the couch. I adjusted my legs to straddle his hips.

I laughed and pulled away from him. His eyes were a happy hazel, and his lips were soft and parted.

"What?" he asked.

"Have I told you that you're amazing?"

"Not this week."

"Remind me to put it in my planner."

I kissed him again, taking it slower this time, being a little more thorough, making sure to enjoy his supple lower lip and his honey mouth.

He ran his strong hands up my torso and slid my shirt easily over my head. His lips trailed down my neck and my eyes fluttered closed in anticipation. He slid my bra strap down my shoulder as his kisses moved slowly southward.

And then his phone started to ring. The distinctive ring of a damsel in distress.

He stopped kissing me and rested his head against my breastbone. His breath traveled down my chest and his fingers curled around my waist.

I kissed the top of his head. "You should get that."

"Are you sure?"

"Didn't you just tell me that the Avion wouldn't call you for trivial things?"

Chaz sighed and I slipped off his lap. As he strode angrily across the living room, I pulled on my tank top.

I tried not to listen to the conversation but that naturally curious thing prevented me from letting Chaz have any privacy.

"About what time? No, I've been with my fiancé. Can I come now?"

When he went for his keys, I rose off the couch.

"I'll be right there." Chaz slipped his phone into his back pocket.

"My house was just broken into."

"Crap. Was that the police?"

"Yeah. Neighbor reported it."

"Want me to go with you?"

Chaz paused in his trek to the back door.

I nervously filled that silence, suddenly afraid that he wouldn't want me there with him. "I mean I can stay here and wait for you to come back, but we all know I'm just going to hound you afterwards."

"No, you should come. And speaking of hounds, can you call Tucker?"

I nodded and went to grab my purse from the dining-room table.

THERE WAS ONLY one cop car outside, but its lights were making every shadow on Chaz's street dance like a patriotic parade.

Chaz walked up to the front door, which had been kicked in. "Let me clear it first."

I nodded. As high as I was on being a kick-butt Prima, I was also going to be good fiancée if it killed me. This was his house, his violation; therefore, it was his show.

See, I was learning.

Tucker said he'd meet us there, so I stayed outside on the lawn.

An old woman in a blue housecoat and pink slippers shuffled toward me from the house next door. Her silver-streaked hair was wrapped up in soft pink curlers and she smelled like Ben-Gay.

"What happened?" she asked, her wide brown eyes looking up at me.

"Looks like someone kicked in his door."

"Oh my. Well, good thing you two weren't home."

Actually, I kinda wished we had been there. The two of us would have taken out a burglar in about four seconds flat. No muss, no fuss. This was just extra paperwork.

"Should we be worried?" the old woman asked.

"I don't know. I'll make sure we let you know what happened."

"Thank you. Seth has always been such a good neighbor. Still mows my yard every week."

I looked over the woman's shoulder and smiled. I didn't correct who had actually been mowing her yard for the past six years. "He's a keeper."

"Violet!" Chaz was waving at me from the door.

"Take care of yourself," I said over my shoulder as I walked across the front yard.

The woman shuffled back toward her house and I wondered how many more eyes were on us at two in the morning and which pair had called it in. It made me tighten my sweater around me as I joined Chaz in the doorway.

"Can you take a sniff around?"

I raised an eyebrow. "Seriously?"

Chaz just glared. "Do you want me to say please?"

"Maybe later." I winked at him before I entered the familiar scene.

The police officer was sitting in an armchair filling out paperwork.

He rose. "Are you the fiancée?"

"I do have that honor."

"Mr. Garrett looked around and said he didn't see anything missing. Said you might be able to."

"I'll try."

When I was sure the officer was nothing more than an average Joe, I took off my dampening charm and released my borders.

Without the charm to dull my senses, the information jumped to me. There had been someone here, but I couldn't smell them. The lack of scent scared me. It was something unnatural. Not a shifter or elemental; they left a trail, a smell in their wake, being the more natural of the Wanderers. This was something that left a trail of cold spots through the living room and into the guest bedroom.

I followed the cold spots, and they led straight to the trunk. Chaz's father had locked away a book responsible for enslaving half the shifter population of Dallas in that trunk. Why were they looking for the book? How did they even know it was here?

I walked back into the hallway and picked up on the cold spots.

Holding my hands out, I felt where it—he, it was definitely a he—had walked through the house to the back bathroom. It was then I noticed that it wasn't cold; it was a lack of heat, like the life had been sucked out of that spot. Every space had an energy, and this one's had been sucked out.

I ran my hand across the sink and felt another cold spot on my half-used bottle of shampoo.

That was just creepy.

I went back out into the well-lit living room as fast as I could and found Tucker talking to the police officer. His eyes flashed to me for a moment, and his energy was spiky. Something the police officer said had set him on edge.

Chaz, too. His arms crossed over his chest so tightly I was sure he would rip his jacket. I walked over to him and rubbed my hand across his shoulder, using some of the friction to warm up my hands from the creepy cold spots.

"Got anything?" he asked quietly.

I nodded. I kept my lips tightly clamped between my teeth to keep from telling him because I didn't want to say anything in front of the officer. I was pretty sure that Officer Joe would not understand unnatural cold spots running around the house.

About fifteen minutes later, the officer gave Chaz a case report number and I asked that he stop next door to calm the neighbor's nerves.

When the door was shut, I was finally able to speak. It felt like I'd been holding my breath for ten minutes. "It wasn't a shifter or an elemental. But it was one of us. Something that leaves an ice-cold trail. And they went for the trunk in the closet."

"The one with the wedding dress?" Chaz asked as he headed for the room.

We followed after him. It didn't strike me as odd that Chaz would think of it as the trunk with his mother's wedding dress and other family heirlooms. But for me, it was the trunk that I used my weird psychic powers to open and discovered the most evil book on the planet like it had been calling to me.

He went to the trunk and examined the still intact lock. He looked relieved, if a person whose house was just broken into can look relieved.

"He walked down the hallway and messed with my shampoo, too."

"It could have been trying to catch your scent." Tucker said.

"And now its officially creepy."

Chaz looked to Tucker over my shoulder. "There haven't been any other break-ins in this neighborhood, have there?"

"No." Tucker was being suspiciously still. I think he was taking my cue. This was Chaz's call, his scene. We were just there to help.

Chaz ran his fingers through his hair, then put his hands on his hips. "What were they after?"

"The grimoire?" I suggested. That book could destroy the planet, one destructive spell at a time. It was worth trying to burgle.

"The one that's missing?" Tucker asked.

I nodded. "It's a scary book to go missing, but it's even more scary that they knew where to look for it."

Chaz gestured that we go back out to the living room. "Too bad they didn't steal the TV," he joked.

In our relationship, jokes were good. If he was joking, everything was going to be fine. I looked over at the bulky twenty-year-old TV set. "That really is a shame."

I was just about to offer that we could make it disappear when my phone rang. I pulled my phone out of my back pocket and frowned. It was my neighbor.

"Miss Finn? Is something wrong?"

"Your dog keeps barking."

My dog? Shadow? Why was Shadow at the house?

"I'll get home right away, Miss Finn." I hung up. "Shadow's barking at my house."

"I thought you installed a . . ." Tucker was going to say doggie door. We'd actually cut a hole in the wall for a nice doggie door so Shadow and, ironically, Nash could get into my house any time they needed. "Shit. This is a false flag. The guy's at your place."

I'd never moved so fast in my entire life for Chaz's car. I yelled an order to Tucker across the front yard. "Go watch Jessa."

. . .

CHAZ'S CHALLENGER COULDN'T go fast enough for my taste.

My brain and my mouth went a mile a minute. "Are they back? Did they reorganize now that Carlisle is gone? Was this an isolated attack? What kind of Wanderer leaves a trail like that?"

"Is this how your mind works?" Chaz asked, his knuckles white on the steering wheel. "All loud and constant?"

"Yes."

"How do you stay sane?"

"Who said I was sane?"

Chaz cracked a smile, which again was my goal.

"I'm sorry it broke into your house."

"It's not an *it*, Violet. It's a being. And I'm sure he has a name and when I figure out what it is, I will not stop until I find him."

"Is that how your mind works? All loud and vendetta-y?"

Chaz snorted as we pulled up to my house. I stepped out of the car and Shadow came running up to me. His energy was manic as he jumped and pointed with his cute black nose and ran around me.

"I know. There was someone in the house."

I started walking toward the door and Shadow blocked my path.

"Shadow, if he's still in there, I promise to leave a little for you to stomp on too."

I stepped over him and tried for the door one more time.

Shadow growled and bared his teeth. In the waxing moonlight, I saw something dangling from his white teeth.

I knelt down and reached out for the strip of cloth hanging out of his mouth.

"What is it?" Chaz walked up behind me.

I stood up and faced Chaz. "Apparently, Shadow got a piece of our intruder."

His eyes flashed golden in the streetlights. He was just itching to use his power to go off and find the guy.

"Now, now, Action Boy," I held the cloth behind my back. "Let's check our house before you go gallivanting off."

"But the fresher the cloth the easier it is for me to track them."

I walked toward the door. "And when you haven't slept in three days when you finally catch him, and he . . ."

There were scratch marks on my front door. Long, deep grooves into the red paint. I traced the imprint of a boot into the wood. He was strong, but not strong enough to break through the wards that kept out evil intentions.

"Is that a . . ." Chaz ran his fingers across the impression.

"Going to rethink chasing after it?"

Chaz nodded. "Let's just get inside."

I knew we weren't done with the conversation. I knew I was going to have to burn this piece of cloth to keep Chaz from hunting down the thing that broke into his house, but as he gently ushered me through my front door, I knew that I had until sunrise to convince him to not go alone.

CHAPTER 5

FIRE ROSE AND licked the ceiling of the warehouse. The tall aisles of product only created more defined pathways for the fire to follow.

The girl ran and ran hard. Every turn she took only landed her face to face with the fire.

She took a left and then another left and was met with the wall of flames that seemed to be toying with her.

"What do you want?" She screamed out as she pressed against the wooden pallets.

A face appeared in the fire, a beautiful face with dark wide eyes. The curl of the flames formed into lips that seemed to smile as they spoke, the voice pressing down on her like the flames that surrounded her.

"I want you to pay for what your kind did."

"We did nothing," the girl screamed back.

"She's dead because of you."

"We didn't kill her."

The flames rose higher and burned hotter. Her sharp canines pressed down against her dried lips as she tried to find another way out.

A figure walked out of the flames. A woman with dark hair and dark skin, who carried the flames with her in her eyes. "The Prima is dead. Someone will pay."

The flames encircled both of them and as the vampire girl screamed, the woman with the dark skin simply held her there until the girl was nothing but a handful of ash.

I WOKE UP with sweat across my brow. I'd gotten close to no sleep, but this dream was dark and real, and my fingers itched to write it down. Chaz's head weighed seventeen more pounds as I pulled out from under it. It would just have to be another "coffee with a side of coffee" kind of day.

I grabbed my dream journal from the dresser and slid into my slippers. I'd slept in my clothes just in case our little visitor decided to try again. I grabbed my robe off my door and went downstairs.

There was something brewing in the air. Something more than coffee.

I looked out the glass window to the purple morning sky and wished I could read the clouds like I read all those novels. This was the beginning of something. Something big. Something planned.

Crap.

I heard keys in the front door and Tucker ducked in. It made me look at the clock. Six a.m.

"Wanted to make sure you were okay?" he said softly, walking quickly past Shadow sleeping on the couch.

"We're fine. Anything at Jessa's?"

Tucker shook his head. "Talked with the doorman, nothing strange. They were just targeting you and Chaz."

I sighed as I hit the "on" button on the coffeemaker. I didn't have the energy to make a latté. "You should probably go home, get some sleep."

"I'll sleep when you sleep, Prima."

I could have fought him, impose my will, but that would just take too much energy. So instead I made him coffee. Tucker took off his utility belt so that he could sit at the dining-room table.

I put his coffee before him, some of the liquid sloshing out with my rough delivery and sat next to him. "You look awesome, by the way. All geared up and police-y again. How does it feel after almost six months off?"

Despite what was going on around us, Tucker smiled and his brown eyes twinkled. But what I saw wasn't anything compared to what I felt. His joy reverberated through the ties that bound us together, like someone doing double-dutch in my chest. "Really good."

"I know I should have asked sooner, but what did happen with the IA investigation?"

Tucker shrugged. "They couldn't find any real evidence against me. Just hearsay. I'm completely bottom rung again but I'm working."

"Good."

"And I'll keep an ear out for any of our kind of trouble."

I frowned. "I want to take the high ground here and tell you that's how you got in trouble before, but after last night, I think I'm going to need that contact."

"I'm not letting any of us get hurt anymore, Violet." There was a particular growl in his words.

"I know, Tucker." I looked down at the coffee. Something was missing. "We've got an appointment with Delmont this morning if you want to come."

"We?"

"Chaz and I? But since it's pack business, you should come too."

Tucker shook his head. "I'm going to sniff around Chaz's place a little more and see if anyone else got a visit last night."

"Who? The entire pack?"

"If I need to."

I looked down at the black coffee. I was so tired that I'd forgotten milk. Screw it, I needed the caffeine. "Take Nash. He wants more training time."

"He upstairs?"

"No, actually. No one was here last night." I sat up. Where were they? Kandice had taken over the guest bedroom and Nash was usually on my couch. If it wasn't for Tucker's snicker, I would have called them that instant.

"What's that for?"

Tucker was smiling into his coffee. "Come on, Violet. He just rescued Kandice and she's probably really, really grateful. You're the storyteller, you write it."

When his meaning sunk it, I grimaced. "No. Not Nash."

Tucker laughed and he took a long swig of the hot coffee.

Now the images of Nash and Kandice were firmly planted into my brain, I desperately needed to change the subject. "What's this?" I pointed to something on his belt.

"Taser."

I pulled the bright yellow plastic gun from the holster on the opposite side of his gun and turned it over in my hands. It looked like it should have NERF written across its plastic handle. "So the needle thingies shoot out and send the electricity through wires?"

Tucker took the Taser from my inexperienced hand. "Yes, when you pull the trigger, the prongs shoot out at one hundred thirty-five feet per second and conduct a five-thousand-volt shock." Then, he smiled. "What they don't tell you is that you can just use it as a stun gun when you take off the cartridge."

"Really?"

Tucker pulled off the plastic cartridge at the end of the barrel and flipped a button on the side. He pointed it up to the ceiling and pulled the trigger. A white-hot stream of electricity crackled between two silver prongs at the end of the open barrel. It was pretty and the snap of the pulse make my hairs stand on end.

I was mesmerized by the violet sizzle.

"It's enough voltage to take down a grown man. And can be used several times."

"What about a grown animal?"

Tucker frowned. "Is there something you're not telling me?"

"No, never. Just . . ." I looked down at the table as he set down the Taser. "I know I'm not the biggest fish in the fishbowl and I want to make sure that if I have to get into it again, I . . ."

"A Taser will reduce the use of deadly force."

"Exactly."

Tucker took in a deep breath as he holstered his weapon. "You can't blame yourself for her death, Violet. Of any of us, Cristina knew what she was doing. Could literally see the choices she was going to have to make."

"But I didn't. That's what got her killed. How can you put so much faith in someone who—"

Tucker grabbed my hand and slammed it down on the table, squeezing it so hard my knuckles cracked. My eyes locked with his as my Legacy burned around us at the sudden pain. "Yes. She died. But she died free. She didn't choose you because you were the most powerful or the best at strategy. She chose you, we chose you, because you gave us the freedom to. People die and it hurts like hell and it reminds us how much we've got worth living for."

Tears of exhaustion and pain streaked down my cheeks. Tucker was slowly but surely absorbing my way with words, possibly through magical osmosis.

"Now, as your Riko, I should be giving you the 'buck up and deal with it' speech because you've got others who need your help. Others who might need a firmer hand to make sure they make better choices than they did before. But as your friend, I know you can't even think about risking another person's life. That you doubt yourself, which I'm again going to remind you is one of the reasons I trust you. You will never let the Legacy go to your head. You will put others first even if that means not sleeping and not eating."

I sniffed and wiped my tears on the sleeve of my robe. "You really are good at those pep talks."

"Here's another. You need some sleep, and you need to eat."

"Can't. Have to go become a millionaire today."

He released my hand and leaned back in the chair. "Fine, I'll sleep when you sleep," he repeated, like it was some sort of gauntlet tossed out on the table.

"You have no idea the number of all-nighters I pulled in LA."

"And you have no idea how many nights I was out partying and then had to be on duty the next day."

"Touché, Mr. Briggs."

As I sniffed again, I took in a whiff of Tucker's scent, a steady, dark chocolatey espresso blend. The first time I'd really sensed his good guy potential, he'd smelled like coffee, the one staple in all the incarnations of my life. It wasn't until now that I realized what that meant: he was the rock. He was the constant and the North Star.

Where Chaz was my heart and would catch me when I fell, Tucker would stand beside me loyally because I had set him free, and he chose to be by my side.

Tucker tapped his knuckles on the table. "Violet, you okay? Your eyes went a little glassy there for a second."

I chuckled, pushing the under-caffeinated and overly philo-sophical thoughts aside. "Peachy. Just need a little more coffee."

DELMONT WAS NOT happy to be there on a Saturday. He had to come down to the front of the building to let us in and the silence in the elevator was only made worse by a horrible rendition of *In Your Eyes*.

But I didn't care. Fresh coffee in hand, I was ready to become a millionaire. Maybe I could get some sleep then.

He showed us into an immaculate office complete with fake plants and textbooks (again, got to love that super smell, not a real printed page in the room) and we sat at a massive mahogany desk.

Compensating much?

"I had my secretary mark all the places you'll need to sign. And you'll need a witness."

I watched him as he placed the documents before us and pulled a pen from the desk drawer. It slipped from his finger when he handed it to me. His movements were stiff, nervous almost. It wasn't the grace I expected based on our last encounter.

"Guys, can I talk to Delmont alone for a moment?"

Chaz frowned and looked at Delmont and back at me. "We'll be right outside."

Tucker's furrow wasn't any less deep, but he followed Chaz out into the waiting room.

Delmont sat down across from me. "Can I help you, Miss Jordan?"

"Something's wrong."

"It's Saturday."

"This is hardly your first Saturday at work, Delmont. You'd have to work a lot of Saturdays to get this office. What is it?"

Delmont looked down at his long pale fingers. "I've been contacted by several people this week about Haverty's estate."

"Did they miss the memo about me taking over the Pride?"

His crisp blue eyes darted up to mine. "No. They heard you only have the majority by one. They are trying to lose that one."

"You?" I gasped.

"Others are willing to pay handsomely for my services."

I frowned. "Then why am I still sitting here?"

His voice was louder than I'd expected, a tone that made my hackles and power rise around me. "Because for the first time ever, I'm sticking with my choice. And I'd appreciate a little faith and less snark."

I had to watch my grip on my plastic to-go mug. My hand shook at the scolding. People don't yell at their Prima. More flies with honey, I repeated to myself.

I let out a soothing breath. "Who called you?"

Delmont shook his head. "You don't have to worry, Miss Jordan."

"Of course I have to worry. If they are contacting you, they are contacting the others."

"I have put a stop to that."

I gulped. "How?"

He scratched his sideburns wearily and I watched as he carefully crafted his sentence. "I offered a truce on your behalf."

"Oh really? Do anything else on my behalf I should have been contacted first about?"

Our connection twisted just beneath my breastbone. He was holding something back that he wanted to tell me. It was almost like he wanted me to pull it out of him, but he'd locked his jaw so tight nothing was getting through.

I took a deep breath and set my coffee mug on his desk. In a swift movement, he grabbed what I thought was just a crystal paperweight and put it under the mug.

"God, you're just like . . ." I was going to say Devin. My fabulous best friend had a thing about coasters that I will never understand.

But Delmont was nothing like Devin. Devin was good and trusting and human. I wasn't sure Delmont was any of those things.

"A truce with whom?" I kept calm, watched my tone, and looked straight into his blue eyes.

"I was right when I told you that the elementals would elect an Akasha. Her emissary contacted me for a meeting."

"Which one is it?" There had been some talk as we whiteboarded what was left of the Wanderers in Dallas, trying to figure out what would happen to the rest of them now that the Pride was destroyed but our pack was still intact.

"Inez Walker. A fire elemental."

I closed my eyes and tried to see the fight in the ballroom of Forest Farms. Looking back six weeks ago made the battle scene fuzzy, but I did remember there being fire, something on fire whizzing past my head.

"She wanted to know the numbers. See if there could be a division of assets. The others did too. The Clade Leader, the Coven Mistress. All of them have contacted me."

"Why didn't they contact me?"

Delmont was silent and simply lined up a few pens at the top of the paperwork.

"Seriously, if they are going to start coming after my people, then I will not be bureaucratted into the corner and left to do nothing."

He looked away.

"Damn it, Peter." I slammed my hand down on the desk and jumped to my feet. "They knew you well enough to approach you, but if you can't support me . . ." I stopped myself. That foot-in-my-mouth habit was harder to break than I thought. I leaned forward on his desk and he leaned back in his chair. Slow down, Jordan.

Give him that one extra chance that you give everyone else. "If you were in my shoes. If you had a broken pack that needed to be pieced back together one life at a time, would you trust her?"

His gaze rose to meet mine. "She does seem to want the best for the elementals."

I licked my lips and sighed. "Fine. Set it up. But as my new emissary, you're going with me."

"What? I can't just drop everything and—"

I pulled at that taut twine of magic in my chest that connected him to me, and he went silent. "Please set up the meeting at the coffee shop. I'd at least like a home court advantage."

"Yes, Miss Jordan."

I relaxed and sat down in my chair, taking my coffee from its crystal coaster. "I think I'm ready to sign those papers now."

I called to Tucker and Chaz, who bounded into the room.

"Everything good?" Chaz settled back in next to me and Tucker watched from behind.

"No, but I'm ready to sign some papers."

"You'd better stretch first," Delmont said as he readied the stack again.

AN HOUR LATER and I was a billionaire. Seven back accounts, seven properties and seven majority stock holds. The number repetition was a little creepy.

"Is there anything else I can do for you, Miss Jordan?" Delmont asked as he placed the signatures in stacks that held some secret meaning.

"Now that I officially own it, I want to sell the Forest Farms."

Delmont looked up from his organizing. "Are you sure? That's worth a million alone."

"I'm sure. I just want it to go to some boring human who doesn't know what happened. Can't feel the scars we do."

Delmont licked his lips. "Done. Anything else?"

"Let me know when the meeting is."

He nodded and rose, signaling the end of our time together.

. . .

"WHAT WAS THAT ABOUT?" Tucker asked in the elevator down.

"Apparently the other breeds have been actively organizing and their go-to guy was Delmont to get the skinny on the Shifters."

We hit the foyer of the building and walked for the cars.

"Define actively organizing," Chaz asked.

"As in I'm a Prima, they have an Akasha and a Clade something and a witch mistress?" When I tried to say it out loud, it all sounded wrong, which meant that it was probably right up my alley.

"How can we trust Delmont?" Tucker growled.

My feet stopped like I'd hit a glass wall. It wasn't that the thought had just finally crossed my mind that Delmont wasn't what he seemed to be; I knew that. I froze because it seemed Tucker might know part of the story that I didn't.

"I think it's okay."

"How do you know?"

How did I know? Delmont was hiding something. He purposely rubbed me the wrong way and he'd gotten me into something I wasn't sure of. But after what he had said, I was still sure that he would never turn against me.

I'm really not the brightest color in the box, am I?

"The nose knows." I shrugged as I leaned against Chaz's car.

"But I need to have a session with our resident librarian of the weird if he's not otherwise occupied."

"Anything else?" Tucker asked.

My stomach growled in response. "A session with some food. Someone recently told me that I needed to eat more."

Tucker almost smiled despite the furrow. "I know a burger place around the corner."

"Of course you do."

CHAPTER 6

"MISS, YOU'RE NOT allowed to have that in here," the librarian called across the entry.

Twenty ounces of mocha firming in my grasp, I just glared at her, and maybe growled, as I proceeded to the back, where Nash took care of the special collections. The only warning of my coming was the tendril of energy I'd sent him as Chaz dropped me off.

When Delmont had told me about the others in the city, I realized all the lore I knew on Wanderers had to do with Shifters and Fey. I knew the others existed, had felt their power or been at the angry end of it at some point, but I didn't know about the rest of my universe.

Suddenly, that seemed very dangerous.

Which was why I sat across the library table from Nash. "I need everything on Elementals and Vampires and Witches."

Nash was ready. He looked at home among the stacks of books that flanked him on the table. With only the minute and a half warning I'd given him, he still managed to have bright sticky notes stuck into the pages of the volumes.

He smiled, like he'd been waiting his whole life to tell

someone everything he knew. "Elementals, even though they are the closest to the shifters, are the polar opposite. The elementals' magic can only control one element. The element isn't passed down, just the power. But like us, it takes in some and not in others."

"So you could have a mom water elemental and a father wind elemental and what? Get a baby tornado?"

Nash reached for a book and flipped it open to some crazy-looking diagram. "Not exactly. The offspring would be doubly powerful, but ultimately would only be in control of one element."

It was a pretty picture, but I was a little slow when it came to translating what I assumed was Latin. "So a family unit might have all four elements. Then how do they choose their leaders?"

"The elementals choose the strongest of the elements to lead them."

"Whoever can whip up the best firestorm?"

"More like who can squelch the other contenders."

I winced. I didn't want to be squelched. "Do we know anything about their way of doing things? Do they brush each other?" I didn't know if I wanted to send my animal power out into a burning ring of fire, but weirder things had happened.

Nash shook his head. "I know they don't commune like we do, but they have their own set of rules. I think you have to have all four elements to even have a Kiln. I tried to find something written down, but elemental manuscripts don't survive well."

"Can't weather the ages?" I smirked.

Nash's dimples flashed for only a moment before getting back to business. I tried to keep the smart-aleck remarks to a minimum so he could do his thing.

"What do you know of Inez Walker?"

His eyebrows jumped. "She's who they chose as their Akasha?"

I frowned. "Do you think she was one of the ones Carlisle

would have needed to defeat to take over the Pride?" I asked. It was a harsh question. Carlisle had systematically killed or conquered everyone else in the Pride before our showdown.

Nash shook his head. "He wouldn't have seen her as a threat. She isn't a legacy."

"What's does that mean?"

Nash licked his thin lips again. I was thinking that I needed to get the boy a water and some lip balm. "She wasn't born with a legacy. Her parents weren't Wanderers."

I was just about to point out that Tucker's parents weren't Wanderers, but I had a feeling it was more than that. When I didn't say anything, Nash filled in the blanks. He looked down at his long fingers and rubbed them together. "The fire chose her."

"Like the earth gave her magic?"

"It's been recorded a few times. *The Mother chooses her children*, I think the phrase is."

"Like the Mother who created the Wanderers?"

Nash nodded. "There are several viewpoints about what her name actually is, but the all-seeing, all-powerful who created the Wanderers as harbingers of the earth chose Inez to harness the fire. The Mother has a plan for us all."

"Oh." And I thought I was the only chosen one in Dallas. Guess I really am part of the few and the proud. "Now that's a story."

Nash smiled. "And if she is the one the elementals chose as their Akasha, it's going to be an interesting meeting, from what I remember of her."

"What do you mean?"

"Don't take this the wrong way, but we have proof that you don't play well with others. Need I mention Sully and the warthogs?"

I faked a gaff at his suggestion that I wasn't the perfect negotiator. But the encounter with a rogue pack of warthogs had landed Nash with a pretty wicked scar and cursed Shadow to his furrier form.

"Inez isn't exactly the warmest personality."

"Ironic. Don't you think?"

I didn't even get the briefest of smiles from Nash.

"I'm being serious. If she thinks you're a threat, you're toast. Nothing figurative about it."

I sighed. I knew this was serious. I also knew I needed sleep and coffee was no longer doing the job of keeping me awake. Exhaustion ached along my shoulders and in my hand as I grasped my—what was this—fourth coffee for the day.

"Got any books in this place on how to make friends and influence evil?"

Nash shook his head. "No. I can only point out what you already know. The elementals are like their elements like we are like our animals. You think you're catty, she's the embodiment of fire."

"So keep calm and carry water. Got it."

Nash's chin dropped down to his chest again. I'm sure this was not what he envisioned this moment being like. He probably saw himself as Yoda, and I was turning this into a session with Jar Jar.

"What's the sitch on the vampires?" I leaned back in the chair and waited for the info dump.

"Nothing you've ever written."

"Seriously?" I gasped. My entire world view just turned on edge. Half the stuff I was known for at Cloak & Dagger was on vampire covens.

Nash chuckled. "Just joking. There's actually a lot of truth in what you wrote. Your brain really was wired for this stuff."

I let out a sigh of relief. "You had me going there for a second."

Proud of himself, he went on. "Vampires are actually closest to fairies. They can control others' perceptions of them. It's what makes them so perfect-looking and always so suave. And the inviting-them-in thing is about half true."

"Which half?"

"They can come in, but not for long. It sucks their power if they are not invited."

"What about the stake thing? Please tell me the stake thing is true."

Nash looked at me like I was an idiot. "What doesn't die when you ram a stake through its heart?"

I pouted. "I guess you're right."

"But if you really want to kill them, you cut off their heads with an iron sword, which, ironically enough, is their preferred weapon of choice. Iron really works on all fairies."

"And the blood thing?"

"Totally true. It's how they get their power, by taking it from the blood of others. It's not really a hunger thing, more of an energy thing. They need the energy to keep up appearances, their super strength. The longer they live, the more power they get."

I grimaced. I was so glad that I was just a panther. "Who do you think their Clade leader is?"

"Their Clade Seat or Source. The translation is a little off." Nash reached for another book and opened it to a page with a sticky note. He pointed to a picture of a small terra-cotta bowl with what I knew to be the ancient Wanderer language scrawled across it "The Clades are like family blood lines. So their leader is not only the one who probably turned them into vampires, but also the head of the family. For Dallas, it is probably Emilio. He is the oldest. It usually works like that."

"How many are in Dallas?"

"Six? Really didn't participate too much. I only saw them at the monthly moons, but I know they were running some company somewhere."

I bit my lower lip. "If they had a company, I probably own half of it now."

Nash's jaw hit the ground. "You took the estate?"

"You are now looking at the newest millionaire in Dallas."

Nash leaned across the table. "Can I give you a list of books to get for the library? This place doesn't even have a complete set of *Lord of the Rings*."

"Blasphemous. Consider it done. Who are we missing? Oh, witches."

Nash nodded and pulled forward another book. I knew he was just doing it for show. But again, I was respecting his information flow. "There was one coven in Dallas, but no one has heard from them in ages. If they were here, they didn't advertise."

"But is it all I hoped and more, with the symbols and the dancing naked?"

"No, but thanks for the visual. Shifters are born with their magic on the inside. Witches can collect the raw magic of the earth and form it to their will. Anything they can imagine—if they have the will and the knowledge to harness it, they can do pretty much anything."

"So they are the ones to watch."

"They all need to be watched, Violet."

I sat up in my seat and set my coffee aside. "I know. When Delmont sets up the meetings, I want you and Tucker there."

"Delmont?" Nash said as he pulled his hand away from mine.

I felt more than just Nash's furrowed brow. He'd chilled and hardened when I said Delmont's name. "What is it, Nash?"

He shook his head. "No."

I didn't have to give him more than a look before he confessed.

"Delmont was a big part of the reason that . . ."

Nash couldn't say his name, but I didn't have a problem with my blood brother's name. "Spencer. Delmont was a big part of why Spencer . . ."

It took him a moment to get it out. "Of why Spencer had to protect us in the first place. Delmont is vicious and did everything he could to destroy us."

"'Destroy' is a very harsh word, Nash."

Nash struggled and it killed me. Nash was our heart, and if he was in pain, then I was in pain. I opened up my hand to him and rested it on the table between us.

"Thank you for telling me, Nash. Tucker just growled at me when I mentioned his name."

There was a twitch on Nash's lips.

"And frankly, the guy's had me on edge since our first meeting. He's too perfect. It's annoying."

"Tell me about it." Nash finally reached out and took my hand.

I squeezed his long fingers. "I don't trust him a hundred percent. But he knows things and—"

"The evil you know is better than the evil you don't," he finished.

I smiled. "You know, I never fully appreciated that statement until recently."

Nash brought his wide hazel eyes up to mine. "You changed us from the zombies we were. Maybe you can turn him into something that isn't a complete dou—"

"Nash," I chided. "Language. You're in a library."

I WAS AT home for exactly thirty minutes before Jessa knocked on my door. And I was so looking forward to a nap.

"Hello bride-to-be," she greeted as she sauntered into my living room. Her black hair caught the rest of the daylight as she posed, her big bag swinging on her arm.

I sighed. In all the hustle of the day, in all the flipping through that blasted planner, I'd forgotten that Jessa and I had plans. "I need coffee."

Jessa frowned as she followed me into the kitchen. There wasn't much protein in there, but damn if I didn't have the best coffee station this side of Oak Lawn.

I started to grind the beans for coffee number five.

Jessa waited to speak until after the beans were properly pulverized. "What's up? Why are you so tired? You and Chaz enjoying the you-and-Chaz a little too much?"

I grimaced. "No. But good to know you're warped."

I snapped the beans into place and flipped the switch to brew them. "It seems that along with playing Prima, almost having my house broken into, not to mention the Legacy, I, at some point, became a millionaire."

I ran her through the meeting with Delmont.

"Seriously?" Jessa smiled.

"Seriously."

"And Stalker Boy?"

"He's completely on board."

Jessa's eyebrows jumped. "Wow. That was a little unexpected."

"Why?"

"I'd thought he'd tell you to distance yourself from it as much as you can. It's practically blood money."

"Thank you!" I flipped on the steamer. When I stopped, I pulled two to-go mugs out of the cabinet. "I've been saying that the whole time and he's still all supportive and *you can do this*."

Jessa looked down at her hands. "He doesn't understand the temptation."

My skin tingled. It was a very un-Jessa thing to say. "Huh?"

"I think you forget we're linked sometimes. I know what you go through. Hell, right now, I can feel how tired you are, and he won't understand that. I don't think Chaz fully appreciates just how fine a line you walk, because he's never had to walk that line."

"Which is probably why I love him. He will always be squarely on the good guy side."

"Thank God, because I don't want all this wedding planning to go to waste."

I was just about to sip my latté when I got the gist of tonight. I don't know why it took me so long to put all the pieces together. She had a bag that was bigger than normal. She was wearing comfortable shoes instead of the in-style espadrilles. "Are we going wedding planning?"

A smile spread across Jessa's face and she beamed. Literally. Part of the fairy-princess gig. "I've got the whole evening set."

"Joy," I snarked.

"I LOOK LIKE A CREAM PUFF." I was trapped in a prison of tulle and satin. The corset dug into my ribs and the feathers along the top tickled my nose.

"It's gorgeous." Jessa fluttered around me, fluffing this and that.

"I can't see my feet," I complained.

"Why do you need to see your feet?" Jessa said.

I looked at the mirror and grimaced. Jessa peeked out from around my whipped cream disaster.

"You need to try on dresses to see what you like," Jessa said as she went to sit on the love seat provided for families.

I sighed. My shoulders were starting to ache and the three ibuprofens weren't doing anything for it. "Can't you just pick out something fabulous and make sure that the pictures look good?"

"No, Violet. This is your special day. It has to be what you like."

I looked back at the dress. "This is not what I want."

Two more dresses later, I still wasn't sure what I liked.

"Definitely not this," I said as I waddled like a penguin over to the love seat next to her. Jessa sighed. It was supposed to be a mermaid cut, but I felt more like a mummy.

"You have to have thought about it, Vi. What girl doesn't know what her wedding is going to look like?"

I raised my hand. My arms were the only thing moving in this dress. "This one."

"Seriously." Jessa dropped her chin to her chest and raised her eyebrows. "In the six weeks you've been engaged, you didn't think about what you wanted."

"I haven't really had a lot of time to myself, Jessa. With the new pack and the other Wanderers and the holes in the Veil, being engaged sort of took a back seat." I reached down the front of the dress and pulled at the bodice so I could take a deep breath. I slipped down on to the cushion next to her. "I thought about who I wanted there. You, Iris, Tucker. I can see people."

Jessa sighed for the millionth time that evening. "This was supposed to be a bonding experience."

"Aren't we bonded enough?" I asked.

"No, like girlie bonding. One night without that magic stuff. This is what girlfriends do. They go wedding-dress shopping and have champagne and fun. We used to go out and have fun, remember?"

"I'm not sure regular girlfriends close a wedding boutique to have a fully catered buffet while one of them tries on dresses that are three times her mortgage."

Jessa shrugged. "I can't help that."

I smiled. "Fine. But this little number." I gestured to the slinky gown. "It's not it. And it smells funny."

Satin binding my knees together tightly, I wriggled to the edge of the couch. "How do you walk in this?"

Jessa rose and offered a hand to help me up. "Think little Chihuahua. Tiny steps on your toes."

Jessa helped pull me to my feet. It was a struggle given the height differential and the fact that the heaviest thing Jessa ever lifted was her purse.

Finally, we managed me off the couch. "Thanks."

"Try the one with the blue sash."

"Are you serious?"

"Go," she pointed with her firm forefinger. "Humor me."

I threw up my hands. "Humoring. I'm humoring."

The next two dresses were hideous and by the seventh, I was exhausted. Wearing formal wear wasn't exhausting; the contortions needed to get in and out of it was. I leaned against the couch next to her and sipped the cool champagne. My head was spinning, and after the week I'd had, I was pretty sure it wasn't just the champagne.

"What's wrong with this one?" Jessa asked, probably expecting another goring critique.

"Actually..." I looked down at the cream-colored dress and was able to take in a deep breath. "This one doesn't suck."

"Hallelujah."

I turned around and looked at myself in the mirror. It was a simple strapless ivory dress that went down to the floor, but I could still see my toes beneath. I turned to the side. "I think I like it."

Jessa joined me at the mirror. "Nice simple lines. There is one problem though." She turned my back to the mirror. "You can see the marks."

As I turned my head to look over my shoulder, the four scars down my back were visible, highlighted against the ivory of the dress. "I haven't seen those in a while."

They still unnerved me. I had almost forgotten about the scars down my shoulder, it seemed so long ago, and yet I felt the burden of it every day.

"Vi?" Jessa asked.

"It's okay," I said as I looked back at her. "I'm not saying they are war wounds, but they are part of who I am, and I'd expect anyone at my wedding probably already knows what they are."

Jessa nodded. "I'll write down the style name of the gown."

"Just don't tell me how much it is yet."

"Aye, aye fearless leader." Jessa walked back to the couch to get the wedding binder she had made. It was lavender satin with a white lace wedding cake on the top. How *not* me is that?

But her snide remark did beg a question. "Why do you call me 'fearless leader'?"

Jessa looked up from her binder. "Because you hate it."

"Has your family ever been part of a pack?"

Jessa froze. "Why?"

I swallowed and licked my lips. "Haverty was able to control other breeds within his pack. I don't know if I can."

Jessa slowly walked toward me to get the dress information. "Are you seriously thinking about taking over Dallas?"

I shook my head. "I don't know. Delmont said there would be chaos. But it sounds like the others are doing the same thing that we are. Electing a leader and moving forward."

"And do we trust this Delmont person?"

"I don't know. He's tough to read. One minute he's Team Violet, and the next he's making deals with the devil. But what if he's right?"

Jessa shook her head. "It's not you, Violet. I know what you are capable of, and as much as I joke, you're doing a great job with the boys, but . . ."

She moved away to put her binder back on the couch. "I don't know if a Key Holder should be bound to a pack. We are sort of supposed to be neutral. It's why we don't deal with the Cause. We maintain the Veil, keep the powerful ones out, no matter their personal philosophies."

"What about Chaz? Have you heard of Guardians in a pack?"

She sat on the edge of the couch. "You'd have to ask him. But he's sort of already chosen his side, the Cause."

I rolled my eyes. "Right. Those lovelies."

Jessa smiled. "He chose you too, so it can't all be bad."

I put my hands on my hips and looked down at the gorgeous dress. If I tried hard enough, I could see something like a wedding. Holding flowers. Probably purple ones. Maybe with some catnip.

CHAPTER 7

THERE WERE TWO reasons I was taking this meeting at the coffee shop instead of my home office in my turtle pajamas. The first was that in all the excitement, I'd run out of coffee beans for the coffeemaker. The second was that there was no longer a moment's peace with Chaz buzzing about the house doing God knows what, Kandice pacing in the guest bedroom, and Nash and Tucker alternating who was constantly checking up on all three of us.

So I curled up in my other office, the corner table where I'd taken a million meetings in the past month, and talked to the LA think tank. With my ear buds, I probably looked crazy, but half the people in here were talking to themselves.

"Violet!" they all yelled simultaneously.

I smiled. The guys at the production company had known me since I was Drew's lowly assistant and worked with me at every cheesy step of the way through a million scripts. Now, I'd handpicked a group of people who could see *MoonBlood* onto the small screen. Putting your paranormal autobiography on TV does require some finesse.

"Hey guys! How's the weather?"

"Too damn sunny as usually."

"Same here. Where should we start?"

Silence filled the line.

"Guys?"

Finally one of them spoke up. His voice was shaky. Did I have so much clout I could intimidate grown men from across the country?

Go me. "We had some concerns with the main character."

"Charles? What's wrong with Charles?" It already felt like they were kicking my baby.

"We think we need to make him tougher."

I laughed. "Tougher we can do. What else?"

"We need to see more of Raven?"

"You mean the hot redhead in the leather everything?" I knew that was coming. I'd grown up in this culture. I know what nerdy boys want. They want the hot unattainable who they strive to attain and get. "Done."

"And we need to get the bad guy to be less bad."

I gulped. By working out Charles's pain after being bitten by a werewolf, I'd been masking my own. While his villain was a black-haired, blue-eyed alpha female who wanted nothing but power and got hers in the end, mine had gotten away and still haunted me. I didn't know if I could soften anything about my memory of Spencer.

Guess I needed to put all the fictionalizing to work. "I think I can come up with something."

"And the location. We think it should be in New York."

"Why?"

"It's got such a modern feel to it. We want it to be in a modern place."

"I still think it should be in Portland. It fits Charles more."

Another voice spoke up. "How about we see what the budget allows for and write accordingly?"

I nodded. "Agreed. Let's do be practical about this?"

There was a snicker on the line. "About a werewolf torn between evil and good? Of course, let's be practical."

The group of us laughed.

There was that sense of camaraderie that I missed. "What can I do for you next, guys?"

"Story arcs. Three or four for each character."

I scratched down the assignment in my planner. As I flipped through the pages, I tried to find some time to carve out to work. I think I had Sunday morning off and a little time on Tuesday before the full moon, which was approaching faster than I really wanted.

"Done. Anything else?"

"I think we are good at our end. We will hammer out the business stuff, but we'll need to get scripts out pretty soon to dangle in front of the money people."

"Noted. Want to schedule a time to talk next week?"

The group laughed. "We can't think that far ahead, Violet. We don't see the big picture like you can. Just call us when you can."

"Okay." I flipped through a few pages of the planner and scratched in a time to call them again. They might have that flexibility, but I certainly did not.

"Hey, we were wondering if you're planning a trip out here anytime soon. We'd love to do this in person at some point."

"I can't think that far ahead, guys. Talk to y'all later."

I hit the "end" button on the phone and rested my head in my hands. At least I'd managed not to lie to them. Bonus points for me.

But where the hell had *y'all* come from? Maybe I had been here too long.

~

I WAS DRIVING HOME when I got another call. This one

threw me more than Kandice's or anything Jessa could possibly think up, and lately, with all the holes in the Veil, her phone calls has been pretty exciting over the past six weeks.

Waylon's panicked voice shrieked in my ear. "Violet? Is Lexie with you?"

I stalled my car at the stop sign as fear made my muscles lock up and I couldn't downshift smoothly. "What?"

"She's not in her room. I've looked everywhere I can think of. Is she with you?"

"No, Waylon."

"Violet, I don't know what do to."

Finally, something I could handle. Muscle memory put my gearshift into neutral and I jammed down on the clutch. "Actually, I do. I'm coming to you."

The car behind me honked at I tossed the phone into the passenger seat and turned the ignition. When my baby was purring again, I threw her into first gear and did a U-turn in the intersection.

I loved my little car.

As I was flying over to Waylon's, I called Chaz. "Hey, meet me at Waylon's and bring your tracking gear."

"What?"

"Bring that bag you bring when you tell people you're going to hunt someone down."

"Oh. What's going on?"

"Lexie's missing."

"I can be there in thirty minutes."

"You'll be there now." I heard him grumble on the other end of the line. "Wait. What are you doing?"

While I came to a stop at a stoplight, I turned on my super hearing to try to figure out where he was. He was driving. I'd know the exhaust of that engine anywhere. "Chaz? Where are you going? Did the Avion call you?"

He sighed. "I was tracking that thing that broke into our houses."

"Are you kidding? What were you thinking?"

"That it broke into my house?"

"But alone? It was strong enough to make a boot print in my front door. What was going to stop it from making a boot print in your head?"

"I did perfectly fine before I met you."

I had to pause for a moment as I threw my car angrily into second gear. "And you're trying to get back your lost freedom?"

"No, Violet. I'm trying to protect myself."

"At least call someone. Tucker's off duty."

"They are not my pack, Violet!" The truth finally reared its ugly head.

"Don't be stupid, Chaz." I knew it wasn't the best thing to say. I really knew it when he hung up on me.

WAYLON WAS PACING the foyer when I got there. "Oh thank God, Violet. I was just about to call the police and I . . ."

His eyes glanced behind me and I felt Chaz walk up. "You two move fast."

"When family needs us, we're here," I answered.

Waylon's brown eyes landed back on me. "We had this fight, and I could just hear someone who wasn't me yelling at her and. . ."

"It's okay, Waylon. I remember how many times I wanted to run away at her age."

"You never ran away," Waylon frowned.

"I had you," I smiled. "And now I'm returning the favor."

"Why?"

"Because she's got her Aunt Violet. And I will find her."

Chaz cleared his throat behind me. His anger radiated out

around him like a heater at my back. "Why don't we go up to your place and see if she left us anything?"

"No we need to be out hunting and—"

I put my hand on Waylon's arm. "No. You need to calm down, I need a coffee, and we can look at her room for clues."

It was a battle convincing Waylon to stay in his hotel room without busting out the "don't worry, my fiancé has psychic GPS and can find anything."

But unfortunately, it left Chaz and I alone to discuss things as he kicked that GPS into gear.

"You were a little forceful with Waylon back there," Chaz said as he drove, his eyes glowing as he steered us this way and that, following his psychic trail to her.

"Jordans are blunt, said so yourself. Besides, got the job done." I plucked the little panda bear from the console between us and held it in my hands. It had been Lexie's baby toy and Chaz locked onto her in three seconds flat. "Where is she going?"

"She's not far now," he said softly.

I picked at the panda's worn ear. "I'm sorry that I yelled at you."

"Technically, I yelled first."

"I was only trying to say that if you needed help, they aren't just my boys."

Chaz shook his head as he turned exited the highway. "I'm not in the club, Violet."

"Neither is Jessa."

"But you guys are Key Holder and Keeper."

"But we weren't before I was attacked, and I'd still have taken a bullet for her."

Chaz squeezed his knuckles around the steering wheel. "Get to the moral of the story, Aesop."

"You guys hang out, play football. Joke around with each other. They don't just hang around you because of me. They don't feel they owe you for anything. You've got yourself a family now, little orphan boy. Use it."

Chaz was quiet for a good long while as he wove through the streets. "I was already on my way back from hunting down the thing that tried to break in when you called."

Anger sizzled around me, making the insides of the car hot enough with my Legacy that Chaz flipped on the air conditioner in defiance.

"You'll be happy to know that Shadow fought me on it. But I took the cloth from your dresser and followed it."

I took in a deep breath. He was right. He'd done this for years before me, and his father before that. "Well, you're in one piece, so I'm guessing he didn't stomp on you."

"Not just one, a group of them, but they were gone. It was a loft-apartment thing with lots of computers. Look like they'd been gone for about a day."

"What were they?"

"I don't know. I don't have your preternatural senses. None of the usual signs. But it was like they'd up and gone. Food in the fridge, clothes still in dressers, shoes still by the door. Just gone."

Listening to his voice was calming me down. Helping me remember what he was before me, before I'd completely turned his life upside down. "How do you know they weren't just at work?"

Chaz shook his head. "Didn't feel right."

"Do you think they'll come back?"

"No. Don't think they found what they were looking for."

"And now they are just wandering around town, shoeless?"

It was quiet for a little while. "Guess if I'd called Tucker, he might have been able to sniff something else out."

"Actually, Nash has a stronger sense of smell."

"Good to know." Chaz relaxed and when he did, so did I.

This was the part of him that I'd first fallen in love with, the fighting-the-good-fight part.

"What did you mean that Waylon saved you?" he asked.

I picked at some food or wax embedded in Lexie's poor panda's fur. "They never let me go back home. After my parents died. My stuff was just brought to their house. I had it in my head Mom and Dad were just waiting for me to come home, like some lost princess story."

"Sounds like you."

"One night I'd had enough, and I packed my bag and I started to walk home. Waylon found me about four hours later walking down the highway."

"What did he say?"

"He said that if I was so intent on running away, he was going to run with me. He wouldn't let me be alone. We spent the night at this completely vile hotel room, playing gin rummy all night and eating pizza. I'm pretty sure he called Aunt Glory when I was in the bathroom."

"How'd he get you to come home?"

I looked over at Chaz. "He said he would drive me there to see the house, but it wouldn't look the same. Wouldn't have the life it had with the three of us in it. And if he had to choose, he'd want to remember it like it was at Christmas when Mom would string lights on everything, and the tree was in the front window. Not like it was now, dark and cold and empty. I told him to drive us home the next morning."

"What happened to you two?"

I sighed. Chaz was my family now, right? He was marrying into this mess. "He left me. Aunt Glory was there, but Waylon was with me and the moment that I was getting happy, he left for college. Part of me knew he would come back, but it wasn't the same after that, and then I went to college and that was that. I did the leaving. I'm the schmuck in this scenario."

Chaz reached out to take my hand. "You're making up for your schmuckiness."

I took in a deep breath. I certainly was trying. "I'm learning about family at the same rate as you."

"Uh, Violet?" Chaz stopped the car and pointed to the building next to us. "Lexie's at your coffee shop."

I looked up at the building next to us. My coffee shop? Lexie had found her way to my safe spot? Goose bumps ran up my arm and I tried to push away what that meant and the complications that might follow.

"You okay?"

"Why this place, Chaz?" My voice wasn't more than a whisper. My brain flew in a million directions at once.

"We can't deny they are Wanderers, talent or not. Maybe she just went to a place that felt safe to her."

I licked my lips and nodded. It was purely coincidence. There was no way she was just called to the coffee shop because her Wandering blood told her it was safe, right?

"I'm going in."

Bastian, the manager, was behind the counter rearranging the coffee mugs. Business was slow as usual. "Hey, Violet. What can I get you?" he greeted.

"Actually, that's what I'm looking for." I pointed to Lexie curled up in the back corner. She was definitely related to me. She had her bag on the floor and was reading a book the size of *War and Peace*.

I adjusted the charm at my throat and walked over to her. "Hello, Lexie."

"Hey, Aunt Violet." She pushed up her glasses and looked at me defeated. She curled her feet up and hugged her boney knees.

"You okay?" I slid down in the chair next to her.

She scratched an ancient scar on her knee and kept her eyes

down. "I just needed fresh air. I couldn't be cooped up in the hotel room anymore."

"And you didn't think you could call me?"

Lexie's eyes darted up to me. "What?"

"Didn't occur to you that you've got a pretty amazing aunt who would gladly help you escape your tower for a while, if you'd ask?"

Lexie's lips parted.

Honesty was the best policy, right? Maybe I needed to take a moment to teach this kid something if she was going to be in my life. And as I looked at her, a blend of Waylon and Aunt Glory and maybe a little of me, I knew that I wanted her to be in my life.

"I know about moving around. It wasn't until Dallas that I felt like I belonged anywhere."

"Why'd you wander around the country?"

I wondered if she knew what she was asking, what words she was using to conjure the story. But I told her the truth anyhow. "I was searching because I was alone. And I found it."

"What was it?"

"A family. I found people who loved me, despite my many flaws."

"And you found love." Lexie shifted in her seat and I saw the book that she was reading. I couldn't even imagine the idea of love and searching that the latest teen fad was filling her head with; it had done a number on me at her age.

"What?"

"You found Chaz. Do you think you were searching for him?"

I thought about the man waiting out in the car, giving me the space I needed while staying close enough to save me from myself. The man who needed to fight but was staying still for me.

"I think so. And when I found him, I opened up for a lot of others."

Lexie bit down on her lower lip. "Is Dad angry?"

"Yes. You have no idea just how scared he was when he called me."

"He's going to yell at me when I get home."

"He probably will."

Lexie closed the book. "Guess you'd better take me home."

"Not necessarily," I said as I curled my feet up too, matching her little cat position. "If you don't want to go home, we can stay here. We can go to my house, whatever you need to do to feel better."

Lexie thought about it for a while. While she was thinking, I ordered a hot chocolate for her and a double latté for me. Chaz walked in at some point and stayed over by the newspaper rack.

"Soccer. I miss soccer."

"You want to go play soccer?"

"Can we?"

"I think I can arrange a pick-up game."

"WHO ARE ALL THESE PEOPLE?" Lexie asked as we walked across the soccer field. The lights were only going to be on for about ten more minutes at the park just around the corner from my house, but ten minutes might be all I needed.

"Remember when I said I'd found family. These are them. Tucker, Nash, Kandice, and Shadow."

Lexie gave a small wave. "You have a dog?"

"He chose me, actually. I do not claim ownership."

Shadow danced around her legs and Lexie cracked a smile as she reached down and scratched behind Shadow's ear. "Dad won't let us have a dog."

Tucker and Nash chuckled softly, and Tucker spun the ball in his hands. "So I thought we were playing soccer?"

Lexie smiled. "I get Aunt Violet."

"Your loss," I sighed as we put our stuff on the bench and walked out to the middle of the field.

Lexie played hard and she was good, like too good. Against a super-fast Guardian, a panther, and three dogs, she'd scored three goals before we even knew what was happening.

I pulled out of the game and Shadow took my place as I went to make the phone call.

"Vi? Please tell me you found her," Waylon sounded tired, like worrying had zapped all his energy.

"We found her."

"Oh, thank heavens. Where is she? I'll come get her."

There were a million questions I wanted to ask him. Watching Lexie, there was something special about that kid as she completely schooled a field of men at soccer. And how did she know about the coffee shop?

"How about I keep her for the evening? I'll order pizza and we'll talk. Maybe she just needs a girl right now."

I heard Waylon run his fingers through his hair. "Okay."

"Relax, Waylon. Isn't this why you came to Dallas? So your daughter would know her family?"

He just sighed as a response.

"What did you guys fight about?"

"She doesn't understand there needs to be rules, needs to be order. Especially now when so much is up in the air."

I frowned. That didn't sound right. But I wasn't going to argue with his philosophy of being. But I could be the aunt she ran to when she needed a little freedom from the rules.

The pops from the lights echoed across the now dark fields. The group walked over, already sweaty.

I wrapped up my conversation with Waylon. "Got to go. I'll return her tomorrow."

"Thank you, Violet. You have no idea what this means to me."

As I looked at my line of boys and thought about another one of them disappearing, I knew exactly what Waylon meant.

"You owe me one." I hung up the phone and looked at the group and then caught a whiff of them on the wind. "God, you guys smell horrible."

"Yep," Chaz said as he sat down next to me and put his sweaty arm over my shoulder so I could get a clear whiff of his armpit.

"How about some ice cream and then back to my place?"

"I'm staying with you?" Lexie asked.

"For tonight, yeah. And then I need to take you home, okay?"

Lexie nodded as she grabbed her bag from the ground.

NASH SLEPT ON THE COUCH, Kandice was in the guest bedroom, Shadow was someplace, and Chaz had volunteered to sleep in my writing chair.

"You're a saint," I whispered to him as he took some pillows off the bed.

"Yes, I am. And I'm taking care of *my* niece too. Hey Lexie, pecans or cinnamon?" he asked.

"Cinnamon?" Lexie answered.

Chaz smiled back at me. "She really is a Jordan." He gave me a quick kiss, just long enough to leave me with the feeling of his lips and his stubble before he left.

"You guys really going to get married?" Lexie asked.

"Does seem to be the plan."

I pointed to the bed and Lexie hopped on and snuggled underneath the soft blankets. She was fighting sleep and I knew it. I flipped off the lights and walked around to my side of the bed.

We both snuggled in, facing each other, blankets up to our chins.

"How come you already feel like family, Aunt Violet?"

"What?"

"I've only known you like a week and you already feel like family."

I shrugged. "Dunno, Lexie. But it's mutual. I think you're stuck with me."

Lexie smiled. "Dad was mad, wasn't he?"

"No, actually. Just relieved. Dallas isn't the safest place on the planet."

"You live here."

Good point. Dallas was dangerous for her because of me, though, how did I say that in a way that wasn't going to bind my words around my feet and let her trip me up? Avoid it.

"What drew you to the coffee shop?"

Lexie pressed her lips together. "I dunno. It was just inviting. And when I got there, I knew it was safe. And the manager was really cute."

I chuckled. She was right. He was pretty cute. "But you weren't afraid?"

"I was afraid until I got there."

"Why?"

"Don't know. It was well lit. And it smelled good."

"Smelled good?"

"I like the smell of coffee."

I laughed. There really wasn't any doubt that this was mine.

Something tingled down my spine, and then I smelled roses. "We have company."

I jumped out of bed and opened the door just as Jessa was fumbling with a tray of hot chocolates and a cosmetic bag the size of my head.

"Are you having a sleepover without me?" she asked as she pushed through.

"Jessa, this is my niece, Lexie. Lexie, this is my best friend Jessa."

"I'm so happy to meet you," Jessa squealed as she set the cosmetic bag on the bed and doled out the hot chocolates.

I closed the door behind her and took my hot chocolate.

"How did you find out?" I asked as I carefully sat back down on the bed.

Jessa waved it off with more alacrity than I'd ever seen her blow off something. "Never mind that. We have a young impressionable girl. This is a once-in-a-lifetime opportunity here, Vi."

Lexie giggled.

"Toes and nails now." Jessa slipped off her slippers and it was then I realized that she was already in a pair of satin pajamas.

CHAPTER 8

*L*EXIE FELL ASLEEP somewhere around midnight. Her toes were now a vicious shade of hot pink that hurt my retinas to even look at and she had flowers on her fingers.

"How's she doing?" Jessa asked softly, sitting next to me on my window seat as we both watched her sleep.

"She's amazing," I said. "And I think she wanders."

"Oh." Jessa's perfectly arched eyebrow arched. "Really?"

"I've yet to feel anything off of Waylon, but she found the coffee shop."

"Seriously?" Goose bumps covered Jessa's arms. "Guess it's official."

"What?"

"You've turned the place into a haven."

"What's that?"

Jessa sighed. "Think of a church. It is holy because people believe that it is. You've made it into a safe space because you and all your power believe it is a safe spot."

I sighed in echo to her sigh as I got the whole picture. "And just like Wanderers will come to me when they need help because I'm a Prima, they will go there if they need help."

"Bingo."

"Poor Bastian."

I sighed as I leaned my head against the cool window. Poor Lexie.

There was a cool ripple that echoed out from Jessa, like she was the pond that the stone had been thrown in. "Crap," Jessa hissed as she clutched her chest.

I would have laughed and said something to the effect that I really was wearing off on her and not the other way around, but the light in Jessa's now lavender eyes told me different.

"The Veil."

IT WAS A flutter of pink and taffeta. She spun in the mirror and smoothed her hand over her hair, perfectly done at the salon earlier that day. She adjusted the charm at her neck, hidden in the sparkling necklace that lay perfectly at her throat. Everything was perfect.

When the doorbell rang, she jumped and spun around again before the full-length mirror. She briefly touched a picture of a woman on her dresser and flew downstairs to answer the door.

Her father beat her there. He stood in front of the door with one of her uncle's shotguns.

She frowned and put her hands on her hips. "Dad, Seriously? Don't you think that's a little overdramatic?"

He looked down at the shotgun and then at his daughter. "I think it adds the perfect dramatic touch."

"You've met him. It's just prom. I know the rules and I know what happens if I miss curfew."

"And I already know that you will miss curfew."

She smiled up at her father. "You only know that I will miss curfew because you missed curfew on your prom night."

Her father looked away for a moment and dropped the shotgun to his side. "You understand that I have to."

"Tyrant." She smiled as she walked up to him. "I will go to the dance. I will have a good time and I will not do anything stupid. I promise."

"I know." He sighed as he ran his fingers through his sandy brown hair.

She leaned up and kissed him lightly on the cheek, making sure that she didn't get any lip gloss on him. "It would have been more effective if you'd flipped the safety off," she whispered in his ear.

She smiled and headed out for the perfect prom night.

JESSA PUNCHED ME in the arm. "Wake up. We're here."

"What? I'm awake," I said as I sat up and looked around from the front of her BMW.

"Fifteen minutes in the car and you were out like a baby."

"Having a hard time sleeping."

"Bad dreams?" Jessa offered as she got out of the car.

I opened the door and threw my tired legs out onto the pavement. As I stood, it took the wind to tell me exactly where we were. "Are we at a hospital?"

"Sort of and you're avoiding the question," Jessa said as she grabbed a Coach messenger bag from the back of her car. Survival in style. "Are you having dreams about *him* again?"

"No. I'm having a hard time getting sleep." I followed Jessa into the alleyway behind the huge red Dumpsters that read BIO-HAZARD. I held my hand over my nose as the smell of clotted blood surrounded us.

"Like you need some chamomile to relax?" Jessa asked, her hands pinching her nose together.

"No. Like everyone else needs to calm down so I can get some sleep."

Jessa just shrugged. "You're the Prima. This is the life you chose."

I really didn't expect to get any sympathy from Jessa. She wasn't the sympathy friend. She was the let's-kick-ass-and-look-fabulous-doing-it friend.

I shook my head. Technically, I think it was the life that chose me, but right now wasn't the time to argue because as we turned the corner, I knew exactly what had drawn us out that night.

I reached for the charm around my neck and slipped it off. As the spell dissipated, the chilling breeze from the open Veil fluttered all around me, like torn bits of gauze tickling at my skin. "I think we are getting stronger."

"I'm getting stronger," she corrected. "You're just playing catch-up."

"And you're getting catty," I joked as I followed her to a random spot on a wall. I didn't need to see the rip in the ether to know it was there. I reached out and it twisted between my fingers like organza with a soul.

"Come on, wonder girl, let's get this fixed up." Jessa found a crate in the alley and pulled it up to the wall so she could reach the edges easier.

"Does it need blood this time?"

Jessa looked around the wall and ran her hand across the empty space. "Let's just try it the old-fashioned way."

As both of us leaned up to begin to weave the tear back together, tying the loose ends and bonding them with little bits of magic, like trying to rework holes in pizza dough, I caught a scent of something rotting. I almost thought it was the BIO-HAZARD bin until it got more intense.

"I think it's time to change deodorants," I joked before a large bloody hand clamped onto my shoulder.

Seven months of Jeet Kune Do kicked in, and I grabbed the wrist and ducked back and to the right. I twisted the arm of the foul-smelling man and nearly threw up from the stench. He smelled like that wondrous combination of old cat urine and the meat you left in Tupperware before you went on vacation. Only it was right up my super sensitive nose.

From behind, I saw rotten flesh down his neck and the chunks of scalp exposed. Even the wrist locked within my fingers seemed to writhe and I looked down to see the macerated skin tear away from his muscles with twist of his wrist.

I dropped him fast and pushed him forward. He slammed into the brick wall just to the side of the Veil.

"What the hell is that?" Jessa shrieked as she scurried closer to me.

The thing's skin still hung between my fingers. I shook the flesh from my hand and wiped the blood off on my jeans.

"Zombie?" I offered.

As it turned back around, a slow lumbering turn, it did share three common characteristics with the modern-day zombie myth. It stunk like rotting meat because it was rotting. The dull cataract eye lolled in our direction as it started back toward us.

The second characteristic was that it was slow. It didn't move, it lumbered. It was nothing compared to my shifter reflexes. It didn't seem super strong, just persistent, which led to the third characteristic of the zombie movies I knew and loved so well. It was coming at me teeth first, like it wanted to take a chunk out of me.

"Are you serious?" I asked the universe, not really wanting a response, just wanting it to know that I, Miss Horror Movie Writer, thought it was being ridiculous with this one.

I dodged another attack and kicked him against the wall again.

"Careful of the Veil," Jessa chided.

"Why don't you keep fixing it and I'll . . ." I trailed off. How did you kill zombies? "Bash his head in?"

"Sounds like a plan, but point the blood spatter away from me?"

I shook my head as the thing recovered. Jessa. Less about the details, all about the looks.

Just as I was looking for something to kill this thing with, another caught me around the waist and threw me to the ground like a sacked quarterback.

As I was wriggling away from its arms, I clawed at its face and brought an eyeball impaled on a talon.

"Awwgh," I cried out. I shook my hand and flung the eyeball off into the night.

Drawing on my power, I threw the thing off of me and looked around. There were five now, one of me, one Jessa. How'd these guys get the drop on us?

I reached my power out around them to find their magic. Mine was a silver center of life and light. These were dark, like a black fire that burned within their chests that needed to be fed constantly before the light went out.

"I think they are ghouls," I said to Jessa.

"I think they need to be dead," she snapped back as she looked over her shoulder and wove the Veil as fast as her little hands could.

I looked around for a weapon. I was pretty sure I could kick their heads in, but these were new shoes, and I didn't want to get ghoul blood on my new sneakers.

Where was Chaz when you needed a good shot gun? Oh, right. Taking care of my niece because he is the most amazing man on the whole planet.

Guess this one was all me.

I lunged at the first one. I would have said it caught him off guard if he even had a guard. He stumbled back and I landed on top of him. I grabbed his head and rammed it into the pavement, harder than I actually wanted to. I felt the crack of the skull in my palm, like crushing a fortune cookie.

Dark black ooze drained out of his cranial cavity and I jumped up quickly and wiped my hands on my jeans. I needed to remember to bring wet wipes with me. Add that to the survival in style bag.

Another one was close. I stomped on his foot and rammed my palm into his chest. His ribs cracked under my attack as he flew backward, and his ankle snapped when I didn't let up on his foot. He went down, another head against the pavement. It didn't get up.

The other two went down with relative ease, which would have begged the question why don't bad guys attack all at once, but that would have given these guys both a motive and cognitive thinking, which I really wasn't ready to bestow upon this particular band of misfits.

Until the last one looked me in the eyes.

He was either younger or older, but he was different. He wasn't as fragile as the other ones and nearly had all the skin left on his face, though part of his cheek did hang down. His suit was ragged, with brown fluid down the front. His eyes were still juicy enough to burn darkly with the hunger that raged beneath them. If I was a gambling woman, I would have said this was their leader.

But you know me, I don't play games and I certainly don't gamble.

He rushed at me, but then quickly turned toward Jessa. I dashed for him and tackled him to the ground.

Which, once he'd pinned me, I knew was where he wanted me in the first place. He was stronger than the others, and even with my super strength, he was able to hold me down.

"Prima," it hissed, only it didn't have the suppleness to the lips to actually make out the P and the M sounds, so it came out like "Reena."

"You really should just give up now," I said as I stopped

fighting and started looking for weapons within arm's reach and a way to get out of this situation.

As this thing, this once-man, looked down at me, I got the feeling it needed me. His friends were just out for a midnight snack: I was used to that scenario. But there was a look in his eyes, a pinch in his voice that told me he didn't want to hurt me.

Just as I was about to say something, the brave and daring fairy princess I call my best friend decided to come to my rescue with pepper spray, barely legal pepper spray.

"Eat this," she prefaced before she shot a long and close burst of pepper spray into his face.

Now, if I wasn't a werepanther and was just a girl, the spray that sent my attacker running out into the night with a scream that literally curdled my blood would have landed all over me, sending me into an eyelid-boiling, skin-bubbling, rage-inducing fit as I tried to wipe myself clean of the pepper oil.

But I am a werepanther and I have super senses. So take that, and multiply it times ten.

I screamed as the pepper burned my eyes, which only caused me to inhale a mouthful of it. The pepper burned down my throat like I'd swallowed Chernobyl.

I rolled to my side and kept my eyes closed and tried not to touch my face. The little Chaz had mentioned to me about the matching pepper sprays he'd given to me and Jessa was Don't touch your face if you accidentally get sprayed. It's oil and it spreads fast like oil.

However, he neglected to mention that if you got sprayed with it, it would feel like a million bee stings all over your body at once and you'd want to scratch out your eyeballs.

Somewhere above my own crying and the raging forest fire on my face, I heard Jessa's mantra, "Oh God Oh God Oh God Oh God," and there was a bottle of water splashed on my face.

"No water," I choked out. "Milk."

I don't know how she got me to my feet, but we were

moving. I couldn't suck in enough air to curse her to high heavens. I couldn't open my eyes to aim my foot at her butt. I could only stumble blindly in the direction she pulled me.

There were bright lights. The hospital? Had she taken me inside the hospital?

Someone who wasn't Jessa sat me down and I batted a hand away when they tried to touch my face. I cracked a puffy eyelid and only saw tiled floor and a blue uniform.

"Here," Jessa said as her rainwater energy pattered around me.

Suddenly, there was something cold and thick running down my face. When I gasped, a bit of it fell into my mouth.

"Ice cream?" I gurgled out.

Jessa wove her fingers through my hair and pulled my head back and smeared an entire ice cream cone over my face like some fancy new exfoliant.

Between the cold milkiness and her soft excited energy pattering along my skin, the burning very slowly dissipated.

"Ice cream, Jessa?" My voice was still raspy, and according to Jessa's smart phone, would be until the inflammation went down from the pepper's oil.

My skin was puffy and sore like a bad sunburn, but with the super healing, that would be gone soon. We sat across from each other at Braum's, known for their homemade burgers and their all-night ice cream. They are not known for their triage, though the woman working behind the counter hadn't flinched when I came in screaming.

"You said milk and this was the closest thing."

"I'm still getting over the fact there was a Braum's across the street from a Botox place."

"Not missing the irony," she said as she ate her ice cream. She'd at least offered to pay for dessert after smashing the first round all over my face to calm the burning of the spray.

"What was that thing?"

Jessa's ice cream seemed to turn sour in her mouth as she put her spoon down and pushed the cup away. "I think you had it right with a ghoul. I've only heard stories."

"What are the stories?"

Jessa ran her hands up her arms. "Ghouls tend to rise when things are unbalanced. Their hunger contradicts something good."

I frowned. "So the universe thinks we are too good now?"

Jessa shook her head. "I'm just telling you what I know."

"So the universe wants everything to come down around me ears. Awesome."

"All I know is that the universe is about balance. It's one of the reasons that the Veil is so hard to keep up. It's not supposed to be there. We put it up to keep the humans safe."

"So they wouldn't get snacked on in back alleys?" I asked.

Jessa just gave the look that clearly said she wasn't in the mood for joking. "I'm just saying, if the ghouls are rising, something is out of whack."

"Huh." I smiled through my stinging skin. "You said 'whack.'"

Jessa rolled her eyes and gave up.

CHAPTER 9

"*V*IOLET? ARE YOU all right? You look like you've been crying." Chaz cupped his hand under my chin and forced our eyes to meet. His furrow was back and from the bags under his eyes, he hadn't slept either while us girls had been away.

"Met with the rough end of some pepper spray."

"What?"

Jessa pushed me through the doorway. "That would be my fault."

"Why did you pepper spray her?" Chaz asked.

"We were attacked. She was being *helpful*." I made sure my air quotes around the last word were particularly emphatic.

Jessa scoffed. "It was in the heat of battle and the thing was trying to eat her face."

"It wasn't trying to eat my face," I snapped as I flopped down on the couch.

"It was trying to eat her face," Jessa repeated as she perched on the arm of the chair.

Shadow raised his head from the fireplace and then nestled back down again.

"Lexie still asleep?" I asked.

"Hasn't budged."

"Maybe she didn't notice I was gone." I sighed. "I need a shower."

"Yes, you do," Chaz said. "You smell like death warmed over."

"I'm pretty sure I was *attacked* by death warmed over."

The space between my shoulders was beginning to ache and I was getting that crick in my neck I'd get on editing marathons for three days straight with no sleep. "I'll take a shower on one condition."

"What?" Chaz asked as he offered his hand to help pull me off the couch.

"You make a full breakfast. We're talking eggs and coffee and pancakes, and coffee."

"Got it," Chaz smiled. "Get upstairs."

Jessa just waved and headed for the door, to no doubt take three showers to get the smell of the ghouls off her. I was as quiet as my leaden feet would allow as I slowly climbed the stairs. The kid must have my super hearing. The second I slipped in the door, she started to stir.

"Is Chaz making breakfast?" Lexie asked as she sat up and rubbed her eyes. Her hair was kinked up on one side and I was thankful that she didn't get my curly hair.

"He's getting started on it right now."

"Did I keep you awake? Dad says I talk in my sleep, but I can't prove it."

I sat on the edge of the bed next to her. "You didn't keep me awake. How are you feeling about going home this morning?"

Lexie sighed and rolled her shoulders, stretching. "I know Dad has rules and rules are important, but he's got to let me make a few mistakes for myself. I'll never learn anything if he keeps me locked away."

"I think you're too smart for your own good. You must be a Jordan."

She rubbed her nose and then lay back down on her pillow. "Tell me a story of growing up with Dad."

"We didn't grow up together."

"Tell me about something about Dad as a kid."

I looked across the barren side of my bed and meant to slink across the lush covers, but I think it was more of an elephant tromp because Lexie giggled. The moment my head hit the pillow, I knew it was a bad move. My body relaxed against the memory foam and the aching seemed to stop for a moment and the smell of squishy death faded away.

"Does your Dad still like card tricks?"

Lexie rolled her eyes as she mirrored my position. "He tried to do them at my last birthday party."

I laughed. "He could guess my card every time. I think he even carried around a deck of cards with him, and if I started moping, he'd pull out those cards."

As I thought back to those bright and golden days, I couldn't help but feel I'd wasted every single one of them. Being so damn angry at the universe. Ignoring the family that was really just there for me the whole time. Just waiting until I reached out for them.

Which I never did, because, I think we've already established, I'm stubborn.

With a resolute sigh, I looked at Lexie. I wasn't going to give her the choice. I was going to be in her life kicking and screaming. "I'm going to take a shower and you can go down to breakfast when you smell the cinnamon, but not a moment before. Must remember to keep the boys waiting for it."

Somewhere between pancakes and coffee, Devin called. I hadn't talked to my better human half in ages. "How is my favoritest pediatrician in the world?"

"Still kicking. How is my favorite super hero in the world?"

"Still purring."

Devin laughed. I closed my eyes and leaned forward to hold

my head in my hands. His voice soothed me, only slightly revived by the hot coffee and hot cakes.

"Haven't heard from you in a while."

"I've been swamped." I looked up at Lexie and paid close attention to my nouns. "Turns out that I wasn't exactly prepared for my new job."

"How could you be prepared?"

A few months ago, I'd told Devin everything over several bottles of wine. He knew about the Wanderers. He knew about my curse and knew about the pack. And he still stuck around. Didn't mean I was ready to go public with all this. Devin was special and knew the importance of keeping secrets between friends.

"And because of that, I've been a sucky friend."

"You've had a lot on your plate."

"Doesn't excuse the suckiness. Want to meet me for coffee?"

"Got a little time this afternoon?"

I had to get up from the breakfast table to find my planner. When I finally found it and then the date, I moaned. "Crap."

"If today's not good, that's okay." Devin was too under-standing and frankly too good for me.

"No, I missed an appointment last night."

"What?"

The question echoed from the phone and from across the dining area. I reached across the table and handed Chaz my planner so he could see what I'd missed. Just a checkup with one of my pack members about a job.

"I missed an appointment with a . . ." My eyes fell to Lexie. "With a student."

"Why are you being weird?" Devin asked.

"My niece is with me."

"Your niece? I thought you were an only child."

"This might be one of those coffee conversations."

"Noted. When is a good time?"

I reached back out for my planner and Chaz frowned as he handed it back. I scanned the pages. "Saturday around ten?"

"As you wish, fearless leader."

I smiled as I hung up.

"Who was that?" Lexie asked.

I sat back down at the table with my planner. My day was packed and I was about to miss another meeting with LA about the TV show. "My friend Devin. He's a doctor."

"You have two boyfriends?"

I laughed. "No, I have one fiancé and one boy who happens to be a friend."

"And Tucker? What's Tucker?"

I looked up to Chaz, who just shrugged. Note to self: not good lying on his feet. "Tucker is a co-worker."

"Is he a writer too?"

I sighed. "Actually, he's a police officer, but he helps me research police business to make my writing more real."

"And the others?"

"Tucker's family."

When Lexie finally looked back at her pancakes, I sunk my head, exhausted. It was all becoming too clear. The Haverty rule of not consorting with humans and not letting them know the truth about Wanderers would never work for me because lying was exhausting. That was what, five lies to Lexie in a matter of minutes?

I wasn't winning the aunt of the year award. Maybe next year.

"I KNOW THAT I've been a little incommunicado, but I've given you gold, you just have to spin it, Rumpelstiltskin." I ran my fingers through my hair and rested my head on the desk.

Five minutes into my conversation with Drew, my boss in

LA, about the story arcs for *MoonBlood*, and everything ached. It was more than just a bad breakup that landed me in Dallas. I needed space from Drew. He thought about every detail every time and had to be on top of all of us to make sure that we toed the company line. Hence the reason that I developed a wicked coffee addiction while working for him

"I'm not paying *me* to spin it, princess. I'm paying you to spin it."

I sighed. "What if I just gave you all the rights to do with it what you wanted?"

The line was silent, and in that silence, my eyes closed, and the warmth of my office surrounded me like the universe wrapping a warm blanket around my shoulders. The white buzz of my computer stopped as the screen faded to black and took a little nap as well.

"I don't want the rights to *MoonBlood*."

"You paid me to write it. I wrote it. Technically, it's already yours."

"Do you even hear what you are saying, Violet?"

The concern in his voice drew me from the darkness behind my eyelids. Drew didn't show concern often. I slowly sat up. What was I saying? I would never give up one of my characters. Especially one that hit so very particularly close to home. "I'm sorry, Drew. I don't want to give up *MoonBlood*. I'm just tired."

"Well if you lived in LA, I could . . ."

"I will never live in LA again, scumbag old boyfriend or not."

"I just worry about you, Violet. I know you're not the intern I hired all those years ago, but I still worry. How about you send me some season-long arcs and I'll have Violet Four see what she can do with them, and then you can rip them apart and make them brilliant before we give it to the Write Pack."

"Violet Four?"

"There's just no replacing you."

My eyes watered. It was the nicest thing Drew had ever said

to me. Between that and the concern, I'd think he was a completely different person.

"Now, I need to go. I think I just heard a click on the line."

He hung up quickly. I laughed as I set the phone down. Good to know that his paranoid ways had not changed.

The floor creaked behind me and I sniffed. I still hadn't gotten used to Lexie's smell yet. I turned to face her in the doorway of my office.

"Chaz wanted to know if you wanted to drop me off."

"Do I have to?"

Her shoulders fell and her gaze hit the floor. "I'm sure I could call Dad."

Crap. I stood. "No, sweetheart. I meant I'm kinda getting used to having you around. Not sure I want you to go home."

Lexie smiled up at me—an ear-to-ear grin, and if I wasn't sure she had psychic blood running through her veins, I would have said it was something almost fey-like beaming in her eyes.

"Let me get dressed."

CHAZ HAD GOTTEN a phone call from his modeling agency, so I let him off the hook of dropping off Lexie. I adjusted the charm at my throat and waited for Waylon to answer the door. Lexie hadn't remembered to pack the hotel key in her haste to run away.

When the door opened, I experienced something that only solidified why I needed them in my life. Waylon's eyes filled with water as her threw his arms around Lexie. She hugged him back with the same vigor, and one would think each was trying to squeeze the air out of the other.

"I'm sorry, Dad."

"I promise the tyrant has left the building," he whispered back.

I smiled. Seemed it wasn't a Violet way with words, it was a Jordan thing.

When the two broke and I wiped my eyes too, Waylon hugged me. There was a warmth there that I only vaguely remembered, a baked-cookie sort of feeling as I hugged him back.

"This is why I need you, Violet. To rescue us."

He let go and pulled me into their suite. I went a little reluctantly, knowing the two of them needed to have a conversation. Lexie slipped her shoes off where there was a pile of shoes and tossed her bag on the chair.

"Lexie?" Waylon said as he walked to the kitchen.

"Tyrant," she shot back as she picked up the backpack and headed to what was probably her room on the other side of the suite.

"You have no idea what this means to me, Violet." Waylon poured me a cup of coffee and splashed in milk and two sugars. It was just what I needed.

I took the warm mug and stirred. "She's kind of awesome."

"She really is. I don't know what I'd do if I lost her." Waylon put his hand on his hip and looked at me.

I felt that familiar feeling, cool stones running down my back. I was starting to think that my dampening charm was on the fritz. Have to talk to Nash about that.

"Wish you could spend the day with us." Waylon sighed before he went to fix himself another cup of coffee.

"Something keeping you from asking?" I took a sip of coffee. It wasn't the best but the sentiment made it sweeter.

Waylon frowned. "I'm sure you have a busy day ahead of you."

"Nonsense." I dug around in my cavernous bag and pulled out the infamous planner. "I'm sure that I can—" My day was still packed and there was no moving anything around to tomorrow. "I'm booked. But . . ." I flipped through the next few days. "I can do dinner on Tuesday?"

Waylon smiled. "I'll give you a call on Monday."

My shoulders sank and I looked at my watch. I had just enough time to get over to the coffee shop for the next meeting. I chugged his coffee as quickly as I could. "Thanks for the java."

"Lexie. Aunt Violet is leaving," Waylon called across the suite.

The girl ran back across the apartment and threw her arms around my middle. Every cell in my being wanted to cancel all the appointments to spend the day with her, but there was no rest for the wicked.

"Thank you, Aunt Violet."

"You are very welcome, and I'll see you on Tuesday for dinner."

Lexie gave one more squeeze before she abandoned me for her father's side. His large arm rested on her shoulder. They were going to be fine, despite the burden of their last name. I was going to see to that.

HANNAH AND EVAN needed only one word to describe them: nervous. Their noses twitched under their horn-rimmed glasses. Their eyes shifted from their clasped hands to mine wrapped tightly around my coffee mug. It all made me twitch.

This was my second meeting with this couple, and I still had a hard time getting over their furrier sides: rabbits. But with my history with the furry creatures, I was proud I was sitting fairly still before them.

"How is the housing situation working out? You said you were looking to move in together now that you didn't have to be messengers."

Hannah nodded, brown curls falling in her face. She didn't bother to brush them away or try to meet my eyes.

"So does that mean you found a place?"

She nodded again. And she was the talkative one of the couple.

The small amount of information I had pulled out of them was that Hannah was the rabbit first, and Evan followed just a few months into their dating. Haverty was using them as messengers to deliver his dirty dealings and Hannah still bore the scars of some of the responses, which is why, though the spring was hot upon us, she was always wearing a sweater.

"So you've found jobs as well? Evan, weren't you looking into working at Sprouts?"

He nodded. "They hired me. I'm stocking for them."

"Good. At least I know that you're eating."

They both nodded.

"Did you remember to get off the full moon?"

Both jumped and looked at each other. There was a quiet little conversation in their eyes and I couldn't help but smile at their silent dialogue. Chaz and I didn't have a secret language. We'd have to be in the same room at the same time for that.

Hannah looked back at me. "No, but I'll call in right now."

"How can you forget the full moon? I set one rule to be followed."

I didn't hear how harsh my voice was, but I saw it in their entire being, felt in it the soft spider thread ties between us. They were scared. I closed my eyes and dropped my head. It was more than that, something more subtle than fear with an edge of disappointment. Who was the tyrant now?

"I'm sorry." I sighed. "But seriously. How can you forget something that I've been reminding you about for weeks?"

"We've been trying to do what you said. Find a house. Get jobs. Open bank accounts. We're doing our best."

I bit my lower lip before I snapped that their best wasn't

good enough. Lately, my best had been fair. Maybe it was their good enough and I needed to work at making their best better.

I watched as Evan squeezed Hannah's hand. They'd gotten that part right. Find someone to be better with.

I licked my lips. "Please remember to get the time off for the full moon. We are carpooling from Riverchon Park. Do you know where that is?"

"Yes, Prima," they answered in unison.

There was something in their tone that made me feel even worse about my leadership style.

"We did have a question for you," Evan said.

Hannah knocked his knee with hers and gave him a wicked frowning.

"Yes, Evan?"

"Are you going to be able to do something about this?" Evan lifted up his sleeve and the dark Demon Lock stared up at me from under his plastic watchband.

I gulped and had to stop my hand from reaching out to it. "I didn't know."

I couldn't feel it like I had with Tucker and Tyler. But if anyone fit Haverty's need for prey, this one did. Haverty only marked the weakest of his pack as tributes to the demon Jovan.

"What about you?" I asked Hannah.

She shook her head. "He knew one of us having it was as good as both of us having it."

My heart hurt for a moment and I had a feeling it was their pain and not mine. "Do you guys remember Nash?"

They both nodded.

"I've got him trying to figure out how to break it."

Evan nodded and rolled his shirt sleeve back down.

I reached for my planner. "Keep looking for an apartment. Hannah, let me know how the job thing is working out, and I will see you in . . ." I flipped open to the monthly calendar and tried to calculate the days until the full moon. "Five days? The full moon is in five days?"

A furrow appeared between Hannah's brown eyes.

I leaned back in my chair and stared down at the planner. Five days? Five days to prepare the farm for the invasion of twenty shifters. I was pretty sure Iris knew we were invading, but I should probably call her to get a pep talk about how she wasn't going to help me out with this.

"Okay. I'll see you guys in five days."

The two nodded and fled the table. There wasn't another verb for it. Evan grabbed Hannah's hand and they bounded away in record time.

I leaned forward and rested my head in my hands. What the hell was I doing? An unplanned full moon, scared pack members, ghouls.

I didn't think there was even a hand basket for where this city was heading.

WHEN I STORMED into the library like I usually did, the head librarian just rolled her eyes and let me go back to special collections with my twenty ounces of coffee and bad attitude.

It got a little worse when I saw Nash and Kandice canoodling over a book. How could he be flirting when he was still researching the elementals for me and still hadn't given me an answer to breaking the Demon Lock without binding more souls? If I didn't have time for romance, neither should he.

But then Nash laughed and the feeling of it echoed in the golden thread that bound his magic to mine. Nash was happy. His energy was warm and steady. And Kandice—her silken silver strand was smooth, without the constant thrum of fear that usually ran through it.

Maybe this was Nash's person. The hound dog and the

hawk. There was a certain poetry in it. I almost wished I didn't need to bring my doom and gloom, but just call me a little black rain cloud.

"You two look comfy," I said as I walked into the special collections area.

The two jumped away from each other and stared at me like I was going to yell. Their bodies flinched, waiting for it. First Hannah and Evan, and now Nash? I really was doing something wrong.

I slunk over to the table and pulled out a chair.

"Violet. We were just looking into elemental lore," Nash said quickly.

"You were flirting, but as long as the research is getting done, I don't mind it." I smiled and leaned back in my chair. "How done is the research?"

Nash looked at Kandice and they both relaxed. Another couple with a secret language? Chaz and I were missing the boat on this trend.

"We've found out how to hurt them?" Kandice squeaked. Her voice was tight and she was so very unsure of herself. "The elementals."

I focused in on her strand and enhanced it. She smiled. "We found that if you can completely disconnect them from their element you can hurt them."

"So if she's a fire elemental, I just have to douse her in water?"

"It's not quite as Wizard of Oz as that," Nash said. "But yes."

"Bummer."

"But," Kandice chimed in, "you could wrap her in wet cloth and she wouldn't be able to call on her element."

I nodded.

"And then you could go in for the kill."

I winced. "Not really ready for the killing part, but if she comes at me, I'd like to be able to stop her long enough to run."

"You running?" Kandice asked.

"It happens. Not in my shining moments, but it happens." I turned to Nash. "Ready for the doom and gloom part of this afternoon?"

Nash gulped.

"I've got more with the Demon Lock. I'd like to be able to break it by the full moon."

"That's five days away," he said quickly, sitting up in his chair.

"Apparently."

Nash reached up and pinched the bridge of his already thin nose. "I'll try. I mean, without the grimoire, I don't know how much else is out there about that."

"Well, it looks like you have a helper now. Twice the brain power should mean half the time."

Kandice brushed a strand of blonde hair behind her ear, revealing flushed cheeks. "Thank you, Prima."

"For what?"

"No one's ever given me credit like that before."

"When you give credit to yourself, others will give credit to you."

Nash chuckled.

"What?" I asked.

"You sound like Iris." He smiled.

"Well," I said, grabbing my bag and my coffee and standing up, "I do like to pretend I'm getting better at all this."

Despite everything else that has happened today, I thought.

I left Nash and Kandice to their research and their twit-terpating.

Driving home in my little Miata, I was finally ready to admit I was exhausted. I needed sleep. Needed to stop with the coffee and try some water or, heaven forbid, chamomile tea.

I needed to get home so Chaz and I could work on the secret language that I'd seen all day. I let my brain drift into a nice little wonderland where it was just me and him and maybe a set of Egyptian cotton sheets, working on our cutesy together.

However, I also wandered into the other lane and nearly sideswiped the truck beside me.

Startled and sufficiently awake, I made it back to the townhouse, where the garage was empty. Maybe Chaz had gone for groceries. We were running dangerously low on food.

I dragged my feet through the courtyard between the garage and the house and saw flowers on the dining-room table. I slid the glass door open and felt the pressure of the amped-up protection spell above the entry.

There was a small plant on the table. It was stalky, with small purple flowers. I plucked the note from the table and the plant identifier from the soil.

"Got a call. Cause, not underwear. Should be back tomorrow. Will expect the cavalry if I'm not. Get some rest. Love, Chaz."

I looked over at the plant marker. Catnip.

Tired laughter echoed through the blissfully quite house. Screw the secret language. He knew the way to my heart was through a joke.

I took the catnip and the note and went straight to bed.

CHAPTER 10

SHADOW WAS ON the bed when I woke up. His tail wagged as he began to jump. He might have been enjoying his role as guard dog too much.

"Oh my God, what?" I said as I sat up and adjusted my tank top.

Shadow jumped off the bed and ran to the bedroom door.

I was about to tell him to use his doggie door when I heard the pounding at my front door. The next round of it shook the whole front of the house.

Rubbing my eyes, I adjusted the charm at my neck and slowly walked down the stairs. I caught a glimpse of the clock on my way.

Six thirty in the morning.

Who the hell was knocking on my door at six thirty in the morning? I ran my fingers through my hair and looked out the peephole. Crap.

I flung the door open and Peter Delmont was standing on my doorstep.

"Someone better be dead," I growled.

He just smiled. His workout attire was already soaked in

sweat and I was going to blame it on my drowsy sensibilities when I admitted that he smelled amazing. "Wanted to drop these off. The paperwork was filed yesterday, so you officially own all seven properties."

I eyed the folded manila envelope he clutched. "You couldn't wait for a decent hour of day?"

"Frankly, I thought you'd have a lackey get the door."

"I don't have lackeys," I said as I grabbed the envelope.

"You shouldn't be here alone. Where's that fiancé of yours?"

I frowned. He was asking entirely too many questions. "How did you even know where I lived?"

"Paperwork. The devil is in the details, Miss Jordan."

I leaned against the door frame. His blond hair was combed back despite the exercise and his blue eyes looked almost teal in the morning light. He really was a specimen.

"Well, I appreciate the house call, Counselor. Now if you'll excuse me, I have a day to start."

Peter licked his lips and put his hands on his hips. He looked over my shoulder and his eyes landed on the silver protection charm in the foyer. "That's big stuff."

"It's why I don't need lackeys."

Peter smiled, his lips still pressed together as he fought his amusement. "You really just do things your own way."

"Pride myself on it. Will I be seeing you at the full moon or did your secretary not get it on your calendar?"

"I'll be there, sans caravan."

"Right, because your undoubtedly phallic sports car can't be caught on the same drive as the rest of us."

This time, his smile was wide enough to have some teeth in it. "Have a good day, Miss Jordan."

"Mr. Delmont."

He turned to go just as Tucker was making his way up the sidewalk still in full police regalia. Oh, this would be interesting.

I took off my charm for a moment just to feel the story

between them. It took a moment for my energy to adjust to being unhampered by the spell.

The two men slowed as they approached each other and static electricity sizzled between them as they passed, eyes locked and fists clenched. They really hated each other.

Tucker made his way up the sidewalk, not taking his eyes off Delmont until he was standing before me. "Why is Delmont leaving your place sweaty at the crack of dawn?"

I laughed. "Are you serious?"

I walked into my place and Tucker followed, closing the door and locking it.

"He stopped by to drop off the keys to the properties. The signatures went through. It's official." I tossed the keys on the dining-room table and walked into the kitchen to start a pot of coffee.

Tucker leaned against the counter next to me. Shadow joined us and Tucker reached down to give him a good scratch behind his ears. Still brothers, no matter the shape.

"And he decided first thing in the morning was best?"

Discovering that coffee had not magically reappeared in my kitchen, I huffed and turned toward Tucker. "Listen. I know there is bad blood between you guys. Nash didn't tell me every-thing, except that he was responsible for keeping you guys on the outside of the old pack. Did you hear the keyword in there? Old pack."

"Still think he's a do—"

"Language," I snapped. "What is it with you guys and that word?" I turned back to get two mugs from the cabinet. There was Plan B for caffeine, but I hated to result to such measures. "But he's ours. He chose me, Tucker. That has to mean some-thing to you."

Tucker let out a long, slow sigh. He wasn't convinced.

I put a kettle on, and with a heavy heart, dumped in two scoops of instant coffee. As I waited, I took a moment to appreciate my Riko. I'd been wearing that damn charm for so long I'd forgotten how powerful Tucker really was. Slightly pissed off, his power pulsed around him like a heartbeat.

"Besides"—I smiled—"he's the low man on this totem pole."

Tucker seemed to take great pleasure in that as the smile spread across his face. "Where's Mr. Garrett?"

I frowned. It sounded so odd, and my first response was going to be that Mr. Garrett died almost seven years ago fighting Haverty. "Mr. Garrett?"

"Your fiancé?"

The kettle started to whistle. "Why'd you call him that? He's just Chaz."

Tucker looked down at his coffee. "Well, it doesn't seem right to just call him Chaz anymore."

I poured the hot water and stirred. "Why not? He's still just Chaz."

"But he's your Chaz."

"Damn straight, but you've never called him Mr. Garrett." I handed him the mug. It was odd to be having this conversation with Tucker after the conversation I'd just had with Chaz.

Tucker pressed his lips together and looked for his words in the steaming coffee. "He's not a Primo even though he's your mate."

Oh, well, that was out of left field.

"Don't get me wrong. He's like a brother, bled for us, fought with us, but he's not pack."

I took a sip of coffee. I'd been waiting for this, for the ancient politics of all this to finally mangle the situation. "What would that take?"

Tucker's smooth answer made me think that he'd prepared for this question already. "He'd have to be committed to us and break his alliances with the Cause."

"Why?"

Tucker put down his coffee. That's how I knew that this was

important to him. I rested mine on the counter, letting him know it was important to me too.

"Because you can't have two alliances, Violet. It doesn't work. You'll pull yourself apart trying to be true to both."

"Sounds like you're not just talking about Chaz."

Tucker licked his lips. "We all understand why you weren't able to host the first full moon, but you haven't even told me of the plans for the next one."

"We're going to the farmhouse."

"And what then? Do you even know how to commune? What are we going to eat? The devil's in the details, Violet."

Shivers wracked down my spine at hearing that horrible phrase again. and my coffee danced in my hand and spilled over the side. I grabbed a towel from a drawer and wiped up the spilled coffee, through it wasn't good enough to cry over.

Tucker leaned against the counter. "You can't half-ass this, Violet."

I put my coffee mug in the sink, only half drunk. "It wasn't my intention to half-ass this."

"The road to hell is paved—"

I put my finger up and stopped yet another annoying cliché. "Did you want to look at the properties with me today or just be Mr. Judgey?"

Tucker dropped his head. "Let me change."

I LOOKED DOWN at the double macchiato in my hand and then up at the condo not three blocks from where I lived. Haverty had also been drawn to the intimate townhomes in Uptown for one of his seven safe houses. I tried to let the similarities stop there for now.

Tucker took the first step toward the front door. I sipped my hot beverage, let it steel my nerves, and followed after him.

The inside smelled like mildew and wet carpet. I covered my nose with my hand, visions of spore-induced zombies dancing through my head.

"Pipes must have burst," Tucker said as he freely sniffed the air.

He ran his hand along the wall and found a light switch. The living room was sparse: a couch, a TV on a plastic milk crate. It looked like my first place in LA when I got the job working for Drew at Cloak & Dagger Productions.

"Guessing no one's been here in a while?" I asked as I walked into the living room.

I crushed something under my sneaker. When I lifted my foot, I saw a bag of vegetable chips. Fresh vegetable chips from Sprouts. "Or still living here."

Carefully, I opened my borders and let my power wash over the bottom floor. Even with the dampening spell, I could still feel the hide-aways.

Two rabbits. Young. And mine. My stomach churned. I closed my eyes and sorted through the fifteen strands that floated like spider's silk through my power. When I found the correct two, I pulled at them slightly and there was an audible gasp from behind a half-sized door under the stairs.

I looked at Tucker and he nodded.

"You can come out," I said nicely.

It took them a while, but slowly the tarnished handle turned, and I saw four small brown eyes peer out of the darkness.

"It's okay," I cooed. It didn't sound like my voice. It sounded like disappointment, but not at them, at myself.

Slowly, Hannah and Evan unfurled themselves from the small cupboard under the stairs. They stood before me, smelling like wet fur and moist wool. The smell was new since I'd last met with them, but the look of guilt wasn't.

"Hannah, you told me that you were living in Plano."

"Actually, all we said was that we'd found a place."

I pinched the bridge of my nose. I wouldn't fault her on the technicalities. "How did you know about this place, Evan?"

"Followed Carlisle for a while. He used it to have parties."

I cringed at the name and I think they all felt it through our connection.

"You know a pipe has burst someplace," Tucker said.

"Yes, sir," they both answered, eyes still cast down.

I studied them. I'd never seen two people more suited to their animals. Or a couple who needed a fresh start.

I looked over at Tucker and raised an eyebrow. He held out his hand with the keys in his palm. I plucked the keys out of Tucker's hand and held it out to the couple. "The place is yours on a few conditions."

They twitched with anticipation.

"You clean it up. Make it livable."

"Yes, ma'am."

"You keep it that way."

"Yes ma'am."

"And if one of your pack mates needs help . . ."

Their eyes darted to mine. "We will give them a home."

The sentiment hit me like a warm shot of tequila. It started in my chest and spread out to my extremities. I couldn't help but smile.

There were lights in their eyes, or maybe it was a hum in the connection between us. I liked it. It felt like being a Prima. Felt like I might be doing something right.

"You've got a week to get that smell out of here. If you can't pay the bill, get it to me."

Hannah looked over at Evan and he nodded. She reached out took the keys. "We will."

I looked around the place and back at them. It would be the perfect nest for two rabbits, who could make more rabbits. The thought of a whole host of rabbits sent a chill down my spine.

"Something wrong?" Tucker asked.

"My burden. Let's leave these two to it and head over to the next one."

"Thank you, Prima Jordan," Hannah called out.

"I'll see you in a few days. Full moon, remember?"

As we left, I think I heard a happy squeal from the two inside.

SOMEWHERE IN THE middle of the third property, my stomach growled.

"See, I knew you weren't eating," Tucker grumbled as we walked through the kitchen.

"I'm fine," I said. I grabbed a packet of peanuts from the bottom of my bag. "See, not starving."

But the peanuts smelled too good and the roasted honey smell of them filled my senses. I was hungry. Too hungry.

I threw a handful of nuts in my mouth. "What's this?" I asked as I turned the handle of a small door that looked like a pantry off the kitchen.

When you are about to engage four ghouls in battle, might I recommend not doing it with a mouthful of honey-roasted peanuts?

Four slimy humanoids rushed out of the white door.

"Violet," Tucker yelled.

I put my hands out against the barrage and a thumb sunk into shoulder meat. That's why I shouldn't have had the peanuts. Bile rose up in my throat at the rotting breath of the thing that came out at me.

Two rushed past me toward Tucker and I managed to kick one of them back into the pantry.

The ghoul's milky eyes seemed to look at me as his hands came out again.

Instinct took over and I struck him with an open palm

strike, only to feel his ribs crack beneath my palm and not stop him coming.

He swung a limp arm at me and I pulled back, but not far enough, and his long dead nails raked my cheek, drawing blood.

I should have been more in control. I should have been well fed and well rested and maybe been taking the time to shift every now and then, because the moment that I smelled blood, the panther took over.

I fell back against the kitchen counter and into the silky blackness of my animal.

WHEN I CAME to, I was kneeling naked over a decapitated body with a slightly cheesy taste in my mouth. Crap and double crap.

My heart raced as I looked around the scene to piece together what was going on. Body parts lay all over the empty dining room.

The smell of filth was all around us. I looked down at my pale skin to find it slick with this black ooze. Why I was naked?

Movement to my left drew my attention as Tucker shifted back into his human form.

"Violet?" His voice was high and tight as he turned away and shielded his eyes. "What the hell happened, Violet?"

I stood. "Shirt."

Tucker took off his button-up shirt and tossed it at me. I slipped it on as fast as I could, and my mind seemed to work better not naked.

The moment I was covered, Tucker turned around. "What the hell was that?"

"I don't know."

I looked down at myself, the hum of the shift still in along my skin. And I was starving. Anything that I had remembered to eat in the past day was burned through with the energy of the shift.

My stomach churned as I looked down at the torso of a ghoul at my feet. There were very distinctive claw marks all over the body. Blood I could handle, had spilled it and had it spilled, but rotten body fluids were a new kind of gore that even on my second exposure was still hard to manage.

Tucker stormed over to me. "You lost control, didn't you? I mean, you were the fastest I've ever seen you, but you lost control."

I rolled up my sleeves, nearly ripping the poor things off with my anger. "What do you want me to say, Tucker? That I've been too busy to eat or run or shift in the past six weeks? Fine, you're right. Feel better?"

Tucker ran his fingers through his hair. He let out a long sigh. "No."

"Tell anyone and I'll have to eat you, but your point has been made. Okay?"

Tucker looked around the room. "What are these things?"

"Ghouls, according to Jessa."

"In the middle of the day? In Plano?"

"Guess they don't care about zip codes."

I nudged the body at my feet and black ooze seeped out of the flesh and into the carpet. "Can you call Jessa? See if she can get the Cleaners over here? I'm going to try to find my bag."

Tucker nodded and called Jessa. I went back into the kitchen to see if there was anything left of my pants.

There was another body in the kitchen. It almost matched the black granite countertops of the new construction.

My clothes were shredded and probably the reason the panther went after them with a vengeance. Those jeans were fairly new. At least the purse was relatively not soaked in ghoul guts.

Careful of the oozing body on the tile next to me, I dug

around in my pants pockets for the keys to my car. As I was grabbing my Chucks, something caught my eye on the chest of the thing lying next to me.

Pretty sure it wasn't going to move because the left side of its head had been smashed in, I carefully reached over and flicked what was left of its shirt off of something carved into its chest.

The Demon Lock. I would have known it anywhere. This thing was marked by Haverty? This thing was pack.

My brain, the part that had been bred to be a horror movie writer, to think the thoughts that normal happy people never think about, began to churn out a story. And when it got to the end, I turned around and threw up everything that I'd consumed in the past two days into the perfect inlayed kitchen sink. It was mostly coffee, but the peanuts made a reappearance as well.

"Violet?"

I wiped my mouth on a sleeve and looked up at him. "They were part of the Pride."

"What?" Tucker seemed more concerned with my illness than my realization. He opened a few of the cabinets and found an unopened case of bottled water in the fridge.

I tore the plastic top off a bottle and gulped down the cold water.

When I was pretty sure that my stomach was going to stay where it was, I turned to Tucker.

"Check out the mark on its chest. He's got the Demon Lock."

Tucker slipped into policeman mode and I felt him harden his stomach to take in the sight. I was going to have to learn that trick.

He knelt down by the body and took a good hard look at the mark. "Holy shit."

"Yeah."

Tucker stood and leaned on the counter next to me. "What does it mean?"

"Would you like to hear my gloom and doom version?"

He didn't nod. I wouldn't have wanted to hear it either.

"I think that's what happens when the demon of said Demon Lock calls upon the mark. He sucks all the magic and life out of them, and they are left like this, hollow and hungry."

Tucker gulped and I watched the slow bob of his Adam's apple. He reached up and stroked the white, long-dormant scar upon his own breast. "Are you sure?"

"No. But when my gut goes for the worse possible scenario, it's usually right. And my gut is saying that this is Jovan's work."

"Why would Jovan do this?"

I looked down at the body. It made sense now. Why I didn't feel any energy from them. Why I hadn't, even in a better condition, been able to feel any attack coming. Jovan was calling in Haverty's debt to him. Must take six months for news to travel to the Neveranth that I had killed his little partner in power.

Or six months for Spencer to find the demon he'd been searching for when all of this started.

My entire body tightened, and I shook hard. Part of it was the exhaustion, part of it was the solid proof that my worse half was scheming again.

"Vi?"

I looked up at Tucker. I wasn't ready to say that story out loud yet. "I've got four pack with this mark, Tucker. I need to get to them."

"You need to rest."

"How? I've got four people bound to me that might turn into meat suits if I don't act on this now."

I started for the door and Tucker grabbed my arms hard and turned me toward him. "You need to go home."

The doorbell rang. We both looked toward the front door like we were prepared for a stampede of elephants through it.

"Do the Cleaners really move that fast?" Tucker whispered.

I wriggled out of his hands and stepped over parts to the front door to look out the peephole. Sure enough, Kurt and the rest of the fearsome fashion Foursome were outside with Jessa, who, bless her pointy head, had my emergency duffle bag from her place.

I threw the door open. "Brace yourselves."

"Oh pfft," Kurt said as he pushed past Jessa and I.

But all four of the perfectly coiffed men stopped when they saw the carnage in the living room. They were experts in making girls pretty and cleansing the evil out of a place with their special brand of fairy magic. This was certainly the worst thing that I'd thrown at them.

I pulled Jessa into the foyer and kept her there with a hand on her arm.

"Please tell me that's not ghoul guts?" she said with the most disgusted look on her face as she looked at my black-streaked self.

"It's ghoul guts."

Jessa did a full body shiver of disgust before she handed my duffle over. "What is this place?"

"One of the Haverty properties. Value might have gone down if they knew about the ghouls hiding in the pantry."

"And my mother wonders why I don't cook."

I walked into the living room and the Cleaners were still looking at what was left of everything. The four men in their identical suites just looked around and tried to figure out how they were going to clean up the mess I'd made. Kurt stared at a particularly interesting black splatter on the ceiling.

"Can you handle it?" I asked Kurt.

"We got highlights on you. We can handle a little dismemberment."

I snorted and went into the bathroom. The water was turned

on even though it was more than obvious that no one had ever lived here. I got some hot water going and rinsed off.

Everything hurt. My head, my skin. The panther had come to my rescue again. Or had she come to the aid of those poor creatures, put them out of their misery? Maybe that's why she pushed me away, to make the hard decision for me. Lord knows that if this lot of ghouls had looked at me like that other one in the alley had, I don't know if I could have ripped them into a million pieces like she had.

I shook my head. Pronouns were getting in the way again. I had chosen to block it out because I'm not strong enough to make that choice right now, to end a being's life, mercifully or not.

A knock echoed through the bathroom.

"Still in there?" Jessa asked again.

"Still standing." Barely.

"Hurry up. The Cleaners want us out of here."

I hurried as best I could. I dried off with Tucker's shirt and pulled out my emergency cat suit. Jessa's gift to me: a black velour track suit from Bebe, magically charmed to shift with me. The stretchy material softened the aches and pains.

She opened the door as I was brushing my teeth.

"Tucker filled me in on what happened. You really think those things are Wanderers?"

I nodded, then spit and rinsed. "I do."

"Was Spencer involved?"

A nervous laugh bubbled out of me as I put my toothbrush back in my bag. Hot tears welled up in my eyes and I sat on the sink and looked at her.

"Whoa, Vi." Jessa jumped and came into the bathroom, shutting the door quickly behind her.

"I know he's involved somehow. Antagonists just don't fall out of the story, Jessa. They always come back. He's behind this, and if I don't find out soon, I'm four pack members down and might not make it out myself."

"Hey," she rubbed my arm. "Haven't seen defeatist Violet in a while. I was just getting used to kick-ass Violet. Where'd she go?"

"She hasn't slept in five, six days, hasn't eaten in two, and woke up naked in front of her Riko."

"Is this one of those pep talk moments? Tucker's pretty good at those."

"Been getting private pep talks?"

I said it quickly, as a joke, but a flush ran through Jessa like I'd never seen before. There was a sprinkle of roses and raindrops in the air around me and a bright lavender twinkle in her eye.

"Seriously?"

Jessa pulled her hand away from my arm and pressed herself against the bathroom wall. The smell of roses faded away, but the lavender twinkle didn't. "We just talk."

"Are we talking business or more like what's your favorite Italian dinner and can I buy it for you sometime?"

"No. Just talk. About pack stuff and magic and maybe about music."

My jaw dropped. "You and Tucker?"

"There is no me and Tucker. We just talk. And he might have gone on a few patrols with me when you were busy."

"Oh my God, Jessa." I smiled all the way down to my aching toes. "That's great."

"There's nothing to be great. He helps me keep you sane and he's a gentleman and . . ." Jessa dropped her face into her hands. "I sound stupid, don't I?"

"No. You sound like a girl with a crush."

She looked up at me and her little face hardened. "You will not make fun of this, Violet."

"I promise."

"I'm serious. No dog jokes, no 'has he shown you his gun,' and so help me God, if you make a 'getting tail' joke, I will shove you into the Neveranth myself."

She was serious. It was more than her idle threats. There was something that fluttered in her energy. Something light and hopeful.

And so help me, I was not going to be the thing that squashed it.

"I promise," I said softly, and I reached out my hand to her.

She took it cautiously.

"I won't even mention it, until you want to, and I'll keep it mum from Tucker."

"But he's your Riko. What if it all ends badly?"

I smiled. "You were here first."

Tucker's voice carried across the bedroom. "The Cleaners really want us out of here."

"Coming," I called back and winked at Jessa before looking at my bedraggled image in the mirror. "I've got a million calls to make, four people to hunt down, a—"

Jessa stopped me. "You're going home. You can restore the natural order of things from your couch with a full stomach."

CHAPTER 11

I HAD TO flip through my planner to remember the phone numbers of the four pack members that needed to be watched over. Thanks to my smart phone, I found the number of the nearest Sprouts to the town home and found out that Evan was still at work. I'd send someone over there to explain things to Hannah.

I pulled up to the curb in front of my house and stayed in my car to make the next call.

How the hell was I going to explain this? Hi, you might turn into a zombie, so if you could just stick around another pack member, that would be great.

The phone call picked up on the first ring. "Prima Jordan? I was just about to call you," Jane said. There was a slight lilt to her voice, some accent that I hadn't asked about yet that curled around her words. She was quiet and just so very proper. There wasn't any other way to describe her.

"Something wrong?"

"My mark hurts."

I gulped. "I know. Where are you?"

"At home."

Jane lived alone on some property on the outskirts of town. It was perfect for her animal side, a white horse, but it was a good thirty-minute drive from here. I was running out of bedrooms, but I needed her with someone.

"Okay, Jane. I don't want to freak you out, but I don't want you alone. So you've got a choice. You can come to my place and sleep on a couch for a few nights, or Gator lives over on your side of town, over in Forney, I think."

"Which one is Gator?"

"Tall redheaded guy, looks like a construction worker."

"I am not sure about that."

I nodded. "Okay. Well, I'll text you my address and you can pack a bag for a few days."

"What about work?"

"Work is fine, but I don't want you alone at night."

"Should I be scared, Prima Jordan?"

"No, don't be scared. In fact, I need you to do whatever makes you happy, so if you've got a favorite pair of pajamas, or if you need to get your nails done, I need you to stay positive."

"That might be the strangest advice I have ever heard," she said.

"Well, welcome to the pack. I'll see you tonight."

"Yes, ma'am."

I flinched at the title and hung up to call the next one. "Hola, esta dia buena a la Rosarios."

I could hear the bang and clang of the busy restaurant behind him. "Mr. Rosario, it's Violet Jordan."

"Prima," the older man greeted me with his thick Spanish accent.

"Do you know where Julian is?"

"Working. Did he do something wrong?"

I laughed. The three Rosario boys were troublemakers in the most wholesome kind of troublemaking, but like Hannah and

Evan, Haverty had only seen the need to mark the middle son with the Lock.

"No, Mr. Rosario. Just make sure that he's not alone for the next couple of days. And call me if anything happens."

"Is it the Lock?"

These guys really were all on the same wavelength. I wished I could take credit for some of that, but not yet. "I'm just being careful. Will we be seeing you and your wife at the full moon?"

"We can't all leave the restaurant, Prima."

"Understood. But I'll need the boys there."

"Si, Si. They will be there."

"Good. Take care of yourself."

"Adios, Prima."

I leaned my head back against the headrest as I hung up. Three down, one to go.

Knuckles rapped against my passenger door and I saw Chaz standing out on the sidewalk. I unlocked the door and he opened it and climbed in.

"What are you doing?"

"Phone calls. Welcome to my new mobile office."

He too leaned his head back on the headrest.

I'd missed him. One day away and I'd missed the golden in his eyes, the warm musky smell of him.

"Jessa said you got attacked by ghouls. Again."

"Yep."

He let out a long sigh. "On a scale of one to ten, how bad was today?"

"Fifteen."

He sat up straight in the seat. "What? Why? She said it was four against two?"

"Remember a really long time ago when you told me that the panther needed to fulfill its three primary urges?"

"Yeah. Think it was Iris, but yeah. Why?"

"I haven't been running or eating nearly enough or anything

really that would satisfy the panther, so when she got a chance to stomp on something today, she took it."

Chaz gave me a hard look. "Did you wind up naked?"

"Pretty much."

"Did Tucker jump down your throat about it?"

"Pretty much."

He looked down at the console between us. "Guess I suck more at this fiancé thing than I thought."

"How is me ending up naked your fault in any way?"

"I'm supposed to take care of you, help you get to the best version of yourself and since we've been engaged, you've nearly missed the full moon, stopped sleeping and eating, and lost control of your shift."

I smiled and slipped my hand into his. "Then why don't you take me inside and cook me dinner?"

"Because I need to talk to you about my trip." He squeezed my hand.

That wasn't good.

"Here in the car? We have nearly two hours with no one in the house."

Chaz settled into the passenger seat, as much as he could in the small space. I couldn't afford the Miata with the leg room. "It's quiet here."

I popped my seat into a more reclined position and readied for a story. "Shoot."

"Andrea needed me to find a pack of ghouls roaming her city."

My skin prickled. "Did they have the Demon Lock?"

Chaz frowned. "Yeah, actually. Turns out they used to be . . ."

"Members of the Order and now they are nothing but mindless shells of their former selves hoping to chomp on some Wanderer flesh?" I filled in. I popped the seat back to a sitting position, remembering why I had been in the car making the phone calls in the first place.

There was a beautiful furrow between his hazel eyes. "How do you know this?"

"Figured it out after this afternoon. The four ghouls had the Lock and my brain went to its usual dark place."

"What happened to them?"

"The demon on the other end of the Lock. The whole reason Haverty promised off members of his pack was to get more power and I'm thinking Jovan is calling in his debts now that he knows Haverty is dead."

"Why?"

"Well, when I thought it was just here, I would have said he'd found out Haverty wasn't the big dog anymore and was cashing in his chips."

"But now that it's happening all over the place?"

"I don't know."

Chaz sighed. "So do that thing where you make stuff up with your writer brain."

"Seriously?"

"Yeah. Look at the big picture and puzzle piece it together like the plot lines in your movies."

I sighed but humored him. I closed my eyes and saw the ghouls again. And the Demon Lock. And what I thought Jovan might look like. In my head he was this evil dark beastie with horns like the devil from *Legend*.

Why would the evil lord of the netherverse need to call upon power from our realm, and slowly? Chaz didn't mention hordes of ghouls, just a small pack. A few here and there. Chaz hadn't mentioned a change of power in San Antonio, and in the six months I'd been on the circuit, he hadn't mentioned a power shift from light to dark.

So I'm evil and going one by one through old ties that probably don't mean much to me, but I'm still getting more powerful.

"He's either pulling on their ties because he's teaching

someone else, or he's trying not to get caught. But if he enjoys chaos as much as everyone seems to think that he does . . ."

"He's teaching someone how to control others."

The vision of the ghoul with the Lock on his chest flashed across my brain and my stomach churned again.

"What else? That's your 'something else' face," Chaz said.

I licked my lips and told him what I wasn't ready to admit to Tucker. "What if he's teaching Spencer?"

Chaz gulped. "That's a conclusion I'm not ready to jump to. "

I knew Chaz and he would need proof. "Can you see if you can fill in the blanks?"

Chaz nodded and somewhere in the conversation, all the golden had faded from his features as he was put to work. "I can ask around, get on the white hat broadband and see if anyone else has noticed a ghoul influx."

I chuckled. "We just said ghoul influx in a grown-up conversation. Our lives are weird."

He squeezed my hand. "At least they are ours."

I smiled, a warm happy smile for just one moment in the quiet car with my fiancé.

THE FIRST ROUND of housemates landed at about six thirty that evening and the ebb and flow was constant after. Nash and Kandice finished up the dinner that Chaz made for me while I took a very hot shower and a fifteen-minute cat nap. Chaz went to his house when I wasn't alone to get some laundry and supplies. Tucker showed up and paced, because that's helpful in a crisis, and by the time Jane made it to my place, it was eight in the evening, and everyone had settled into sitcoms and ice cream bars Nash had picked up on the way home.

"Like I said," I narrated as I lead Jane upstairs, her dark eyes wide. "It's a little cramped. Kandice is in the guest room right now. Shadow has his bed downstairs."

"Which one is Shadow?" she asked.

"The dog, but he's actually a man just cursed to stay in the shift."

"Oh."

"Which leaves my office for you. I've got a recliner in there. It's worn but sleeps pretty comfortable."

I opened the door for her and went around grabbing my laptop and power chord from the desk and a few notebooks so I could work from the kitchen table. "I'm right across the hall and the bathroom is the one with the vacancy sign. It was Chaz's idea after a few unfortunately incidents early on."

Jane nodded and set her bag down on the recliner. "I still wish I knew why you told me to come here. I mean, I am hardly anyone."

"First of all, never think that. You are Jane and the prettiest white horse I've ever seen. Secondly, you belong here as much as any other pack member. And thirdly, Jovan's been calling on the Demon Lock and I want to do everything in my power to keep you safe from him."

Jane went pale. Her sun-kissed skin went sallow, and she collapsed into the chair next to her. "I knew you told the truth but. . ."

I knelt down before her. "I'm not going to pull punches. I want you to know the truth so you can fight for yourself."

"How am I supposed to fend off Jovan?" her voice was small and quaking.

I took her hands and strengthened the ties between us. "Well, by being happy, feeling safe. Jovan gets into your fear and your heartache, so be happy. I've got a library full of books, a living room full of friends, and a freezer full of ice-cream sand-wiches and chocolate. It's an urban paradise."

Jane finally cracked a smile, which was all I was going for.

"Now, if you'd like to join us downstairs, I'll be working and Tucker will be pacing and Nash will be looking at us like we are idiots, but there will be ice cream and coffee. I'm always good for coffee."

I WASN'T EVEN through my story arc or my first ice cream bar when my phone rang.

"Hewwo," I managed with a full mouth.

"Vi, It's Devin. Have you been to the coffee shop today?"

Had I? "I think I was there yesterday. Why?"

"Today's the last day. They're closing their doors at midnight."

My entire body tensed. "What?"

"Massive sign. Didn't Bastian tell you?"

I stood and ran through every memory of the blond-haired manager. "No."

"Well, I suggest you get down here and have one last coffee with me before this place is gone."

I looked up at Tucker, who looked like I'd just flipped on the Defcon 5 buzzer. "I can't, Devin. We're in research mode tonight before the full moon."

"Oh, right, well. I'll drink a double in your honor."

My neurons screamed out at the missed opportunity for caffeine, especially knowing what I was going to be doing the rest of the night. The rest of me could use a Devin fix.

"Well, twist my arm. I'll be there in ten." I hung up the phone and looked at Tucker. "I need to go out for a little bit. Tell Chaz when he gets back?"

"Now? Where?"

"I'll be fine, Tucker. I just need thirty minutes and a coffee, and I'll be back good as new."

I went to the front door to slip on my Chucks.

"You can't leave, Violet."

Tucker was just about to be between me and coffee. Maybe my Riko didn't know me as well as he thought he did. "I'll be at the coffee shop. It's as safe as this place."

He tried to protest again but it fell flat when I grabbed my purse.

"Thirty minutes. What can happen in thirty minutes?"

CHAPTER 12

THE COFFEE SHOP was the saddest thing I'd ever seen. Bastian had dragged out every seasonal decoration he had and hung it on the walls. Hearts and fireworks adorned the window around the Last Day Open sign stuck between the wooden blinds and the window.

I opened the door and felt the shimmer of the protection spell I'd put up six months ago. I saw the mirror that Jessa and I had put up to make sure that she could see into the shop before she magically materialized in the bathroom. I saw the spot where Chaz and I had our first fight.

Devin rose. Ever the drama king, he was dressed in all black with a pair of black sunglasses on. He stretched out his hand and pulled me to him, kissing me on the cheek.

"Whatever are we going to do, Violet?" he said as we walked to the counter.

Bastian had on three different hats with a crown over all those, all strapped with elastic bands under his chin.

I leaned against the counter. "Why didn't you tell us, Bastian?"

"Figured quicker was better. Like a bandage, my mom used to say."

I shook my head. "This isn't right, Bastian."

"Bank sure seems to think it is. I'm getting out before I go completely under." He still mustered a smile. "Last caramel macchiato on the house to my best customer."

I sighed. "Make it a double."

"And Stretch here?" Bastian asked.

"Something fancy," Devin said.

We both slid down the bar to the pick-up counter.

I took one last survey of the place, burning it into my brain, into my energy. Would the magic still pull Wanderers here if they turned this place into a tire shop? Or would the magic fade when I no longer called it home?

When my eyes finally landed on Devin, there was a furrow between his brown eyes that rivaled the Mariana trench. "You look skinny."

"Thanks?"

"No, like Kate Moss skinny. When was the last time you ate?" he reached out and pinched my bony elbow.

"I know. I've been a little preoccupied with work lately."

"The furry kind or the writing kind?"

"I wish it was the writing kind."

Devin slipped into doctor mode. He gently took my wrist and looked at the clock on the wall. He pressed his fingers into my throat and looked quickly into my eyes. "You're cold."

"I'm fine."

"No, your basal temperature the last time I checked was one hundred degrees even. You're not even burning at normal levels."

"I know, Devin. I'm working on it and I was kind of hoping that a relaxing cup of coffee with my human friend might help with all this stress."

Devin frowned and then slid his arm around my shoulder. "But you have all those gorgeous men around you all the time."

"I know. It's exhausting." I laughed.

Bastian served us up our last cup of coffee and we went back to my little table.

"I met all my pack here. Where am I supposed to go now?"

"I scope out men here. Where am I supposed to go now?" Devin fired back before he sipped his coffee. "Oh, bravo, Bastian."

The man tipped his head to us and went to his next customer.

Devin sighed as he looked mournfully into his cup. "I'm sure you're needed back at the fort, so catch me up as quickly as possible."

And I did, I rushed him through the pack meetings, the ghoul attacks, and ended with the piece de resistance. "So now I'm a millionaire."

Devin's jaw dropped. "And you're still wearing those old Chucks?"

I laughed. It felt good to just be Violet for a few moments, not taking or needing anything from him.

"Then why are you bemoaning the loss of your favorite coffee shop?" And Devin uttered the most sinful words I'd ever heard. "Buy the coffee shop."

The smile spread itself across my face. My toes curled with happiness as I suddenly saw a future that I could live with. A never-ending fount of free coffee. Now that was magic.

But then I remembered the spiel I'd given Chaz and why he wasn't going to get a yacht for his birthday. "It's not my money. It's the pack's money."

"And didn't you just tell me that you met every single one of your pack members here?"

"Yes, but it's just a coffee shop."

Devin leaned forward. "It's more than that. It's a special

place for you. You have memories here. And now you have the means to make sure others can have those same memories. That some other crazy writer can meet a debonair book lover and form a friendship that lasts forever."

I smiled and reached across the table to take his hand. It was so warm. "This is why I need you, Devin. A fresh perspective. All those pretty boys and not a one of them thought just buy the coffee shop to keep them safe."

Devin flashed me an award-winning smile and I was just about to comment on his debonair attitude, when a cold rush of energy washed over me like an ice-cold bucket of water down the back of my shirt.

"Violet?" Devin put down his cup of coffee but kept a tight grip on my hand.

And then there was a flood of roses. I took in a deep breath and pulled out my cell phone.

It rang in my hand.

"What is it, Jessa?" I asked. I was already on my feet. Devin followed quickly.

Her voice was tight and rushed. "Rip in the Veil. Not a tear. I'm trying to find it now."

"I'll be there in . . ."

I stopped when I saw Waylon walking through the door. He wasn't Waylon though. He was a cold stony energy down my back and there was something wrong with his eyes.

I dropped the phone from my face and tore at the charm around my neck. Freed from its dampening spell, I truly knew his power.

Son of a motherless goat, the man was powerful, like me-on-a-bad-day powerful.

"Waylon?"

His wild eyes landed on me, and they weren't the light brown I was used to, but a white cloudy look, like a saucer of milk. "Blood, Violet. I saw blood and this big friggin' snake thing."

I gulped. "Waylon?"

He ran his shaking hand through his hair and the cool rivulets of power dissipated as I watched his brown eyes return to normal. "I didn't want you to find out like this, Violet. But it was bad, there was a . . ." His eyes landed on my coffee companion.

"Devin," Devin stuck out his hand quickly.

"Devin, this is cousin Waylon. Waylon, this is Devin."

Waylon shook the man's hand quickly and I turned to Devin.

"It's hitting the fan right now, isn't it?" Devin asked.

I shook my head. "You've been hanging out with me too long, but yes," I looked over at Waylon, the man I thought I knew, and then back at Devin, the man who knew me too well. "I think it's a keep-your-cell-phone-on kind of night."

"I love you," Devin said as he kissed my cheek and grabbed his coffee. I watched as he put a twenty in Bastian's tip jar, which seemed extra full tonight.

With a jaw of steel, I grabbed Waylon's arm and pulled him toward the quiet back corner of the shop. Even though there were only a few patrons there, I didn't want them talking about blood and snakes over their coffees.

"Slowly, Waylon."

As he spoke, his power sunk so deep inside him that I couldn't feel anything emanating from him except his regular body heat.

I listened to him like I'd never listened to anything else in my entire life. Knowing that whatever he said was going to redefine my entire world.

"I got the Jourdaine Legacy after Aunt Lily died, Violet. Her future visions."

My stomach churned over on itself. My mother's legacy went to Waylon?

"I wanted to tell you. God did I need to tell you. But . . . when I found out about the panther, I knew I had to find you."

"What?" I looked deep into Waylon's brown eyes.

"I had a vision about you being attacked. I knew you'd been changed over."

Thoughts spun through my head. Waylon a psychic? Waylon, who we had gone searching for his daughter with? Waylon, who used to give me Indian burns?

I did the only thing that made any sense right now. I punched him as hard as I could on the arm.

"Oww," he whined as he held his arm.

"That's for keeping it from me. And this . . ." I said before I stomped on his foot. "That's for not coming sooner. Do you know how many times I could have used a psychic in the past six months?"

"Do you know how many times I knew that?" His tone, his eyes killed me. He really had been trying to get here. He really did want to be here with me.

I threw my arms around him and hugged him. It finally made sense why he was here. Why now. And it wasn't any of the sinister things we'd thought. He wanted to be here because he was my cousin. My family. And he wanted to protect me just like all those years ago.

I released him and he sucked in a huge breath. "You're a little stronger than I remembered."

"I'm a little more of a lot of things than you remember. Now what's going on with the blood and the snakes?"

Waylon didn't falter with my quick change of pace. It really was a Jordan thing. "It was horrible. You were there and there was this huge snake and then there was blood . . . and why are you taking this so well?"

"Been through a couple of these prophecies now. The first of them was laid down by our ancestor, actually. Most of them have my blood all over the place. What else was there? A mirror maybe?"

The blood drained from Waylon's face and he nodded. "It was a museum of sorts and there was this mirror thing, I think."

"Any clue on the location?"

"Don't know."

"Can you try?" I pushed.

He furrowed. "I don't know Dallas. There was a garden with statues and the mirror was outside."

I closed my eyes and searched through everything I knew about Dallas, which, thanks to my freelancing articles, was more than the average person knew. "Nasher Sculpture Center. Wrote an article on the installation of a new reflecting pool."

I started for the door. I grabbed my bag and coffee and headed out of my favorite coffee shop. I smiled at the possible new possessive: *my* coffee shop.

Waylon caught up to me on the sidewalk outside. "What is going on, Violet?"

"Do you really want to know?" I asked as I got my keys in my hand.

"Yes. I came here to help you." His brown eyes started to water. "I've seen the future, kid. And without you, it's grim on a good day."

I licked my lips. He wanted the truth. I laid it out for him. Let him choose to fight.

"My sire Spencer Haverty is in the Neveranth. For a long time now, I think he's been trying to get back, or at least learning how to get back. He can use a pond or a mirror to break the Veil and get across but not without a sacrifice. Jessa and I can fix it if we get there in time."

Waylon's jaw hung open.

"So go home, keep Lexie safe and I'll see you for dinner on Tuesday."

He licked his lips. "Who are you?"

"Just Violet," I shrugged as I jumped into my Miata and sped off toward the Nasher.

❧

JESSA MADE IT THERE FIRST. Her penthouse was only a few blocks from the sculpture center. The spring night was warm and there was the slight scent of a storm on the horizon. Got to love those April showers.

"Why'd you call in the cavalry?" she whispered as we hid in a dark corner of the parking lot waiting for the big guns. "It's just another rip in the Veil."

"Turns out innocent cousin Waylon is a full-blown psychic. Gave me a little heads-up that it's not just another rip."

Jessa went cold. "What?"

"My cousin got my mother's legacy. So all that psychic stuff that I can do is just genetic predisposition."

"Holy cow, Violet."

"Yep. We are going to have a major family sit down after this."

Jessa leaned against the wall. "So Lexie is special."

"More than we knew. What kills me is that I couldn't feel him. I mean, he was human by every sense I had."

"Fairy blood might cover it up."

"What?"

"Fairy blood could explain why he's hidden from Wanderers. We are pretty good at hiding in plain sight."

"Are you saying that his father was a fairy?"

"Wouldn't take much," Jessa shrugged. "What do you know about him?"

I tried to remember. "Nothing. I'm not sure I ever knew."

"Scandal." Jessa wiggled her eyebrows, but as soon as Tucker's truck pulled up, she got all serious.

Tucker had brought everyone from the house. Kandice and

Jane looked scared out of their minds, Nash looked a little too excited to play hero, and Tucker was armed to the teeth with every piece of weaponry Chaz had brought to the house so far.

"What is it?" he asked.

"Rip in the Veil," I said. "And possibly a cross over."

"You didn't say that," Jessa said as she punched my arm.

"It's said now. So the plan is to sneak in and stop it before it gets even worse."

"Got it."

I looked at the others' faces. "No. Kandice and Jane need to go home." I pulled out my car keys and handed them to Kandice.

She backed away from them like they were a snake. "No, Prima. I'm in this. If nothing else, I can provide surveillance."

My gaze fell to Jane. "You don't have to do this."

The woman ran her hands up her arms. "I know, but I still came."

I gave her a small smile. "Thank you."

I turned to Tucker. "Vision said it was a big snake thing."

"Great. Know how to kill one of those?"

"Generally, I'm finding that decapitation works for most things." I shrugged.

As I turned toward the sculpture center, I felt like I was missing something important. I had my Riko, the Key Holder, my wise man, and a horse.

Another wave of energy flowed out from the sculpture center.

What I didn't have was time.

I slipped my shoes off at the edge of the fence. "Ready?"

"You don't want to know the answer," Jessa said.

Security had already been disabled. The green shrub maze that held the wonders of the Nasher collection was black and I was glad for the puddles of light from the almost full moon as I slunk along the edges of the stone pathway.

Kandice circled high above the garden and said she'd signal

if she saw something. We really hadn't worked out more details than that. Plans never really seem to work out well for us anyway.

I took a left at the Rodin and then another left at the Picasso. The blue-period sculpture was particularly impressive in the moonlight.

I stopped as I hit the opening for the reflection pool. There was nothing there. Slowly, I let my borders down. I was wrong. The Veil had been shredded, and without my borders, I smelled the blood spilled on the ground and the power that permeated the air.

We were too late. The evil had already been done. The sacrifice already made. My skin crawled with the residual energy still clinging to everything.

Slowly, I stepped toward the reflecting pool, and my bare foot landed in a puddle of warm blood.

I grimaced as I slowly brought up my foot and wiped it on the clean stone walkway beneath me.

Only when I leaned over the reflecting pond did I get the full brunt of what was going on here. It was the smell that gave him away. That heady, sharp, exotic smell of acrid plants and musk.

Spencer. This literally had him all over it. The water was infused with it, the air around this place. It smelled like every nightmare I'd had in the past six months.

Had he been the one to cross over? There was enough blood.

But I'd know if he was that close. And he would know that I'd know because he was a part of me and I a part of him.

But who was the sacrifice?

There was rustling in the bushes, but it wasn't Tucker. I knew it before I'd called his name. The beings were dark, almost nothing more than shadows in my periphery. And they were cold. Anti-life. Like the trail throughout Chaz's house.

What the hell was Spencer playing with now?

A spray of water hit me before the jaws of the massive snake.

I put my arm up, but the beast still caught my arm in its jaws and the sheer force of it knocked me off the stone bench around the pond. As we landed, the huge fangs pierced my forearm.

The snake's body was easily three times the weight of a normal man and triple the length. It landed on top of me and tried to rip my arm off with a violent shake of its massive head. The snake reared back, taking me with it and opened its mouth. I tore my left arm free from its mouth and reached out with my right hand to rake my claws down one length of its head, a claw sinking into the fleshy part of its eye.

The thing hissed and I matched it with an equally horrifying scream. I got to my feet on its left side, and it took a moment to resituate itself. I needed less than that moment to shift.

My hind paws spread, I leapt at the thing's throat. My fangs met with scaly flesh and I bit down hard. Thick hot blood poured out of it in fast spurts. The thing spasmed as I rode its falling body to the ground. I raked my claws down its exposed underbelly.

That's when it started to coil, just about the same time my shifters broke into the circle. I was wrapped up in three thick coils quicker than I could say double crap.

With every movement, it grew tighter and tighter around me. I released its bleeding throat to get a better angle to escape.

Gunshots blasted next to me and I felt the impact of Tucker's buckshot into the beast. The snake cringed and uncoiled for a moment.

I pulled on all my strength to push the beast away from me. When I had a little room to wiggle, I shifted back into arms and legs and fought even harder to crawl out of the coils.

The snake curled in on itself, hissing at both me and Tucker.

I held my arm and tried to shake off the pain. "I got this. Get that Veil closed."

Tucker threw me the shot gun. I caught it with my left hand and nearly dropped it. There was a tingling sensation up my arm, and I didn't think it was carpal tunnel. I looked down for a brief moment to see the two perfect fang bites through my forearm. It was going to leave a mark.

I took in a deep breath and flexed my hand. My arm was going to be fine, and this thing wasn't going to see daylight.

The snake opened its wide, white mouth and its fangs glistened in the moonlight.

"Stop showing off."

The snake lunged out again. Because of its size, it wasn't as fast as the snakes on the *National Geographic* channel, but I was still as fast as all those panthers.

I rolled forward and to the right. It left the beast extended in the wrong direction and left me with a quick opportunity.

I pointed the shot gun at the back of its head and fired. The force threw me back a few steps as it slammed into my shoulder. My right ear rang with the echo of the blast,

But it didn't stop the snake. The smell of its blood filled the space between us, but it wasn't dead.

What kind of monster was this? By the increased numbness in my arm, it was poisonous, and by the bear hug it had just tried to squash me with, it was a constrictor. Twelve-gauge buck shot didn't hurt it and it had been bleeding from a neck wound for nearly five minutes and didn't seem to be slowing down.

So what's nearly indestructible, larger than life, and hangs around rips in the Veil? My instincts told me and I really wished my instincts were wrong once in a while. It was a Bigger. I'd fought one of these before and finally killed it after it had done a clog dance on my chest.

I also knew that if it had come through the Veil, Spencer had not. His plan hadn't worked. That was a little piece of happy that made me fight harder.

I tried to shoot at it again, but it was only a two-fer shotgun.

The snake struck at me again and I deflected the massive head with the butt of the gun.

I grabbed at one of the massive fangs and ripped. The sickened sucking sound of the fang coming out by the root echoed through the night.

That's when shadows came out of the hedges. I thought it was just my slightly poisoned eyes playing tricks on me, but the shadows solidified into beings that surrounding us. An easy twenty against our five. Crap didn't even begin to cover this one. Triple crap wasn't even enough.

Without another thought, expletive or no, I pulled at every tie I had. I called my pack to me. Peter was in his office; the Rosario boys were watching TV. And Tyler—Tyler was drinking alone somewhere. I sent out the message like a text through our connection: *Your Prima needs you; wear comfortable shoes.*

I called them to me because I was about to get my ass kicked.

But I left that part out.

"Sonuvabitch," Tucker said, but I felt his fear as he too looked around the dark circle.

"Hello, baby sister." The things, these shadow creatures were all speaking at once. Not in his voice but it had the same smug tone as Spencer.

My skin tightened at the mere phrase. My stomach lurched. Everything good within me revolted at the words that echoed around in the night.

"Lovely evening. Like my new toys?" The beings pressed closer.

"Not really."

Keeping the snake in my periphery, I looked over at Jessa, who was pulled tightly into Tucker's arm and away from the pond. It had a glow to it. Something soft and lavender.

"Jessa. Close it, now."

"Vi."

"Now!"

Jessa jumped and grabbed a silver knife off Tucker's belt. She drew the bright edge of it down her wrist and let the blood fall into the rippling water.

"Look at the fairy dance."

I looked back at the snake and slowly turned to see Nash and Jane frozen, a line of the shadow men behind them.

A dark ribbon of smoke curled up and turned solid around Jane's neck. She gasped and had to stand on her tiptoes as the black fingers tightened around her throat.

Immediately I sent a stream of energy to them, to all of them, even Jessa, whose blood I could feel running down her arm as if it were my own.

"Now," Spencer ordered.

The shadow things attacked, and the snake struck again. The snake caught me in the shoulder. I was knocked backward on the stone ground and the force drove its fang deep within my shoulder.

I cried out as the poison burned through my shoulder. No getting away from this one. But hey, it was only one fang full of poison now. I only had moments of action left, if the numbness in my left arm was any indicator.

I went to shift, knowing that I could inflict the most damage with claws rather than sarcasm.

The snake was on top of me again, just about to coil. I was about to shift when one of the shadow things touched me and I couldn't. Like the magic was gone. Sucked out of me.

I kicked at it and the thing was as solid as a man but without features like a shadow.

"A snake heart's in the torso," Nash called out before I heard a shadow man strike him so hard I tasted his blood.

My good hand gripped the fang in my hand. The torso? Where the hell is a torso on a twenty-foot snake?

The first coil managed to get around me and began to squeeze.

I stabbed wildly at the shadow thing with its claw wrapped around my ankle. A cold chill was creeping up my leg.

I ripped at the snake's head with my quickly dying hand and stabbed at its eye and throat with the fang. It was like trying to kill a bear with a butter knife.

As the snake coiled tighter and tighter, I felt the rest of my pack close in.

A silver blade flashed out of the darkness and into the back of the snake's neck. I followed the blade up the steely arms and straight into the eyes of Tyler. My lost boy Tyler.

The snake released the bite on my shoulder, its spinal chord now severed.

Tyler went after the beast at my leg.

I pried the jaw from my shoulder. Nails on a chalkboard had nothing on the sucking sound of a fang coming out of your shoulder: it's officially the worst sound in the world.

As I sat up, the world spun, but I was focused enough to take the fang still in my hand and stab it through the snake's hide and rip down as far as I could. If I've learned anything from the movies, it's to make sure that the monster was actually dead.

The blood looked black in the moonlight and I reached in and pulled out what felt like the thing's heart. The smooth muscles beat slowly and stopped in my palm. I felt the light fade away into just another dead monster in front of me.

A hand appeared before me. Tyler's face was splattered with blood. "Can't touch those shadowy things unless they are feeding, but then you can still kill 'em quick enough."

I slid my bloody hand into his and he carefully pulled me to my feet. My knees went weak as the poison ebbed further down my side, making my upper torso go numb. His hand slipped easily around my waist as I leaned against him. "Tyler," I breathed.

"Prima."

"Hell of a homecoming."

"See things haven't changed."

I looked up at him, at his warm brown eyes, at the dimples that were set around his mouth. When he looked down at me, I knew it was exactly that. A homecoming. My boys were back.

It strengthened my core. "Get me something to kill these things with."

Tyler winked and was gone from my side. Tucker had obviously reloaded and was blasting away the ones he could. Nash was making mincemeat of one in the corner, while being only slightly minced himself, and in a gleaming white shirt, Peter was there with a short silver knife already covered in black.

A shadow thing flew at me and I ducked, though frankly it was more of a crumple. It flew over me and straight into the pond.

"Crap," Jessa cried out.

"What?" I pulled myself up.

"The other side keeps changing, from Neveranth, to places here, back to the Neveranth. It's not stable."

"I suggest you make it stable before—" I shouldn't have said it. I shouldn't have even thought it, because then it would have just been my few against the shadow men.

If I hadn't thought it, there wouldn't have been an explosion of water and five vampires rolling out of the pond. They crawled gracefully out of the surface of the water, silver swords in hand.

"Holy . . ." was yelled across the garden.

"Crap," I completed as I watched dumbstruck from the ground behind one of them. I knew exactly what they were. My borders shot, I could feel their ice-cold energy radiating in their chests. They looked out at my pack members, who stopped fighting for a moment.

"Who killed Emilio?" The man was slender with bright white hair that looked odd against his black attire.

My first thought was he was trying way too hard. I pushed

myself up off the stone ground and held my now nonfunctioning arm. "Who's Emilio?"

"Our Source. Which one of you is Jordan?"

His ice blue eyes grazed over the men, even the shadows faded for a moment.

I licked my lips. "That would be me."

I really didn't expect everything to be like I'd written, like Nash and I had talked about. I'd expected speed, but in the blink of an eye, the man's hand was around my neck and I was slammed to the ground, the stone breaking beneath me as well as a few ribs within me. I was almost glad for the poison's numbing agent.

Tucker tore after him and was met with the silvery slice of a blade to the back of his knee by another vampire warrior. He fell hard to his knees and I felt the blood run down my leg.

The man with the blue eyes leaned over me and I realized that they weren't just blue; they were glowing blue, like Jessa's glowed lavender. There was that fairy likeness.

His fingers dug into and around my throat. "I will take your blood for taking his." His own fangs pressed down on his lower lip. Good to know that part was true.

I gurgled out. "I didn't do it."

"At least he took a bite out of you."

The panther lashed out and I clawed four neat lines down his face with my injured arm. I couldn't feel it, but it was still a fighting hand.

The vampire flinched enough that I was able to arch and get a leg around his neck. With a prayer to my sensei that one didn't need actual feeling in their extremities to leg lock someone, I trapped his slender neck behind my knee and locked my foot behind my other leg as I rolled him backward.

He arched over my straightened leg and I rammed my fist into his gut. His hands darted out for his dropped sword, but I caught his hand in a thumb lock.

"I did not kill your Emilio," my voice was scratchy, liked I'd had a cold for four days. "We've both been set up."

"He said you'd say that," the man who had struck down Tucker said.

My eyes darted upward and the man flinched. "Spencer?"

From the periphery of the fight, the shadows spoke again. "Isn't this fun, little sister?"

It was enough of a distraction to allow my grip to falter for a moment. The vampire cartwheeled over me and ripped his head from the lock. He knelt no more than an arm's length away.

"Who are you?" The vampire's eyes burned brighter as he wiped the blood from his cheek.

"I am Violet Jordan, Prima of the Dallas Pride. And you are?"

There was a cry from the skies and I looked up to see Kandice's dark shape against the moonlight. More? More were coming?

The darkness swarmed. It seemed to come out of every crack in the stone and solidify into men.

Chaos erupted. The blue-eyed vampire went for his sword and began hacking and slashing everything that came near him. I heard the screams of my pack members as they too fought off the dark creatures. I pulled myself to the edge of the pond, where Tucker had rallied next to Jessa again.

From across the pond, Jessa looked up at me with lavender flashing wildly in her eyes. "Throw them in the pond."

I nodded and with the rest of my strength, I pushed the information out to my fighting pack along with as much extra power that I could muster. Weakened by the action, I struggled to get to my feet.

With a long deep breath that slowed the action around me, I released the Haverty Legacy that beat wildly to be set free. The power blew my hair over my shoulders and drew the attention of everyone in the group. It spun around me, ready for the fight.

A large brown hawk swooped down and dropped a yellow

something at my feet. I carefully picked it up and smiled. Tucker's Taser.

I didn't have to wait long to see what would happen if you hit a shadow man with a stun gun. One came at me. I ducked and stuck the thing in the chest with the pointy ends and squeezed the handle. The moment the metal prongs hit its chest, it exploded in a puff of black ash and cinders that floated upward and got caught in the power that swirled around me. Like a vampire in the movies.

But ironically, not like the ones in real life. The shadows swarmed one of the vampires and he was left a normal corpse on the ground.

I only had a moment to rip off the spent cartridge of the Taser as another shadow flew at me. I ducked and stuck it in the chest with the exposed metal prongs and pulled the trigger. Black embers rained around me and I smiled. So, they are vulnerable when they are feeding and don't like electricity. Good to know.

"Now," echoed the many mouths of Spencer.

The shadow men all turned toward me.

Half my body numbed by the snake's venom, I readied for the impact of the remaining shadows that hadn't been hacked, sliced, or tossed into whatever Jessa had cooked up.

Four hit me at once and I jumped to throw them off balance. We landed hard on the ground and I cracked my head on the pavement. Again.

As soon as their hands landed on my skin, the cold ache of their feeding pulled at me.

I struggled as much as a one-armed girl could, but the more I did, the less feeling I had in my left leg. I jammed the stun gun against as many as I could, but another dark figure just took each one's place.

"Lock it down, Violet." Peter's voice echoed above me, above the dog pile of shadowy things. "They want the Legacy."

Trying to ignore the leachy feeling, I tightened the lid on the Legacy, tucking it far enough away that they couldn't get to it. But it meant that I didn't have access to it either. I was just Violet now.

A shadow hand covered my mouth, and my eyes flew open. I tore at the hand and kicked with my good leg, only to find that they had taken enough energy that it was no longer my good leg.

I heard splashing water and a round of gunfire. The others were still fighting, so I would too. My nails dug into the hand over my mouth, and I bit down hard. Finally, the hand retracted from the mass of black above me.

I saw Tyler rip one of them off me and then heard someone yell, "Take it over there."

The chill from their hands had nearly covered my whole body now; I barely had enough energy to wave my arm around. It looked pale against the backdrop of shadow men and it wasn't a moment before one of them grabbed ahold of it.

My head spun, with exhaustion, with hunger—but mostly with poison. I felt like I'd been on four all-nighters in a row and the world was more than a little fuzzy.

In the moment of a blink, the last shadow man was pulled away and disposed of. Tucker pulled me to a sitting position. My head lolled against his warm chest.

"Violet. Say something." He looked up. "She's cold as ice."

"I can't feel my feet."

"They are still huge," Jessa said as she knelt down beside me.

I wanted to reach out my arm to hold her hand, but it wasn't really working right now. Tucker's heartbeat was loud against my ear and I closed my eyes to listen to it better.

"No, you don't," Tucker said as he shook me violently.

The rest of the pack hovered around me. I did a quick head count, and everyone was there. "Baddies gone?" I managed out.

"Interdimensional rift." Jessa sighed. "Half-assed it really."

"Into what?"

"Dimensional food processor?"

I grimaced. "Never say that to a writer."

Peter stood and put his hands on his hips. "We need to get her someplace safe. Police are going to be here any minute."

There must have been a general consensus on something, because Tyler hoisted me up and carried me like a limp doll. He adjusted me so I could see over his shoulder.

I thought I was smiling as I watched Tucker walking behind us. His heavy arm was draped over Jessa's shoulder as he limped. Blood covered her pink shirt and flecks of black were smudged across her cheek. Tucker reached up and pulled an ember from her black hair.

I relaxed into Tyler's arm as I watched the budding romance. I'd missed Tyler and I felt his golden proximity between us, the warmth in our connection. It was the first and only bit of warmth I could feel. And then it felt like his warmth was seeping into me.

His steps faltered and he dropped me hard on the ground and I rolled. Concussion number two. Or was it three?

Nash dropped beside me. Blood covered his face, and he was going to have a very heroic black eye for a few days. He touched my shoulder and energy surged straight into my chest. He crumpled next to me as the burning grew within my chest.

"Violet?" he whispered as he cringed.

I felt better, clearer, warm. Able to focus on Nash's pained face.

Peter knelt over me and smacked me hard. "Stop it, Violet."

"Bastard."

"You're killing them."

My head lolled forward as I saw Tyler curled up on the ground a few feet away. He looked pale and there were dark circles underneath his previously warm eyes. Our connection was hot, radiating with warmth and the power that I'd give him. I was taking it back, taking it all back. And I couldn't stop it.

I looked up into Peter's blue eyes, his golden hair, and felt the connection between us. As soon as I felt my core pulling at the rough connection, smelled his soft leather scent around me, a bolt of lightning hit me in the side.

My entire body was set on fire as every nerve ending conducted what had to be a million volts of electricity.

Everything retreated inward and I slipped back into the numb blackness behind my eyes.

CHAPTER 13

"WHY DO YOU always come home bloody?" Chaz's tone was somewhere between anger and exasperation.

"Not always." My throat was still sore from being choked and I still couldn't move, thanks to the poison.

Chaz leaned forward and rested his elbows on his knees. He rubbed his hands together and exhaled loudly.

They'd brought me to Chaz's house because it was closer, and it could house the twelve people who came with me. He'd put me in the guest bedroom because he didn't want a parade of people through his bedroom. It made sense, but this bed was lumpy, and even though I couldn't move anything, every single bump and lump in the bed jabbed into my sore body.

I rolled my head to look at him. I knew what he wanted to ask. But I wasn't going to start the fight this time.

Chaz licked his lips. "Why didn't you call me?" He voice was amazingly calm, but the gravel in it was unmistakably anger.

"Didn't have time."

"Not good enough. You've got half the pack here and no one called me."

"I'm sorry, Chaz. My focus was on the rip in the Veil and the snake thing trying to eat me."

His knuckles went white. It wasn't the right answer. So I tried another. "There is a solution to that problem."

His golden green eyes flicked up to meet mine. "What?"

"Haverty was able to control his connection with different breeds, so I should be able to. I mean it might require a little research, but—"

"No, Violet."

"You'd be able to know when I was in trouble."

"No." Chaz rose from the chair and began to pace. "I can't."

I licked my very dry lips and the exhaustion settled in around my shoulders again.

He rubbed his stubbled jaw. "I mean, I shouldn't have to, right? I'm your fiancé. Isn't love supposed to be enough magic to keep us safe?"

"I think when Piper told us that, it just meant that the panther wouldn't get in the way. Didn't say anything about safe. In fact, a wise little fairy princess said that life is dangerous, sacred destiny or not."

His jaw clenched and he stared very intently at the wall just above my bed. He was picking his words very carefully. "I can't have you coming home bleeding."

"I can't promise that I won't."

His arms crossed over his chest so tightly that I thought he actually might bear hug himself into unconsciousness.

I tried to sit up, but nothing was working yet. "But you missed a key word there. Home, Chaz. I will always come home to you. The home that we built."

He looked down at me and I knew it wasn't going to be enough for him right now. But it was the best that I had. The best I could muster as I lay motionless on his guest bedroom again, recovering from some wild animal attack.

There was a tap on the door and the soft noise echoed

through the silence between us. Chaz went to open the door and Devin's gleaming face was on the other side.

"How's the patient?"

"She's all yours," Chaz said as he walked out of the room.

Devin shivered. "That was brutal."

"That was my loving fiancé."

Devin had his medical bag with him. He moved the wooden chair closer to my bedside and put his bag on the nightstand.

"What's the damage, doc?" I asked.

"You need to stop talking," he said quietly as he pulled on latex gloves. "Actually, no. Now that you're conscious, you need to tell me what the hell did this," Devin said as he started on the shoulder and the two-inch thick bandages taped there.

"You've been out there with my pack and they didn't tell you?"

"They went quiet as soon as I walked in the door. Nash was the only one who talked to me and it was all about the weather."

I licked my lips. "There's a Wanderer term for it that translates to Biggers. And they are pretty much just that. Shifters who chose their animal form in the Neveranth and are as big as tanks."

Devin was taking the news pretty well. "So, large powerful primal snake thing?"

I smiled. "Bingo."

"Why can't it just be vampires with you?" Devin cracked a smile.

"You have no idea, honey."

Tyler brought in a bowl of fresh water and towels. I couldn't help but smile.

He just nodded at me. "We decided to take shifts," he said softly, like the noise alone would hurt me. "The next shift should be in about an hour."

"Who's here now?"

"Kandice, Nash. Jane. Um, Jessa, Tucker, and Peter went to

do something. The brothers went home. Poor things had never seen that much action."

"And you," I had to force a smile. "You're here."

Tyler just pressed his lips together.

"Will you at least stay until we can talk?"

He nodded and then left the room.

"That's the one you've been missing?" Devin asked softly. He was slow, meticulous as he cleaned. Carefully peeling off the bandages and cleaning the wound again. Out of the corner of my eye, I saw stitches. There was no getting out of a scar this time.

I squeezed my eyes shut and let Devin's soft fingers work their own kind of magic. "Yeah."

"But he came back when he was needed?"

"I don't want him to be back out of sense of obligation. I want him back because we are his family." I opened my eyes after Devin covered the wound on my shoulder.

"He's back. And still hotter than hot."

"Yeah, the broody thing is working for him."

Devin smiled as he rewrapped the shoulder. "You're still cold."

"I'm half-naked."

"No. Your body temperature. You're practically clammy."

"I'm a little low on the juice right now."

"Don't you have that battery pack?" Devin asked as he packed up the bandages.

"What?"

"That legacy with all the evil stuff. Don't you have that?"

I tried to shake my head, but it didn't work. It just sort of rolled to the side. "I can't."

"Fear doesn't sound good on you, Vi." Devin closed up the bag and took my hand. "What are you really afraid of?"

I let out a big sigh and told him the complete truth. "I'm afraid that I can't be a dream girl and a Prima."

"You, my love, can be anything you want to be. Prima, lover, writer, aunt, sister, friend, cousin, fiancée, or kick-ass heroine. If anyone can do this, Violet Jordan, you can."

My eyes watered and I already felt better. "I wish I had your faith."

"You do, Vi." Devin squeezed my hand and then stood. "You need rest. I'm telling the others not to bother you for a while."

Devin was just about to leave when my door flew open. Peter filled the doorway. His black T-shirt was clean, and his jeans were fresh. He'd showered, but I had the instant suspicion it wasn't just to clean up but to cover up.

As the two men looked at each other, my skin tightened.

"Devin," Peter breathed. He took two steps back and ran into the door.

"Peter?"

"Oh. My. God," I breathed.

I saw it between them, felt it between them. This was Peter. *The* Peter. The lawyer who Devin had confessed was 'perfect,' if I remembered correctly. The same Peter who had stomped all over Devin's heart so badly he hadn't dated since.

My stomach churned, half at my own recollections of what Devin had gone through and the other half from Peter himself, from our connection. Peter was afraid. Twenty shadow men and he was as cool as a cucumber. Facing Devin, he froze and pulled at the connection between us.

"What are you doing here?" Devin asked, switching his doctor bag from one hand to the other.

Peter pointed to me. "Prima Violet."

Devin's eyes jumped from my pale figure back to Peter's. "You're a . . ."

"You know?" Peter took a step toward him.

Devin didn't step away. He looked the wolf straight in his blue eyes. "Of course I know. I'm here, aren't I?"

"Well so am I."

"Good. She needs her pack."

The men sort of stared at each other for a while. Devin was doing great. Peter's heart was beating in his chest and his upper lip was moist. His sweet leather scent filled the room as his blood ran hot.

I saved him from himself. "Thank you, Devin. How about you come back later today?"

"I'll be back in four hours to see if you need antibiotics."

Devin left the room and Peter took in a deep breath and I felt the relief in my own chest.

He stayed by the door for a few moments, then shook his head and walked into the room, closing the door behind him. "I've just come back from the vampires and—"

"You broke up with Devin!" Yelling took more energy than I thought it would and I collapsed against the lumpy pillows.

Peter stopped mid-stride. "My private life is private."

"Your private life nearly destroyed my best friend."

"We have more important things to talk about than . . . that."

Peter walked to the side of my bed. He looked down at the chair Devin had just been sitting in and crossed his arms over his chest as he stood.

"No, Peter. Lesson one of Violet Jordan's Pride, you do not dismiss the people who make you happy."

A deep crease formed in between his blue eyes. "How do you know he made me happy?"

"Because I felt your fear when you saw him again."

Peter's hands gripped his arms even tighter across his chest.

But it was more than his actions that stopped my meddlesome ways. The bond between us turned and tightened, felt like I was trying to pull an anchor from the bottom of a very deep ocean.

"Fine. You don't want to talk about it, but Devin's part of this, so you'll need to make some sort of peace with that."

Peter licked his lips and just kept staring at me.

"Tell me about the vampires."

His story was something out of one of my novels. The Clade Source, Emilio, had been taken by a swarm of darkness, just like the ones we fought. Valiance, the second in command, tried to stop them but they vanished through a mirror. A blond man then appeared in the mirror and told Valiance their leader had been taken by someone named Jordan and he could help the Clade get him back. And that led to them jumping through a mirror and into the fight.

"But we're good for now? Did you make another little truce on my behalf?"

Peter shook his head. "They proposed the truce, maybe after I mentioned that you owned their company."

I groaned. There was a reason that government wasn't my best subject in high school. Politics wasn't my favorite thing.

"Where did the snake come in?" I asked.

"I think I can answer that." Jessa pushed through the door with Tucker right behind her.

I smiled. "Thank God you're okay."

"You look like a crash-test dummy and you're worried about me?"

"Can't help it. Key Keeper, remember?"

"We've got some bad news," Tucker said.

"Good thing I'm sitting down."

Jessa carefully sat on the bed next to me, arching her legs over mine and leaning against the wall. Tucker took the vacant seat next to me.

"Wait. Someone needs to get Chaz."

"He was on the way out when we came in."

I closed my eyes. He wasn't making this easier by running again.

With a deep breath that made the wound in my shoulder flare with pain, I opened my eyes and looked at Jessa. "Give it to me. I'm ready for the info dump."

"Spencer knew Emilio had a pretty strong house and they would avenge him, as any good Clade would," Jessa narrated.

"Check."

"He also knew he needed a blood sacrifice to open the Veil for something major to cross over."

"Done. Figured that out last fall."

"What I don't think he realized was that if you send a snake across, you get a snake in return."

"Huh?"

Jessa tucked her hair behind her ears and used her hands to explain. I got the distinct feeling she liked being the info girl in this situation. "Last fall, Spencer went across and a big-ass panther was sent back."

I nodded, or I meant to nod. "Very distinctly remember that."

"I think Spencer wanted to use Emilio because he had power and house who would attack when fed the right information, but I think he was trying to come across himself. Because the exchange wasn't even, I think it sent the snake instead."

It made sense. It maintained the balance the universe liked. "But if we know this, then he knows it now too."

"Which means you'd probably have to be the sacrifice to actually get him back here." Jessa blurted out the words and then flinched.

"Awesome." I rested my head on the pillows again and looked up at the ceiling. I always knew it was going to end up being me or Spencer. I knew there could only be one.

Wow, I was even epic in my head.

"What's the story with the shadow men?" I asked Jessa.

Jessa pointed to Tucker. "Tag, you're it."

Tucker nodded his head and rubbed his hands together. "Remember the ghouls."

"Never going to forget those lovelies."

"They are marked with the Demon Lock that Jovan used,

right? Well, we might have quarantined one of the shadow men."

He waited. I think he was waiting for me to scold him.

"And?"

"They've got a mark too. Not the same one, but I think it's the same principle."

My skin goose bumped as my brain did what it did best. If Spencer had minions that were bound to him with something like Jovan's Demon Lock, then that meant only one thing. "Spencer's a demon."

Jessa put her hand on my knee. "Guess he's been a little busy on the other side. Where you've been getting more powerful for having formed your pack, he's been putting together his own made up of those things."

"There's something else that we haven't discussed yet." Peter's voice was dark, low and quiet. "Violet stole power from the pack."

I'd known what I'd done from the moment I woke up. I felt different, off, wrong, and I knew it was more than the aftereffects of the stun gun, the marks of which were still red and angry on my torso. "I didn't know what I was doing."

"But it's not the first time you defaulted to something that Spencer could do," Tucker said.

I looked over at him. "I am so sor—"

Tucker held his hand up and I stopped. "It wasn't you. It was Spencer."

"No, Tucker. It was me. Stop putting me up on this pedestal. I did that. I took power because I'd expended myself. Let me take responsibility for this."

Tucker looked away. Jessa squeezed my knee.

"Spencer wouldn't have cared," Peter said. "He just took, and he'd never apologize."

"Let me apologize, Tucker."

Tucker's dark gaze rose to mine. "Accepted, but you rest and you eat and you shift so it never happens again."

Nash slipped into the room and closed the door. Smart boy. "And if he's gotten to the point that he's taken power from others, he's much bigger than he was before."

"We are bigger than we were before." Good to know the poison hadn't numbed my moxie.

"Numbers aren't going to win this one, Prima," Peter said.

My skin goose bumped. He'd finally called me Prima and the title held so much more weight with his voice than it ever had before.

"But your suave might, and Nash's info. And we've still got something he doesn't have."

Peter chuckled. "What could we possible have?"

"A reason to fight."

Peter dropped his chin and looked away.

"We're going to need marching orders," Tucker said.

I smiled. Where I might default to evil, Tucker still defaulted to his military precision. "We need to solidify the Veil."

"Done," Jessa said. "I'll call my mom. See if she's got anything else I can throw at it."

"And the ones with Jovan's mark?" I asked.

Tucker nodded. "I'll corral them. We've only got two days until the full moon."

I nodded. Was I even going to be in shape enough to run a full moon? "I don't know if 'corral' is the right word but thank you."

"I'll get on the mark he used. See if there is something we can work to circumvent it," Nash volunteered. "See if there is another way to actually break it."

"And I'm going to leave all the rest in your very capable hands, Mr. Delmont."

Peter nodded.

"Good." I sighed. "I need some rest. Doctor's order."

The men slowly filtered out. Jessa stayed and curled up next to me on the little bed. I adjusted my body as much as I could, but she ended up pressed against the wall.

"How are you really?" she whispered. "And don't think you can lie to me."

"Exhausted. Scared. And still a little numb."

Jessa sighed and wrapped her arm around my midsection. "Don't you ever almost die on me again."

My eyes watered. Jessa was shaking. She'd finally let her guard down now that the boys were gone, and I didn't blame her. I held her the best I could with one arm bound like a mummy and the other trapped under her.

"I will do my best."

"I thought the Veil was bad and then the snake thing and then vampires. I was pretty sure that they were myths until last night."

"Nice to know you have a learning curve as well."

Jessa was quiet for a moment and I let my eyes close. Devin hadn't given me any painkillers and each muscle was quietly waking up from its slumber and reminding me that my pants had in fact been beaten off me. I was hoping I could sleep some of the pain away.

"What did Chaz say?" she asked.

I licked my lips. "Someone should have called him before I was filleted, and he doesn't want to be part of the pack."

"Oh."

"Yep."

"So where did he go?"

"I have no idea."

IT WAS SUSPICIOUSLY quiet in the house and I was getting bored. Between the six hours of unconsciousness and six more hours of actual sleep, I'd gotten more rest in the past day than I had in two weeks, which meant that the brain was officially firing on all eight cylinders again.

And the poison had finally worn off. Which meant I could move all my limbs, but the residual effects of the ass-kicking were still there, which meant I didn't want to.

I knew I'd heal faster with the Legacy. But I deserved to suffer a little for this one. Call it self-penance. Call it self-pity. I was going to heal this one out without the magical mojo. It would teach me a lesson. I am edible. And I hurt people.

When someone finally knocked on the door, I was almost relieved. "Come in."

Tyler stuck his head in and then followed. The book bag on his back almost got closed in the door; he was trying to be so stealthy.

"Hey there." He kept his voice at a library level. He came to sit on the chair next to the bed.

I was feeling more and more like an invalid every time someone came to visit. It took all the strength I had, but I pushed up on the bed so I wouldn't look completely defeated, though I was pretty sure the huge white gauze wrapped around my shoulder and the complete bed hair didn't help my case. "What can I do for you?"

"I wanted to say I was sorry."

"You have nothing to be sorry about."

He hung his head. His hair was a little less golden than I remembered, and his frame a little more slender.

"You needed time. But I'm glad you came when you did."

Tyler sighed. "I came too late."

He set the bag between his feet and reached inside. I gasped as he pulled out the grimoire that I'd given Cristina, the one that had been lost when she'd been taken. He carefully set it on the bed between us.

The dark energy radiated from the pages and the darker

memories followed. Cristina had taken it to help us research breaking the mark. She'd done everything that I'd asked of her and then ended up dead right in front of me.

When I looked up at Tyler, I knew he was thinking the exact same thing. But he couldn't say any more than I could, so he talked business. "The mark Tucker found on the Shades—it's in there too."

"Shades? Better than 'shadow men.' " I shrugged.

"So is how to banish them, how to open a portal in the Veil, and how to create a demon."

I gulped.

"It's got to be the sister book to the one that Spencer has. The one he used to first open the Veil."

I nodded. "Yet another thing Spencer and I both have."

"He doesn't have this." Tucker pulled a knife out of the bag as well. Its long silver blade flashed in the light from the table lamp next to him and I saw the familiar scrollwork down the edge. The last time I'd seen this, it was sticking out of Cristina's chest.

"The Haverty Blade?" I could barely speak as Tyler and I shared our grief for a moment.

Tyler licked his lips as he put the dagger on the bed. "Things are going to get dark, Violet. I think we all know that. You're going to need this."

I ran my finger along the silver, and it burned my skin. Sure enough. This was the real deal. "Did the others tell you about what happened? What I did to you?"

"They didn't need to. I knew. Which is why I'm giving you this now. You need to know what weapons you have."

"My plans don't go well."

Tyler looked up at me. "I know that. God, do I know that. But I also know that if you didn't know that, you wouldn't be holed up in this bedroom pouting."

"I'm not pouting."

Tyler raised an eyebrow. "You're pouting. It's a little pathetic."

I sighed. "I need rest, Tyler."

"I know. I've felt how strained you've been these past three weeks. I know that you are trying and it's not working."

I frowned. "It's working. I'm just getting the kinks out."

"Hate to point out the obvious, but it's not. Haverty could do this and take vacations to the Bahamas three times a year."

"Haverty enslaved people and blackmailed and intimidated and oppressed everyone until they were scared little nothings who couldn't fight back."

Tyler threw up his hands. "And it was damn effective. For him. You need to find your way of doing things."

I looked down at the book between us. I needed to find my way a little sooner rather than later.

"I'll be at the full moon. Thought about going down today and helping to get ready," Tyler said as he rose, picking up the empty bag. "And then I've been thinking about getting a job."

"Which noble profession?"

"The paying kind. Tired of living off Tucker."

I nodded. "Sounds like a good goal."

"Small steps." Tyler left me with a small smile. "I know what I need to do, and you know what you need to do. Just take that one small step."

Maybe that's what I needed as well, small steps out of this bed.

CHAPTER 14

FTER LOOKING AT my wounds in the mirror, I knew Jessa was going to kill me. There was no wearing a strapless dress after this attack.

The two fang marks looked like bullet wounds through my forearm and the one through my shoulder wasn't pretty either.

Of course, Jessa did have miraculous ways to hide dark circles under your eyes, so maybe for one day she could make me into a beautiful bride.

If I had a groom.

Chaz had been missing from his house for nearly two days.

Kandice and Nash had been on Violet watch most of the time; the others came and went. The Rosario brothers had been hilarious as they told me what happened on their end of the fight, filling me in on what I didn't already know, complete with reenactments of Julian being strangled by a Shade and his brother hitting him over the head with a chair they'd found in the bushes. It was a laugh that I desperately needed.

I needed to go home. I needed to pack for the full moon. I needed to sleep in my own bed that wasn't the lumpy guest bedroom. I still couldn't manage to sleep in Chaz's bed alone.

Peter was the one who was there when I was ready to go home.

"You're up?" he asked as he looked up from his laptop. He'd made an office of Chaz's coffee table. And if I thought Peter in a sharp-cut suit looked odd in the coffee shop, it looked even more out of place against Chaz's orange couch and wood paneling.

"Don't sound so disappointed. Got the super healing thing too." I sat down on the arm of the chair.

"How up?" he asked.

I would have shrugged but the shower had exhausted me. My arms felt like cement columns hanging off my sore shoulders.

"Walking, talking. Not much else. Why?"

"The elemental Akasha contacted me. Seems she got word of what happened with the vampires and wants an explanation."

"I can't meet with her right now. What kind of impression would that make?"

Peter thought. The gears churned in his head. He was a planner. Maybe his plans worked out. Mine certainly didn't.

"I think it's perfect. Go wounded. Let her know that you are vulnerable."

"And when she stomps all over me and declares herself Prima?"

"She won't."

"Why not?"

"Because she can't keep the vampires in check and obviously you can."

The plan didn't make sense in my head. "I'm confused."

He licked his lips and the thought again flashed across my brain that he was gorgeous. It was the strangest thought, but it made me smile. "She believes you defeated the vampires that night and they are following your lead already."

"Crap, Peter. What part of the conversation when I yelled at you about putting words into my mouth didn't you get?"

"I didn't tell her that. But I may have led her to believe it."

I frowned. There was that gray Peter was so very good at. That fine line he liked to walk. "Where?"

"Still your call."

"The coffee shop? No, it shut down." And then the brain started working again. "How fast can you buy something?"

"Depends."

"My coffee shop went under. But it's sacred and I want to buy it."

"Do you want me to buy your childhood home as well?"

I smiled. Peter's snark felt good, like things were getting back into the Violet rhythm of things.

"It's not just sacred to me, Peter. It's a protected place for Wanderers now."

Peter's lips parted. "Oh."

"I want to buy it. Keep it open for us."

Peter looked down at his laptop and reached out for his phone.

"What's this place called?"

I PACKED UP MY THINGS, basically what was left of my clothes from the snake attack and went back out into the living room.

Peter was pacing but had the widest smile on his face. "Great. Have the papers sent over to my office by Friday, but I'd like the keys by the end of the day."

He ended the call and looked over at me. "It's yours, Prima."

I let out a deep relaxing breath. Finally, something going right for a change. "Thank you."

"Do you want me to call the Akasha?"

And the sense of accomplishment flew right out of me. "What day is it?"

"Tuesday."

"I think I've got something on Tuesday." What was it?

Peter pulled my cell phone off the charger on the side table. "Your cousin called a couple of times."

My chin hit my chest. "Dinner with Waylon and Lexie."

"I think this is more important."

"I don't. Can you take me home?"

MY HOUSE SMELLED AMAZING. Candles had been burning to cover the lemon-scented cleaning supplies that Chaz liked to use when he was deep cleaning the house.

Peter stopped in the doorway and winced at the smell. "What happened?"

"Stress cleaning." I walked into the living room. "Chaz?"

Mixed in with the candle smell was the smell of fresh flowers. Fresh cut flowers only meant one thing. He was gone. He'd take a job at a time like this?

Of course, he would. He needed to be needed and what I had done had unequivocally told him that I could fight my own battles. I walked over to the dining-room table and found a note tucked between the loops of the next-door neighbor's honeysuckle plant.

"Needed to talk to Andrea. I'll meet you at Iris's."

Guess he'd forgotten about the dinner with Waylon as well.

"Prima?"

I looked across the living room to see Peter still hanging out in the front entryway.

"Something wrong there?"

"Just want you to keep your space your space."

I frowned and walked back to the doorway. Peter put my bag inside the foyer, which meant that he could enter, he just didn't want to.

"Meaning?" I asked.

Peter shook his head. "I'm the last person to give relationship advice."

"We all learn from mistakes. They don't have to be ours."

Peter put his hands on his hips. "I know Chaz isn't pack, but if he was, I'd say that he was scent marking."

"Huh?"

"We invaded his home, his territory. So he's wiped us clean of this space."

"I was thinking that it was the first time he didn't have to clean around people but go on."

"After what you two have been through, I don't think that you should let anyone else stay here. I think this needs to be your refuge."

"I think you might be right."

"We've got Tucker's place and Chaz's place for the overflow."

"I like that pronoun use, Mr. Delmont."

Peter just rolled his eyes.

"Set up the meeting with the Akasha for tomorrow morning and I'll see you at the full moon."

Peter nodded and walked back to his car.

Tucker was going to hate that I was on my own, but I needed a little quiet time. And if I was going to have to have the conversation with Waylon and the Akasha I knew I needed to have, I needed to heal now.

I sat down in my comfortable living-room chair and took in a deep breath. It was time to stop pouting and get down to business.

Small step number one: get strong enough to hold a cup of coffee.

I released the borders on my Legacy and let it burn around me, through me. The power swirled around me freely, openly. As the Legacy ran through every nerve ending, every muscle, my shoulder healed, and power burned down the muscles in my back and the holes in my arm.

It was mine. They were mine and he wasn't going to hurt us anymore.

~

LEXIE WAS IN the living room watching some teen dream movie that she had convinced her father to rent on the way over. Waylon and I were in the kitchen waiting it out.

"How did that snake thing go?" He'd been dying to ask all evening, but Lexie was more than talkative over dinner.

"Great. Got eaten and then vampires showed up and Spencer sent his lackeys to polish me off."

"Wow."

"Please be more specific next time."

Waylon shook his head. "I can't believe you, Violet."

"What? The panther part?"

"No, the fearless leader part. I came here thinking I was going to be the big hero, telling you things you never could have dreamed of and you've already lived them."

I squared up and asked him the hard question. "So what is your schtick? Lay it out for me."

Waylon put down his coffee. Of course there was coffee involved in this situation.

"Psychic. Future only. Just like Aunt Lily. And I can't really control it."

I swirled my coffee. It was the first thing I did when I felt like Violet again. Made a pot of coffee. "Do you dream it?"

"All the time."

"But you are hidden. I can't feel you or Lexie and my preter-natural senses are pretty damn good."

"It's this." Waylon pulled up his sleeve. On his upper forearm, there was a black swirly mark that I knew too well.

"You've got a permanent dampening spell?"

"Yep. And every pair of shoes that Lexie has gets one too."

Waylon rolled down his sleeve. "I'll tell her when she's ready. Maybe when she has her first dream."

"When did your dreams start?"

Waylon gulped and looked away.

"Waylon?"

He licked his lips. "My first one was about a week after Aunt Lily died."

I remembered that. My life with him was getting easier to remember from the black hole of oblivion I had shoved them into. I was still sleeping in the living room before his mom cleaned out her sewing room so I could have some privacy. Waylon woke up screaming and I took him a glass of milk because that's what my mother would have done.

"Pretty much every night since then."

"When was your first about me?"

"Three years ago. You were fighting off this pack of dogs."

I snorted. "That was my first date with Chaz."

His jaw dropped. "You got attacked on your first date?"

"And he still stuck around." The joke fell out of my mouth before I could realize that it wasn't exactly true. He wasn't here now.

He sighed and grabbed his coffee and started to spin it. Man. He really was a Jordan. "I saw little things here and there until . . ."

I gulped. "Until what? You're going to have to weave a better story than your company sent you here."

Waylon came out and said it, which, though I appreciated it, was still shocking. "Until I saw you thrown through the Veil. Packed up everything the moment I saw that."

The thought of it washed like cold water down my spine. "I haven't done that yet."

"I know."

"So it's still going to happen?"

"Yes."

My stomach flopped over on itself and I couldn't breathe. I was going to be thrown through the Veil? As Spencer's tribute?

"We can't let it happen." Waylon's brow was cement.

"Well, duh," I said as I put the coffee down on the counter.

"No, I mean. I've seen what happens if Spencer wins. Every incarnation is bad." When Waylon was serious, a vein popped out on his forehead. That wasn't there thirteen years ago.

"How bad?"

"Jovan takes over and runs everything. Like the whole world."

Okay. Well, I was pretty sure he wasn't just going to bake everyone cupcakes. "Would it make you feel better to know you're not the only one who has prophetic dreams?"

His eyes brightened. "You too?"

I waved my hand to get rid of the notion that I was psychic. "It's little things. Crazy dreams. It's not really about the future—more like my brain tuning into things I'm too dumb to listen to. The first time it was fairy tales that my mother told me."

Waylon smiled. "I remember those. Every night."

"Came back to me when I needed them, like little whispers from the past. Helped me beat Haverty the first time."

Waylon listened for the movie Lexie was watching. It was currently the musical number between the heartthrob and the underdog as they fell in love. This was one of those moments I wished I didn't have super hearing.

"I read somewhere that psychics get their power because they can hear what the Mother is telling us," he started.

I put my finger up when I heard Lexie's movie stop and her bouncing across the first floor. She landed in the kitchen doorway. "Whatcha talking about?"

"Dreams," her father said.

Lexie walked into the kitchen and leaned against her father's arms. "I had a weird one last night about the cleaning lady in the hotel."

"Weird as in clowns or aliens?" Waylon asked.

All three of us laughed. It felt good. Felt natural. And as angry as I should be at him for keeping all of this from me, for keeping this precious girl from me, I was glad that they were here now, when I could appreciate them.

I'D WRITTEN THIS character once, a vampire queen. She was cool and calm and calculating and had learned to be as still as stone. It calmed her allies and infuriated her enemies. It was also one of the first times when what I'd seen in my head ended up on the screen—granted, it was a small screen venture, but the actress did an amazing job of capturing it.

I thought about that stillness as I waited for the Akasha. Even though my neck was killing me and my arm was aching because I burned through ibuprofen faster than I could take it, I didn't want her to see how nervous I was. I had to fight my leg to keep from bouncing as I waited at a table in the middle of the coffee shop, my coffee shop. I wanted to look calm and put together despite the white bandages that wrapped around my arm and shoulder.

After Peter had made the phone call, the keys to the coffee shop were in my mailbox. Say what you will about Peter's fidelity, the boy could push paperwork with the best of them. Attached to the blank manila envelope was a yellow note with "1100 am" written on it.

So I waited for my meeting with the Akasha and ran speeches through my head. But nothing seemed to come off right and there were always too many cat metaphors.

The bells on the door broke the unnatural silence of the place.

The first thing I noticed about the Akasha were her eyes. They were almond-shaped and nearly yellow colored against her dark skin.

She stopped in the doorway and shivered. "Violet Jordan?"

"Yes, ma'am."

She looked around the coffee shop and then saw the protection symbol above the door. "You're working some heavy mojo here."

"I needed to make sure that we were safe."

"Meaning you and me, or you and your pack?"

"Any Wanderer who wandered in."

She pressed her lips together and looked up at the symbol, then back at me. There was a quizzical look on her face, and she took in a deep breath before walking across the espresso-soaked floor.

I rose to greet her. I'd left my charm at home. I wasn't going to need it for the full moon, so I hadn't packed it. Which left me woefully unprepared for the sheer heat of her. I felt her when she was within three feet of me. When Nash had warned me that she was the embodiment of fire, I didn't think that she was actually as hot as fire.

She stuck out her hand. "Inez."

"Violet Jordan." As I slid my hand against hers, my power went out around her. I'd brushed everyone in the past six weeks, so it was a natural reaction for me.

But she was the first one who'd burned me back. The dry air brushed my cheeks and, in its wake, came the sizzle. It was like the slow burn after a pepper spray and it stayed on my cheek and arm long after she'd released my hand.

"It's a pleasure to meet you, Akasha."

The woman winced. "Please don't call me that. I hate all the formal stuff."

"Then, please call me Violet." I gestured that we should sit.

Inez did, but she still looked around the shop. "What's up with this place?"

"I came here often enough, before and after the shift, that I somehow created a haven for all Wanderers."

"How?"

I was honest. "I have no idea, but people tend to end up here when they are lost."

Inez tugged on the cuff of her scarlet leather jacket. She crossed her legs at the ankle and tried to rest her hands in her lap. She was nervous. I was making someone else nervous. "Which means that it's a safe place for your people too."

"What about vampires?"

"I suppose that if a vampire was in trouble, they might gravitate toward this place, but I'm not really eager to find that out."

"Delmont said you tangled with them."

"I did."

"Said their leader ended up dead."

At least I didn't have to lie. "He did."

Inez adjusted in her seat and as she looked at the window where I'd spent most of my time in the past two years, I saw a slick scar just at the collar of her jacket. It wasn't the pretty vampire bites you see in the movies, but a half circle of violent edges. The story of it jumped into my brain before I could even blink.

She'd been attacked by vampires. What good vampire wouldn't want a victim that would keep them running at human temperatures for a while? That's why the mention of me consorting with vampires had her nervous.

Maybe Delmont was wrong about this approach. Or maybe he knew the story and what kind of effect it would have on this woman. It did seem like his M.O.

"I didn't kill him," I finally said.

Inez's gaze jumped back to me. "What?"

"He was dead when we got there. But his Clade did come, and we did fight."

Inez swallowed. "Are you going to let them stay?"

I shook my head. "I don't know."

She looked at me with wide eyes.

"I know that you have your own pack and probably have just as many concerns as I do about how we are all going to deal with each other."

"Kiln. A group of elementals is called a Kiln."

I nodded. "Okay. I know that you guys are probably going through the same growing pains we are, and frankly, I don't think we need to worry about more cooks in the kitchen."

Inez studied me for a moment. "He said that you were different."

"Who?"

"Tai-Jen, the wind elemental."

I was shocked. It hadn't occurred to me before that my own sensei would also be part of her Kiln. "He would know me probably as well as anyone."

Inez leaned back in her chair. She wasn't fidgeting for the first time now that I was the focus of the conversation. "He said you were strong but stubborn, and you pushed yourself to be faster."

"Did he mention how many times he threw me against the wall?"

"He did take a bit of pride in that." When Inez smiled, she lit up the whole room. And just like Nash, I felt like I'd been given a gift—that she didn't smile that often, didn't have enough occasions to.

"He's right. I do push myself. Pushed myself a little too hard. But I'd imagine you can understand that when you've got people relying on you, you want to be strong for them."

"I can."

I was getting "good guy" vibes from her. I wished I could

blame it on some psychic ability, but really it was all in my gut. Still wasn't going to trust her. Not until I knew the story about the scar on her neck. The scar was a little too deep to just make rash decisions.

We didn't want another warthog incident.

"I'm not going to propose an alliance. I'm too new at all of this to get interspecies politics involved. But if you've got troubles, know that you can call on me, and I'll let you know . . ."

"The next time a giant snake decides to attack you?"

"Something like that."

Inez took in a long breath and let it out slowly. "After what Delmont said, I wasn't sure I was going to like you, Violet Jordan."

"What exactly did Delmont say?"

Inez raised her eyebrows. "He said that you were powerful and would make a good ruler over Dallas."

I sighed. "I don't want to be a queen, Inez. I just want our people safe."

She frowned. "You've got the money, the power, and over half the Wanderers in this area on your side, but you'd give up the crown?"

"If there was someone I knew could do it better, yes."

Inez chuckled. "If your 'better' is not getting eaten by a snake, I'd like to take a swing at it."

"The next time a Bigger comes across, I'll let you have a shot."

Inez settled back into her seat. I felt the play of her energy in the air around us as she drew her finger across the table. "Why did you come alone?"

"I'm never really alone."

Inez huffed. "Tell me about it. They won't let me go anywhere without Cheech and Chong outside."

I knew exactly who she was talking about. Their shadows blocked half the window outside. "The big earth elementals?"

"Yeah."

"I called them Rock and Roll last time they were trying to beat in my brains."

"Decent guys actually."

"Aren't they all in the beginning?"

Inez shook his head. "You'll never fully know what Haverty did."

I nodded. "I won't pretend. I also will never do what he did. Goes against everything that I stand for."

Inez looked up and I saw the fire in her eyes, literally. "What do you stand for, Violet Jordan?"

I licked my lips and told her the same thing that I had repeated to my pack when I'd first met all of them, when I sat down at these very tables and explained what they could do now. "It's not about the power. It's about the choices you make and the lives that you build. It's always about the home that you go to after the fight and the family in that home."

Inez looked away as her eyes began to tear. "And if you don't have a family because they were taken from you?"

I reached across the table and took her hand. Her power flared around her and my skin began to burn like holding your hand over a gas flame. But I kept it there. "Then you build one. And you fight for them."

"There does seem to be a lot of fighting in this world."

I released her hand and held up my injured arm. "More in mine than most. Sacred destiny or not, life is rough."

Inez nodded. "I hear you."

"I will want to know what you guys are up to."

"What makes you think that I will tell you?"

"Remember that stubborn part that the sensei mentioned? It's true."

Inez sat up in her chair. "Do you have any concerns?"

"Can I still train with my sensei? I need a good throw-down every now and again to keep me in my place."

"I don't see why not. Wouldn't mind enrolling myself."

"Are fireballs not effective enough? Because last time I saw you, it looked pretty darn effective."

Inez smiled. "They are effective, but they burn the good as well as the bad."

"Gotcha. Versus a good throat chop that can be aimed at one throat."

"You have an odd way with words, Miss Jordan."

I watched her. There was something else that she wanted to talk about. Something more, and it didn't involve ninjitsu. "Anything for me? Questions, comments, concerns?"

Inez looked down at the table. "Be frank with me. How many have you lost to the Lock?"

The images of the ghouls flashed across my brain and my eyes snapped shut for a moment. When I opened them, Inez's knuckles were practically white, knotted together on the table between us.

"None, actually. Been attacked by a few, but all of mine are still standing. Why?"

Inez shook her head. "Nothing."

She was lying. I'd never seen a lie scream behind someone's eyes like it flashed behind hers.

"You've lost some?" The way her jaw clenched, I knew my answer. "How many?"

"Five."

"I'm sorry." I couldn't hide the blood draining out of my face. Why did Jovan need all that power?

"I wasn't strong enough."

"You cannot blame yourself for sins you didn't commit."

Inez rose and I followed suit. "I need to let you go. From what I understand, you have a pack meeting tonight."

"You know, full moon and all. It was a pleasure meeting you."

"See you again, Violet Jordan."

Inez walked back out the door and I saw her, and the two brutes pass by the sunny window.

Now that went swimmingly, I thought to myself as I walked behind the counter of the shop. My Plan A of just being Violet Jordan actually worked for once.

I deserved a celebratory coffee.

Everything at the shop was still in its place. Even the fridge was still running. The grinder still worked, and the milk was still good.

Freshly made latté in hand, I leaned across the counter of my coffee shop and just took a moment and a sip of coffee—surprisingly, my first of the day. It wasn't horrible.

I looked across the quiet shop and knew that something was wrong. It was more than the espresso, which didn't have Bastian's flair to it.

It was this place. This place needed people. I needed to open it back up and get Bastian back behind the counter to fix me a decent caramel macchiato every morning.

And if needing a decent cup of coffee every morning made me a queen, then so be it.

CHAPTER 15

THE FARMHOUSE NEVER looked so blissfully wonderful before. Its two-story frame stood out against the afternoon sky and it glowed with a homey warmth. It was probably just the sun behind the house because we were pushing late afternoon when we finally arrived, but to this exhausted girl, it was the most beautiful sight on the planet.

I parked closest to the house and watched as the six other cars that had followed me from Dallas found places to stop along the undefined driveway.

I grabbed my overnight duffle and the black canvas bag with the scary stuff I didn't trust to stay at home in it and climbed out of my little car.

"Want to me to corral the others?" Tucker asked behind me.

"Yeah. Let me prepare Iris. And please stop using that word."

Iris didn't need preparing. She shuffled out onto the porch in her black orthopedic shoes and looked hard at the line of newbies.

Tyler was behind her, wiping his hands on a dish towel. And there was why Iris didn't need preparing.

I met her at the top of the stairs.

"Hairball," Iris grumbled.

"Old lady."

I leaned forward and gave Iris a small kiss on the cheek. She still smelled like dust and cashmere and I took a moment to burn it into my brain. That smell was home. I joined her on the top step, and we looked out at the new recruits.

"They're a pretty tame bunch," I started. "We've got enough sleeping bags for everyone to sleep out in the barn."

"They're not sleeping out in the barn like a bunch of animals. We'll find places inside."

I was going to protest there was nothing wrong with the barn, but the set of her jaw and the squint of her eyes looked like she was preparing for something, so I wasn't going to fight her on this.

"We got groceries for everyone, working on a potato salad right now," Tyler said.

"Iris, you didn't have to."

"Don't think you're not reimbursing me, little miss millionaire."

I looked to Tyler, who only shrugged. "She deserved to know."

I couldn't blame him. Iris was damn intimidating despite the silvery bun and apron. She probably broke him with one taste of her sweet tea. "We probably need to discuss some of that."

Iris nodded. "Already have the iced tea ready. Chaz going to make an appearance?"

I again looked to Tyler, who threw his hands up and went back into the house.

I forced a smile. "You know how those Garrett boys can't resist a free meal."

Iris frowned. She knew both Chaz and I too well to know everything wasn't all right. "Strapping you two to chairs to work it out is the last thing I want to do, but it's still on the list."

"Understood. Ready to meet the troops?"

"Guess so."

"I COULD REALLY use that whole *How to be a Prima* talk now." I rocked my chair hard on the porch.

After getting everyone settled and fed, which was more of a feat than I'd imagined, Tyler took some of the more skittish ones out to the fields to work on some borders and control. He volunteered for the job, actually, surprising me and Tucker most of all. Peter worked on his computer in the living room, and somehow Nash gained access into Iris's secret back room of Wanderer knowledge that I hadn't even ventured into. I'd given him the grimoire the second I'd gotten out of my car and he grabbed it like it was the last piece of birthday cake with the extra icing.

Keeping up the front of put togetherness before the pack had made my skin begin to ache, and when Iris suggested that we take to the porch for some girl talk, I didn't refuse.

"I keep telling you. It's different for each person. This is your pack. Your set of rules."

"Then at least tell me how you did it."

Iris's eyes trailed across to the light of the dying sun. "It took me a while. We were just shifters though, and I had the Cause on my side."

I shook my head. "We don't play nice with the Cause."

"You don't play nice with anyone."

"Managed to keep the elementals at bay." I was still proud Inez, and I hadn't ripped each other's heads off.

Iris sighed. "I kept it simple. Meetings once a month. Let them live how they wanted. Set out some pretty simple rules."

"Which were?"

"Don't eat anyone. Don't tell anyone. And don't put me in a situation that I won't like."

"That's it?"

Iris looked over at me with an arched snowy brow. "It was a simple code. Everything seemed simpler back then."

"Before Haverty, you mean."

Iris shook her head. "He changed the game. Made it more about power than it had ever been before. And that was before he started in with the demon." She shifted in her rocker to face me. "It's going to be hard for you to serve your people."

"What?"

"You've got the heart in the right place, but your pride and power aren't going to help."

"Iris, that hurts."

She sighed. "I'm old and tired of wasting all this wisdom on the birds."

I wanted the wisdom. I wanted to absorb every ounce of wisdom that I could get. But a rumble echoed across the field, a rumble I would have known anywhere. Chaz was back.

"You need to go to him." Iris slowly pushed herself up and off the rocking chair next to me.

"Know something that I don't?" I watched her shuffle toward the kitchen door.

"Yes. Now mind me for once in your life." The slamming of the screen door punctuated her command.

Chaz had to park at the end of the long line of cars down the driveway. Which was probably a good thing. I needed a moment to convince myself he hadn't left me again when I needed him. He'd just gone to do his job, just like I had gone to do mine.

At least he came back in one piece. I came back a little chewed on.

His boot steps were heavy as he climbed the porch stairs. He dropped his bag on the wooden slats and trudged toward me.

As I stood, his slid his hands around my waist and rested his heavy head on my shoulder. I fought a wince as he slammed it down on the shoulder with the still tender wounds. He took a deep breath and let it out slowly as he tightened his arms around me.

"Chaz?"

"Just be still."

I pressed my lips together and wrapped my arms around him. Only as I relaxed into his embrace and my power pulsed around us did I feel how incredibly exhausted he was.

I wanted to know what happened. I wanted to know if anyone had touched him because I'd just have to rip their head off. I wanted to know because suddenly I was scared.

I heard him grunt as my embrace grew a little too embracey.

"Sorry," I said as I loosened my arms around him.

Chaz pulled away and his golden green eyes looked down at me, complete with the dark circles I was getting known for having as well.

"What happened?" I kept my voice to a whisper.

"I chose you."

I pulled away further to focus a little better on his words. "Huh?"

His hands rested on my hips as his gaze rested somewhere around my left ear. "I went to Andrea. Explained I couldn't work cases anymore. Couldn't be running all over the country."

"But . . ."

He raised an eyebrow, and I swallowed my protest.

"I'm out."

I frowned when I realized what he was saying and looked down at the inside of his left forearm where the Cause's mark used to be branded into his skin. His skin was perfect, like there had never been a spell there at all.

"I'm choosing this life, this fight."

The smile that overcame me was contrary to the tears that welled up in my eyes. I wrapped my arms around his neck and for a moment the sunset was brighter, the birds were chirping, and there wasn't an evil bastard trying to bleed me through the Veil.

"Vi," he squeaked.

I jumped back and giggled. Actually giggled. "Sorry."

"I'm still not ready to be part of the pack."

"Okay." I nodded. "I need at least one person left to Taser me."

The furrow that appeared between Chaz's brows might have beat his world record for the fastest and the deepest.

I sighed. "It's a long story."

"There's more. You've got to give a little, Violet. You've got to make some decisions too."

"What?"

"Things have got to change. It's not working, for me, for you, for them." Chaz sounded like he had a plan as he pulled me to the railing of the porch and sat me down. "First of all, give up that planner. The guilt on your face when you missed an appointment was painful. It's not you. You're not a planner."

"Thanks for reminding me."

"You're welcome. Second. You're going to ask Drew for a hiatus."

I gasped and tried to stand but Chaz clapped his hand on my injured shoulder and pushed me back to the railing. "But I'm a writer, Chaz. It's who I am."

"Being a writer is *part* of who you are. I know your writing brain has saved our asses a few times, but the world won't end if you don't oversee *MoonBlood*. It actually might end if you don't focus on this story, our story."

I wanted to protest. But he was right. I wasn't just a writer anymore. I was a Prima and an aunt. I still smiled when I thought about that. "Well, when you put it like that . . ."

"It's not forever, Violet. Probably better that you keep writing, but you don't have to work anymore. The money took care of that. And if you still see it as blood money, then look at it like this: the money is helping you be a better Prima, which makes them a better pack."

"I bought the coffee shop." The confession seemed to jump out of my mouth. "To make sure it stayed a haven for the pack. I suppose using a little of it to pay off my mortgage wouldn't make me totally evil."

"Exactly," he nodded. "And I really don't care if you fight me on this one, but I'm moving in. The boys can have my house and it's going to be hard, but you're right. There is no *us* anymore. There is *we* and my part in this *we* for now is to be your Guardian. Protect you, even if it's from yourself."

As the tears welled up in my eyes, I nodded and stood. He let me.

"Agreed. On all terms, Mr. Garrett. And no more house guests, either."

Chaz let out a long breath. "Good. Because I was getting really nervous about walking in on another one again."

He pulled me to him and kissed my cheek. I took in a deep breath of his musky scent and burned it into my brain.

"Now what was this about you being Tasered?"

So I told him. Caught him up on the intel from the Shades, the location of the grimoire, what happened with Inez, and even gossiped to him about Jessa and Tucker.

"Huh," he said as he wrapped his arms around me.

We'd ended up in one of the rockers together. As I talked, his warmth surrounded me, and I was probably the most relaxed and rested that I had been in six weeks.

"Yep." I rested my head on his shoulder. It was amazing that a five-feet-eleven woman could curl into such a tight space, but it was the best tight space to be in.

Chaz sat up and listened. We were still keenly aware of the silence. "Where is everyone?"

"Tyler has them doing something."

I felt Chaz shift underneath me.

"How is he doing?"

"He just lost the love of his life. He's doing what everyone else would do. He's burying himself in something constructive so he doesn't have to think about it and I'm not going to stop him. Maybe that's what I've been doing? Over-managing everyone so I don't have to think about losing anyone."

"Because you think you caused it?"

"No," I sat up and looked down at Chaz. His raised an eyebrow, catching me in another lie. "Yes. But at least Tyler is good at it. His whole nurturing side came out the moment he saw some of these guys. I think we've found our Shala."

"What about Iris?"

"She thinks she should stay out of this. A fresh pack."

"But we are here."

"I didn't say that she doesn't care about us as people. She just doesn't want to get involved in the politics."

Chaz looked out across the field. The spring sun was going down and I was postponing the inevitable while on the porch with my love.

"You need to go, don't you?"

"Yep."

"Want me to stay in the house for tonight?"

"Yep."

"Want me to make breakfast in the morning?"

I nodded with a wide content smile and leaned down to kiss him. It was a simple kiss. We didn't need the big theatrics anymore, because we'd already made our choice. Though I was pretty sure that with a little convincing, I could get some serious theatrics going.

Chaz pushed off the porch chair and I was forced to stand.

Plans were foiled again.

"Go be that girl I just gave up my sacred destiny for."

"Yes, sir."

. . .

TYLER HAD THEM ALL standing just on the other side of the barn. He knew I needed to have Prima time. That I needed to be me for a little while before I was what they needed of me. That's why he was going to be our new Shala. He seemed to know what we needed to make us better.

I waited on the periphery of their circle and slipped off my tennis shoes. It was still amazing to see all of them together. It hadn't happened yet. I'd taken them all on individually, but together like this, their eyes wide in the full moonlight as they listened to Tyler and the rules for that night, they were a force to be reckoned with.

I slid my hand over Tyler's shoulder and his speech stopped. "I think most of us got this."

I flicked my eyes over to the youngest, Remy, and then back at Tyler. If anyone was going to need his help tonight, it was going to be Remy. And frankly, I wasn't sure how a white-tailed deer was going to fare during hunting season.

I turned to my pack. "I've got nothing you haven't already heard. I can't show you anything you haven't already done yourself."

The crowd was getting antsy. The full moon was pulling on all of us, and it was stronger than I'd ever felt before. Twenty times stronger, to be as precise as possible.

I released my borders, getting rid of any pretenses that I was not their leader and just another shifter.

The Fang sisters rolled their necks as they stepped out of their wedge sandals and pulled off their huge dangling earrings. The Rosario brothers took off their shirts and looked like something from that teen dream movie we'd been watching with Lexie.

"Simple rules, people. No bringing back souvenirs. But you come back. And if something happens, then you call out to me or Tucker and we will get you back."

I heard Peter pop his neck to my right and the relief of it jittered down my spine.

"And I know that this is going to sound cheesy, but look at the person to your left."

I looked over at Tyler, who was looking over at Remy.

"Now look at the person to your right."

I looked over at Tucker, who wasn't even trying to catch a peep down Praline's shirt, though the smallest of the Fang sisters wasn't trying to hide her ample assets.

"What do you see?"

"Dark roots," Praline snapped.

Lucy, another petite blonde with more rhinestones per inch than I've ever seen, whipped her head around and stung Praline on the arm with her sharp, perfectly manicured nails.

I chuckled. "What else?"

"People," Kandice said softly.

I smiled. "And what don't you see?"

"A pack of mutts," Tucker filled in.

"Exactly."

I looked around and knew it was time. The commune was the fundamental of the pack. If all of Nash's big books had taught me anything, it was that. The difference between a pack and every other group of Wanderers was that the Prima shared her power.

The pack was only as strong as its weakest member and it was the Prima's responsibility to keep her pack strong. And not to do what I'd done and take from them. A sharp stab of fear ran through me and I looked to Tucker. What if I did it again?

What if my default was still set at take instead of give?

Tucker put his hand on my shoulder and gave me a little shove forward. That was his older brother coming out, telling me to get the job done. That he was right behind me.

Hesitantly, I shared my power with them, and they accepted it. It was easy, felt natural to be around them, open with them like this. Feeling the thin strands that connected us become stronger. The power coursed along their skins, ran rampant up their bare spines, slipped around them like liquid silver. It filled in holes from stress, sadness, making each of them stronger as they let my power wrap around them.

When I felt Remy's head go a little dizzy, I pulled back to just being radioactive. Their eyes were wide and their animals ready. I'd done it. I'd actually done something right. I really was their Prima.

"Now play nice and protect your pack mates."

"And last one back to the house has to do breakfast dishes," Tyler put in.

With a little flick of my hand and a crack of my energy, I sent my pack off into the fields for their first shift together.

The Fang sisters didn't even make it to the tree line. They shifted into their wolf forms within two strides. Jane and Gator were galloping the other way across the field and the rest of them scattered to the wind. Even Peter eventually trotted off into the darkness, his silver mantle catching the moonlight.

Except my boys.

Tyler put his hands on his hips. "I got the kid, right?"

"Lords, yes. I saw the way that Lucy was eyeing him, and I wish she had carnage on the brain."

"I'll stay at the house," Tucker said.

"Only if you want to. Chaz has it pretty well secured."

Tucker's eyebrows jumped. "Chaz is back?"

"Yep. Chose this fight above all others. He chose us."

Tucker gave a deep nod before he pulled off his shirt.

Nash's voice was the oldest I'd ever heard it. "And there is going to be a fight, isn't there? Something major if the Cause is letting their players go. Something they can't handle."

"Yes." I couldn't lie to him. Not like this. Not after what I'd just preached about. "There is. Something they can't predict, and if Chaz's assumption last fall is still true, they just want it to play out and be over with."

"God, I hate those guys," Tucker grumbled.

Nash shrugged. "Guess I'll keep reading."

"And I'll keep training those who need it," Tyler said.

"And I'll keep giving those inspirational speeches." Tucker smiled.

"I dunno." I shrugged as I rolled my shoulders. The pull was undeniable now. The panther wriggled in my chest to get out, to run free with her pack. "I thought I did pretty well at this one."

Tucker's eyes twinkled with self-righteousness. "I knew it."

"You don't know squat." I punched him on the arm. "You're it."

Three strides toward the tree line, and I was on all fours running like a dark streak against the moon-filled night with my pack behind me and the open night before me.

CHAPTER 16

*K*HALIDA HADN'T SLEPT in three days. Just knowing the Jovan was coming terrified her. She knew her operations were airtight and there was no way in the Neveranth that he could trace any of the rebel activities back to her region.

But still, she feared his motives behind this trip to his Southwest Territory. Did he doubt his power here? Didn't he trust her hold over her region?

The steam of her hot coffee swirled in the breeze that curled around her, playing with her satin robes. She stood on her balcony overlooking the gardens to the east of the estate, or what would have been the gardens before the fire-breathers destroyed it in the last uprising.

She usually didn't watch the sunrise. But she had seen the sunset, so it seemed fitting. From here, she could see what was left of the skyline against the purple morning. She remembered when it had glowed with neon lights and life. Now one of the most stunning southern skylines was nothing more than the skeletons of a great Metroplex.

That damn cat. If she'd only gotten her act together.

As she watched, Baine led a group of soldiers in formation through *their morning jog around the property. She wasn't one for exercise, but she was one for the appreciation of sweaty bodies glistening in the morning light.*

Baine looked up to her balcony and nodded to his Queen.

Khalida raised her cup to the group of men with a small smile.

Bringing up the rear of the group was Clay. His brick-colored hair was plastered to his forehead and provided one of the few colors in this misty morning.

Even from this distance, she felt him. Felt the way his blood surged when he saw her. But he simply nodded and ran on with the rest of the men.

Khalida shook her head. She was getting slightly attached to that one and it had nothing to do with their night together. He reminded her of what she used to be. Stronger. Tougher. And so incredibly obstinate her clan sacrificed her to the demon that resided in her chest.

Maybe it wasn't such a good thing to dwell on the past, especially when the current Prince of Darkness was going to be on your doorstep in less than an hour.

I WOKE UP in bed to my ringing cell phone. I reached across Chaz's bare chest and smacked my lips. They tasted like ash. Better to dream about demons and tasting ash than dream about Spencer and getting a mouthful of brimstone. I slowly pulled the phone to my ear.

"Violet?" Waylon asked.

"Yep?"

"Did you happen to dream about . . ."

"Succubus named Khalida?"

Chaz finally woke up at that little happy thought.

"I pegged it at six years," Waylon said quickly.

"Huh?" I sat up and scratched behind my ear. Apparently, I'd made it to bed in a tank top and undies. Bet Chaz loved that.

Waylon went on. "My visions, the clarity, the length can sometimes tell me when something is going to happen. I peg that in six years."

"So help me with the story here, kid. I die, she takes over Dallas? I really wish people would stop prophesying my doom. It's a crap way to start the morning."

"Huh?" Waylon said.

"What part of the *damn cat* didn't you catch?"

"Oh, right. Still getting that part down."

I stretched and wiggled my toes. "What? Don't believe your little cousin can rule the world?"

"I'm getting closer to believing that every day." Waylon sighed. "I'm going to go through my journal and double-check all the Khalida dreams I've had."

"You've dreamt about her before?"

"Almost every day since I've moved here."

My skin prickled and I rubbed my bare upper arms. "So she's evil? One of Jovan's henchmen?" She didn't feel evil. It felt natural to be in her point of view, but then again, my evil meter was pretty much in the middle.

"I don't think so, but she's the only one powerful enough to rule this area, besides you of course."

"It's too early in the morning for flattery, Waylon." I stretched. "I need to check on my pack."

"Well, have fun not getting dead."

"You too. Let me know if you see anything else." I hung up the phone.

"So what is it about you dying again?" Chaz asked as he rubbed his eyes.

"I've been having dreams again. I thought it was just writer Violet getting back on track, but it seems that Waylon is dreaming them too and he thinks they're about the future."

"So what's the dying part?" he repeated.

"I had a dream about a demon who takes over Dallas."

Chaz sat up, his eyes suddenly golden. "What did he say?"

"Pegged the doom and gloom at six years, but I've had a couple of these dreams now and some have been great. And some have been not so great."

"Tell me the not so great ones."

I licked my lips and readjusted to look straight at him. "I had one about our wedding."

"That was a bad one?"

"No. I was trying to create the argument that I don't think they all definitely happen, because I don't see us ever getting married in a church or in that much tulle. I think they are just possible futures."

"Violet?"

I sighed. "I had one about Inez burning a vampire girl to death. Before I knew it was Inez."

Chaz's eyebrows jumped. "I thought that things were good with the Akasha?"

"Which is why I don't think that all of these come true. The Inez I saw in that dream wasn't the Inez I met. I really do believe that they are possible futures."

"Psychics don't dream about possible futures, Violet. They only see the real future."

"Well." I adjusted to sit within his arms. I put my hands on his bare shoulders and looked into those golden eyes. "A psychic from my own family said I would be part of a demon rising, and we managed to avoid that one." I smiled at him. "Agreed?"

Chaz licked his lips but eventually nodded.

I smiled. "And if my spidey senses are right, no one else is up this early."

Chaz listened. "Agreed."

I pushed him back down to the bed and leaned over him. "And it has been a very long time since we've had any one-on-one time."

"Agreed."

I leaned forward to kiss his nose. "And you did just choose me above all others."

"Agreed."

"And I never did get to properly show my appreciation." I threw my leg over his and straddled his hips.

When Chaz finally got the picture, his eyes widened. "Violet, there are twenty people sleeping in this house."

I just smiled. "Panthers are known for their stealth."

I leaned down to kiss him, and boy, did he kiss me back. Apparently, I wasn't the only one in this relationship who had counted the days since one-on-one time went out the window.

He trailed his hot fingers up under my tank top and ran his thumb over a nipple that seemed more than ready for the attention.

As I made the move to get rid of my underwear, the antique bed let out a loud squeak of protest. Chaz and I froze, as if one squeak could rouse the entire house.

"This might not work, Vi," he whispered.

"You're just embarrassed because you grew up here."

His golden eyes landed on me and I thought I saw a blush across his cheeks. Being mostly evil, I leaned down and caught his ear lobe between my teeth. It was his weakness. And I knew it. Hence the evil.

He threw us to a sitting position. The bed and I both protested.

"Come on." He moved me off his hips and then off the bed.

I frowned. "Are you serious?"

He stood before me and winked. "Trust me."

His leg swept mine and I fell backward, but his lightning-fast reflexes caught me before I hit the ground. Slowly, he rested me on the floor and pressed his body against mine. My heartbeat wildly in my chest, which only pumped the blood harder to every nerve receptor that was now against his completely perfect body.

"This isn't my first silent session."

My eyebrows rose but my snark was quickly sated by his lips on mine and his knees slipping between my legs. He nestled in on top of me and his lips trailed down my neck as his hands went for my underwear.

Something in the shift of his weight ground my shoulder into the thin carpet. I winced at the carpet burn.

Chaz popped up. "What?"

"This might not work."

The furrow in that man's eyes was something akin to learning that his precious Dallas Mavericks would never play another day.

"One more idea."

He took my hand and pulled me up and then on top of him. I would never tell him I got a thrill out of being manhandled, out of his strong hands telling me exactly what he wanted me to do.

I straddled his lap as he sat on the floor by the bed, leaning back. His hands ran up my arms, my almost healed shoulder and across my clavicle before he grabbed my chin and pulled me to him. His mouth was hot and honey as he kissed me and grew taught beneath me. His golden power trailed down my skin as he opened his borders to embrace me as well.

I wished that I could have been so pure. My hands went for his boxers, taking their sweet time trailing down his hard chest, tracing the circle of his nipple, and then traveling down the perfect cut of his abdominals to his elastic waistband. He didn't protest as I rose up and we slipped them down his long muscular legs.

My underwear didn't have a chance. The lacey things I'd purchased under the guidance of Jessa's obsession with panty lines ripped under Chaz's suddenly needy hand.

With the pesky underwear out of the way, it was like we were dancing as I shifted easily under the direction of his hands and he guided himself in.

I gasped louder than I'd meant to, and he smiled as he looked up at me. In that moment, I felt complete, relaxed, and only here with him.

Slowly, his hands rested on my hips and lifted me up and down. The heat below my navel began to rise and spread out as he repeated the motion and we found that exquisite rhythm between us.

One hand traveled up my back, keeping us close together, keeping our lips no more than a breath apart.

I took a little initiative, speeding up the downs, but his fingers dug into my hip and slowed me. He obviously wasn't minding the fact we were in his childhood home.

I didn't care anymore. He was with me. He was mine and as I opened up my Legacy to him, I felt his power meet me. And I needed that, I needed him.

His hand slid between my thighs and his thumb began to circle my raw bud of need.

And wow, was I ready. I kissed him hard as the waves of pleasure hit, trying to be as quiet as possible. His fingers dug into my back and hips as my nails dug into his arms and neck. He slammed me down on him and I felt his body tighten as he climaxed.

As the waves subsided, I pulled away and looked at his blown pupils. I leaned forward and kissed his salty skin and rested my head in the curve of his shoulder.

Chaz kissed me one last time before he lifted me up and set me on the floor next to him. He pulled my legs over his and held me tightly. We stuck together with the slight perspiration that had formed. I rested my head against the side of the bed next to us and enjoyed the feeling of being nothing more than a blob of electrified putty in his arms.

"I think I might have needed that," he finally said.

"Needed to assert some dominance?"

Chaz just raised an eyebrow. "Needed to make sure that you still need me."

"I will always need you, Chaz. I might be the most kick-ass girl you know, but I will always need you. If nothing else, the lawn mower isn't on remote control yet."

He tightened his grip around my waist and rested his head on top of mine. He chuckled. "What am I going to do with you?"

"Love me, feed me. What do you need?"

Chaz sighed. "Nothing. I've got everything I need right here."

I took one more moment to be loved. To be wrapped up in my lover's warmth. To know that no matter what was going to be thrown at us we could do this together.

"However, if you get up now, there will still be hot water in the shower."

"Probably enough for both of us."

Chaz smiled. "Harder to be stealthy in the shower. Go, you need to check on your pack."

With an overdramatic sigh, I pulled my Legacy back behind my borders and slowly unfurled myself from his arms.

I TRUDGED DOWNSTAIRS to start on breakfast after a very hot shower only to find that Iris had beaten me there.

"You're up early. Usually sleep in later after a shift."

"I don't really sleep anymore. Anyone else up?"

"Tyler was up. Went for a jog."

Iris stepped aside from her work of rolling out the dough for biscuits and pointed for me to finish the job. I took over, remembering how to powder the juice tumbler before cutting out the doughy circles and putting them on the greased cookie sheet. Everything I knew about the kitchen, I'd learned from Iris.

She stood next to me and watched, her arms crossed over her apron.

"What do you think of Tyler?" I asked.

Iris was silent.

"I'll wait. I'm learning patience."

"He needs to be Shalar."

"Is that the male version of Shala?"

Iris just ticked her tongue at me, but I felt the chiding more than anything else. She wasn't shielding anymore. Didn't need to. And she if was really going for the say-anything-old-lady act, then I'm pretty sure I just got a slap on the keister.

"He's good. The Mother has given him the gift."

"You keep talking about the Mother, I'm going to start to worry."

Iris sighed and she shuffled over to the kitchen table to sit down. Her descent was slow, and I didn't like the way that she relied on the table to lower herself. "I've been a little slower lately and thoughts like that keep catching up with me."

"Like what?"

"Like since I met Tyler, I feel that I don't need to be on top of you every second."

"Iris, come on. I'm not doing that bad, am I? I got everyone here and shifted and back again."

I shouldn't have said it. I knew it before I heard the boot steps, before I felt Tyler's furry energy from outside the kitchen window.

He tore through the back door. "Jane's missing."

Panic hit me in the face like the smell of his morning sweat. I closed my eyes and went through my curio cabinet of connections to my pack. Jane's braided satin strand was steady. As I reached out to her, if I didn't know better, she was sleeping.

I frowned. "She's safe, calm."

"She's not in her bed. Doesn't look like it's been slept in."

I put my hands on my hips. "Nonsense. I put everyone to bed last night."

"Then where is she?"

"Maybe she found another bed to sleep in," Iris suggested.

Tyler shook his head, and then he grimaced. "No. Everyone else was asleep."

"Except you," I pointed out.

He dropped his eyes and his voice dropped about three decimals. "I don't sleep well."

Oh, I thought, right. "Let's not panic. First step first. Try to look for her."

"Who are we looking for?" Chaz asked as he walked into the kitchen. He came right up behind me and put his arm around my waist.

"Jane isn't in her bed," I said softly.

"No problem. Let's go find her."

I slipped away to get my shoes and met Kandice in the hallway. Her wild energy beat around me exactly like the flap of her wings. "Jane didn't sleep in her bed."

"I know, but she's okay. We're going to find her."

"How are you so calm?" Kandice said as she followed me through the house.

"Because we are all here. Because she is calm wherever she is." I grabbed my shoes from the floor in my room and slipped them on. "And because I had Tyler build us a barrier around the farm so we'd know if anyone got off the property."

"What?"

"Contrary to what it might have seemed at the museum, I'm actually pretty good at this big-picture thing."

Kandice gasped and put her hand over her mouth. "No, Prima. I'm not . . . I would never—"

I smiled up at Kandice. "I know. It's okay."

Kandice let out a deep breath and dropped her hands to her sides. She looked twelve and like she needed a sandwich.

"Why don't you come join us as we look for her?"

Kandice nodded, her short blonde ponytail swinging merrily.

. . .

WE FOLLOWED CHAZ through the knee-high grass to the west of the house.

"What do you think is crawling around out here?" Kandice asked.

"Probably nothing willing to take on a panther."

"Or a dog," Tyler said as he followed carefully behind.

"And I guess I could just fly away." Kandice dared to join in on the conversation.

Chaz snorted. "Guess I'm toast."

I scratched between his shoulders. "Very handsome toast."

We were getting closer to Jane, who was still sleeping. I tugged at our connection to wake her up, or what I thought would wake her up.

There was a small gasp on the wind and then Jane's dark hair appeared at the top of the blades of grass. The gentlemen stopped but Kandice and I walked forward.

"Violet?" Jane's large brown eyes looked up at me before she looked down at her naked body and she curled up into a little ball.

I took off my light sweater and pulled off my T-shirt. It would cover most of her and frankly, both the guys here had seen me in less. Jane pulled the shirt over her tousled hair and then tried to pull it down to cover her backside.

I pulled the tie from my own still wet locks and handed it to her.

She carefully reached out and took it as she worked her hair into a braid.

"Are you okay?" I asked as she smoothed her hair nervously.

"I think. I am not sure what happened."

I knelt down and put my hand on her shaking shoulder. There was a slight something around her, in her energy.

Carefully, I looked into her worried eyes and saw what had

taken her. When my brain locked on to what it could be, my Legacy flared around us both and Jane gasped. It was dark and smelled of sickeningly sharp plant sap. "Spencer."

Bile rose in my throat as I thought about how he'd entered me, torn through me, using my body as his. And now he'd done it to one of mine. The violation felt no different.

"Come on, let's get you inside."

IT TOOK THREE cups of coffee to get my nerves under control.

Tucker had done the wise thing and sent the others away while the usual suspects gathered in Iris's living room. They probably felt like they were watching a tennis match as I paced this way and that, fueled by caffeine and a hatred that still burned hot around me.

"You're going to singe my curtains," Iris said as she passed around a tray of iced tea.

I took in a deep breath but couldn't stop the swirling of the Legacy around me. The heat of it made me think better and I was beginning to think that I shouldn't have been suppressing it all this time.

"We need to know the facts." Tucker had his police voice and it just managed to make me more angry.

"Spencer possessed Jane," I snapped.

"And she's got the mark, right?" Nash asked.

"It's the only way he could have gotten to her."

Nash huffed. "But that's the mark of Jovan, I'm pretty sure that's demon specific."

"I'm pretty damn sure it was Spencer."

"She could have let him in," Peter said from the doorway.

"You weren't invited here," Tucker said he stepped between me and Peter.

"I know. And I don't care. She's going to want to hear this."

Peter side-stepped Tucker with the grace that I had origi-nally attributed to him. It put him dangerously close to me and within the bubble of my frustration. I felt his strength and his truth along the still roughhewn ties between us.

"I got a call from the vampires. Their last one with the mark was taken last night."

The air was sucked out of my lungs. "All of them now?"

Peter nodded.

I leaned against the brickwork of the fireplace and let the edges dig into my back.

"Maybe your tie to them is stronger than the Clade, stronger than the Coven," Tyler said.

"Stronger than the Kiln. Inez lost ones as well." Peter shook his head and ran his fingers through his hair. He took a seat on the armchair next to me and waited, his blue eyes watching me along with all the others.

Think, Violet. You'd just prided yourself on the big picture. Why can't you see it now? What was going to help me see what I needed to see?

"Jessa. I need Jessa."

"One fairy princess coming up," Chaz said as he went into the other room.

"Why are you bringing outsiders into this?" Peter asked.

"She's not an outsider, and as she'll like to remind you, she was here first." My eyes fell to Iris. "Any words of wisdom?"

"Lords, no. I'm just glad it's not me this time."

I frowned. "This time?"

"Jovan wasn't always the top dog on the other side."

I walked over to the couch she was sitting on and Tyler relinquished his seat. In fact, all the boys exited as if they knew I needed this alone time, that this was Prima time. "I could use a good story right now, Iris."

"It's not a story. It's a cycle. Just like everything else. A cycle of balance. Jovan ate his predecessor. His predecessor spread his teacher's bones across the world, never to be found."

I flopped back against the hard cushions and put the rest of the story together, along with some really hardcore similarities to one certain space odyssey from a galaxy far, far away.

Jovan was powerful. Jovan saw a way to take over both dimensions in Haverty. When Haverty proved too stable, he turned to Spencer. And if Spencer was half the man I was, he'd been a little too good at the evil stuff and Spencer figured out a way to beat the demon at his own game. Like Jovan had surpassed his master, Spencer had surpassed Jovan and was using the Demon Locks as his own personal buffet table, a smorgasbord of Shades to feed from. And thanks to our connections, Spencer knew what it took to get back to this realm. It was now the padawan against the master. And if last night was any sign, the padawan was winning.

I looked over at Iris, my mentor. "Tell me it's only a metaphor. I really don't fancy eating you."

Iris threw her hands up in the air. "You've already surpassed me. You've got people you can trust. And a man who loves you. I knew it the first time you shifted in the barn that you were meant for this."

"Sure did give me enough grief."

"If I didn't, how would you know that I loved you?"

I smiled and curled up on the couch to rest my head in her lap.

Her fingers ran through my curly drying hair. There was a magic there and it wasn't anything having to do with shifting; it was the power of family.

As her fingers ran through my hair, the stories fell into place, the puzzle pieces, snippets of dreams, the little lore that I did know, and my gut, the sheer pull of my gut glued it all together.

"Got the answer yet?" she said as she stroked my hair.

"Give me a second."

"Need another cup of coffee? I know you think better with coffee."

I smiled. "I'm good."

"Well as you use that gigantic brain of yours, I've got a kitchen to clean, a lunch to prepare, and three loads of laundry." She patted my head and I sat up.

Iris pulled herself up off the couch and shuffled halfway across the living room, then turned around. "And I'm going to have to call a plumber because of all the hair down the drains."

"Send me an invoice."

"Don't think I won't, Miss Moneypants."

I smiled and watched as Iris walked toward the kitchen with the pretense of fixing lunch. But somewhere deeper, I think she'd just officially passed the torch.

CHAPTER 17

I FELT THE shimmer down my spine as Jessa used her magic to get into the house. Chaz brought her to the living room.

"So this is where you disappear to?"

"Welcome to the Bat Cave."

"Homey," Jessa said as she looked for a place to put her bag. She dusted off a chair before she set down her Fendi.

I rolled my eyes. "Did Chaz fill you in?"

"You need a Memory Clock?"

"We need to know what happened to Jane last night and she doesn't remember. Then I need you to get back and fortify the Veil. The Shades will be looking for any crack anywhere to get Spencer through."

Jessa bit her lower lip and looked hard at me. "This is going to be bigger, isn't it?"

I nodded. I opened the connection between us so she could feel the trepidation, but also the strength I knew we had together. My sense filled with rose petals and raindrops.

Jessa nodded as she strengthened her connection to me. "Well, you know what I always say?"

"Keep your enemies close but your lip gloss closer?"

"No," she smiled. "Go big or go home."

I laughed just as Chaz came in with Jane and a huge mirror. I was pretty sure Iris didn't want to know what we were about to do to her mirror. Again.

I went to Jane. She'd showered, but her eyes had dark circles under them, and she held her arms to her chest like she couldn't get warm. I put my hand on her upper arm and felt the sting of the active mark under her shirt.

"Did they tell you what we are trying?" I spoke like I was speaking to a skittish horse, which was really quite accurate.

"Something to help me remember."

"But you have to want to remember."

Her large dark eyes looked over at the mirror and then back at me. "Will it help you break the mark?"

"I don't know. I know it doesn't hurt if you're ready to see it."

"You have done this before?"

I nodded. "Jessa helped me remember my mother."

Jane looked away from me and down to the couch. "I do not want you to watch."

"Why?"

She rubbed her arms again. "I do not want you to see how weak I am."

"Jane, I . . ." but I felt it in our connection. She was ashamed of the possession. Where I'd taken mine to anger and nearly torn myself in two, she'd taken hers straight into shame.

But I respected her wishes. "If you need me, I'll be a holler away."

Jane nodded and I went back to Jessa, who was prepping the mirror with Chaz's help.

I whispered to her. "I only need last night. And be gentle. Stop if she freaks out, but I need to know what he wanted."

Jessa nodded.

"Oh, and we are having the wedding in the barn."

I walked away to the sound of Jessa's "What? Are you kidding?"

I FOUND THE Fang sisters sunbathing in the front yard. The chill from Jane had settled into my own skin and I needed the sun's warmth to chase it away. "May I join you?"

"Pull up a towel," Praline pointed to a stack of fancy beach towels that definitely didn't come from Iris's closet. These three friends knew how to make the most of a rough situation.

"Thank you."

I spread the towel out and next to her and lay down in the sun.

Charlotte leaned up. "Don't you want to give us a lecture on skin cancer or something?"

"I'm not pale by choice. Just don't get the opportunity to stop often." I stretched my arms up and took a moment to just be.

Praline snorted. "Tell me about it. I got three kids at home."

"Three?"

"Yeah. Three completely spoiled little brats and I love every hair on their heads."

"Are they . . . do they Wander?" I asked.

"No. I was bitten by blondie over there, and I've been really careful not to be around my family when I'm a little extra nippy."

"I can hear you," Lucy snapped. "And don't think that we don't enjoy mommies' little monthly vacations."

Praline smiled. "It does have its perks."

Lucy picked up a bottle of sun tanning oil and the intense smell of coconut drowned out the waving fields of grain. "Dropping my girls off at their grandmother's is my favorite time of month."

"Are yours?" I asked.

"Not a one of 'em. The Mother got that one right. My girls are gorgeous, but not bright."

Praline laughed. "That's an understatement."

"Like your Brock is going to win a Nobel."

"It could happen."

I laughed along with them and felt the contentment in their connections to each other and their connections to me.

"You know what I like about you, Prima?" Praline said. "You've got your priorities straight. Family first, fur second."

I liked that. I sat up and looked across at the three women. They were what I had been trying to accomplish in every other person here. Family first, fur second. These women, with their blonde hair and four-inch heels and their rhinestone everything, were already practicing what I had been preaching all along. They were given this lot in life and by God, were they going to make the most of it on their terms.

I was as frank with them as they were with me. "Something bad is coming, something bad will always be coming, actually, but I'm pretty sure that's another inspirational speech all together. I want to let you know that you don't have to fight. You've got kids and . . ."

"And a pair of high heels that can stab a man's eyes out," Praline said as she sat up from her seat. She pulled her sunglasses down her small nose and looked me straight in the eye. "That bastard threatened my kids. So if you need me to stomp on someone, you just call. And Lucy here can cheerlead them to death or something," Praline waved her hand and lay back on her beach towel.

Lucy whispered over to Praline. "Bitch."

"Slut," Praline whispered right back before she smiled.

I loved it.

The notion that I needed to stop Spencer at all possible costs washed over me and I was left with a taste of sour pennies in my mouth. Even if it took everything I had, I had to protect this.

I had to protect these girls sunbathing on their Mommy's Weekend. I had to protect Peter and his delicate heart. I had to protect the Rosario brothers so that someday their children could run the family restaurant or be lawyers or musicians. It was more than just protecting them physically. It was about protecting their right to even have that.

I hopped up from the beach towel and thanked the girls for their generosity. I headed straight for the house. I had an offensive to plan.

Tyler came rushing out from wherever Tyler was rushing from. "We've got something to show you."

In Tyler's shadow was Remy, the nervous teenager. He kept his eyes down and his hands jammed in his pockets. His entire existence was so familiar that my power went out to him in solidarity for all of those who were gawky and knew the entire Green Lantern oath by heart.

"What is it?"

Remy handed over his cell phone.

I looked down at the screen. It was a text conversation between him and a Twila.

"Who's Twila?" I asked as I scanned through the conversation. It was mostly nothings but sweet ones.

"My girlfriend," Remy finally said.

"And one of the witches in the Coven," Tyler filled in.

The conversation between them just got a lot more interesting.

"What's this about shadows?" I asked as I kept scanned through the messages. These kids were more prolific than I was. "Have they been attached by the Shades as well?"

"I think so." Tyler nodded.

I looked to Remy. "Do they know how to fight them?"

"No, I think it killed one of them."

"Text her back, tell her they can only be harmed when they

are feeding or with electricity." I handed the kid back his phone and I'd never seen anyone text that fast, including Jessa.

"Why didn't anyone tell them before this?" I turned to Tyler.

He shook his head. "We've never been on good terms with the witches."

"Or the fey apparently, and I've got one in the living room. It ends now, Tyler. Anything we know, they know."

"Done," Remy said and he handed the phone to me for inspection.

I nodded and we headed back to the house. "Make sure that they know what happens."

"But what if one of them is like working for that other guy?" Remy said.

Tyler actually laughed. "This kid's good."

"If one of the witches has sided with Spencer," I filled in the name for him, "then hopefully her leader will know." I opened the door to the kitchen to find the usual suspects eating around the table, including Tucker and Nash, with a book the size of the table itself.

"And how will you know if the Mistress knows?" Tyler asked.

"I guess I'll need to get everybody together. Make sure they know the signs."

"What did you just say?" Nash asked.

I froze on my way to the refrigerator. What had I just said? It had just flown out of my mouth with very little thought behind it. It was just the natural progression of the conversation.

Or was it just the natural progression of everything else?

"I think I just said that I needed to unify Dallas?"

The room went silent. All eyes were on me. My mouth went dry, and I continued on to the original quest of something wet from the fridge. I grabbed a liter of orange juice and drank it straight from the bottle.

Iris was the only one brave enough to jump on me. "Use a glass, girl."

I set down the empty jug on the counter and looked around at the sea of eyes staring at me. "Maybe not unify, but at least get us talking, on the same side."

"Like what you did with the Akasha?" Tucker asked.

"Inez," I corrected. "She's just Inez."

"She threw a fireball at my head," Tucker said.

"I'm sure she was aiming for the other six-foot-four guy." I shrugged.

Tucker ground his teeth. "No, what I mean is that to you, she is just Inez. To us, she is the Akasha."

"Listen, I get that there are politics between Wanderers, but—"

"You're not listening," Peter interrupted. "To you, she's just an ally. She can't hurt you because you could probably deflect the fireball with your Legacy. For us, she could barbeque us with a thought."

I frowned. "Never thought I'd see you scared of anything."

"I'm not scared. I just have a hard time trusting them." He crossed his arms over his chest and leaned against the door frame.

"There is no *them*." My voice came out louder than I'd intended, and the entire group flinched. "They are people. There is us, and there is Spencer. He's the enemy here, not the elementals."

The kitchen grew still. I could hear the birds chirping outside, now that all the predators were inside the house. I could smell the soft warm breeze as it wafted through Iris's curtains.

In that stillness, the parts of the story locked in place in my head and my entire body jumped when it clicked.

Nash rose. He was the only one who'd moved in ages it

seemed, and he stood to look me straight in the eye. It was like he'd figured the puzzle out too, my brilliant boy.

"You're walking yourself into a logical nightmare, Violet." Nash licked his thin lips. "You can't protect every Wanderer from Spencer without uniting the pack again, but you can't fight Spencer without risking people's lives." He walked around the table and came closer.

Chaz's heat enveloped me as he slid his hand into mine. "But you can draw a line in the sand."

I looked up at him, into his golden eyes. He was juiced from some unknown source. "What?"

"I thought you were the queen of all cinema. You draw a line. Do what you do best."

"Frustrate them to death?" Jessa said from the kitchen door.

She darted around Peter's broad frame and walked across the white tile floor, grabbing a kitchen towel to swiftly cover the blood on her hand and standing dangerously close to Tucker.

Chaz continued. "You make them choose. Keep the magic out of it. No pack stuff. Just make them choose which side of the line they want to be on when the fighting happens."

"It's too simple," Peter said. "Which is why it might work."

I turned toward Chaz. "Are you seriously telling me to Plan A it? To go in there and just tell all the leaders the truth? When has that ever worked?"

"With the Akasha," Tucker said.

"But . . ."

"You said so yourself. *It's just Inez.*" Tucker smiled. I think he was enjoying this just a little too much.

I licked my lips and leaned back against the tile counter, Chaz's hand still firmly grasped in mine.

Nash spoke again. "Start with offering up the information about the Shades."

Jessa sighed. "How about we just pull out the big guns and tell them what Spencer is planning?"

All of us took a keen interest in Jessa and I think she drew out telling us the information for dramatic effect. Good to know you can never take the princess out of this particular fairy.

"You were right. It was Spencer. There was enough of his energy left in her to see what he was up to. It took a few go-rounds and that poor girl is exhausted, but—"

"Jessa! Seriously get to the point."

"He's trying to come back. Plus, Jovan *wants* him back on this side of the Veil."

The collective intake of air should have rid the kitchen of oxygen but no one passed out.

"As a messenger kind of thing?" I'm not sure who asked the question, who had regained their wits first. Sure wasn't me.

Jessa looked up at the ceiling for a moment. "I got more of a 'get the boy away' thing."

"So there has been a power struggle on the other side," Tucker said.

I began to pace. There were so many people in the kitchen that the pacing room was only three good strides, and I was pretty sure that I stepped on someone but they didn't protest.

"So Jovan takes the little devil under his wing. Teaches him things like how to steal energy, things that his father never taught him. He gets really good at it, which is why I defaulted to it when I was dying, but now, he's gotten too big for his britches and surrogate daddy wants him out of the nest. So he's pulling on his debts to help my older brother three-heel-click it back home."

I looked around at the gaping mouths.

"Don't explain it to the others like that," Jessa said. "There was just way too much wrong with that whole thing."

"But I'm right." I looked around at all the other eyes, but

particularly Nash's. I knew that he'd find the flaw in the logic. He shook his head.

I smiled. We had a plan. "So we get back to Dallas. Tell the heads what we know and—"

Tucker spoke. "Fortify you. You're the one he needs to get across."

I nodded. "Agreed, but if I've got all the Wanderers keeping a look out for weirdness, then that should be easier."

"Maybe we could ask a certain long-lost cousin to see something useful?" Chaz asked.

"First steps first, though," Nash said. "Do we want to break the Demon Lock? Make sure Jovan can't get any stronger?"

I gasped. "What?"

"Cristina solved it for us." Nash walked back around to the side of the table. "It was in the margins of the paper you had stuck in there."

The energy between Tyler and me tightened. I pulled at it as well, like he was keeping me upright as much as I was keeping him standing, both knowing that we could do this together.

"Seth Garrett had it half right and Cristina finished it off."

"What?" Chaz joined us at the table to look over the book.

Nash's gaze bounced between me and Chaz like a tennis ball that didn't quite know when to stop.

Chaz's eyebrow arched severely, and I thought he might sprain something. "I mean I knew that he helped people out, but he broke Jovan's mark?"

I nodded. How was I going to say this without completely sending Chaz into another dark and broody because maybe I had left out a few vital details about his father? "Cristina was helping me figure out how. Our concern was that we could break it, but it would bond them to me, and I can't have more than four."

"Why not?" Chaz asked, his eyes growing more golden as the conversation went on.

Why'd he have to ask that question? "Because the way that your father did it actually just broke the bond with Jovan and didn't actually remove the lock."

Chaz wasn't stupid. He'd lived with monsters and demons his whole life. He knew how this stuff worked. "Dad pinned the mark on himself. Like the boys pinned their mark on you."

I nodded.

"And the boys drained you, so the others drained him?"

Iris finally broke in on the powwow. "Seth knew what he was doing." The crowd parted for her as she carefully made her way to the table. "Came to me, told me what he'd done."

"Did it kill him?" Chaz's hands wrapped around the top of the kitchen chair and I watched the tension run up from his white knuckles to his shoulders.

"Made him fight like hell." Iris reached out and put her wrinkled hand over Chaz's hand. "He fought harder afterward. He was connected to others. Knew the power of a pack. And he knew that Haverty had to die."

Chaz got silent, that stony silent that he always got.

I curled my arm around his. "Nash, how do we break it?"

Nash licked his lips. "Fire. Burn another mark on top of it, just like Garrett did."

"But it wasn't enough," Chaz growled next to me.

Nash looked to me for permission to continue. I nodded and he slipped into Mr. Info Mode.

"The lock connects two people's magics, their souls if you will, allowing for a flow of energy. Undoing the mark just unlocks them but it's like two loose shoelaces. Still dangling out there. The key, the part that Cristina figured out, was how to loop the magic back in on itself and create a whole person again."

"My brilliant girl," Tyler breathed. Something light and fluttery passed between us as we both surged with pride and sorrow stirred together.

"How?" I asked.

"By redirecting the person's power into themselves."

"But how?" I repeated.

"Because you're the freak with the stories," Jessa said. "We do stuff together that no one's even heard of before."

I burst out laughing, as did the whole of the kitchen. "And I'm also the one who says stuff wrong?"

Jessa just rolled her eyes. "I'm saying that you have a knack for this. If your little brain can dream it up, I'm pretty sure you can do it. Screw the books."

"Like that lightning thing with Carlisle. Shifters aren't supposed to be able to do that," Tucker said from behind Jessa.

"And no one but a Fairy Warden is supposed to be able to weave the Veil but you can."

I shook my head. At this point, I wasn't too keen on the two of them teaming up. "I'm not chancing this one. We need more than just Violet's brain to rely on. It's too important."

Nash cleared his throat. "Cristina already thought of a potential solution. You'll have two loose ends. So if you put a banishing field using charged protection stones, Jovan's energy won't be able to stay where you break the mark."

"And it would be like a little energy vortex for their own energy to bind them back to themselves and not to me?"

Jessa smiled. "See, you are built for this."

"What about anyone else within a five-mile radius?" I asked. "What protects them from Jovan? From his loose end finding someone else?"

Nash's face turned to stone. "You can't protect everyone."

I was going to have to choose between my pack and innocent people. My stomach churned and I felt something like a squid kick around in my gut. Did I put my pack above the others in the area?

I tightened my embrace of Chaz's arm. His power beat around him, his emotions breaking through his steely borders for the moment. I'd fought too hard to let this happen, to have my people take from me. And Seth Garrett had fought too hard to have me stop trying.

"Do it." The words made my mouth dry, and my stomach turn over on itself. A million other thoughts ran through my head.

Nash and Kandice nodded and took the book away. Tyler escorted Jane back upstairs.

The rest of us just looked at each other in silence for a moment.

"You can do this," Chaz finally said.

I dropped my head to his shoulder. "I wish I had your faith."

"You do. And apparently that of everyone else you've ever met."

Chaz pulled his arm away from me. "Who thinks Violet can pull this off?"

Chaz raised his hand and everyone else in the room did too. It was ridiculous to see a group of grown-ups raise their hands, but the visual was damn effective.

"Who's going to be right there, just in case Plan A doesn't work out?"

Everyone kept their hands up.

"Fine," I said as I pulled Chaz's arm down. "But this isn't a joke. I know I tend to tread on the lighter side of things, but not about people's souls."

Tucker stepped up. "As a person who happens to actually have their magic connected to yours, I know you can do this. You just have to want to."

PETER CAME IN when I was scratching my back against the rough edge of Iris's fireplace. "What can I do for my favorite emissary?"

He stalked across the living room and joined me by the fireplace. He kept his voice low between us, probably a good habit in this house. "Still wanted to make sure you were keen on this unity thing."

"Not pushing for unity. I just want to make sure that everyone is safe."

Peter watched me for a second as I rubbed against the mantel.

"Are your scars itching?"

I stopped and a chill ran down my shoulders. They were. That's exactly what it was. The fours scars down my shoulder tickled almost.

"Mine do that right before a major litigation," Peter said.

"I think mine are trying to tell me that I'm mortal."

"Well," Peter said as he ran his fingers through his blond hair. It fell back into its perfect order. "You are trying to do not one but two things that have never been done before."

"Break the marks and unify a city?"

"Defy a demon and declare war on your maker."

"I think that second thing has been done before. Granted, it was probably in a movie, but I'm sure it's been done before."

"You need an army if you think you can stop him," Peter said frankly.

I looked up from where my eyes had been raking the bricks of the fireplace. "I've got one better. I've got a silver-tongued wolf who can charm the skin off a snake and will get all the heads together by the time I get back to Dallas."

Peter's jaw turned to stone as he clenched his teeth. "That would take a miracle."

"No, it won't, and you want to know why?" I reached over and placed my hand over his heart. It pounded under my fingertips. "Because I know what your insides look like, Peter. I know why your bond to me is so different from all the others."

He licked his lips. "Why's that?"

"The others are strands. They keep themselves loosely connected to me for their own reasons. But our connection is a million strands twisted together through strife, and frankly, some serious frustration. Do you understand?"

Peter's lower lip quivered for a moment and his borders dropped around him and I was awash in the scent of leather and sandalwood. He'd never been so vulnerable with me.

"You are the tested rope, Peter. And you are the stronger for it. You can work those miracles."

In a sharp move, Peter took my hand from his chest and put it against his smooth cheek. He closed his eyes and took in a long, steady breath. "You reminded me of my older sister." His breath traveled down my wrist as he narrated the story that I'd been waiting for. "She was fierce and free-spirited and everything I couldn't be because of . . ." He took in a deep shuddering breath. "She was on the outside what she was on the inside."

"What happened to her?" I whispered.

"Nothing. She's living happily in Seattle with her two kids. But until you, until . . . I didn't think I'd be comfortable enough in my skin to even think about that kind of happiness."

His blue eyes fluttered open and I smiled up at him. "Feel free to quote me back to me."

"It's not about the power. It's about the lives you build."

I brushed my thumb across his cheek. "And if I can do anything to help in those choices, or help you build anything, you only need to ask."

Slowly, Peter let go of my hand and let it trail down his chest before I pulled it into the back pocket of my jeans.

"Thank you, Prima."

I felt the word, felt the power burning in my chest as he repledged himself to me, to this fight.

Peter dropped his head and walked out of the living room past a very confused Chaz.

I called out after him. "If you want his new cell number, it's on my phone."

Chaz raised an eyebrow but walked to join me by the fireplace. "Does that need explanation?"

"He's going to set up a meeting with the other heads."

I rested my head on Chaz's chest. That morning when it was light between us, when it was far away and just us, seemed a million years ago.

"You're exhausted," he cooed.

"I'm exhausted. Are they ready yet?"

"No. They didn't have enough salt for the protection circle."

He kissed my temple and wrapped his arms around me. I pressed myself against his strong chest and took in a deep breath of that wonderful scent.

"Remember when it was simple stuff, like four mutts chasing after me?"

Chaz chuckled and I closed my eyes to just be quiet for a moment. Just be still. And loved. And just Violet.

Chaz pulled me over to the couch and set me down. He pulled my legs over his and I rested my head on the back of the couch. "Can I tell you a story for a change? I think you might need it," he offered.

He ran his hand through my long hair and pulled lightly the ends, sending prickles of calm down my scalp. "I met this girl once. Klutzy thing that couldn't seem to keep her shoes on."

I laughed. "Probably not the brightest crayon in the box."

"Hey. Interrupting the narrative flow."

I rested my head back on the couch. "Continue."

"So this girl didn't know just how special she was. Couldn't see the big picture. Sure she could tell you the entire canon of Star Wars, but she couldn't see what was really going on around her.

"And it amazed me that when the world was falling around her ears, she was still her. And when there was blood and violence, she was still her. And now that she is facing down another prophecy about death and another resurrection of a demon, she is still her."

"And what is that?"

"Funny. Sharp. And she still puts others first."

"So what are you going to do about this shoeless, klutzy girl, because she sounds a little dense?"

Chaz smiled and everything went golden for a moment. "I'm going to marry her and make sure I put her first."

A tear squeaked out of the corner of my eye. "Still keen on that idea? After all this?"

"Because of all this.

I curled into his chest and tucked my head into his neck. A few more hot and happy tears streamed down my face and I buried it into his chest. Why did he always manage to make me cry?

"I want to get married in the barn," I said into his Illinois T-shirt.

I waited for the laughter, or some joke about animals, etc.

Nothing came. I sat up and looked at him.

"I love it." He shrugged. "Now you have a phone call to make to your boss. Don't think I'm letting you out of your promise."

"Yes, sir." And I kissed him. More than I had kissed him in a good long while.

CHAPTER 18

*I*T WAS BIG spell time. Nash had drawn the circle in a field, and it spread out as far as I could see. The boy had a talent for spellcraft, or at least for following instructions to the letter.

Tyler gathered the four with the mark. Jane still quivered from her run-in this morning. Charlotte, the other Fang sister, stood there, her heels digging into the dirt. Julio was joined by his two brothers. Hannah and Evan held each other's hands.

Others stood outside of woven patterns of the circle.

Jessa squeezed my arm. "I think I have something that will help."

"I'm taking all I can get."

Jessa reached up and touched my forehead. There was a familiar chill that forced my eyes closed as a cool power covered my face. "It will let you see the unseen. Like I did that one time."

I opened my eyes and Jessa glowed a little more radiant than usual, like I was looking at the world through 3D glasses. Everything had a deeper dimension. The circle beneath my feet glowed white and I knew this was going to work because even I had a hard time pushing through the barrier as I walked toward my people. The circle really did know evil.

"So you know how this is going to work?" I asked my huddling masses.

They all nodded obediently.

"Then I guess I just need a willing participant."

The four looked around at each other. I wouldn't have volunteered to be first either.

"Fine, I'll go," Charlotte said. "Nothing's gonna hurt more than giving birth to Terrell. Have you seen the head on that kid?"

I smiled. Laughter was good for me right now. Relaxed me.

Charlotte stood before me in the center of the central circle. With the spell that Jessa had placed on my eyes, I could see her wolf in iridescent pink on her chest, like a truck-stop T-shirt.

Nash brought me a cordless wood burner and a picture of the symbol that I needed to burn over her mark. I'd made it very clear that I was not going to have that evil book anywhere near this spell work.

"A wood burner?" I asked as I touched the smoldering tip of the pen-sized tool. It burned a hole into my pointer finger, but the black dot disappeared quickly with my healing.

"Better than what he did it with the first time," Charlotte said as she pulled up her shirt and turned around.

Her mark was planted at the base of her spine, just above the waistband of her almost indecently short shorts.

"Do you want to sit down?"

"Guess it would be better than you kneeling to look at my butt."

Charlotte sat cross-legged on the ground and I sat behind her, tucking the paper under my toe.

"If this doesn't work—" I started.

Charlotte turned her head to sweep her long dark hair out of the way. "If this doesn't work, you tried. More than he ever did for us."

I took in a deep breath and focused on the dark mark. It seemed to swirl under her skin, like a life force of its own, the black not just ink undulating under the surface, but evil locked under her skin.

"Think about something nice. This is going to hurt."

I steadied my hand on her back and let out a breath. This was just like drawing on someone, only it would smell like barbeque.

When I made the first line across the swirling black mass, it burned with a white light.

Charlotte cried out and her energy spiked around her, her power pulling at mine. It took everything I had to keep behind my shield, not to reach out to her. This was working, but at what cost?

"You okay?" I asked.

"Friggin' peachy," she responded.

If she would have said fine, I would have stopped right there and tried something else, but the defiance in her voice pushed me forward. She was one of mine and she could do this.

I made the second and the third marks and she cried out again, her nails digging into the ground at her side. With each stroke, a fine white line settled over the Demon Lock.

And the Demon Lock was fighting back. The strands that connected her to the demon were red and angry as they swirled around on the mark, tendrils of red-hot energy reaching out. Her life force and the demon's were fighting each other in the circle mark on her back.

"Last one."

Charlotte nodded and, even though I couldn't see her tears, I could feel them running down her cheeks.

As the wood burner drew one last line across the mark, I

heard the pop when the spell was completed, the crack of it when the mark was broken.

Charlotte gasped as I watched the darkness fade from her mark as a tendril of hot energy shot out and across the field like an angry arrow.

Take that, you lousy piece of demon.

I looked down at the mark and saw the part of Charlotte that needed healing. Light, wispy fingers reached out like a scared child and looked like an exposed nerve as its tendrils waved outstretched, searching.

I scurried back on the ground, but I knew that I couldn't be far enough away. She needed to heal herself. "Charlotte, focus. The symbol will help you, but you have to focus. Bring your power back to yourself."

Her shaking shoulders and her clenched jaw told me she was, but it wasn't enough, and I couldn't risk sending my power to her to make her stronger, to risk bonding her to me.

A baby pink strand of power jutted out at me. I flinched and held my hand up, like I could have caught it.

When I opened my eyes, the tendril was stopped, still lunging out at me but like a dog at the end of its chain. I was stopping it. I was preventing it from touching me by my sheer will. Commanding her energy like a real Prima.

And if I could stop it, maybe I could turn it back to Charlotte.

I had to try. *Use that big brain of yours, Vi.* Everything else was a visual. The brick tower that kept my power safe. The curio cabinet of my pack members that kept them protected in my head.

I thought of my hand like a mirror and pushed forward. Slowly, the tendril backed off.

On my knees, I crawled across the ground back to Charlotte.

The tendril darted a few times, but I caught it again and

pressed forward until my hand hovered right over Charlotte's exposed power.

"Can you feel that?"

Charlotte nodded.

"Take it. Just reach out for it and take it. It's already yours."

With one deep breath, Charlotte expanded her power around her, and the tendril was absorbed into her.

Charlotte collapsed and I waved for Nash to bring bandages. He pressed the bandage against the fresh mark and carefully ran the tape around the edges to make it stick.

I shook Charlotte's shoulder. "Talk to me, Charlotte."

She pushed herself up from the grass and turned to look at me with a little wince. She looked around, and I could see the wolf still emblazed across her chest. Brighter. Stronger. Pinker.

"I think . . ." she started. "I'm good." She nodded. "Yeah. I'm good."

I resisted the urge to do a happy dance. It was all too easy. But then again, no one had ever tried before. Except for crazy Violet.

Nash however, did not resist showing his excitement. "Ready for another?"

I DIDN'T HAVE the energy for another big speech that night. Only half of the pack stayed for the night after the full moon, and I saw the other half of them off with brief instructions: Don't do anything stupid; you'll know if something happens, and you'll have to choose.

The Fang sisters went back to their kids. The Rosario brothers went back to the restaurant. Hannah and Evan went back to their burrow with instructions to recreate the white stones that Nash put around Iris's house. Gator took Remy home with instructions to tell his girlfriend Twila that the Prima wanted to meet with their Coven leader, but I was sure that he'd already texted her something to that effect.

But I kept Jane for another night. She slept for the better portion of the evening and barely ate her dinner, her hands still shaking. Her mark took a little longer and fought me a little bit more, but eventually, it broke. It was the first time I'd seen her smile.

Iris was quiet. I brought her tea on the porch as the sun went down.

"Tucker and the boys offered to fortify the barn."

I smiled. I hadn't even asked Iris if I could get married there. This place was more like home than any I'd ever found. Guess if I was going to start with the Plan A stuff about keeping everyone in the loop, I might as well start here.

"Chaz and I want to get married in the barn."

Iris didn't react except for the single tear that squeezed out of her eye that she quickly caught with her knobby knuckle.

"And I supposed since you're the closest thing he's got to family, I should probably make sure it's okay with you we're getting married."

"You're two grown adults. You don't need my permission."

"But we'd still like to have your blessing."

Iris looked over at me. "I don't know that I can give it."

It wasn't like a stab to the chest; it was an actual stab to the chest. "Iris," I winced.

"There was a reason that I never married, Violet. Wasn't because there wasn't opportunity."

Iris put down her tea and turned toward me. "You know that I hate preaching and you know that you're already doing a better job of this than I ever did, but a Prima has to stand alone. The ultimate decisions have to be yours."

"Why?"

Iris almost jumped at the question.

"Where does it say that I can't have a Primo? That I can't share?"

Iris shook her head. "You just don't know."

"Then tell me, Iris. Help me learn."

Iris's jaw clenched and her hands clasped on the arms of the rocker. "I was the reason Dallas fell. I was the reason Haverty wormed his way in. My weakness, my mistakes alone."

"Just because you took the blame doesn't mean the others were blameless."

"But they could sleep well at night when it was my fault."

The truth of it trickled down my skin and bumps. "You gave them peace."

"Until Haverty turned to that demon for more power."

"It was still peace, Iris. And, not to get too epic about it all, but you've done good by me, by this pack. Given me some peace. Hell, Iris, you've been Chaz's family."

Iris looked out across the backyard as the night darkened. "I'm just trying to say that the hard decisions have to be yours, as the Prima. You will always have the biggest sacrifice. The buck stops with you."

I nodded. I knew this. And I told her.

Her blue eyes shone in the moonlight. "Chaz can't be that sacrifice."

"Never, Iris. I want him to be in on that big decision. I want him to share everything."

Iris nodded and her eyes went back out to the field. "I just hope that's enough."

"Think of how much stronger the two of us would be."

The screen door opened, and the man of the hour walked out, and our conversation stopped.

"So you want to get married in the barn?" Iris said.

Chaz grinned as he knelt between us. "You always said I was raised in one, so it seems fitting."

"Have you figured out what rings you're going to use?"

I looked down at Chaz. "Haven't really talked about it."

Chaz winked up at me. "Doesn't mean I haven't thought about it. I figure since you've got my mom's rings, I might wear your dad's."

"Not sure we should have so much heirloom silver out there."

Chaz stopped smiling.

"I've got my parents," Iris said, still gazing at the backyard, as if she was actively trying to hide the tears in her eyes. "Not like I've got anyone to pass them down to. It's gold, so it won't kill you."

"That's a bonus."

Iris pulled herself up from her rocking chair. "I think I'll go to bed. See if you can keep the howling to a minimum tonight."

"Yes, ma'am," we answered in tandem as we watched her toddle into the kitchen.

Chaz got up and pulled her rocking chair closer and reached out to take my hand. "So you're really going to unite Dallas?"

"That's Plan A."

"What do you want me to do?" Chaz looked across the field. "I need my marching orders like everyone else."

"Thought we covered that this morning. Right next to me when I kill that bastard."

Chaz faked a shiver. "You know I like it when you talk all tyrant-y."

"Maybe that psychic was right all those months ago. Maybe you just need to protect me."

Chaz nodded. "Check. Protect the girl. Done."

"Which means that you have to stay really close to me. Like all the time."

"Should probably shower with you just to be sure no water demons try to attack you."

I laughed. "That's a good start."

I rested my head against the rocking chair and listened to

the quiet. I was exhausted. The hand that Chaz held still ached from this afternoon, but his warm hand was helping with that ache.

"I'm okay with Dad, you know."

I looked over at my golden fiancé.

Chaz looked at me. His fingers tightened around mine and there was glassiness to his eyes. "I mean, I get it. He was fighting the good fight. Just wish he would have thought about me for a second before he did it."

"I think he was. He was trying to make Dallas safer for you. So you could grow up."

"I was already grown up and working my own sacred destiny."

"Doesn't mean he didn't still see you as his little boy."

Chaz sniffed and looked over at me with a small smile. "How did you get all-knowing about family? I thought we were orphans together."

"I think Waylon reminded me. He's got this image of me in his head as this chubby teenager. I think he always will, despite the fact that I can kick his ass across the county without breaking a sweat." I pulled at his hand. "And you're not an orphan, Chaz. You've got Iris. And you've got me. And a niece and even a cousin, if you'll have him despite the bad timing with his prophetic visions. And that's not even the pack, the boys."

"Please don't harp about the pack, Violet."

"Okay. I won't harp. Besides, I've got the rest of our life to harp on it. And now that I've given up my job for you, I've got a lot more time on my hands."

CHAZ STOPPED BY the coffee shop, or I made him stop at the coffee shop before we even went home the next evening. The shop looked good with the lights back on against the dark street and Bastian looked even better behind the bar. He smiled and tossed the steaming towel on the espresso maker as I walked across the floor.

"Miss Jordan," he greeted.

"Don't you even start." I leaned forward on the counter and looked around at the life ebbing from the place.

"Caramel macchiato?" Bastian asked.

"Extra whipped cream."

I followed Bastian down the bar.

"How did you do it, Violet? I've watched you pay for coffee in handfuls of pennies before."

"Someone died," I answered honestly.

"Oh my God, I'm sorry." Bastian's eyes went all puppy dog.

"Everything's fine. Did you get all the paperwork sent in?"

"Yeah. Your lawyer is a shark though."

I laughed. "You have no idea."

We paused our conversation as he steamed the milk.

"I can't thank you enough, Violet."

And here we got to the part that I'd been practicing in the car ride home. The reason that I really made Chaz stop here. "It's not completely altruistic. I will unfortunately need to exert some powers of ownership."

A furrow formed between Bastian's sandy brows. "Like what?"

"Like I'm going to make some modifications to the back room, and I might ask you to hire a few people. Close up early on occasion. But the coffee making is all up to you."

Bastian nodded. "Whatever you need, Violet."

I smiled. "Might be nice to have a permanent parking spot out front."

Bastian laughed and it echoed off the espresso-soaked floors and the arts-and-craft-covered walls and surrounded me with a warmth that made me feel like this was all going to work out just fine.

I bathed in that glow for exactly the time it took for Bastian to finish up my coffee and for me to walk to Chaz's car parked out front.

My cell phone began to ring. I fumbled for it in my purse and finally found it.

"Hannah?" I answered. She was supposed to be at work. That's why she had to get back early from the full moon.

"Is that this freak's name?" The venom carried through the line could have melted the phone in my hand.

My power went out to Hannah and Evan. As I sorted out the power strands to find them, I asked calmly, "Who is this?"

"You know who I am."

I did. I could smell it as I made the connection with Hannah and Evan, scared but together. I wasn't scared of Kandice's boyfriend. I was scared because they hadn't called out to me.

"Tighty whities. I do remember you."

I got into the car with Chaz and carefully set my coffee in the holder. He knew something was wrong.

I held out my hand. "Drive," I mouthed.

"What do you want?" I asked TW as Chaz took my hand. His power filled the car and he got the location: the Uptown townhouse.

"I want Kandice to pay for what she did," TW hissed.

"What? Wise up and get a decent boyfriend?"

"What?"

Oh, guess he hadn't heard about that. "If I get there and a single curly hair is out of place on their heads, I won't just chase you down the street naked. Tonight, I'm feeling hungry."

I hung up. "They've got Hannah and Evan."

Chaz shook his head. "How did they even find them?"

"I will never underestimate the power of stupid again."

CHAZ STOPPED AT the darkened end of the street. There was what looked like a tailgate party outside of the townhouse. Five trucks surrounded the front of the house. It looked out of place on the narrow street filled with smart cars and Mini Coopers.

I slipped out of the car. The smell of alcohol wafted down the street. Who actually tailgates at a lynch mob? At least they'll have ice to nurse their wounds.

Chaz went to his trunk and opened it. I walked around to join him, using the open trunk to hide us. As if that bunch was smart enough to be on the defensive. "I can't kill them, Chaz. But I don't know another way to stop it. Just scaring the wits out of them didn't go as planned."

He pulled out a small dart gun and a baseball bat.

"How long have you wanted to use that?" I pointed to the gun.

"Only like three months." Chaz tucked the gun into the back of his pants. His hip holster already held his everyday gun. "But how are you going to do this, Vi? If intimidation didn't work the last time?"

"I really will just have to eat him." It was worth the look in Chaz's eyes and the laugh that bubbled out of my throat. "I don't know, Chaz. They took my people. I'm not playing with them this time."

"And frankly, I don't want you burping redneck all the way home."

I snorted. "I love you."

I stared down at the street and thought. These guys were smart enough to find them, but stupid enough to actually think that they could take on a Prima.

Of course, they didn't exactly know I was a Prima. I wondered what Tighty Whities had told them happened that night in order to get them roused enough to mob it up.

There was a lightning flash behind me, and the night was filled with the smell of ozone. I jumped and turned, ready for a fight. The Legacy sizzled down my arms at the new feeling of power.

Two women walked toward me. A tall redhead and a younger girl. They were powerful. The feel of it preceded them like a warm breeze.

"Prima Jordan," the young girl said as she scuttled forward quickly. "I'm Twila."

I relaxed, curiosity calming the cat for a moment. "Remy's girlfriend?" I asked as I walked a few steps toward them.

"Prima Jordan," the woman said. "I am Mistress Willowbourne."

Every muscle in my body flinched to keep in the snicker. The tall redhead in the ankle-length dress looked every part the Coven Mistress. The green cape was a bit much though.

"I wanted to thank you for the information about the Shades. It proved invaluable."

"Well, you're welcome, and I'd really like to extend the olive branch and talk, but I've got a little situation here."

"I know." Willowbourne's eyes flicked to the circle of trucks. It really was that obvious on this street.

I gaped. "How?"

But I knew the answer in the twist of Twila's pale fingers at her waist. "Remy's in there."

I gulped and turned back to look at the house. The Legacy burned down my back and I had to clench my hands into fists to keep my anger down. A third one? Why couldn't they call out to me?

"I do seem to owe you," Willowbourne said.

I licked my lips and turned very slowly back to the tall woman. "What?"

The woman looked down at Twila. "It seems our star-crossed lovers are going to take the day. If you need some help, I might be able to assist, if the Mother wishes."

I looked over at Chaz. He only shrugged.

Willowbourne rubbed her hands together and there was a ripple in the air around us. She was calling on her power and the trees around us seemed to give it to her.

"Well then, let's hope the Mother wishes three of my pack to be saved from a group of rednecks."

Willowbourne smiled. "Seems that the wind is right."

Chaz's hand curled into mine as we walked toward the house.

Willowbourne said she needed thirty minutes and we promised to deliver the rednecks to her in one piece.

We were almost to the townhouse when Tyler came running out of the bushes. "Something's wrong with Remy. I texted him and he didn't text back. He always has that damn thing in his hand."

I winced. "He might have gotten himself kidnapped?"

"What!"

"Shhh. You're blowing our plan to get him back," I hissed as I grabbed his arm and pulled him into sync with us as we walked toward the house disguised as young twentysomethings on a Wednesday night.

As we walked up to the front door, I feigned a stumble and launched my purse into the back of one of the guys' heads.

He turned around and his plaid shirt had seen better days. He reeked of beer though he had nothing in his hands.

"Sorry about that." I laughed as I bent down to get my purse.

"No problem," he grumbled.

That was before I sunk my fist into his midsection. He doubled over and I elbowed the back of his skull. He dropped like a sack of smelly potatoes.

I looked up at the boys who were looking at me with their mouths open wide enough to catch flies. "What? Did you really think that negotiating was going to work with these guys?"

"No. Just remember to save one for me," Chaz said.

I winked at him as we walked in through the unlocked door.

"WHERE EXACTLY DID you learn how to hog tie someone?" Chaz asked as I wrangled the last of the bunch.

I cinched the knot tighter. "Waylon taught me, actually."

"Do you think he *saw* that you'd need the skills?" Chaz asked as he stood over them.

I'd never thought of that before. "I don't know. I think he did it because we were bored."

I pulled out my phone and dialed my Riko.

"Officer Briggs," he answered.

"Tucker, I need you to pick up a few drunks."

"What?"

"I need you to arrest someone."

"That's not in my . . ."

I spoke slowly. "Tucker. I need these guys to wake up in jail in their underwear with no memory. I know that might compromise your morals, but this is what I need."

"Yes, ma'am."

I hung up. I knew I was swimming with a sort of gray but as I watched Hannah walk up to one of the men still unconscious and kick him really hard in the shins, I also knew that my gray was worth her standing up for herself.

I felt Willowbourne walk into the little townhouse. She looked around at the men scattered across the floor. "Your methods are effective, if a little brutal."

I crossed my arms. "Don't judge my methods and I won't mention the cape."

Willowbourne raised her eyebrows.

That whole foot-in-my-mouth thing. I'd done so well. "I'm sorry. I get a little snippy after a fight."

"I forgive you."

Chaz came up behind me and squeezed my shoulder. I needed his steady reminder that Plan A actually seemed to be working right now if I didn't ruin it.

I stepped to the side and let the witch do her thing. Willowbourne walked through the group, running her hands over the heads of the men. "Which one needs the biggest wipe?"

I pointed to TW.

"Who does he need erased?"

"Me." Kandice appeared in the doorway of the house, Nash close behind her. Their fingers were so tightly woven together that I felt the ache of it in my hand.

Willowbourne summoned her and when Kandice looked at me, I nodded. We needed to show trust among the species, and I was going to offer it up first.

Kandice went to her and the woman put a hand on her shoulder and then placed her white hand on the man's head.

I felt the pull on Kandice and then the push of a spell into the man's brain. Willowbourne's eyes went white for a moment, just like Yasmina's had. It was pure Mother power and it smelled like rosemary.

It only lasted for a moment and I was going to comment on it, but Chaz put his hand over my mouth. I did need him to protect me from myself.

When Willowbourne let go of Kandice, Nash rushed to her side and pulled her against him. The witch completed the circle of men and then wiped her hands on her cape. Looked like it was good for something. "My part is done here."

"Thank you, Willowbourne."

"I will see you soon, Prima." The woman and her train of skirt walked out of the door and into the night air.

I looked over at Twila, still curled around Remy. He'd fared pretty well through this whole ordeal, only a small bruise on his cheek, which would probably just made Twila love him even more.

"I think you should probably go with your Mistress," I suggested.

Twila's arm only curled tighter around Remy's.

There was a crack of lightning in the front yard and the girl jumped. She kissed Remy on the cheek and scurried out of the house.

"I need to learn that lightning thing. That was handy."

Tucker's police lights filled the living room. Tyler flinched at the familiar pattern of red and blue against the walls.

Tucker walked in the room and stopped cold. "What do I actually need to know?" he asked carefully.

I wove my very simple story. "These eight men got drunk and broke into Hannah and Evan's house."

Tucker lifted one eyebrow. "They sure did do a lot of damage."

I nodded. "They sure did, but they are not going to remember it. They were really drunk. Scouts' honor."

Tucker scratched behind his ear. His nervous tick. "Was that a cape I saw leaving?"

"Maybe."

Tucker shook his head. "Okay. I need everyone out who doesn't want their name on the record."

Hannah and Evan stayed. Nash offered to house them at the apartment for the evening until sunlight could help them rebuild their living room.

WITH THE BOYS gone and the pack safe, I fell onto my lavender bedspread and didn't protest when Chaz pulled off my shoes.

"Has it started yet?" Chaz asked as he kicked off his boots and pulled off his shirt.

"Has what started?" I asked as I rolled over to stare at the ceiling.

"Where your brain goes crazy?"

I sighed. It had already been going that direction on the car ride home. I'm as cool as a cucumber as I beat the fool out of a bunch of rednecks, but now that there was quiet, the gears started churning out painful thoughts. "Already there."

Chaz made quite a showing of unbuttoning and unzipping my jeans. He pulled them down my long legs and I smiled as he had to tug to get the skinny jeans off my big feet.

He rolled me over and pulled off my jacket and let me fall back to the bed in my T-shirt and underwear.

The churning thoughts might have stopped for a little while as I watched him peel off his UT shirt and let his jeans fall to the floor, the moonlight streaming through the window high-lighting every perfect muscle in his torso.

He crawled across the bed and pulled me into his arms as we rested on the cool pillows. I hadn't even wiped the blood off my knuckles yet and I picked at the brown flaky mess as he held me.

"I did this, Chaz. Tonight was all my fault. My bravado because I wanted to do something by myself."

"But Hannah and Evan are fine, better. Kandice and Nash are stronger than ever."

"And I had to break my promise to Tucker that I would never ask him to do something against his morals. What makes it worse was that Peter saw it coming."

Chaz sighed, his breath cascading down my arm. "But I think the Willowbourne likes you."

"Really?"

His fingers ran softly up and down my arm. "She's hasn't left her circle since I've been working Dallas. Tonight was a big deal."

"Really?"

"It's how she survived. She hid."

I sighed. "I just can't help but think that Haverty might have had the right idea about keeping us hidden and the penalty that came with it."

Chaz sat up. "What?"

I huffed and shifted to a sitting position on the bed. "Calm down. I'm not saying that I'm going to go all tyrant. I'm saying that . . ."

What was I saying? That Haverty had to be a bastard because he didn't have others to help him? That he had to crack an iron whip because if he didn't, humans were being murdered all the time? Was I feeling sorry for the guy?

"I think I'm saying that I won't have to because I trust others. Which, according to Iris, is the last thing I should be doing."

"Iris?"

"Yeah. Gave me this big speech on how I needed to do this alone because it would be easier on everyone."

The information didn't sit well with Chaz and it weighed heavy across his brow.

I licked my lips. "I think with everything that's happened tonight, maybe, Iris and Haverty had the same problem."

"What was that?"

"They were alone."

Chaz smiled. "Say it again, fearless leader."

My skin goose bumped and again I made a choice, and the echo of it hung around us. "I think we need to unify Dallas."

Though Chaz was golden for a moment, his eyes turned dark. "Where does Spencer come into all this?"

Hearing Chaz say his name sent another shiver down my spine. "The others have to know. They need to know what he is capable of."

"Are you going to tell them about your connection?"

"Hopefully they already know, but I'm not going to keep it from them. Hell, maybe one of them knows how to break it."

Because I already knew a way to break it. I curled back into Chaz's arms and we lay back down on the bed. There was always a Plan C going round and round in my head. A plan that was guaranteed to break the bond.

CHAPTER 20

"*HERE ARE THE Harrison files, your double-shot macchiato, and the conference call is set up for speed dial on two," Pamela said as she set down the manila folders and his steaming hot coffee on his desk for the long evening ahead.*

Dylan barely looked up at her as he nodded his head. If he didn't nail this . . .

"Will there be anything else?" she asked, looking at the clock. It was already close to midnight and the dark seemed extra dark outside his tenth-floor window.

"I'm good," he said as he reached out for the paper cup.

Pamela pushed the paper cup within reach of his grasping fingers.

Dylan brought it to his lips without taking his eyes from the file he was flipping through.

"See you tomorrow then."

Pamela left and Dylan finally lifted his eyes off the files and watched his assistant walk out of his office.

"SO YOU CAN CLEARLY SEE by the figures this is the only way to go,"

Dylan spoke into his headset, kicking his heels up onto his desk and relaxing his hands behind his head.

The investors in Japan said they had to think about it until their next morning, but Dylan knew he had them, part of his sixth sense.

He would get the deal he had been working on for the past three months and he would get the promotion.

He took off the headset and picked up an empty coffee cup.

With a bank shot off the wall, he tossed the cup away and wondered if Pamela would be able to come with him when he moved to that corner office. She was just a temp, but the girl had skills, and those stockings with the stitches up the back of her long legs.

Dylan stood up and looked out of his office window. The skyline sparkled at the wee hours of the morning. He looked across the street at the iron-framed building covered in mirrors. He saw his building in its reflection and wondered whether, if he looked hard enough, he could see his own rising star.

He looked closely, trying to count the floors on the reflection to see if he could find his office.

The building before him exploded in a shower of glittering glass.

Dylan jumped back from his window as it too cracked under the force of the explosion. The edge of his desk caught him as he watched the rain of mirrors.

All Dylan could think was how much bad luck that would be.

AT THE THIRD ring of my cell phone, my heart was pounding. Some part of my brain had finally associated the chirpy sound of the standard ring tone as a precursor to death and danger.

Smart brain.

"Hello?" I scratched my head and yawned.

"If it isn't my favorite cousin." Waylon sounded far too chipper this morning.

"Are you calling me because you had a dream about the Infomart exploding?"

"No, I'm calling you because I'm on your porch and I wanted to make sure you were wearing pants."

I sighed and pulled the covers off my bare legs and slowly dropped my feet to the floor. Chaz hadn't stirred yet and I didn't want him to. Poor thing needed sleep like I needed more sleep.

Grabbing a pair of lounge pants off the back of a chair, I shuffled out the door of the bedroom and headed downstairs. "Why the hell are you on my doorstep at this unearthly hour?"

"Just dropped off Lexie at her first day of school."

I pulled on the pants in the living and looked down at Shadow, resting in his bed in the living room. He just shook his head and lay back down.

I ran my fingers through my hair in the mirror in the foyer, checked my teeth, and picked the sleep crusts from my eyes. "Which one did you pick?"

"The private Catholic one."

"So the soccer coach liked her?"

I opened the door and Waylon answered me face to face. "Loved her."

I dropped the phone from my ear and motioned for him to come in.

He followed me through the living room and into the kitchen. "I stopped by to make sure you got through the full moon okay. But should I be asking about your dream about Walmart?"

I groaned as I started making coffee. "Please don't. But can you confirm that you have not had a dream about the Infomart? Big building with lots of mirrors?"

Waylon put his hand up in a Boy Scout oath. "I have not. Why?"

I sighed. "Chaz has this theory that if real psychics only

dream about actual futures, then whatever I am might dream about possible futures."

"Who told him we don't dream of possible futures?"

I stopped and looked up at him. "He read it in some book."

"The book is wrong. I dream about all sorts of futures. Those history psychics only dream of past things, but the rest of us dream every possible angle of events."

I nodded. "Good to know that not all the crazy stuff in those books comes true." I started the process of measuring out the beans and suddenly got a hankering for Bastian's coffee cake.

"In your case, I think all of yours are linked to Dallas."

I frowned. I'd only told him maybe three of the dreams that I'd ever had. "What?"

"Well . . ."

There was a lie coming. I knew it. I could tell when his gaze floated somewhere to the left of my elbow. "If you dare make up some story, I'll know."

Waylon sighed and spoke fast, as if saying the truth faster would take the sting out of it, for him and me. "Lexie took your dream journal when she was at your place."

"What?" I spun around to glare at him and launched a half cup of coffee beans across the kitchen floor.

He danced backwards, missing the barrage. "I asked her to."

"What?" I shrieked. "Why? And why couldn't you just ask about it?"

"I wanted to prove my theory."

"About what? That you can't even trust your family?"

"That you are tied to Dallas." He reached around to the back of his pants and produced my dream journal.

"And you stuck my journal down your pants. Geez, Waylon."

I grabbed my journal from him and flipped through the pages. There were Post-its on a few of them, highlights. "This might actually be worse than when you read my diary in seventh grade."

"Your diary in seventh grade wasn't half as interesting as this one."

He then pulled a moleskin diary out from his back pocket. "Some of the dreams match. I've dreamt about Seth and Jesse."

"Who are Seth and Jesse?" I asked as I continued to look through my highlighted journal.

Waylon seemed to laugh. "You haven't figured out that one yet?"

"I dream in stories, Waylon. My brain is programmed for script writing. Complete with characters and a three act structure."

"Seth and Jesse are your sons."

I felt like he'd poured a cold glass of water down my back. "What?"

Waylon flipped through his book. At the beginning of his, he read out loud, "Seth saves Jesse from . . ."

"Stop," I said. "I have kids? Wait, don't tell me. I don't think I want to know." Me and Chaz had kids? And if we did, of course we would name them after his dad and my best friend.

"But I've dreamt of them. You've dreamt of them."

I had to suck in a breath to shake the chill of the future from my shoulders. "I've dreamt of possible futures, Waylon. Snippets of things that might be. I don't want . . ."

Waylon softened. "I get it. Not knowing is better than knowing, if it doesn't happen."

It was just too much. I was barely keeping it together with the pack, let alone two little me's running around the place. "Let's keep to the apocalyptic stuff though. Get to that."

Waylon flipped to another page. "You've only dreamt of Khalida once? I've dreamt of her a million times. Each time she's on a different side."

I hadn't written the Khalida dream down so I closed my eyes to see if I could find it again. "She wasn't exactly on Jovan's side but still running Dallas."

Waylon closed his book. "I've got a theory, but it's a long shot, nowhere near the box."

"Darling, I live outside the box. Shoot."

Waylon licked his lips and hands out wide before him, said "You dream of a possible future based on the decisions you're going to make."

"Huh?"

"What happened right after the Khalida dream?"

I had to think, which was hard without coffee, so I turned around to finish making the neurological agents. "We had an incident with Jane and then . . ."

"What?"

"We decided that we needed to unify Dallas?"

"Holy cow, Violet? Seriously?" Waylon leaned against the refrigerator.

Finally, the coffee started to brew. "How did you figure out this brilliant theory?"

Waylon beamed with pride. "Lexie actually. She had the idea after she read the one about her. Something about a pink prom dress."

"How did she feel about knowing the future?"

"A possible future," Waylon corrected. "She didn't like the pink dress. She would have chosen something different. Which was how she figured out that it was all about the choice. If you hadn't made the choice to let her in, she would have run away. There would have been no dress at all."

"She's my niece. There wasn't a choice."

"But there was. You could have just dropped her off and Lord knows that I would have preferred it that way, but you didn't. You followed the impeccable gut of yours and you showed her your family and invited her in. She saw the shotgun in your actual closet that I was carrying, according to the dream journal. So the theory goes, you dream the future of the choice you are about to make, but in how it is going to affect Dallas, or those around you."

The kitchen went silent as I let what Waylon was saying sink it. It was the most strangely specific magical talent ever. And I wondered if somehow Dallas was just like the coffee shop, a haven that had its own way of protecting and communicating.

It's also when I realized that the coffee had stopped percolating. I pulled down two mugs and poured the two cups. I poured in milk and sugar, stirred with the same spoon, and handed him a mug.

"The same with Khalida. You dreamt of a possible future where you didn't exist."

"No. A world where I existed and lost."

Waylon just shrugged. "And then right after, the decision was made to unify Dallas. Nullifying her taking over. I haven't had a dream about her since. Her ruling Dallas is no longer a possible future. These are not coincidences. We both know that coincidences rarely exist when it comes to us."

I gulped. "It's not a coincidence that I'm in Dallas."

Waylon hid his victory grin.

I gave him his story. "It was Jessa. And our foreseen connection that originally brought me here."

"And now the pack keeps you here."

I nodded. "And that whole fiancé thing."

My phone began to ring again. I sighed and answered it. "Good morning, Peter. Do you know what time it is?"

"It's done." His voice was clear without the resentment and gravel it usually had.

I set the coffee down on the counter before I dropped it. "Seriously?"

"You said when you got back to Dallas. Nine tonight, at the coffee shop. Each head will bring a second and I will moderate."

My stomach tightened. I'd thought I'd have a few more days

to write all those speeches and maybe watch *Braveheart* for some inspiration.

"Oh and here's the kicker. Valiance, the second of the vampires, confessed to breaking into your house, looking for the grimoire to break the marks. I told them that if they hadn't tried to behead us, we might have shared the information sooner."

Well, that was a nice little tie-up for loose ends. It boded well for the evening. "You are amazing, Peter Delmont."

"A wolf is only as strong as his pack, Prima Jordan." His words were serious, but I could hear the smile on his lips.

"Have you told Bastian that he'll need to close up early?"

"I left that honor for you."

"Lovely. I'll see you tonight then."

Peter hung up and I set the phone back down.

I looked at Waylon and wondered if he already knew. So many questions ran around my head as to how he worked. "Guess I'm doing it all tonight."

Waylon's eyebrows jumped. "Tonight? Already?"

"Yep. I have one hell of a lawyer."

Waylon frowned as he sipped his coffee. "How come I didn't get a call?"

I frowned into my cup. "I asked for the heads."

"I'm the head of the only psychic family in town."

"We don't know that."

He shrugged at the details. "I'm still going."

"Don't make trouble for me, Waylon."

Waylon set his mug down on the counter. "I'm serious about this. I have a vested interest in the survival of not only this city but of my cousin. I want to be there."

I looked at him. Really looked at him. Would the others believe he was another head? Or would they see it as me stacking the deck? But he was the most powerful psychic in the city, since . . .

"Fine," I said.

Waylon actually let out a woo-hoo.

"Isn't it too early for woo-hoos?" Chaz asked from the kitchen door.

He nodded to Waylon and went to get himself a cup of coffee. He'd pulled on his pajama bottoms but hadn't checked his hair in the mirror.

"Peter has set up the meeting of the heads," I said.

"Boy works fast."

"Man is very capable. Waylon has invited himself."

Chaz leaned against the counter next to me. "I suppose it is your party. What time do we leave? I've got some errands I need to take care of today. Some things I need to move in."

"I'm not sure there is a *we*."

Waylon quietly put his coffee mug on the counter and slipped out of the kitchen.

That gorgeous furrow appeared between Chaz's eyes. "Violet?"

"I'm not sure how it's going to look with me coming in all posse'd up."

He shrugged. "Then I won't go in as your posse."

"I'm pretty sure they know we're together."

"I'll go as the only Guardian left in the city. If you want all the species represented, I'm going."

I sighed.

Waylon stuck his head in the kitchen door. "He's got a point. He is the only identified Guardian in the city."

I put my hands on my hips. "I'm not letting you two bully me. Family or not."

"I'm not. I'm protecting my interests in Dallas." Chaz repeated exactly what Waylon had just said.

My gaze darted to Waylon. "You two planned this."

"No, but I might have known what he was going to say." Waylon winked.

"You're an ass." I pointed at Waylon. "And you"—I turned to Chaz—"I suppose that you're going to throw that whole *you've-been-sent-by-the-Mother-to-protect-me*, so by the gods you're going to protect me."

"No. I'm just going to pretty up the place." He smiled and leaned over to kiss my forehead.

"Waylon, go mess up someone else's morning."

Waylon disappeared from the kitchen doorway. "See you later, fearless leader."

I waited to hear the front door close to speak again.

"What did he want this early?"

I hopped up on the counter and pulled the pancake mix from the cabinet and handed it to Chaz. He smiled and took it. As he was getting out the supplies to make breakfast, I filled him in on Lexie's insight that not only was I connected to Dallas, but that I was dreaming in futures based on my decisions.

Chaz stopped. "So you were right about dreaming of possible Dallas futures."

"I was half right. I would have never thought that they were the futures of the choices that I was about to make."

"It does seem a little twisted," Chaz said as he began to flip the pancakes.

"Also I'm going to be obsessed with trying to figure out what choice I make today that ends with the Infomart getting blown to smithereens."

His eyebrows jumped with surprised but settled back down. "But it's not the worst that's been thrown at you, Vi. You'll overcome this task, just like you've overcome all the others."

"But not without help."

Chaz just shrugged. "Doesn't matter. You've taken on everything that the Mother has thrown at you. These heads are going to be no problem."

He flipped two fresh pancakes onto a plate and handed it to me.

I slid off the counter and went to sit at the kitchen bistro set.

He joined me with two more pancakes. The sun danced in his golden highlights and made his eyelashes even longer and darker.

"Why are you looking at me?" he asked, mouth full of pancake.

"Did you really believe eight months ago, you'd still be making me pancakes?"

He finished chewing. "I knew that I'd be making you pancakes for the rest of our lives."

"Awww."

"WHAT SHOULD I WEAR?" I asked Jessa. "What says I'm like-able but I could totally kick your ass if I needed to?"

"Boots and ruffles," Jessa said as she sat down on my bed.

"Ruffles? Do I even have ruffles?" I started to shuffle through my closet. My eyes had started to hurt from the marathon of political movies I'd been fast-forwarding through. The only thing I learned was that it took great speeches and war paint to win the day. And I was fresh out of both.

"You have the green top we bought last fall."

I turned toward her. "Do you have a complete catalogue of my entire wardrobe?"

"And?" she asked. "You remember every book and movie. I remember shopping trips."

"Touché," I answered as I turned back to the closet.

Bastian had been particularly compliant when I'd asked him to close up shop a bit early tonight. I promised I'd leave the place as I found it if he promised to leave an iced mocha in the fridge for me.

"So what is the plan?"

I found the top that Jessa was talking about. It was this green gauzy thing, but it had her ruffle criteria, and if she knew nothing else about the universe, Jessa knew how to look the part. If she said ruffles, ruffles it was.

I grabbed a tank top from my dresser and started getting changed. "Plan A. Tell them everything. What we know about the Neveranth, Spencer, Jovan. Jeez, Jessa. They didn't even know how to kill a Shade."

"And plan B? When the others are completely happy being on their own?"

"Then they can be on their own as I go after Spencer."

"Go after Spencer? That's not a Plan B, that's a Plan Dead."

"No. It's a Plan B. If the other heads don't want to join forces, then we are going after Spencer, just the pack. If we can't unify Dallas, we can defend it."

Jessa slipped off the bed and to her feet. Maybe this was the one thing that she had gotten from me, needed to deal with things on her feet. "That's a pretty big Plan B."

I zipped up my jeans and grabbed the green top. "He's getting stronger, Jessa. Every day. But I'm getting stronger, too. One of these days, it's going to happen. And I want it to be on my terms."

"And how exactly were you going to go after him?"

"With your magic, Nash's spells, and a really, really big sword."

Jessa's hands clenched at her sides. "And you just assumed that I would go along with this. With a plan that uses you as bait to get him across."

"No. I assumed you would tell me no."

"Then why did you say my magic?"

"Because it's better than my Plan C."

I walked over to the door and shut it. Goose bumps traveled down my arms but it was Jessa's fear that put them there. I sat down on the bed and looked up at her. "Plan C is you send me across, and I do it myself."

My stomach tightened as her energy spiked out and her lips parted. "Violet, no, I mean . . ."

"Try to tell me that you never thought it was going to be Panther Thunderdome."

Jessa shook her head. "No. He's on the other side. He can't get out of there."

"Like that snake thing couldn't get out of there, like the holes aren't all over the place. The Veil isn't strong enough and it's not your fault. The Veil is weak because Dallas is weak."

I reached out and took her hand. I opened my borders and let my magnolia-scented power surround her. "I'm not saying this happens today. I'm still all for Plan A. We go full United Nations of Wanderers and it strengthens the Veil and Plan B and C are moot points."

Jessa licked her lips.

"I'm guessing your silence is more than acquiescence."

"You're talking about Dallas like it's a living thing. It's a little crazy."

I swallowed. "Well, I'm connected to it. We both are. Doesn't it make sense? You're called to Dallas. I get attacked here and end up finding this insane calling where I'm dreaming about Dallas constantly."

"Is that the new dream set? First, fairy tales about princesses and now you're dreaming of I–35?"

I smiled. Jokes were good. Jokes meant she was still on the Violet wavelength.

Jessa looked down at my bedspread. Her hand was still in mine.

And then she made a choice. I felt it stir in the air between us, tighten the silver bonds that held us together as Key Holder and Keeper.

Her lavender eyes landed on mine. "I will be the perfect fairy princess to convince these heads they need to unify because I am neither throwing your ass in or dragging your ass out of the Neveranth."

I smiled all the way down to my toes. I jumped up and wrapped my arms around her. She squeezed back.

"And then you can get to planning that wedding." I let her go and looked down at her. "I want to do it in August."

"Finally, a date I can work with. Is there any way I can talk you out of that barn idea?"

"Nope. The barn stays."

CHAPTER 21

I COULDN'T STOP moving. I'd rearranged the tables in the coffee shop into a neat circle with two chairs at every table. I'd put out brownies on white porcelain plates with the cloth napkins that Bastian kept under the counter for special occasions. I'd even put out little glasses of water on the tables. Isn't that how the UN meetings I'd watched on CNN were set up? Little glasses of water?

"I didn't know she organizes when she's nervous," Tucker whispered to Chaz.

"Neither did I."

I turned to glare at the both of them. "Everything has to be perfect."

"Trust me. This is fine."

I jumped when the bells of the front door announced the first visitors. Jessa and Kurt swept through the front door but stopped as they looked around at the empty room.

Jessa sighed. "I wanted to make an entrance."

"Looked good to me," I offered.

Kurt the Cleaner walked over to me in his perfectly cut suit and gave me two air kisses. "How are you, darling?" he asked.

"Lovely. You?"

"I'm always perfect." His eyes flicked over to the boys behind me. "Is this Stalker Boy?"

I smiled. It had been a while since I'd heard Chaz's other moniker. "Let me introduce you."

MY STOMACH CHURNED when I looked around the room. Though I knew everyone in the circle, it was still an impressive bunch. Inez brought my sensei as her second and I bowed respectfully to him before he gave me grief for not visiting the dojo.

I laughed. "I've been getting in my practice, but I'll try to get back to my regular schedule."

They took a seat and I watched carefully as my sensei greeted Chaz with almost the same respect that he greeted me. With our recent foray into Chaz's past, I wondered if Chaz knew that Sensei was one of the people Seth freed from Jovan's hold, if he could see the ripple effect of his father's actions like I could.

Willowbourne floated in, her green cape fluttering around her, and Twila peeked out from behind her.

"Prima Jordan. It is good to see you again," she said with a deep sweeping bow.

I had to squeeze my nails into my palm to keep from laughing as I watched Twila's eye roll behind her.

"Mom, you're good. Can we sit down?"

Willowbourne nodded and headed for one of the other tables. I stopped Twila with a brief touch on the shoulder. "That's your mother?"

"Unfortunately."

The reason the Willowbourne came to our rescue so easily became crystal clear. She did it for Twila. Because if anything happened to Remy, her daughter would be destroyed. What wouldn't a mother do for her daughter?

My slightly morbid thoughts were distracted by a sudden chill in the room. The two vampires looked like pale statues in the moonlit doorway.

"Good to see you again, Valiance. Please come in."

His light blue eyes stayed on mine as he walked toward me. "Prima. I'd like to introduce you to our new Clade Seat, Andrin."

Andrin swept my hand and brushed his cool lips against my knuckles. I didn't flinch, because I had the distinct feeling this was their brushing, their test of character. So I brushed him back and he felt like a wall of ice before me.

His Aegean blue eyes rose to mine and a smile flicked across his lips. "Pleasure to meet you, Prima Jordan."

I felt like the air had been sucked out of the room for a moment before my Legacy seemed to fill the void between us. "You as well. Please take a seat."

His cool hand slid from mine and I watched Inez's entire body tense as he walked past her and took the last table across the room.

The last but not the least to arrive was Waylon, with Lexie in tow. I met them at the door.

I made sure to hug Lexie before I scolded her father. "Why did you bring her here? She can't be here."

"You're the only babysitter I know."

"She's twelve. She can stay home by herself."

"That's what I said." Lexie rolled her eyes.

I put my arms around her small shoulders and gave her a tight squeeze.

"Not tonight." Waylon frowned.

There was something in the way he said it that made my spine feel like hollow bones rattling. I looked down at Lexie. "Do you feel comfortable staying with Nash and Kandice?"

"Yeah. I bet I can make him do my homework."

I looked back at Lexi and handed her my phone. "Call Nash."

I shut the door of the coffee shop and turned toward my guests. "Shall we begin?"

My heels knocked across the wooden floor as I took a seat next to Chaz. "You all have introduced yourselves."

I placed my nervous hands on the table before me. I'd even wiped the tabletops down. Who's the stress cleaner now?

"I hope Mr. Delmont explained I am not trying any sort of political power play. I simply want to know that we can work together."

"Because of Haverty," Valiance said.

"Because of the ghouls?" Inez asked.

"Because of the rednecks?" Willowbourne asked.

I sighed. It was nice to be not once, but three times reminded that I am not made of awesome. "Yes," I answered simply. "It does seem there are new sorts of chaos abounding in Dallas."

"Then maybe someone does need to step up to the plate," Andrin said.

"Says the man whose been Clade Seat, for what, an hour?" Inez shot back.

I looked over at Inez and watched Sensei put his hand on her arm.

I licked my lips and realized the utter relief and the time that it gave me to think. "I believe at this critical junction all of us are passionate about keeping our people safe and would be willing to do anything to keep them that way. Personally, I'm good with a pack right now, but we can't isolate ourselves."

"Why not?" Willowbourne asked. "Seems to work in other cities."

"But it doesn't," Chaz said. "Every city has their own way of doing things. Mostly, it means there is a dominant breed, and the others just scurry around scared."

The others seemed to take Chaz's words into consideration. I wanted to beam like a proud dance mom, but I just nudged him with my foot before I went on. "I'm simply proposing we share what we know about common foes."

"Going with the enemy of my enemy approach?" Andrin's black eyebrow arched over his ice blue eyes.

"The logic seems sound."

I looked around the room and decided that leading by example might also be a good approach. "I'll go first. The Shades that have attacked a few of us can be killed by letting them feed, and then you can chop their heads off. And with a little electricity, they ash just like those . . ."

Chaz reached under the table and squeezed my knee and I shut up. Probably shouldn't talk about the fictional death of vampires when there were actual vampires in the room. Good save Chaz.

"We were attacked as well," Willowbourne said. "Prima Jordan's information saved our lives."

"Seems you all are getting very cozy, but I still don't see anything to tempt me to share," Andrin said. "And frankly it appears to me you are the epicenter of all the violence in the city, Miss Jordan."

My jaw would have dropped in shock if it wasn't clenched tight with the accusation. I met his eyes, but years of script writing didn't give me any fodder for a rebuttal.

Peter rescued me. "The violence was here, embedded in the lives of those who didn't have a choice but Haverty. And yes, she does have to fight. She puts herself out there so we can be safe."

"She doesn't hide away in some hole and let her lackeys do all the work."

My head snapped toward Inez. There was that bitterness, that deep-seated anger I knew was in her. I couldn't blame her for it. Was that the story behind the scars on her neck? And what possible future had I prevented that had me dreaming of her burning a warehouse to the ground?

"I think Andrin just needs to learn how we do things in Dallas," I said calmly as my eyes stayed on Inez.

"We fight to protect our family," Willowbourne said.

"We protect what we have built." Inez sat up straighter in her chair. "At all costs."

"And we will face what's coming, together." Waylon finally spoke.

I looked over at Andrin and let my green gaze sink into his. "And I'd like to think some day we will fight to protect each other. But again, not mandating it be today."

Andrin was the one who shifted as he looked away and I couldn't help but see a curl to Valiance's lips.

I wanted to smile. A part of me wanted to jump up and squeal with joy that finally something was working out and it was going to be amazing. We were here. Sitting together with some knowledge of calm settling around me.

"Great. Now that's out of the way . . ."

And then the front wall of the coffee shop exploded.

The force lifted me up and threw me across the café. I landed hard on a table and slid off onto my side. Splinters and glass rained down and I curled my head into my arm and waited for it to stop.

When I heard boot steps on the broken glass, I shook off the rubble and stood, but stumbled, thrown off balance by the ringing in my ears.

A blast of icy air picked me up and tossed me into the corner where I usually took my meetings. My head cracked against the wall and I broke every picture frame on my way down to the ground.

The only thought that slipped through my concussed brain was who would be stupid enough to attack the most powerful Wanderers in the city.

An acidic aroma filled the room and my skin tightened around my bones as my power flared. Spencer. He was here, watching, infecting from the other side. Damn thing was as powerful as Jovan now.

I pushed myself to my feet and my power reached out for Jessa, Tucker, and Peter while my eyes searched out Waylon and Chaz. Slowly, the others rose from the wreckage, shaking off pieces from the explosion. Chaz looked beyond pissed as he wiped blood from his lip.

Inez stood calmly in the middle of a fire facing me. The fire seemed like an upside-down cape that started at her boots and flicked up around her shoulders. She'd done this? She'd invited Spencer into this?

"Seriously?" I asked as I stepped over what was left of my table.

A cool trickle of blood slipped down the back of my head and neck. It was going to ruin that pretty green top Jessa had suggested.

I dropped my shields and let the Legacy stretch as far as I could. It spread through the coffee shop and out onto the street.

The power echoed back the information that I needed. There were eight elementals surrounding the place. When they felt my study, five appeared in the broken front window of the shop. "Eight against eight, exactly a fair fight."

"Seven against nine, Prima Jordan," Sensei said as he pushed himself up from the rubbish. "I pledged myself to you before this girl."

I turned to Inez. "You've got one hell of a story to tell if you want to make it out of this walking."

"I'm not doing anything that you wouldn't do."

She didn't have to speak. I knew. I knew because I would do anything to protect my people. She thought she'd chosen the more powerful side. She thought she had to do this alone and she'd gone for the voice in her head that promised the power to be able to do it alone. It was too much of a pattern, just like Iris had said.

Well the pattern was going to stop here. Now.

"Did Spencer at least throw in a set of kitchen knives with the deal he offered?"

A line of fire ran around the floor, encircling the nine of us. The curtains caught fire and Jessa jumped as it circled too close to her.

Tucker quickly stepped between her and the flames. And the two manly vampires jumped onto the black counter of the coffee bar. Apparently, vampires really don't like fire.

My eyes went back to Inez and the whiff of Spencer's influence made my anger flare. "What was it?" I yelled.

"My people are safe. It's what we all want. What he offered all of us."

I gasped. My eyes darted from Andrin to Willowbourne to Waylon.

"I had a dream," Waylon said as he held his hand to his eyebrow to keep the blood from his forehead gash from running into his eye. "He knew about Lexie, talked about how I needed more people to protect her, more than just her aunt."

"And if you worked for him, she would be safe?" I filled in the rest of the promise.

Waylon nodded. "With the implied consequences if I didn't."

"What happened?" I asked.

"I woke up and I fixed Lexie breakfast and I took her to school."

I smiled. He really was related to me, with his ability to be calm in the face of danger.

"Seems none of us were without temptation." Willowbourne pulled her cape closer around her. There was a sharp snap of ozone in the air and rain began to softly pitter-pat around us.

Inez laughed. "Rain, really?"

The flames burned brighter around us, forcing the nine of us closer together.

"And what comes with rain?" Willowbourne asked.

A white streak of lightning shot out of Willowbourne's hand and struck Inez in the chest. Her body flew back, through the place where the door use to me and out into the street.

That's when the others attacked. Six against nine. I figured I had a second to reorganize the troops. I rushed over to Waylon. "You need to get out. Now."

"No, Violet, I . . ."

I grabbed his face and forced his eyes to mine. "I will not be responsible for making Lexie another orphan, Waylon Jordan."

Waylon simply nodded and he did something he hadn't done in fifteen years. He kissed my forehead. "I love you, kitten."

Waylon ran. He jumped over the rubble and ran like a man with his pants on fire.

I smiled. He was going to be okay. He was going to be okay, and I was about to grind Inez's face into the concrete with these lovely yet comfortable boots that Jessa helped me pick out.

I stepped over pieces of my favorite couch and the magazine rack from beside the door. "Tucker, how long until the police come?"

Tucker looked up from where he was pummeling either Cheech or Chong. "Four minutes."

"Not going to need that long."

I walked out through the window, my long legs clearing the frame easily. Inez was on her back on the sidewalk.

I walked toward her slowly. "I just don't understand. Why him? Hell, I could have taken better care of you than him. At least I'm in the same zip code."

Inez looked up at me, the fire's light burning in her eyes. There was a charred mark on her shirt and if she had been human, she wouldn't have been breathing.

"He's more powerful than you."

"I don't care how powerful he is. He won't win."

Inez pushed herself up to her feet and I let her. It would be more fun to knock her down again.

"You've betrayed your people."

"He will protect them."

"Aww. Did he promise you champagne wishes and caviar dreams? It's crap, Inez. Everything he says is crap. I should know."

"You don't know, Violet." Inez rolled up the sleeve of her jacket and I saw a freshly carved mark on her forearm. The Demon Lock.

My Legacy flared around me, fueled by the anger at this vat of stupidity before me. She'd bonded herself to Spencer.

It made the bile in my stomach burn. "He's been in my head, in my dreams. I know him. I know his ambition and exactly what he's capable of. He will not protect you. He certainly can't protect you from me."

The magic of my panther ran down my spine, eased by the frustration at such a powerful woman being seduced by him. I shifted down into my panther form just as she threw a fireball where my head had been. The smell of singed hair was sharp as it filled my nose.

I leapt at her and she put up a wall of fire. I flew through it and we tumbled to the ground as I hit her straight in the chest. She fell back with me on top, claws digging into her jacket. She landed hard on the ground, the impact jolting her teeth, and I looked down into her fiery eyes.

Her magic filled her, and fire spread from her fingers down her arms and covered her entire body.

I sprung from her chest and landed a few feet away, the hair on my legs still smoldering. I defaulted to the only fire prevention I knew. I rolled on the ground until I was sure that I wasn't smoking anymore.

Only to have to leap over another fireball, and then another. This was a little harder than a wind elemental with a death wish.

This felt like she was playing with me. Little fireballs. I'd seen this woman burn down a warehouse and walk away unharmed.

This was a distraction. We were dancing around something bigger.

I shifted on the other side of my car in its rock-star parking spot right out front like I'd asked for. From the smell of completely melted leather seats, it looked like my car had been the source of the explosion, and it still smoldered. Poor Miata.

"What are you keeping me from, Inez?" I asked stretched my neck, kneeling behind the car. My jacket was singed down the arms and my jeans were covered in ash. This was my favorite jacket. It was my power jacket, and these jeans made my ass look amazing.

Now I was pissed.

I rose just as she pushed the fire at me. It seemed to start at her shoulders, burn down her arms, and extended out through her hand as she aimed at me.

I stayed still and just put up my borders. Rock hard, a foot thick and cool as a cucumber, my power wrapped around me and I felt the heat from the fire as it flew around me but didn't touch me.

Then I smiled. Peter said that I could do it. That was a new trick for the books.

When the blast was over, I used the door of my desecrated Miata to leap over the car and land before her. Surprise filled her eyes before I wrapped my power around the two of us.

I let the Legacy swirl around us, and as much as she pulled for her power, it couldn't reach her through mine. Still a foot thick, I let it close around us and the sounds of the fire and the brawl faded away.

While my power suppressed hers, I let my words break her. "We could have been amazing, Inez. Two angry orphans protecting their families. Now I'm going to have to protect your people because you couldn't."

I curled my hand behind her neck and landed a balled fist into her solar plexus. Inez crumpled. And with a throat chop to her scarred neck, Inez fell to my feet, unconscious.

As I looked down at her, I dropped the swirling wall of power around us. It was harsh. I knew it. But she had made her choice. She'd ended up on the wrong side of my line in the sand. There was a sickening thought, and it churned my stomach. It really was my way or the highway.

No. It was my way or Spencer's way. I looked up at the others who had their elementals pinned or down for the count. I was wrong again. It was our way, or the highway.

Sensei walked up to me. He had a smudge of ash down his forehead and a twinkle in his dark eyes. "That was an excellent execution."

"Not the best word choice right now."

"She will be fine, Prima Jordan."

"As long as it's not today." I started toward the rest of my pack.

They were all fine. Bruised but better for it. There was a fire in their eyes, and it had nothing to do with the still smoldering coffee shop.

"We've got about forty-five seconds before we get company," Tucker said.

I was just about to suggest that we regroup when pain filled Jessa's eyes and she reached out for me. I barely had time to catch her before she hit the ground. The moment I took her hand I knew what had happened.

The words Jessa forced out hurt as she dug her fingers into my arm as she gasped for breath. I felt it too, like a dagger dragged through my gut. And I actually know what that feels like.

"There's been another sacrifice to the Veil."

"Why does it hurt so much?" I whispered to her.

"The more powerful you get, the more powerful I get. I've told you this like a million times."

I smiled. If she was dogging on me about this, she was going to be fine.

Jessa was the one who moved to stand. I helped where I could but did not interfere when she reached out to Tucker to keep her standing.

I looked around at the others. This semicircle of mismatched creatures, flushed from the fight, eyes still burning with their power.

"It does seem that trouble follows you," Andrin said as he ran his fingers through his long black hair, creating that still perfection again. Like he hadn't just been dodging fireballs with the rest of us.

"Well, now you know that I didn't lie about anything. She didn't target me. She targeted us. She wanted all of us gone."

I heard sirens coming down the street. I pointed to the other side of a fence. And remarkably enough, everyone followed.

"I'll give us a bubble," Willowbourne said. "They won't be able to see us."

As she worked, I turned to the rest of the group. "This is your moment. I'm going in. I can't let Spencer get free. He's too powerful. Even if it's not Spencer, it's big."

"Do enjoy your evening, Miss Jordan." Andrin turned and walked down the street with a swagger that could have made any girl drool. If that girl didn't think he was a complete coward.

Valiance stayed. It looked like he planted himself on the concrete and forced his eyes to me and not his Clade Seat.

"You really ready to do that? I asked. "He is your leader."

Valiance winced and I looked over his shoulder to see Andrin glaring at us. "I'll live."

"I think I will respectfully bow out," Kurt said. "We are not fighters, but if you need us, we are ever at your service."

I nodded. "I might need to redecorate this place after it stops burning."

Kurt bowed and stepped away from the circle.

A shimmer covered the space around us, and the night grew a little quieter and the air stilled, like she'd put a glass cake dome over the small circle of us.

Willowbourne joined the conversation. "I'm in. I'll bring the whole Coven if I need to. Except Twila."

"Mom," Twila whined.

"You are the heir to the Coven, Twila. I need to secure an heir."

Twila actually stomped.

Willowbourne just raised a red eyebrow and there was something exchanged between them that made Twila drop her eyes. Her mother looked back up to me. "What do you need?"

I looked to Chaz and Jessa.

"Nothing special to mirror magic, except for the mirror," Jessa said.

I looked to Chaz. He hitched his thumb over his shoulder. "I've got everything in the back of my car."

"Got a sword in there?" Valiance asked.

"Broadsword, katana, rapier? Iron or steel?" Chaz shot back.

Valiance nodded. "I'm good then."

I was still awestruck. "Um. If we are going to make this stick, I'll need the Haverty knife. It's the only thing that I know will kill him."

Twila practically jumped. "Oh, I can get it."

I shook my head. "No it's—"

"Actually, she *can* get it," Willowbourne said.

Twila wriggled to the middle of the circle of grown-ups. She put out her hand. "Just think about where it is, really hard."

I took a deep breath. We were wasting time but showing trust like this could secure the Willowbourne on our side for good. God, I was even thinking like a politician now.

I slipped my hand into Twila's and looked into her emerald green eyes. I thought as hard as I could about the knife and where I'd hidden it in the wall behind my washing machine up as far as my monkey arms could get it.

Twila smiled. "You're good."

Her eyes took on the same stormy appearance as her mother's had and the cool spell crept up my arm. Twila reached into the pocket of her hoodie and pulled out the Haverty blade.

I jumped back and broke our connection.

The girl simply held it out before her. "Ta da!"

"Holy cow," I said as I stared at the thin blade.

"Is that the actual one?" Chaz asked.

"From behind your washer," Twila answered.

"Guess there is only one way to find out." I reached out for the blade and touched the flashing edge. The silver burned my skin, and I snapped my hand back and shook the pain away. "Sure enough."

Chaz took the knife and I smiled down at Twila. "That was amazing."

Willowbourne put her hand on her daughter's shoulder as she addressed me. "I would appreciate if you didn't tell many people. It's a powerful skill and—"

Already, my brain was thinking of all the kick-ass things I could do with that power, the simplest being I'd never be without a pencil. "Secret's safe."

Willowbourne nodded. "Now Twila. If Prima Jordan doesn't require his assistance, I'd like you to go to Remy's."

"Thank you, Twila. Tell Remy to set the stones tonight."

Twila gulped as the grown-ups watched her draw a circle in the gravel of the parking lot with the toe of her tennis shoe and vanish with nothing more than a twinkle of light and the smell of ozone.

"I was not sure about Remy, but if he is one of yours, then she is better with him."

I nodded. "He really is a good kid. I promise."

"Do we need to call in the troops?" Tucker asked. "Nash will kill you if he's not here."

"I want all who will come." I turned to Peter. "Except you. I want you safe."

Peter's jaw turned to steel. "No, Violet. I want to help you."

"I need a second line of defense. Go to Waylon. He'll know if you'll need to get the other Wanderers together. If you need to call in the Cause."

Chaz's hand rested on my shoulder. "Aren't you being a little dramatic?"

"No, I'm being prepared. Plan A worked; I want to make sure Plans B, and C, and D are good to go, because I'm not letting Spencer's feet touch Dallas soil."

Peter's blue eyes searched mine and I took hold of his hands. "I have faith in you."

He opened his mouth and closed it again, then opened it again.

I smiled. "Have I actually struck a lawyer speechless?"

"No." He fought the smile on his lips. "I'll call Devin and get him ready for incoming casualties."

I warmed all the way down to my toes and smiled. "Thank you, Peter."

Peter left the circle at a slight jog.

The street behind us was filling with police cars and fire trucks. "Okay. Let's go."

I led the six of us away from the fire. The whole front of the building was up in flames now. Poor Miata. Didn't see that one coming.

The elementals were being taken away in ambulances and the firefighters were already preparing the hoses to fight the flames.

People were starting to gather to watch the flames. We had to look suspicious as we fled the scene, a ghostly pale blond man, a woman in a green cape, and a six-foot-tall woman with a burnt jacket.

Maybe it was Willowbourne's spell still wrapped around us.

Maybe it was the dazzling display of the storefront burning against the night sky. Or maybe it was simply that the fair citizens of Dallas just were not ready to deal with vampires, witches, and shifters.

CHAPTER 22

"ARE YOU SERIOUS?" I asked as we looked up at the Kessler Theater. "Isn't he dramatic enough?"

The Kessler was an old movie house that had been recently resurrected. It had history, which unfortunately made it a perfect place for a rip in the Veil.

Fourteen of us stood outside, about a block away, looking at the neon sign that lit up the neighborhood. This was the first front. Tyler and Nash had gathered Kandice and the Fang sisters.

Willowbourne had called in two other witches. It was odd to see her pull a cell phone from the folds of her green cape, but the others came. Sensei looked small and humble in his nice dojo T-shirt and his usual practice pants. And Valiance looked like the cover of a romance novel with his blue eyes and white blond hair in the moonlight.

"What's the plan?" Tucker asked.

I looked to Chaz. "Should we go with the usual?"

"Seems to work."

Chaz rubbed his hands together. "Okay. We split into three groups. Violet goes in the front all willy-nilly and—"

"Willy-nilly?" I asked.

"You know, with your power all out and scary. And I'll lead a group in through the sides and I'll meet you in the middle."

It was as good a plan as any.

"Anyone else?" I asked.

"I'll put a spell around the perimeter, make it like tar to pass through, should keep the net small," Willowbourne offered. "But it's going to prevent help from coming as well."

"I think the shifters should go in together. Just to keep the element of surprise when the rest of us show up," Valiance put in.

"That's sort of brilliant," I said. "Why aren't you Clade Seat?"

"About a hundred years too young." He shrugged as he went to the back of Chaz's car to arm himself.

The others prepared. Tucker stretched. Nash took off his shoes. Jessa checked her lip gloss in her compact.

As I was reaching down for my own shoes, Chaz pulled me aside. There was a little extra furrow in his brow and a little extra power glowing in his golden eyes. "I don't want you to do anything stupid in there, Violet."

I reached up to hold his cheek, feel that perpetual stubble under my palm. "You know I can't promise that."

Chaz smiled. He slid his hand around my waist and pulled me close. His entire body was tense, hard. He pulled my other hand to his chest and if it was anyone else in the world, I would have said that it was shaking. "But after this, we are getting married."

"Wasn't anything stopping us before."

"Yes, there was. Always has been. You've got the biggest unfinished business I've ever heard of. We finish this. We get married and I take you on the longest honeymoon known to man and Wanderer alike."

My eyes teared up. It was the last thing that I needed right now, to cry in front of the new recruits. "I like the way you think, Mr. Garrett."

He leaned down to kiss me. A good luck kiss, and it tasted like honey.

"Get a room," Jessa hollered.

Chaz pulled away and looked down at me. "I'll be with the other."

"I'll meet you in the middle."

He flashed a quick smile and kissed me on the nose before he pushed me toward the troops. I pulled away from my golden-hearted fiancé and turned back toward the others, still enjoying the good luck taste of him on my lips.

Tyler had tossed his shirt. It really was just for show. "Really wishing you had worked on that 'Roll Out' line, aren't you?" Tyler said as he popped his neck.

I laughed. It's what I needed right now to release the tension between my shoulder blades, which would only make it harder to shift later. And Tyler knew that. He saw what we all needed to be better versions of ourselves.

"We could just say, 'I'll be right back,' " I offered.

Nash rolled his eyes. "Because that works out well in the movies."

Willowbourne joined us. "We have a saying. May the ground support your steps and the wind be at your back."

"I like it. May the ground support your steps . . ."

"And the wind be at your back," they echoed back.

And with their words came a sharp rededication of their promise to me. Without another thought, I pushed my power out to them, making my pack stronger and faster for this fight.

They were going to need it.

THE GLASS DOORS to the theater were unlocked and I wondered what had been done to get this place this quiet at only eleven o'clock at night. The foyer was dark and smelled like ancient cigarettes and popcorn. The Shifters were close at my back as we listened to the emptiness in this part of the theater.

"Be careful. We have no idea who's here," I whispered as we slowly made our way across the space and to the main theater door. "It could be that it's not Spencer, just another Bigger."

I shivered at the thought of the ghouls again. I really didn't want to deal with ghoul guts again. I'd take a giant snake any day.

Carefully, I looked through the porthole window of the main hall. There was a spotlight on the stage, but the rest of the room was dark. Not just dark, but pitch black, like all the light had been sucked out of the rest of the room and tossed onto the stage.

A man in a sharp suit stood next to a mirror, preening himself. Running his fingers through blond hair that was longer than I last remembered, as the suit stretched across shoulders that seemed bigger than the last time.

I growled and the knot of tension between my shoulder blades turned into steel.

Spencer.

"Keep calm, Violet. It's fourteen against—"

"Against Shades," Nash said from the window of the other door. "Looks like he's been collecting an army on the other side."

I focused on the darkness. It was squirming. I jumped away from the door and pressed myself against the carpeted walls behind me.

"More than likely, they won't hurt us. He won't let them. He'll want that honor himself," Tucker said. I saw his knuckles go white as he gripped the trench knife.

Sometimes I forgot what Spencer had done to them, the mind control, the slow mental torture. That this was as much their fight as it was mine. Their fight to officially separate them-selves from that dark time in their lives. They had unfinished business here too.

"Let's get in there," Praline said, a hot pink stun gun in her manicured hand and a bone-handled bowie knife attached to a custom pink leather belt around her tiny waist.

Lucy nodded in agreement. "We only paid the babysitter until midnight."

I looked up at Tucker. "All willy-nilly?"

"Worked last time."

I kicked off the wall and faced the door. With one deep breath, I dropped all of the shields I had around me. It enveloped the eight of us and my pack relaxed. We could do this.

I pushed through the swinging door and was met with the acrid smell of Spencer and the coppery smell of blood. Of course, there had to be blood.

Spencer turned around at the center of the stage, and even from the back of the room, I could see that the other side had not been kind. His beard was grizzled and covered a new scar down the left side of his face. But his navy blue eyes were still the same.

"Dearest sister." His voice was still the same. The same smooth tone filled with confidence and ill will. "You look ravishing."

I flashed a quick smile as I walked toward the stage. "I do try."

What I couldn't see out of the corners of my eyes, I could feel. My pack fed me information through the connection of our power. The darkness didn't hide the Shades. The darkness was the Shades. And he had shipped in helpers. Bodies lined the edge of the theater. Someone had to perform the ritual, but in the one second, I glanced away from him to study them, I could tell it was all him behind their dead eyes.

Full-on possession of others. He really was a demon now. Jovan had taught him too well. A self-made demon with an army of life-sucking Shades, plus two dozen meat suit ghouls. And I had fourteen in total. The odds were not in my favor.

Halfway across the wooden floor, I realized it wasn't a mirror on the stage, but the rip itself undulating with a radiant light. Its cool energy began to trickle around me as I approached.

And then I smelled the faintest whiff of dust and cashmere. My eyes jumped down to the floral mass quivering on the floor of the stage.

My entire body went numb as my brain tried to process what was happening. Iris. Why was Iris here?

There was a soft moan at Spencer's feet, and he just glanced down at the woman as he walked closer to me. "Well, takes a big cat to get a big cat."

My feet stuck to the ground and my stomach hit the floor. *What had I done?* "She was protected."

"Until little Jane moved one little stone out of place on her midnight walk with me." Spencer smiled.

It hit me like an anvil to the chest. I couldn't breathe. Jane's possession not only moved a stone out of place, but also gave Spencer the location of the only other big cat in this area. Why hadn't I thought of Iris? What massive block had kept me from considering Iris as a potential target?

Tucker's hand crept over my shoulder. And then he pushed me forward with a loving you-stop-moving-you-die sentiment.

Spencer couldn't know the stone in the pit of my stomach, couldn't know that he'd already broken off a chunk of the armor and the real fight hadn't even begun. I licked my lips and forced out some snark as I took another step toward him, the sharp smell of blood more vivid than anything else. "So you're adding maiming old ladies to your resume?"

"Seemed fitting. My father took her city, I took her life."

My entire body flinched, and the Legacy ran hot around me. "The two of us will have to start another cycle. You attack me, I kick your ass. You attack my friends, I kick your ass."

Spencer smiled. I'd forgotten that his physical presence made part of me twinge. That his panther had tried to seduce mine. I steeled my nerves against it with the thought of how he'd violated Jane and I.

"We'll just have to see about that."

The Shades swarmed, but we were ready for them. The shadow men came at us with their arms outstretched and mouths hungry.

The eight of us had our stun guns readied and juiced before the first one laid a hand on Tyler.

I jabbed the stun gun into one and it ashed before me. I turned quickly toward Tucker and pried one off his back, slicing its neck with the Haverty blade. The shadow faded into my hands and I quickly turned to slice through another one on Praline's arm.

There was poetry in our motion and when I saw my people not even break a sweat as they dusted one after another, I leapt onto the stage to face Spencer.

"You have done a pretty good job with the leftovers."

I held the blade tightly in my hand and holstered the stun gun. "You've obviously not gotten any smarter on the other side if you think they're leftovers."

"But I have gotten more powerful."

With a small flick of his hand, his power reached around me and threw me across the room. The frame of the stage stopped me, and I cracked the wood with my head before I slid down. Two concussions already down for the night. Maybe I'd break my own record.

"That's pretty decent, big brother," I wheezed out as I gained my footing. "Ever seen this one?"

With the focus of the blade, I threw my own whip of lightning energy at him that Yasmina inspired when she electrified me. Really did give a new meaning to *Monkey see, Monkey do.*

It struck Spencer in the chest, and he flew into the darkness of the wings of the stage.

The rest of the first wave flooded in from the sides and the meat suits went for them. The battle had officially begun.

I rushed to Iris and fell to my knees. I dropped the knife by her head and grabbed her hand. I turned her face toward mine and still felt a small pulse at my fingers. They'd taken her in her favorite house dress and camel-colored shoes. "Iris."

She parted her lips, but nothing came out. Her blood covered my hand from the long slits up both her forearms. If nothing else, Spencer had gotten more thorough in his follow-through.

"I am so sorry, Iris." I brushed a few wisps of her white hair from her still clear blue eyes, gentle of the purple bruise on her cheek.

"Shhh," she whispered.

I looked over my shoulder at the Veil opened by her blood. It was large, larger than what Jessa was used to closing by herself. It pulsed at my back as I looked down at Iris.

Chaz leapt onto the stage and dropped next to us. "Iris." His chin began to quiver.

She moved her hand so Chaz's was under hers and mine. With every breath she took, my power swarmed hotter and faster around the three of us. A few meat suits tried to attack us, but they couldn't get through. My world focused to just the three of us.

"You get Dallas back for good, Violet."

I couldn't answer for fear of the sob that might escape me. I simply nodded.

Her head dropped toward Chaz, as I memorized every wrinkle on her face, every smile line. "Take care of yourself. And the farm."

"Thank you," he managed to get out, but he too was fighting tears. "For everything."

Iris gasped and her body went rigid. I grabbed Chaz's shoulder, knowing we were both about to crack if apart.

She calmed and her gaze fell to me again. "Would to have liked to seen some grandchildren."

I leaned down and whispered in her ear. "I've seen them. Seth and Jesse. They grow up on the farm, and Seth is exactly like his father."

Iris smiled and I kissed her temple.

"Go, Prima. Leave me to my son."

I looked up at Chaz. His jaw was rock solid as he pulled Iris into his lap. He could barely get the words out. "You kill that sonuvabitch."

"Nice and dead this time."

Iris squeezed my hand before I pulled away from her. My bloody hand grabbed the knife and I rose.

The power still swirled around me as I turned to where I'd seen Spencer fly. Out like this, I could feel him. Where he used to be an inky black panther, he was now a tangled mess of power. Stolen power that was icy to my burning energy.

I followed the cold trail of power as I walked through the back of the stage, turning the handle of the knife over and over in my hand, the blood drying and strengthening my grip.

Where the wings of a theater would have held ropes and pulleys, the renovations had replaced all that with aisles of storage containers and catering tables.

I went for the Exit sign and kicked open the door to find Spencer just outside on a loading dock, stuck in the binding spell Willowbourne had put around the place. Figured he would run.

Good to see that some things never change.

I grabbed his collar and ripped him backward, back into the theater. He was not going to touch Dallas soil. He crashed against a wooden crate, and it splintered underneath him. The contents shattered around him- stage lightbulbs- glistening and cutting as he landed. That was a lucky shot if I'd ever seen one.

The panther was ready, willing, and fast. Thanks to the extra power infiltrating every cell, eased by the sheer hate that consumed me, I was on top of him in two seconds. I curled my claws into his new white shirt, still teeming with starch, and threw him as hard as I could against the brick wall.

It was more than appeasing to start his concussion count as well. "All that power and you still can't fly."

He retaliated against that one with a ball of energy that caught me in the stomach and lifted me high into the rafters. After all the sessions in the barn with Iris jumping from rafter to rafter to test my surefootedness, I managed to bounce around in the rafters. But it didn't change the two-story fall all the way back to the ground.

Cats do actually land on their feet. But they need all four of them. I landed safely but the knife went clattering between us.

I eyed him and then the blade and went for it. He did too and we met in the middle, my hand on the handle and his hand on the blade. Letting my talons loose, I scratched at his face, my claws raking across his unshaven cheek, and jerked the knife away, the blade slicing a line into his palm.

I scurried back on all fours, and then jumped to my feet, ready for the next attack.

Spencer stood up and straightened his suit coat. In the dim light that filtered in from the night and the light of the Veil dancing around us, I watched his face heal. The four lines across his perfect cheek sealed back up until they were nothing but faint pink lines and then nothing.

That was new.

He just laughed. And then he started fighting.

I matched him kick for punch and tooth for claw. Sensei had taught me well. I was faster, but not stronger. Where I sliced a claw against his throat, he shoved me back six feet with an open hand.

I stumbled back a few feet. "You've had a teacher."

"I ate a teacher."

I rolled my eyes at his comment until I realized that no, he probably had actually eaten someone with talents and now had those talents. Crap.

What he didn't have was an ounce of his panther left, or if it was there, it was so buried underneath that nasty gooey center of evil that it couldn't get free.

He came at me again and I was able to defend myself, getting in a few nicks with the silver blade here and there, his skin sizzling under the silver. At least he was still Haverty enough for the blade to be a threat, because I sure as hell wasn't enough to make a dent.

I jumped to a rafter above his head and for a moment, I paused. Patience. Sensei had taught me: be patient and your opponent will show you their weakness.

Spencer ran his fingers through his hair again and I knew that he was just about to straighten his jacket.

When his gaze was down and his hands around his lapels, I leapt at him from above. If I could get him on the ground, I might be able to get this knife where it belonged.

My plan didn't work.

Spencer caught me, his hands grabbing my jacket instead and belt tightly, spun me, and threw me toward the stage.

I flew backward like something akin to a windmill, appendages flailing out in all directions as I tried to right myself, tried to catch onto something.

The thick red curtain caught me for a moment, and I stabbed the knife through the material as I fell back down to the stage and rolled out from underneath the curtain and back into the main hall.

It didn't exactly work like it did in the movies, but I didn't hit the floor as hard as I could have.

From my firmly planted seat on the ground, I looked up to see my people wiping the floors with the meat suits. There wasn't a Shade left in sight.

But the Veil was still open. Jessa hadn't managed to close it yet.

"Vi!" Jessa rushed to my side. "Is he . . . ?"

I waved her back as I pushed myself to my feet. "Not even close. And hot on my heels.

A blast of energy threw me into Jessa's small frame, and we slid across the wooden stage until the wall stopped us. It got the attention of everyone in the hall.

"I'd almost forgotten about the little fairy princess," Spencer said as he walked out from the red curtain and across the stage.

Jessa rolled me off of her and sat up. "I'll give you—"

I grabbed her shoulder and shook her before she said anything else that was going to get something else thrown at us.

Tucker, Tyler, and Nash lined up at the edge of the stage, blood-flecked faces sporting wounds that would heal before being given a second thought. I surged with pride as they stood against their former master.

"Boys." Spencer casually hopped off the edge of the stage where my entire pack was waiting for him.

"Spencer," Tucker growled.

"Mutts finally found a home, I see."

They attacked together, even Shadow getting in on the action. But even together, they were no match for Spencer. They flew back and landed so hard on the floor that I felt the jarring of it in my spine.

Then there were lightning bolts and fangs and the fast flash of Valiance's blade. I only saw Spencer stumble back once the whole time they all went after him.

"The Veil seems to be closing itself," Jessa said from behind me.

"What?" I asked, still panting, taking a moment to use the Legacy to heal myself. The aches were slowly ebbing away; the blood in my mouth wasn't flowing.

"This place wasn't a natural rip. It was all spellwork and the spell is fading."

"We are fading. And if we can't beat him, we have to get him back through."

I couldn't watch anymore. They were fine with the Shades and the ghouls, but Spencer was tossing them aside like oyster shells, seeming more full of himself with every attack.

It was Shadow's yelp as his claws skidded across the wooden floor that was my final straw. Grabbing the knife from the stage, I went after Spencer again. I landed three solid punches to his midsection and a knee to his chin, and he still managed to send me sliding across the floor on my ass.

"Need the floor," Chaz called out.

I got up again and looked over at Chaz. And he had something pretty.

I pulled my people back, like yanking on a leash to get them out of the way. Sensei blew the rest of my pack off the floor as Chaz took aim with his modified shot gun and launched a rocket at Spencer's chest. I covered my ears and looked away from the explosion.

In the silence after the blast, Spencer's laughter echoed in the empty space. "Is that seriously all you've got?"

He recovered from the edge of the stage and readjusted his suit jacket. The blast had burned a hole the size of a basketball into his shirt. Now, his flawless abdomen showed through without so much as a courtesy scratch. "I thought you'd prepared better than this, Violet."

"I was counting on my stubbornness to win the day."

I circled around with my back to the Veil, the soft pitter-patter of its energy dancing along my skin.

"Well, this little show has taught me something." Spencer flicked at the torn edges of his white shirt.

"What's that?" I needed to keep Spencer talking. I knew he liked the sound of his own voice off the bare walls of the theater, but more importantly, I was beginning to feel the ache of my pack as they battled, only seven left on their feet. They needed a moment; I needed a better plan.

"You really do know how to throw a welcome back party."

I predicted the attack this time. Like drawing a line in the sand, I forced my shield out before me and managed to lessen the force of his swirling dark energy ball. I skidded backward with the force until my foot hit the edge of the stage.

Spencer laughed out again. "That's what I love about you. Always changing, always finding new ways to use our power."

I growled at his choice of pronouns. "My power."

"When I kill you, it will be mine. You're just holding on to it for me. So let's speed things up again, shall we?"

I felt him draw on his power, like being on the outskirts of a black hole. We all stepped back as we watched darkness swirl around him. It solidified between blinks and another line of Shades swarmed the theater floor.

He could create Shades. That was full-on demon power. The knowledge didn't come from me, but from Nash's hazel eyes.

I pushed out as much of my energy to my pack as I could to make them ready for this; and with it, I pushed out the notion that he needed to get back into the Veil, and quickly.

I stabbed the knife through my belt and pants and the silver stung my skin. But I needed all four limbs free to shift. Maybe four sets of claws might do enough damage.

The Fang sisters shifted as well, leaving the men with the swords. Half fur and half fists, we were a little more productive.

The girls went after Spencer with a viciousness fueled by protecting their family and ruining their Saturday date nights.

Spencer didn't fight animals as well as he did knives and swords. His flesh seemed nearly impenetrable to a blade and a bullet, but my claws slashed into his skin.

His panther was ten times stronger than the girls' wolves but he still didn't shift. Instead, he swung at us and tried to force us away with his power, but we kept at him.

As the men fought off the newest batch of Shades, the girls managed to get Spencer's back to the four-foot-high stage.

How do you make a man jump four feet? If we could just get him back through the Veil.

I went for his ankle and he wasn't fast enough. I actually sank my teeth into the muscle below his calf. Startled, I released him quickly. This guy had just deflected a rocket launch, but my panther teeth pierced his skin like a knife through butter.

Shifters were now his vulnerability. That was the price of the demon power. He'd created his own Achilles heel. I pushed the knowledge out to the rest of the group. Everyone who could shift did and joined me.

Spencer leapt onto the stage. I may have bitten him, but he was still healing too fast for us to really slow him down.

The Veil danced behind him. Jessa scurried to the side of the stage and watched as my pack nipped and snapped and scratched at him.

He swatted Kandice's hawk like he was smacking a mosquito. She went limp and fell like a brick to the stage.

Charlotte leapt at him, taking the moment of distraction. Spencer caught her by the throat and the echo of the snap of her neck rang out like gunfire throughout the hall.

I felt the snap in my chest and fell to the floor in my human form. Like a tight piano string, her connection recoiled, and I felt blood in my mouth and a stab through my chest.

A white-hot fury consumed me, and the Legacy burned

down my spine and boiled the lacquer of the wooden stage beneath my feet.

The rest of the pack knew something was wrong and they backed away from Spencer in fear and anticipation.

My eyes flicked to Jessa as I got into a sprinter's position. She knew it was Plan C time. She knew we weren't going to win this one on this side of the Veil.

As my muscles tensed, I sent out everything I had left to my pack. To Tucker beside me; to Nash as he nudged Kandice; to Tyler, who vocalized his hate in a deep growl. Even to Shadow, who was fighting as hard as any border collie could.

Somewhere in the Dallas night, Peter gasped, sitting forward on Devin's couch; Hannah's hand flew to her chest; and Remy hugged Twila harder. They were going to be fine.

My last thought went to Chaz. Chaz would understand because he knew me better than I did. He would have known that I had a Plan C as part of the big picture. He already known that I was going to do something stupid, but he'd also know that I could not have another person die for me when so many psychics had already seen me dead.

The moment I pushed against my back foot, Spencer knew. His blue eyes widened, and he braced himself.

I threw my panther power forward first, which caught him off guard, and then hit him with my shoulder to his midsection, which gave him just enough lift to get him off his feet.

The Veil welcomed us both with open borders. Like a ball being thrown through deep space, spinning and weightless, I tightened my grip on Spencer's jacket. Everything was bright and sharp and I just squeezed my eyes shut and waited to land.

CHAPTER 23

I SLAMMED AGAINST Spencer's chest, then rolled off him. The dagger tore into my hip from its position at my belt. I pulled out the knife quickly and felt the familiar sizzle of the silver. Start off the fight of your life with a self-inflicted wound. Crap.

I had to force my eyes open and sucked in the air that had been knocked out of me.

We were in a field. The sun beat down hot against my pale skin. The green grass was familiar, as was the smell of the wind.

Spencer had been here before. Spencer had killed two Biggers here. There was a pond in the middle where he'd tried to rip the Veil before. I remembered because he remembered.

I pushed myself up from the grass, wincing at the burning wound in my hip. It wasn't deep, just annoying.

I looked around. No sign of Spencer. He'd been right there.

With a small breath, I released my borders and staggered back.

This place was amazing. Like a haven on crack. Everything pushed back at my power; everything had its own life. The earth, the grass, the wind itself.

Willowbourne's prayer made more sense than ever. *May the ground support your steps.* Because the ground might actually have an opinion on the matter.

I heard a moan on the wind.

Let's hope the ground was in my favor today.

Spencer's blond hair caught the breeze and betrayed his position in the high grass.

I was just about to make some snide comment to incite the fight again when I felt the pop of the Veil closing behind us. It echoed through me and so did the knowledge that my pack was now leaderless. My fiancé was now a widower. Jessa was going to have to scrap all those wedding plans.

My skin tightened as I realized I was alone. For the first time in four months, I didn't have any ties binding me to another person. For the first time in a year, I didn't have anyone to call for help. I felt empty and the emptiness pulled at me. How did people live like this? How had I lived like that all that time?

Iris's words seem to wrap around me. *You will always have the biggest sacrifice.* My family, my ties were the biggest sacrifice of all. Without them, I was just Violet.

But I had given them a family. I had made them a pack, I had brought them all together. They would have each other and that was a Legacy that I made peace with.

Spencer pushed himself up from the grass. He ran his fingers through his long blond hair and then grabbed his shoulder.

"Really didn't see that one coming." He pulled at his jacket, though it looks ridiculous since there was a huge hole in his shirt.

I felt him call for his power and I tightened my Legacy around me like a blanket in the midday sun. "Just so I can get the rest of the story. You were supposed to be Jovan's little favorite, come before him, pave the way in chaos and blood, but you outgrew your britches?"

The blood drained from his face.

"You underestimate the power of our connection, Spencer. And the fact that I've written this time and time again."

"That's right, your little movies."

Anger sizzled down my back and I clenched my fist so tight around the blade that I lost feeling in my fingertips. "They are not little movies. And you know what happens over and over in those movies?"

"What happens, my brilliant little sister?"

My, wasn't he playful? Of course, this was where he had been living for the past six months. This was his home court. The earth warmed beneath my feet. "The good guys always win."

Spencer slid his jacket off his broad shoulders, again wincing with the action. "And you think you're the good guy in this scenario?"

"I didn't just kill a defenseless old lady."

"Defenseless, my ass. She was as guilty as the rest of them."

I shifted as the ground beneath me seemed to vibrate, as if it too disliked his tone.

"She was weak and that's why my father took Dallas from her. Just like I'm going to take Dallas from you."

"Dallas isn't mine to lose. It's the only good thing I've done there."

"What? Make them play nice with each other?"

"I gave them a choice. Gave them the power instead of taking it from them."

Spencer reached his hands out before him. "That kind of thinking doesn't work here."

The time for playing was over when he shot a black cloud of power out at me. I ran and it followed me around the field. I was faster here, my feet making contact with the ground and springing forward, like running on my high school's track-and-field track.

I rolled to the ground and his column of black power whooshed over my head as I stayed low in the grass.

I crawled carefully back in the direction I'd run. I could barely see Spencer's blond hair over the green grass. He couldn't see me.

But why couldn't he smell me? The wind seemed to carry his scent to me, and I knew his heart was racing. I knew there was more blood on him than I could see. He looked around the field for me, but the breeze kept the grass tops dancing. The wind was at my back on this one.

"They need to be led, Violet. They need a steady hand to keep them in line," he said into the wind.

I was within ten feet of him now. I slipped the knife out of my belt.

"They are just animals after all."

I leapt at him.

Unfortunately, he was faster here as well. He grabbed the hand with the knife pointed solidly at him and yanked me forward and off balance. He planted his other hand in my chest and the air rushed out of my lungs.

He slammed me down on the ground like I was a limp doll and the knife rolled out of my hand. His hand went for my throat. Why do they always go for the throat? The second thing that Sensei had taught me after how to flip someone over my hip was how to get out of someone trying to choke you out.

I jammed two fingers into his blue eyes. Sensei had showed me how to fight honorably and how to fight dirty. I had a natural propensity for the later.

One of Spencer's hand flew up and he covered his face. I hit him in the inside elbow and he fell forward. His nose somehow managing to connect rather roughly with my forehead.

Blood sprayed out of his nose, causing him to let me go entirely. I scurried away from him, wiping the blood from my face onto my shirt. It blended well into the other splatters of blood and dirt that had collected on the green material.

The sun glinted off the edge of the blade and I dashed towards it, grabbing it only moments before Spencer. We were just about to launch into another round of "who's got the knife" when the ground rumbled around us. It was at least an eight on the Richter scale.

I stayed on all fours and flinched with the crackle of power through the air. I tucked the knife back into the waistband of my jeans and waited.

Spencer knelt on one knee, which told me who was paying us a visit.

Jovan wasn't what I expected. The goon squad behind him was what I expected, an amalgamation of every evil-looking thing that you could imagine. It was every single monster I'd ever written: a minotaur; a half man, half snake; and every scary thing I'd ever seen in my head. I would never doubt that I was born and bred into this world again.

But Jovan. I don't know why I had a vision of Darth Sidious, all withered and darkly clad, as the demon on the other side trying to take over the world. Guess I really had watched too many movies.

Jovan was a formidable sized man in a simple suit. Apparently evil had a propensity toward tailored work wear. His dark hair was silvered at the temples, his goatee silver from the corners of his mouth down. But his eyes. His eyes were gray, like a storm cloud, and his power swirled around him, making the air around me dense, like a change in barometric pressure.

"Didn't expect to see you so soon, Spencer." His voice crackled against the soft brush of the wind.

The horde of monsters behind him swarmed both me and Spencer, though they seemed to take more pleasure in handling me than him. Slimy hands pulled me to my feet, and something wound tightly around my legs. I didn't want to think about what it could be, but it really felt like a slimy tail. I held in a gasp as the slime began to seep into my jeans.

I was quiet. Chaz had taught me that my mouth got me into trouble. Right now was not the time to put my foot in my mouth. I had a feeling Jovan had a way of making that actually happen.

"And Miss Jordan. I *really* didn't expect to see you here."

But I wouldn't be rude and not speak when spoken to. "I had to see what Spencer kept going on about."

Jovan did something creepy. He smiled. Why is it always so creepy when they smile? "He was supposed to have killed you."

"He's never been one for follow-through. You should know that."

Jovan walked up to me and I could barely breathe through his power. He was suffocating me like I'd suffocated Inez. My heartbeat pounded in my ears and my mouth ran dry with fear —pure unadulterated fear.

"What is so special about you, Miss Jordan? What makes you fight so hard? Spencer here is the best thing I've got, and yet, you're still alive."

"He's got some flaws."

I caught something on the wind, something wild and sharp.

Jovan's eyes darted to the tree line.

He tugged at the sleeves of his suit. The tug told me volumes. Not how he'd gotten the Hilfiger duds on this side of the Veil, but that there was something in the woods that surrounded us he was uncomfortable with.

Jovan looked me square in the eyes and my eyes began to water, like looking straight into a dark sun. "I am very old, Miss Jordan. I don't fight anymore; I win. And I'm not going to win this one."

Jovan took a step back. Jovan, the evil demon who was trying to take over the universe, backed away from me, his gaze darting from me to the trees surrounding the field. "Though it will be interesting to see how this plays out."

The slimy tail and the wandering hands that held me slipped away as the monster horde followed him from wherever he had come from.

I remained still.

Spencer went after him, and with a flick of Jovan's hand, Spencer was thrown across the field by an invisible force.

"Be seeing you around, Miss Jordan."

Jovan was still walking away, a mist forming around him and his horde as he retreated. I had no idea what magic he was using to throw his voice. Or maybe he was just a ventriloquist in his former life.

Spencer ran at me from behind. Or more to the point: I *felt* him run at me from behind. His footsteps might as well have been a stampede of elephants, the way the vibrations ran through the ground and up my legs.

I ducked down and watched him fly comically over me.

He rolled, jumped to his feet and turned on me again. "What the hell is wrong with you?"

"Says the lap cat to the Mayor of Evil Town."

"Why do you ruin everything?"

"Can you sound more juvenile?"

"I did everything he asked of me, and one look at you and all that work out the window."

"It wasn't me."

I looked to the tree line. There was something there. Something bigger.

Spencer's eyes followed mine. "Crap."

Green eyes appeared first, just higher than my head in the trees. Then a tawny pair and then a silver pair. Biggers.

"Double crap," I breathed.

The first one, a lion with a mane the size of a semi-truck, broke the tree line at a slow pace.

"Finally, some justice in this place," Spencer said.

I felt him draw on his power, but I wrapped mine up and tucked it away, until it was nothing more than my panther. I'd killed one of these guys when Spencer jumped through the Veil the first time, and in the dreams, Spencer killed two more of them. They were strong, fast, and twice the size of a Clydesdale.

I knew them, sort of. If all those origin stories were true, then we were the same spirit. Except they were bigger on the outside, while I was furry on the inside. Where I lived on two legs, they chose to live on four.

I stood my ground and let the three approach. The lion's nose was higher than my forehead and the panther's paws were easily double the size of manhole covers. They smelled like wet fur and earth. The wolf, a dark silver gray, stuck his nose into my bloody hip. I remained still, kept my ground, and kept my mouth shut. The moist muzzle went up my side and to my neck and then backed away.

"Why aren't you running?" the wolf asked as he slipped to the right of the lion. They didn't actually talk, but their brains reached out to mine to speak.

And it was rude not to respond. "Why would I run?"

"Why do you smell like us?" the panther asked.

I gulped. "Because I'm just like you. Just bigger on the inside."

Their eyes turned to Spencer, whose dark power was beginning to swirl around him, the stolen life creating a smokey haze in the sun-filled field.

"He's not like us," the lion said.

I shook my head. "Not anymore."

Then two of the Biggers went for Spencer. With his slashing power, he fought them off as they darted and chased him around the field.

The panther stayed with me. We watched the brawl patiently from the edge of the field, her large black head in my peripheral vision. The last time I'd faced down one of these, it was determined to make me a snack. I was hoping that this one wasn't as hungry.

"We want him dead," she growled.

"So do I."

"He has killed many of us."

"He's killed my people too."

"Then why aren't your teeth around his neck?"

"I talk a big game."

"The time for talking is over."

When the words escaped my lips, I knew it was true. "He is me. That could have been me."

If I didn't have Iris. If I didn't have Chaz. We both needed someone. He just turned to a demon.

"No, daughter. He is not you."

My hackles rose at hearing a panther call me daughter. I shivered when I realized that she might be right. I might be her great-great-granddaughter. She could also be me, but I chose something else. Something bigger than myself to focus on.

"But he is your fight, not ours."

An invisible call echoed across the fields, like a silent purr across my skin. The lion and wolf pulled away from their fight and ran toward the tree line, the forest enveloping them quietly.

I took a moment to find Spencer in the weeds, and the panther was gone from my side, taking with her the warm scent of wet earth.

"This is my fight," I repeated to myself. Even though he wasn't a threat to my pack on the other side of the Veil, he was still a threat here. Still a threat to the beings here.

Jovan, the Biggers, they backed away. They knew that the two of us weren't right, the boy who eats souls and the panther masquerading as a girl.

Maybe I belonged in the Neveranth with all the other monsters who had gotten too big for their britches. Mystical realm built to house powerful Wanderers or not, there was only room for one of us on either side of the Veil.

"What kind of deal did you make?" Spencer's voice echoed across the grass, carried by the wind. He ran his fingers through his hair and wiped his bloody nose on what was left of his sleeve.

"No deal. Just the truth."

"Biggers eat half-breeds like you."

"Not if they don't know what the other half is."

A smile passed over his lips. He'd used that same line against the Biggers just months before. "I had no clue how special you were going to be, Violet. You were just supposed to be a midnight snack."

"So you really didn't know about the prophecies or our connection or any of it?"

Spencer shook his head. "I was just hungry."

I stretched my neck, rolled my shoulders, and slipped the knife from my belt. "Guess we've both grown up a little since then."

"Says the drunk girl in the alley."

"Says the reckless playboy."

He threw a cloud of power out at me, but I quickly darted around it. I wasn't stopping this time. Not until the pointy end of this knife was embedded in his chest. But I'd take his abdomen or eye socket as well.

I ran past him and took a broad swipe with my claws down his injured arm. He wasn't as fast as me, he was vulnerable to the panther and he hadn't been tossed around by a Jeet Kune Do sensei for the past eight months. I knew exactly how many hits I could take; he didn't.

I circled around his back and stopped. I knew I could beat him on the ground. It was just a matter of getting him on his back.

He had to spin around to face me again, and when he did, I ran toward him.

We swapped hits to the face and fists to the torso. I kept at him, hoping that between the power plays he'd been making all night and the sheer violence, he would be worn out. Lord knows I was feeling the strain down my back, in the tension down my legs.

After one particularly rough exchange, I skidded back, my bare feet ripping up grass as I stopped. I looked down at the simple knife still clutched in my hand, my bloody knuckles, and my ruined blue jeans.

My gaze darted up to him to find him panting, bleeding, and not looking anything like the boy that ran away through the mirror. He tore off what was left of the white business shirt, exposing the scratches down his chest and his purple shoulder.

I knew what I needed to do; I could see it in my head. I'd done it a million times in the dojo. I just needed him down. "Just fall down already," I whispered, thinking that if I used the words and pushed at them with my will, he would just magically fall down.

He didn't. There is a downside to fighting something that always lands on its feet.

With a deep breath, I launched at him again, slicing the knife upward. He leaned back.

And then he fell.

I was coming after him so fast that I too tripped over the root arched up out of the ground. The root that neither of us had tripped over so far in the fight.

I landed on top of him and rolled over his head.

He was down. And I had about a fourth of a second before he was back up. I stabbed the knife into the ground by his head and jumped on his chest.

His hand immediately went for my face. I slammed his wrist against the ground and ground my knee into his hip to keep him pinned. I wound my arm through his and got him into the most perfect figure four. I pulled his arm up and his knuckles drug across the ground.

His back arched and he cried out. With a sharp twist of my torso, I pulled his shoulder out of its socket. The pop echoed through the empty field.

I released his arm and it fell to the ground limp.

Something else snapped within him, the civil part, whatever was left of the human part and I was faced with what a demon really looked like. Wild, raw, and with a single-mindedness that was aimed at my throat.

His blue eyes turned black, and his good arm shot out at my throat. I caught it easily, but he still managed to flip my entire body over like a full-body arm-wrestling match.

I wrapped my long legs around his waist and squeezed. Arching my back, I was able to keep his one good arm from strangling me, bracing my shoulders against the ground.

I let my claws slide out through my hand and brought them down quickly across his face.

He caught my hand with his and pinned it above my head, grinding my bones into the dirt. His wild eyes focused in on me and his teeth grew sharper. I felt the dark power squirm within him, begging to just take one more soul.

He wouldn't get the chance. The sun caught the edge of the silver blade.

My right arm darted out to where I'd tucked the knife into the ground. I tore it from the earth and rammed the blade into his side, slipping it between his ribs and up to the hilt.

He screamed out above me and reared up, letting go of my arm.

I dropped my legs from around his waist and scurried back.

Panting, I got to my knees and watched as he tried to grab at the blade, the silver sizzling away at his skin. He fell to his back and gasped for breath. Burning began to grow in my own chest as I crawled over to him, the exhaustion of the battle finally settling into my bones as I saw the end.

I reached out and pulled out the knife. Blood poured out into the grass, staining the ground beneath him. I couldn't help but think of how Iris talked about giving it back to the earth.

Spencer gasped for air as he lay back on the ground. The darkness faded from his eyes and his blue came back.

"We knew there was only one ending to this story," I said softly.

His eyes darted toward me.

"The good guys win."

"You're not the good guy," he whispered. "Not anymore. Not after this."

"Maybe not. But I'm the one who's still breathing."

With one final push of energy, I drove the knife into his chest, through his heart and felt it embed into the ground beneath him. There was a symmetry in it that all endings needed.

Spencer gasped, blood trickling out of his mouth. His blue eyes landed on me. His hand clasped around mine on the hilt of the blade.

I took his injured arm and brought our hands to his chest and waited.

The field was too quiet. His last breaths, too loud.

"The Haverty line doesn't end. If that matters to the human part of you left. The empire your father made is still the most powerful in the Wandering world. I intended to make it the strongest. And my pack will continue on with that."

There was one more fluttering look in his navy blue eyes before his breathing stopped and his head lolled to one side. I reached over and closed his eyes.

That's when our connection snapped. The thick steel line that held us together for eight months, that criss-crossed our energies, our brains, broke. The force of it sent me flying across the field.

I landed softly on the ground, as if it caught my broken body. It was done.

My muscles gave up and I just looked up at the clear blue sky.

The grass created a pillow under my head. The sun covered me like a warm blanket over my aching body. Sleep came swiftly.

HAY. I SMELLED fresh hay. I forced my eyes open and saw dust dancing through golden light as it streamed through the familiar slats in Iris's barn, as it filtered between the bars of the cage where I'd first shifted, where Chaz had seen my panther and loved me anyway.

I pushed myself up and looked down at my shirt, my knuckles. No blood, no bruises. Just a white T-shirt smelling slightly of starch, and jeans, unstained by the mud I'd just been dragged through.

"Why a barn?" the voice echoed through the familiar space with an equally familiar tone.

Heaven. Was this heaven? Was Iris was meeting me in heaven?

Someone had surely gotten the paperwork wrong.

I walked out of my cage, and the door moved silently on its hinges. In fact, everything was silent. No squeaky gate, no cooing birds in the hay loft, no rustle of a breeze through the rafters. It had been cleaned out of its usual broken-down farm equipment and the open space looked like a checkerboard of light.

There was a woman standing in the middle of the open floor of the barn. Her dark hair floated in a breeze I couldn't feel, but I could smell. She smelled like honeysuckle, strong sweet honeysuckle.

"Why did you choose a barn?" she asked again.

"For what? For heaven?" I'd never been a believer before, but this wasn't the Neveranth. It felt different beneath my bare feet.

And it was hardly Dallas. There was a completely different feel in the energy of the place, a deep, more thrumming sort of power.

"For your safe place. For most people it's their childhood homes or fluffy clouds."

The woman's sea green eyes landed on mine and I couldn't help but smile. "It's a long story. Where am I?"

The woman matched my smile. Her face was so familiar, but I couldn't place it, like my memories were far away.

"We are in between all that," she said softly.

I wanted to hug her, and my arms seemed to ache for it, but I didn't know why. "In between life and death?"

"In between even that," she repeated.

"Well, we can't be in my brain. It's not this neat."

The woman laughed and it sounded like a wind chimes, twinkling and light. "You are too funny, Violet Jordan."

My name sounded oddly formal on her lips.

Her shoulders dropped and so did her smile. "You'll need to keep that humor."

I looked around the quiet barn. It was so peaceful here and I didn't hurt and there was something about this woman that was just so very something I couldn't remember.

"And you'll need to go back."

"Are you sure about that? I'm not doing a great job of it."

"No." She chuckled. "But the job is getting done."

She moved toward me. I didn't hear the rustle of her long skirt along the ground or the press of her foot against the hay.

"You've done exactly what needed to be done, Violet. And I wish that you could rest here, but you can't." Her long pale fingers reached out past me and pointed to the cage that I had come from.

A dark shadow loomed, trapped behind the bars. The man-sized beast was a tarry mess of teeth and fur and it burned to just look at the void of its existence.

"What is that?"

"The power that he collected. The tortured souls of those he killed."

My stomach churned. "This is what a demon looks like?"

"Demon power, yes."

I had to look away and soothed my eyes on her curly hair and her smooth, milky skin. Her pale green eyes were at my level and her rosy lips were pressed together.

When she touched my cheek, I knew this was more than just a dream. This was more than just a vision or a concussion. This was when I felt the in-between, felt the pull in both directions and felt what she really was.

"You're the Mother," I breathed.

She simply smiled. "I've been called worse."

"The all-seeing, all-knowing being who created the Wanderers knows who I am."

"And has one last thing she's going to ask of you."

I took in a deep breath of air. Was it even air? It was whatever she wanted it to be.

"There was a prophecy about you."

I nodded. "I would stop the demon from destroying the world. Done. Finito. Covered that chapter last December."

"There was another."

I knew it, like she'd brought it back to the forefront of my brain. It echoed in Cristina's smooth voice. "The demon will be freed and we will know and love her."

The woman nodded.

I put the pieces together quickly. "You want me to take that power and go back to Dallas."

"Yes."

I panicked. My heart jumped up in my chest and I couldn't breathe. "I can't harness that. A Legacy, sure. Dealt with that but not a demon. It will kill my panther like it killed Spencer's."

"It's just the power," she repeated.

"It's not, it's all the souls of the people Spencer . . ." The wave of my own words came flooding back to me. I bent over, my hands on my knees and took in a deep breath. *It's not the power; it's how you use it. It's not how you live on four legs but on two.*

"I know you are strong enough to do this, Vi."

"How?"

"Because I made you this strong."

I stood up straight for that one. "If you're responsible for all the crap I've been through, I think you and I need to have a conversation."

"I think I'll pass. I saw the conversation with Yasmina last winter."

I took in another deep breath of honeysuckle. I could taste it on my tongue, the sweet thick scent that reminded me of something.

She looked down at her long fingers as they rubbed together. "I know what I need, but the choice is up to you because the task is up to you."

"Why can't it just stay here?"

"Because when you are gone, this place is gone, and it will find another, weaker, host and continue on its way. Creating unbalance."

"And unbalance equals chaos." Finally one of Jessa's lessons had sunk in. I couldn't have that. Too many innocents had already suffered because of my weakness. "So I have to take carry-on luggage when I go back?"

"And because of the Key Holder, the window for your choice is getting smaller."

"Jessa?"

"She's coming for you." The woman looked off into the sunlight. "And she is very powerful."

I smiled. "You should see her when she's shopping."

The Mother smiled.

"I'm open for suggestions on how do to this?"

Her sea green eyes twinkled. "Think of it like one giant coffee bean. When you are ready, you can make something good with it, filter it. You already know how to harness a power that isn't yours. Just protect it until you know when to use it. It is our people, Violet."

"That's a lot to ask."

"It's you or an innocent. It will keep feeding until it doesn't need a host. Until the Neveranth can't hold it anymore."

I looked at the spiky mess as it hovered in the cage.

"You have your pack to keep you strong. You've got Chaz and Jessa to keep you Violet. You've got a good shot at doing something that no one else has done."

"What's that?"

"Reforming a demon."

I shook my head. "I still think you've got the wrong girl."

The woman's light green eyes sparkled silver with anticipation. "You've always been the right girl, Violet."

I looked back at the beast, the churning mass of wriggling tentacles, then at the woman. I felt the chill of raindrops down my back. "Jessa." The silly girl was coming for me.

And she would always come for me. As would Chaz. And the boys. I couldn't do this, but *we* could.

"Fine. But if you could make the next couple of months a little easier, me and MacTarball here would appreciate it."

The woman nodded.

I looked at the raging power and walked toward it. I really

wasn't the smartest color in the box, cleaning up another mess that Spencer had left for me.

As I reached out my hand to touch it, I saw the perfect sparkling ring on my finger. Chaz. The boys. Jessa. They'd helped me clean up the first mess and I knew that I could count on them to help me again. Because they were my family.

I reached into the dark, slick mass and the hot sinews wrapped around my arms. The Legacy met it with a hot fierceness as I looked over my shoulder at the woman standing there, wearing the same green dress with the white flowers that I had seen all those years ago.

"I have faith in you, kitten."

Tears in my eyes, I turned toward the demon power and was swallowed into the blackness.

∾

"DAMN IT, VIOLET. If you don't wake up, I'll torch your copy of *Firefly* signed by the whole cast." Jessa's shrill voice echoed through my throbbing head.

"You do that, and I'll haunt your ass forever."

Arms encircled my neck, and I was pulled up to a sitting position on the hard ground of the field. And the pain in my everything was back. My eyes flew open, and I saw everyone. Chaz, Tucker, Tyler, Nash. It was like waking up from Oz. But right now, I felt more like the witch smashed under a house.

"Finally," Jessa sighed as she released my neck. She looked exhausted, but relieved.

I looked up at Chaz. In one glance, he knew that something was off. He offered a hand that wasn't occupied by a very large shot gun. I carefully took his hand and he pulled me to my feet roughly.

Chaz held me against him for a moment and I closed my

eyes. He was different. Hotter, his power was out, for a change, out and swirling around him.

"What is it?" he whispered into my ear.

"Cristina was right," I whispered.

The moment I stepped away from him, I could feel the demon squirming around in there, like a hyperactive octopus undulating just below my breastbone.

"What the hell was that?" Jessa asked, as she rose from the ground.

"Did someone have sushi for lunch?" Nash asked as he held his chest.

"Not exactly." My entire family had come through the rip in the Veil to face unknown horrors to find me; there was no way I was lying to them now.

"Spencer made himself into a demon. The Mother asked me to take his power."

"You're a demon?" Jessa gasped.

"Just like Cristina said," Tyler growled.

"And the Mother spoke to you?" Tucker asked.

"Apparently, I've got one more prophecy to live out. And I'm not a demon, just a host of demonic power."

"It is an interesting bit of semantics," Nash said.

There was a hum in the ground, like it was urging us forward. "I think we need to go."

"The phrase *high-tailing it* never seemed so appropriate," Jessa said.

Tucker looked down at Spencer's body. His usually tan skin had gone white in the failing light of day and there was a blue tinge to his lips. Tucker looked up at me and then down at the body. With one quick movement, he lifted the dead body and carried it easily in his arms.

"What are you doing?" I asked.

"I need to make sure he's really dead. For good dead."

"You need proof?"

"Yes, and the others will follow with proof."

I wanted to protest but I needed peace. I felt it more than ever burning beneath my breastbone. I needed no one to doubt me. "I trust you, Tucker."

"I would hope so. Now do what Jessa says."

WHEN JESSA PULLED me through the portal, the demon power did a clog dance in my chest, excited for the opportunities on this side of the Veil. I fell to my knees and bathed in the pitter-patter of Jessa's energy around me as she struggled with closing the Veil.

I looked down at the cement beneath my hands and it took me a moment to realize where we were. "Is this your office?"

"Good thing I totally ignored your mandate to brick this place up."

I could feel the rest of my pack around me and realized how much of their strength I'd missed while disconnected from them. It felt like home again.

With every ounce of energy I had left, I built a hard shell around the power in my chest. It was nothing more than the candy coating for it, but I felt better.

"Violet." Chaz knelt down beside me. "What do you need?"

"Time. Strength. A caramel macchiato."

Chaz waved his hand, and then there were warm hands on my shoulder. Nash, and then Peter, and when Tyler's hand appeared before me, I took it and pulled myself to my feet.

His hand tightened around mine and I met him with my gaze and my power. With all the focus on the demon ball, my Legacy got free reign to wave around as it wanted.

Tyler pushed back. Testing me like he tested the younger members, making sure I was still me.

I smiled. "I'm okay. Tyler. Just stay close."

There was a surge of roses in the room. I turned around to

find the tear in the Veil still open. Carefully, not sure of my footing or anything else, I joined Jessa. "Problem?"

"You know," she said as she wove her fingers through the air. "I really didn't think this through."

"When did our plans ever go right anyway?"

I touched her shoulder, and I don't know if it was the demon or the bond, but I could see the rip in the Veil. Could feel it against my skin as I stood with my best friend, the Key Holder to my Keeper.

"I'm not strong enough," Jessa confessed in a whisper. "This isn't going to work this time. It's been ripped too many times."

"You shouldn't have opened it."

"And leave you there to rot? Never." It was possibly the first time I'd ever heard Jessa growl. She officially had been hanging out with me too long.

Time to put the thinking caps on. "What can we do?"

"Always seemed to like blood before."

I offered up my already bleeding hand and the Veil lapped at my palm, like a cat licking a wound. But then it wrapped around my arm and began to pull me back.

The Legacy and the demon fought, and I felt like I'd been splattered out like a paintball on a concrete wall, all my colors going in a million directions. The Legacy pulled away from it while the demon power fought to dive back in.

"Chaz," I gasped.

His arms were around me in an instant, and in an instant, I was calm, steady again. Apparently, he had the same effect on demons that he had on angry panthers.

It was then I noticed the demon power was a different kind of angry, like rage that wanted to be satiated. It was hungry. But not for power. Not like the Mother had said.

I knew I was daring fate by even thinking the Mother could be wrong about something, but echoes of desire crept across my skin. Memories with children, wives, awards for good deeds, and moments of pride.

Slowly, I pulled away from Chaz and approached the Veil again. The closer I got to the in-between, the more I heard them. Just like my ties to my pack, I could feel their desires, their vanities all swimming around. They didn't want power; they wanted freedom.

"Violet."

The voice didn't come from Jessa, though her hand slipped into mine and her little fingers cut off blood circulation to the tips.

The voice didn't come from Chaz, though I felt his heat down my neck.

The voice came from the other side of the Veil and as I looked through it, I saw my mother standing on the other side. Her long dark hair twisted in the unknown wind and her green eyes smiled back at me.

"Is that . . ." Chaz whispered in my ear.

I nodded. Apparently Chaz was powerful enough to see her too.

"Part of her, I think."

The tear in the Veil only widened as we stood before it. The demonic power lunged out for it and I didn't know why until I felt a tendril of it wander out and weave its way into the Veil.

"Vi?" Jessa's hand in mine, tighter as she watched.

A horrible plan formed in my head as I moved closer to the Veil, feeling the power lash out at me. The demon power didn't like being contained, didn't like being chained. I was going to give it a choice and I knew what the answer would be, could feel it in the pull beneath my breastbone as I saw the plan in my head. Just like a coffee maker. "Key Holder and Keeper, right?"

Jessa's lavender eyes flashed to me. "I don't like your tone."

"I've got this power and you've got the skill."

Jessa was right there with me. "You want to filter that demon through me and into the Veil?"

"No, I want to give you the stolen lives of our people to help protect those who can still fight."

Large tears filled Jessa's eyes. "Damn, you've got a way with words."

"It's a gift. Think you're up for it?"

"Got any idea how to do this?"

"Go big or go home."

Cristina had told me all those months ago that spell work was taking the power and forming it to your will. This was easier than that. The power already had a will of its own. Those stolen lives wanted to be free. I was just about to give them the choice of being anywhere they wanted to be. I just needed to get them there.

I relaxed and let the demon power fill me. It was like undoing a ball of string. The mental image, as comical as it was, helped me figure out what I was doing. One by one, strand by strand, I released the power down my arm and into Jessa, who gave it form. I closed my eyes as the feelings of fingers and hair and fur ran in cool rivulets down my arm and across Jessa's skin.

I could feel the cool magic as she wove, taking the power of a fellow Wanderer and weaving it back into the Veil to protect us.

Slowly, she closed the tear before us, separating me from the in-between.

But the power was still there, still within me. We hadn't used it all. The ball was only half unfurled and I still couldn't feel my panther underneath all that.

"Keep going," I urged.

"What?"

"Keep going. As far as you can. Make the weaving permanent. Spread out as far as you need to."

Jessa kept going. As I kept unraveling, she kept spreading the magic out. I felt Dallas, but also wisps of the Oklahoma plains and the salty air of the Corpus Christi Bay.

My head began to spin from the concentration and probably one of the concussions I'd gotten that day. I released the last of the power to Jessa and I stepped back and into Chaz's arms.

"Is it gone?" he whispered into my ear.

"Yes, they are."

I rested. My body still hurt from the fight with Spencer and the fights before that. I felt sick, like I'd churned out all my food for the past week. I let him be my strength and the panther within my chest purred against him.

Jessa stopped, stretched out to the greatest limit she'd ever been stretched before. When her knees gave out, Tucker was there to catch her when she fell.

It was silent. A still sort of silence without the ebb and flow of the Veil. With the outside power gone, I could feel others, little tinglings of wolves and fire. "Who else is here?"

Chaz chuckled. "They don't follow orders well. You need to work on that."

Chaz's arm around my waist, we walked out into Jessa's actual office and I was met with a crowd. The other leaders, the rest of my pack who didn't have bedtimes. Even the elementals were there.

Tucker had placed Spencer's lifeless body on the floor. I tried not to think about how much Jessa would kill him if he ruined the rugs of her office.

I looked over the crowd, the bloody ones, and the frightened ones. Inez stood in the corner, her head down, still bloodied and bruised from our battle. Willowbourne and Valiance were there, rough around the edges, but still standing.

"Peter, I'd like you to negotiate a more formal allegiance now."

"No need," Valiance said. "Seeing your sacrifice was all the proof I needed, Prima Jordan."

Their energies come out toward me, like the shifters had, but I put my hand up and my walls followed. Like with my shifters wanting energy, I pushed their tributes back to them.

A deep furrow grew in Willowbourne's red brow. "This is what we want."

"I need more time, but I will accept your alliance. I know I couldn't have done this without you."

"He's dead, Violet," Peter said. "There's nothing stopping you."

"I'm stopping me. I'm not ready yet. I will not make their mistakes." I looked into Peter's bright blue eyes. "I've seen the future of Dallas. All sorts of futures. I want to make sure it's the best possible one."

I looked to Willowbourne. "Please tell me you understand. Dallas is already better. And I intend to make it strong, stable."

Willowbourne walked up to me and placed her soft hand on my cheek. "The Mother is with you, Violet Jordan. And I am with you."

I smiled. "Thank you."

Willowbourne pulled away and Valiance gave me a nod as he escorted her out of Jessa's office.

"What are we going to do about her?" Tucker asked, pointing to Inez.

Inez cowered and it killed me. "She gets the same thing that everyone else gets."

Her brown gaze lifted from the floor.

"She gets a second chance, under the very watchful eye of our Riko, with the understanding that I will beat the fire out of her if she ever betrays her kind again."

"Yes, Prima," Inez said softly.

Tucker nodded.

I turned to Chaz and his golden eyes. "Can we go home now?"

His still golden eyes. "Yes please."

Chaz slipped his arm around my waist, which was much needed, because having your ass kicked on multiple plains of reality is truly exhausting.

The whole group of us walked out of the building to dancing lights and flashing sirens. There was a barrier of first responders outside the Infomart. Police and firefighters swarmed us as we exited.

Glass crunched underneath my boot and I looked over my shoulder to see the mirrored Infomart building completely devoid of its mirrors, like a bomb had gone off inside.

Just like in my vision.

"Jessa?"

"What? It takes a lot of mirrors to make a hole big enough to bring a Wookie through." Jessa winked as she followed Tucker to his car.

CHAPTER 25

I KNEW I had conjured the barn as my safe spot, but my couch was heavenly. The boys fought me at the door about needing to keep safe and protected. Chaz very definitively told them to bugger off.

I flopped down on the soft cushions and ached. Chaz locked up the front door, put the ash branch down.

"I didn't think every part of me could hurt at exactly the same time. Even my eyelashes hurt."

"You defied the odds tonight, not once, but three times."

"I probably used up at least three of those nine lives."

Chaz turned toward me, and he wasn't wearing his happy face. "What exactly were you thinking when you leapt through that rip?"

My skin tightened and the sizzle of the pain ran along my entire body. I rose from the couch and everything protested, but I needed to face this fight on my feet. "That my people would be safe without their lightning rod of destruction because they had each other."

Chaz stood before me. Solid. Every muscle tight and his eyes pure gold. "And because I'm not your pack, I don't get consideration?"

"Of course I thought about you, but I thought you'd understand. I knew you'd be okay, broody for a while, but okay. I did what needed to be done to protect my family, Chaz. You, Jessa, Waylon. Not just my pack. My people."

Chaz was the one who looked away. Just like Jovan, just like Inez. "You had no right."

"No right to protect what I had built, to protect the family we made together."

I grabbed his chin and forced his golden eyes back to mine. My chin began to quiver. "Tell me I was wrong. Tell me we haven't done something amazing here."

"You've done something amazing here."

"Don't be ridiculous, Chaz. We did this. You rescued me from that alley. You're the one who pushed me. You're the first person who said I could. This is as much your doing as it is mine."

Chaz took my hand from his chin and wrapped his fingers into mine.

"What's really going on here?" I asked softly.

"I promised to put you first. To make sure that someone was looking out for you when you were looking out for everyone else."

"And you think you failed because I stupidly jumped through a rip with a madman?"

"No, because I'm going to need some rescuing."

Chaz's shoulders fell, and the rock-solid borders that he kept around him fell as well. I was brushed with the warm scent of cashmere and Chaz's musk. The smell was as familiar to me as my own magnolias and my borders melted away at his power.

"Iris?"

"Guess who's got a Legacy of his own now."

I wrapped my arms around him tightly and I squeezed my

eyes shut. I could see him, feel him. The soft warmth of Iris's power connected to his golden center making it ten times bigger than it had been.

Chaz tucked his head into my neck and wrapped his arms around my waist so tightly I couldn't breathe.

When he spoke, his words were not more than a whisper that trailed down my throat. "She died in my arms, whispering about her family. About how proud she was and then it happened. Burned like hell."

"Don't have to tell me twice."

He let out a long sigh. "I don't think I'll shift, but I've never heard of this happening before."

I squeezed him harder. "Since when did we do anything by the book?"

Chaz pulled away and his golden eyes shone in the morning light slowly creeping in through my living room windows. That's why they were golden, still golden. It was his new power shining through. He was the son of a Prima now and had the power to go along with it.

"What happened to her body?" I asked delicately.

"Kurt and the Cleaners, actually. I'll have to call them in the morning and . . ."

I pressed my fingers to his lips. "It's one of the perks of being royalty. You just have to give the orders."

"I'm not a . . ."

"You will be. Well, you can be, if you want it. You've got a claim to the Pride now."

Chaz shook his head. "No. She wanted you to have it."

"Wanted us to have it."

Chaz's eyebrows rose. "Something else that you're not telling me? Another vision?"

I shook my head and pulled Chaz down to the couch. He came willingly, which was good because I didn't have any fight left in me. I rested my head on his shoulder and he pulled my long legs over his.

"Forget the big ole psychics. Self-fulfilling prophecy this time."

His hot lips brushed my forehead. "Well you do have the appropriate blood line for that."

I smiled. A joke. Where there was a joke, there was a way back to normal.

I let my eyes close, let the new warmth of him seep into my muscles and soothe the everything that ached. "We will rule Dallas. Slowly. Patiently and very much together."

EPILOGUE

I SPUN IN the simple cream-colored gown. "This is perfect."

Jessa fluttered around me, pulling at the satin until all the lines were straight and fluffing the veil around my head.

The sun streamed through the windows of my room at Iris's house, our house. The pronouns were still difficult, but we were working on changing that by making new memories.

The full-length mirror reflected back the glowing look of a blushing bride and her maid of honor.

"You're going to ruin the edge of this dress walking through that barn."

"Tyler found a navy walkway for us to stand on."

Jessa popped up. "Navy? But the flowers won't match that."

I turned to her and put my large hands on her petite shoulders. I looked her square in her lavender eyes. "Calm. Down. Everything's perfect. This is what I wanted."

Jessa took in a deep breath. "Okay."

A small rush of feathers swept over my bare arms. I looked at the doorway to see Kandice standing silently with a small smile on her face. Her light purple dress caught the air from the open window and flowed around her plumping figure. "Just wanted to see if you needed anything."

I smiled and waved her in. "I think we're good."

Kandice went to sit on a little chair in the corner.

A wave of nausea passed over me. It wasn't mine. My stomach was fine. Facing down demons and Biggers had pretty much steeled my nerves against wedding-day jitters. I looked over at the thin girl and walked over to her.

When I put my hand on her shoulder and opened my borders, the answer echoed back to me. "You're pregnant."

Kandice's lips parted and she looked up at me with parted lips. "How did you . . ."

"Does Nash know?"

She shook her head. "Only figured it out myself a week ago."

"I'd hug you, but I can't bend down in this dress."

Kandice rose and I wrapped my arms around her. It was there. This little ball of magic that sat around her midsection.

Tears welled up in my eyes, and as I released her, I dabbed at them carefully. "Go tell him. Right now."

"What?" Kandice said. "I don't want to overshadow your big day."

"Go, tell Nash this instant. You shouldn't keep a secret like that."

Kandice scurried out of the room—skipped, really.

Jessa came at me with a Kleenex to fix the little smear in my mascara.

"Guess everyone's getting their happy ending," I said into the mirror, watching Jessa carefully. "I'd like you to recognize I have not been pressing you about Tucker."

"I know."

"And I'd like you to know I've never seen you happier than you've been in the past month."

"I've been too busy planning your wedding to be happy." But

she gave me one glance, and one glance was all it took to tell me there might be another wedding in our future.

A slamming screen door and stomping feet shook the entire house as someone raced up the stairs. There was urgency and an energy preceding the visitor that made my skin prickle.

Chaz flew through the door. His hair was combed, and his tuxedo was perfection.

"You're not supposed see the bride," Jessa squealed as she flew at Chaz to get out of the room.

"Waylon's had a vision."

All three of us froze. Jessa slowly pulled away from Chaz's lapel, even smoothed out the crinkle she'd left there.

"The bloody kind of vision or the demon kind of vision?" I asked.

He paused. "Earthquake unleashes a demon kind of vision."

"Awesome. Do we have a timeline?"

I felt it in the ground before the earthquake shook the house. Cries of panic echoed through the field outside and rattled around in my brain. Sooner rather than later. Okay.

"Jessa, go outside and calm everyone down. I need to talk to Chaz."

Jessa nodded and left the two of us alone.

I sighed and reached out my hand for Chaz. He walked over and rested his head on mine. "You look amazing."

"It's like you're a model or something."

He chuckled and then pulled away to look down at me.

"You knew this was going to happen, right?" I asked as I looked into his now ever-golden eyes. My eyes darted down to the dampening charm now around his neck. I tucked it back underneath his black bow tie. Teaching Chaz to shield had caused a slight riff in our relationship, so I'd let Tyler use his new status as Shalar to help Chaz with his containment.

"It wouldn't be a Jordan affair if there wasn't a prophecy involved."

I sighed as I rested my hand on his chest. "Guess you won't be getting your birthday present."

"What was that?"

"A wife."

Chaz leaned down to kiss me. It was chaste and tainted by the vanilla lip gloss that Jessa had applied. "Don't know. Minister is still downstairs and everyone's here."

"And running." I shook my head. "If I wanted a rush job, I'd have let you talk me into Vegas. This one thing, I want normal."

"Well then, I guess you'll have to ask yourself a question, Violet Jordan."

"What's that?"

"Do you want to take down another demon as a single girl in the big city or as Mrs. Charles Garrett?"

ALSO BY AMANDA ARISTA

Here is the entire series that started it all:

Diaries of an Urban Panther

Claws and Effect

Nine Lives of Urban Panther

Also within the Wanderer universe though a darker and grittier feel,
The Merci Lanard Files follows a trouble-magnet journalist who has to
face the truth about who or what she truly is.

The Truth about Night

The Truth about Blood

The Truth about Shadows

ABOUT THE AUTHOR

Amanda was born in Illinois, raised in Corpus Christi, lives in Dallas but her heart lies in London. Good thing she loves to travel.

During the summer after second grade, she read every book in the young adult section of the library, much to the surprise of the local librarian. So she started making up her own stories and hasn't stopped.

She has a husband who fights crime and a tiny human who is following in her mother's footsteps of storytelling. You can usually find her curled up on her couch with a varied menagerie of dogs writing away.

Along with her BA in English & Psychology and her MA in Education, Amanda is a graduate of the SMU Creative Writing Program. She now lectures at writer conferences and loves discussing craft, character, and structure.

She is represented by Kimberly Brower, of Brower Literary & Management.

Keep Calm and Drink Coffee!